World's Edge

by Ryan Kirk

WORLD'S EDGE

ISBN-13: 978-0692576991
ISBN-10: 0692576991

Cover art by Rizky Nugraha
Interior design by Ryan Kirk

www.waterstonemedia.net

Give feedback on the book at:
contact@waterstonemedia.net

Twitter: @waterstonebooks

First Edition

Printed in the U.S.A

This one is for Mom and Dad,
Still putting up with me after all these years.

PROLOGUE

Akira, Lord of the Southern Kingdom, ran his hand through the grass. He closed his eyes and focused on the warmth of the morning sun on his left side. The morning was early and the predawn silence still held, the fort behind him silent as men rolled bleary-eyed from their sleeping pads. Akira had been up before the sun, driven by curiosity.

He kept his eyes closed as he listened to the soft rustle of a morning breeze through the prairie. If it was possible, even the wind sounded empty and hollow. The grass here was high, coming well above Akira's waist. If he wished, he could sit and disappear from the view of those behind him. For a moment his imagination got the best of him, racing ahead of logic to present solutions to his confused mind. He pictured the Azarians, spread out in front of him - thousands of them, just sitting in the grass, hiding and laughing at their own private joke.

But when he opened his eyes, the rolling prairie in front of him was empty. He looked down at the grass, tall and strong, and thought of the amount of blood this field had been fertilized with.

The grass here would grow strong long after he and his men had rejoined the great cycle. Their blood ensured it.

But there was no death here this morning. The sun rose on three armies that faced no enemy. Akira turned and looked at Fort Azuma, stone walls built tall and strong with sweat and lives. Behind it lay the Three Sisters, mountain peaks Akira could just make out from where he stood. Beyond them, even further to the north, lay the Southern Kingdom. Akira's father had fought for ten hard cycles to retake the pass from the Azarians, and Akira had finished the work through the completion of the fort named for his father. He believed he had ensured the safety of his kingdom. No more would the Azarians be a threat to his people.

Today he wondered if his dream had come true. For sixty cycles the Southern Kingdom had fought and died against the Azarians, fighting to protect their border. The fighting in the pass was as regular and predictable as the seasons. Some winters were harsher than others, but winter always came, and spring always followed it. With the spring came the Azarians. Sometimes more of them and sometimes less, but they always came.

Now, spring was here. Even the prairie, usually burned brown by the sun, was green. The air smelled fresh and clean. But though spring was in full bloom, the Azarians were nowhere to be seen.

It should have meant rejoicing. Behind Akira stood fifteen thousand men and boys who might not meet their ends in this empty grassland. But Akira didn't trust it. He couldn't trust it. The silence in front of him wasn't pleasant. It was oppressive, menacing. It felt like the wind when it stopped right before the storm hit, tearing well-rooted trees out of the ground.

Akira turned and walked back to the fort, causing the bodyguards he had ordered to stay behind to breathe a silent sigh of relief. Questions raced through his mind, but no answers. He couldn't explain it, but when he looked out on those empty plains, he only felt one emotion, and it wasn't relief. It was fear.

CHAPTER 1

Akira studied his maps. They were large, almost as large as the bedroll he slept on. Although he'd not say as much out loud, they were one of the prides of his reign. Maps were knowledge, knowledge of the terrain that could mean the difference between success and defeat in a military campaign. His were the most detailed of any in existence, and with the addition of small wooden figurines to denote armies and units, it gave him all the information he needed to run his kingdom.

The sun wasn't yet up, but the candles in his tent provided plenty of illumination as he puzzled over the maps. He commanded five armies. The Fourth and the Fifth were far away, up north guarding the borders of the Western Kingdom and the Northern Kingdom, respectively. It was quiet duty, but Akira didn't dare leave his borders undefended. The Lords needed to be watched, Tanak especially. Tanak, Lord of the Western Kingdom, was building his armies. Akira's shadows reported Tanak already had three full armies with over six thousand men apiece, and a fourth was in development. It worried Akira, but it was a matter for another day. The treaty had held for over a thousand cycles, and Akira couldn't see anyone breaking it soon.

Down here, at the southern edge of the Three Sisters, Akira held three armies. He had hoped to test his new generals in battle, but no battle awaited them here. His generals would have to find experience elsewhere.

Akira shook his head. There was nothing on the maps he hadn't already thought about. He stepped out of his tent as the first rays of the sun peeked over the horizon. The morning was still. His sleep-starved guards stumbled to attention, but he motioned for them to sit once again. He was in the middle of his armies. There was little for him to fear. No one made it this far unless they were personally known. Ryuu's casual breaking and entering of his castle grounds two cycles ago had caused significant tightening of Akira's personal security. He preferred not having a sword to his neck.

His guards knew his penchant for wandering without company. His advisers objected, but it was a small way he could show solidarity with his soldiers. They risked their lives every day for the kingdom. If he couldn't step outside his own tent without a company of soldiers, what type of leader would he be? His guards would report his wanderings immediately anyway. He never had much time to himself.

Akira wandered to the spotting tower and returned to the view he had looked upon the day before. The morning sunlight bathed the land in brilliant orange hues and Akira couldn't help but think that Azaria was a beautiful land. Empty, but beautiful.

He forced himself to turn away from the beauty below. The land was still empty and nothing had changed. When he reached the bottom of the lookout he was met by members of his honor guard. He almost asked how they had found him, but he knew the answer. They may have given him space, but they couldn't risk giving him freedom. Captain Yung, the head of his honor guard, was a strong soldier, but an even better bodyguard. Akira knew the captain had issued orders that Akira be trailed discreetly at all times.

Akira greeted his captain with humor in his voice. "That obvious?"

Yung, to his credit, did not smile. "There was only one place you would have gone, my Lord."

"You never will call me by my given name, will you?"

"No, my Lord."

Akira laughed. "Well, hopefully these generals will follow orders better than you!"

Yung shook his head and let out a short laugh. "Unlikely, my Lord."

They covered the ground to the command headquarters in short time. Even though the morning was still young, and the camp wasn't awake, all the generals were assembled. The command of a kingdom waited for no one.

When Akira entered the headquarters he scanned the room and took in the three generals of the armies he traveled with. They represented the best of the Southern Kingdom, and Akira considered himself fortunate to have their skills and expertise.

General Toro was the oldest, having seen almost fifty cycles. He had been promoted to general of the First after General Nori had died, making him the highest ranking general in the kingdom. He had the experience in the room that balanced the impulses of the two younger generals, Makoto and Mashiro.

The two of them were as brothers. They had served in the same units growing up and had formed a bond that could only be created on the battlefield. Makoto was the older of the two by a cycle, but he was still only twenty-seven. They were the two youngest generals in the history of the Three Kingdoms, but their skills on the battlefield, both as soldiers and as commanders, had earned them the trust and respect of all. They were both brilliant strategists and charismatic leaders. On their shoulders the Southern Kingdom would continue to grow in strength. Although only a single cycle sat between the two of them, they couldn't have been physically any more different. Makoto was a giant of a man. Akira, who himself was tall, came only to the general's well-muscled chest. Mashiro was thin and of average height, but his speed, both mentally and physically, was astounding. Akira wouldn't want to be on the other side of the sword or strategic table from either of them.

He nodded a greeting and the four of them sat around a table covered in smaller versions of Akira's maps. They all knew the decision that sat before them. There wasn't any time to waste. "Thoughts?"

There was silence around the table, an unusual occurrence for the four of them.

Toro spoke up, echoing the thoughts of each of the generals. "There is no way of knowing the best course of action. We've never encountered this, and we don't have any worthwhile information from scouts to base a decision on."

Akira glanced at the other two, seeing nods of agreement from both of them. "Suggestions, then."

Mashiro spoke up first. "We should march deeper into Azaria with a significant force. This is an opportunity too good to pass up."

Toro disagreed. "It's too big a risk. It presents an opportunity, true, but at what cost? I share Akira's unease about the absence of Azarians. It could be a precursor to greater action - perhaps a trap of some sort to get us to leave our position here."

Mashiro scoffed. "What sort of trap could it be? Our scouts have scoured the lands for leagues. There aren't any Azarians in any direction."

Toro eyed the younger general coolly. "There are many types of traps. It wouldn't be a very good one if we knew what it was. I believe caution is warranted."

Akira turned his gaze to Makoto. The giant was usually the last to speak, but his advice was always well thought out. There was silence as they waited for him to speak. "I agree with Toro." He held up his hand to stop Mashiro's outburst. "Our records of the Azarians go back over sixty cycles, and I have studied them extensively. Nothing like this has ever happened. Something beyond our knowledge is happening. Here we are safe and defensible. If we were to spread our forces we incur unnecessary risk for little gain."

Akira nodded. The majority of the generals agreed with him. Mashiro would chafe, but he would follow orders.

"Remember, the Azarians are not my main concern. If we can build the defenses here so they are impregnable, that is what we will spend the season doing. Speed is of the highest priority. Work your men as if their lives depend on it, for they may. I want you all to figure out a rotation. One army focuses on construction while the others train and simulate maneuvers in the foothills. In a cycle or two we will make our move and our men need to be the best they can be. Understood?"

A chorus of agreement answered his question.

"Good. I'll be making arrangements to leave . . ."

Akira was interrupted by a commotion coming from the field. It was only moments before a messenger walked into the tent.

"Excuse me, my Lord. A scout has returned. He brings news."

"Why the commotion?"

The messenger hesitated. "He made a rather dramatic entrance, my Lord."

Akira gestured impatiently. "Then bring him here, quickly."

The messenger left the tent, replaced moments later by the scout.

One glance was all Akira needed to see why the scout had caused such a commotion. He was covered in cuts and blood and had at least two arrows sticking out of his back. Neither looked fatal, but Akira was impressed he could still stand on his own two feet. He was moved by the scout's strength.

The scout didn't wait for permission to speak. He was shaky on his feet and his voice was soft, trembling like a leaf in a breeze. Akira noticed the fear in his voice right away.

"My Lord, they were destroyed. They were all dead."

Akira raised his hand. "Slow down. Start from the beginning."

The scout wobbled on his feet. Toro grabbed a flagon of wine and almost threw it down the soldier's throat. The man gulped it down without shame, the tremors racking his body subsiding. The scout stood up a little straighter, then slouched again against the pain of the arrows. It was a temporary relief, but it gave the man enough strength to tell his tale.

"My Lord, we were sent into Azaria a quarter moon ago. My partner and I experienced much of what you've probably already heard. The land nearby is empty. No one. We rode through the foothills for a couple of days but saw nothing of note. I'm sorry, my Lord, but we disobeyed our orders and went deeper into Azaria. We wanted to know what was happening. The two of us traveled for two days straight along the main road into Azaria when we saw smoke. We rode towards it."

"We came upon the end of a battle. My Lord, an entire Azarian clan had been wiped out. There were so many bodies we had to get off our horses. We went among the dead, hoping to find a survivor who could tell us more. But we found none. My Lord, it was terrifying. I've seen plenty of battlefields, and there are always wounded. Always. But there weren't any here. Every single person was dead. I don't know if I'll ever get the silence out of my head."

Akira tried to process what the scout was saying. He too had walked through the aftermath of combat, and the scout was right. There were always the living scattered among the dead. They may be dying or just too injured to move, but a recent battlefield was never silent. The air was always filled with the sounds of the wounded. He shuddered, imagining what the silence must have been like.

"We thought we were being careful, but we were spotted. My Lord, I don't think there were more than four or five attackers. But they moved so fast. My partner and I ran. We both made it to our horses, but he took an arrow in the back and fell. These attackers, they weren't human. They moved so fast and were so strong. They chased us, but their horses were tired. We thought we were out of range when my partner was killed. It was an impossible shot. Impossible. I took two myself, but then they were gone and I didn't see them again."

The scout broke down in tears and Akira dismissed him. His story was hard to believe.

The scout was replaced by the captain of the scouts.

"Is the boy trustworthy?"

"He's one of our best, my Lord. I've never seen him rattled before, and he's a veteran. He's seen three cycles in the scouts."

Akira nodded. "See to it he's cared for."

Perhaps there was truth to the boy's story. He didn't want to believe it though. If four or five warriors could slaughter entire Azarian clans, they would be a force of incredible power. Azarians were tremendous fighters and difficult to kill. If they had been wiped out so easily, Akira dreaded whatever was sitting to the south of them. A power that strong could sweep over his kingdom, and there would be nothing he could do to protect his people.

CHAPTER 2

The sword sliced through the air, aimed at Ryuu's neck. He leaned back, letting the wooden blade pass harmlessly in front of him. Seeing a chance, he moved forward into the opening, trying a quick cut upwards. He was fast, but his opponent hadn't stopped moving. She rotated and struck downward, forcing him back again.

Two more passes and he didn't make contact, but Ryuu was getting closer. Every pass brought him a hair closer than the last. It wouldn't be long now. She knew it too.

He was overconfident and lost his focus, just for a moment. It was less than a heartbeat, but she recognized it. She saw every mistake he made, two cycles of experience paying off. His opponent redoubled her attack, strikes blurring together in succession. Ryuu blocked or dodged each of them, but he lost his balance on a tree root, stumbling backwards as his opponent seized the opportunity. She dashed forward, the eager glint of victory in her eyes.

Ryuu resigned himself to the pain of the strike. There was no way he could block her in time. But then Ryuu's mind snapped.

He couldn't describe the sensation any other way. One moment he was in normal reality. The next, the world was moving in slow motion, as if everyone was moving through water instead of air. Not only did he know how his opponent would strike, he knew, with the trained instinct of a warrior, how he would finish her. Ryuu let himself fall, sweeping aside his opponent's sword as he tucked into a roll. He came back to his feet and in three moves had his sword pressed against his opponent's neck.

She blew her dark hair out of her face in annoyance. "You promised you weren't going to do that."

Ryuu lowered his sword, smiling. "Sorry, I tried, but when you had me beat at the end, it just happened. I still can't control it."

She looked at him, curious. "Can you do it now?"

Ryuu closed his eyes and focused. Sometimes it was easier immediately after. He could remember how it felt, and he had some idea of how it happened. Sometimes he could snap intentionally. But not today. He shook his head as he opened his eyes.

Moriko looked disappointed. "I'm sorry."

"Don't worry. I'll figure it out one day."

They walked hand in hand back to their hut, the same one Ryuu had grown up in with Shigeru. They walked in companionable silence, but Ryuu's head was churning, much as it often did. For two cycles they had known peace. It was more than he had expected after they had killed Orochi and Nori. Akira had kept his word.

Ryuu glanced at Moriko. Perhaps more than anything else, it was she who surprised him. After the death of Takako, she had come back to Shigeru's hut with him, mostly because she had nowhere else to go. There was no question of returning to the monasteries, and her family would never welcome her.

They had lived together for moons, an uncomfortable truce between them. Ryuu was still grieving, working through the deaths of Takako and Shigeru. Moriko trained. She had seen how strong Ryuu and Orochi had been and knew there was more for her to learn. Most days Ryuu would work in the garden, his sword collecting dust in the hut, while she practiced every day. She had nothing left but her strength, and with training it grew every day.

After killing Orochi, Ryuu had been broken. As a child, he had dreamed of becoming a nightblade, but when his dream was realized, he learned it was a nightmare. He had seen too much blood, too much meaningless death. The one time he had taken up his blade for a cause, to save a girl who couldn't save herself, he had lost both the girl and the man he called father. The garden brought him a measure of hope, a simple joy in nurturing life rather than taking it.

It was Moriko who convinced him to pick up his blade again. She wanted to learn from him, but more importantly, she had convinced him that he was shutting part of himself away. Almost his entire childhood had been dedicated to becoming a nightblade. When he gave it up there was a hole in his life that gardening couldn't fill. Patiently, she tried for three moons to convince him to train with her, and eventually he gave in.

She had been right, of course. Picking up his blade had felt natural. Even after all that had happened, it felt right, like a part of him was waking up from a long sleep. Ryuu had been torn apart by Shigeru and Takako's deaths, and it was only when he picked up the sword again did he feel like the scars began to heal.

Returning to his childhood home had been both a blessing and a curse. When he had first laid eyes on the small hut he had been overjoyed. He loved being back in a place so comfortable and so safe.

But there was a hole in the hut that wasn't physical, and it seemed to grow larger every day. Shigeru was gone and everything in the hut was a reminder of that. They cooked using Shigeru's old utensils. They made their living by selling the medicines he had made.

Training again began the process of healing, and it brought them closer together. Ryuu had always found Moriko attractive, but the only time he had tried to express his feelings, he'd been knocked on his ass. The memory was strong, and he made no advances, even though he felt himself drawn closer and closer to her through their training.

What they shared was deep. They were both warriors, but even more, they were both nightblades. Their sense gave them a window to the world no one else in the Three Kingdoms could understand. The sun and the moon rose and fell, and as they shared more of themselves, their relationship deepened.

This time it was Moriko who pinned Ryuu to a tree and kissed him. He was stunned. While he could see a strike coming far in advance, he understood nothing about women. But Moriko opened the door, and he didn't turn down her invitation.

Their relationship grew in fits and starts, a seed struggling to blossom in a new environment. But the seasons changed and it continued to grow, continued to get stronger. And now he couldn't imagine a life without her. He never would have guessed he could find someone to share his life with, but he had.

Ryuu squeezed Moriko's hand a little tighter at the thought. The corner of her mouth turned up as she glanced up at him. It was enough. She was quiet by nature, and he had gotten used to her manners. She was strong and silent and gave him the courage to face the battles he must.

Later that night Ryuu lay in bed listening to Moriko softly snoring next to him. He felt emptied and calm as he often did after they came together. He looked at her slim face, covered in part by her raven hair. He brushed it lightly out of her face. She had been growing it long. He decided she was the most beautiful woman he'd ever known. And she was strong too, which magnified her beauty. At her current strength she wouldn't have any trouble fighting someone of Orochi's caliber, the strongest warrior they'd ever encountered. If not for Ryuu's ability to snap, she'd defeat him as often as he beat her.

Thinking of Orochi opened the doors to memories he'd rather not dwell on. He didn't trust the peace they had here. Every night he thought he needed to do something, take some action, but there was none to take. He considered going to the island Orochi had given him directions to, the birthplace of both Orochi and Shigeru. There was a part of him that found the idea appealing, a part that wanted to learn more about the place his adopted father had come from. But the desire wasn't there, wasn't strong enough to motivate him to make the journey. He was happy here.

As he lay there, lost in thought, a shadow crossed his awareness that made him bolt upright and out of bed. Ryuu lived with the sense every day. Most of the time it was a passive ability, bringing in information about his surroundings. Unlike the early days of his training, he didn't have to think about it anymore. It was always there in the back of his mind.

Something was close. Ryuu had his hand on his sword in less than a moment. His training kicked in and he stilled himself, allowing his sense to expand outward. At first, the world outside their hut seemed normal, but then it was there again. It was unlike anything or anyone he had sensed before. At times it seemed like a man, but the energy was primal, uncontrolled.

Ryuu focused. Whatever it was, it was still far from the hut. It was at least fifty paces away, but even that was closer than any man had gotten in the past two cycles. Ryuu rolled off the sleeping pad, coming silently to his feet. As he left the bed Moriko's eyes came open, instantly aware. She started, but Ryuu motioned her to silence. She grabbed her own sword. Ryuu motioned her to stay still. He took a last, longing glance. In the light of the stars her bare skin contrasted against the glint of her blade. She was beautiful.

He didn't bother with clothes. When he felt the shadow was out of the line of sight of the door, he darted out, his bare feet making no sound in the damp grass. He reached the edge of the clearing in a few heartbeats. There was a large tree about ten paces into the woods whose shadow he melted into. He caught his breath and threw out his sense like a net, hoping to catch his mysterious shadow once again.

It was faint, but Ryuu could still feel it. The shadow was still, as if something had caught its attention. As Ryuu calmed his mind, he sensed something he had never expected to sense in the Three Kingdoms again. He could feel the light pressure of Moriko in the hut, her own sense expanding outward, tentative and cautious. But the sense was extending from the shadow as well. So it was another nightblade. There were more in the kingdoms than just the two of them then.

The shadow moved again, continuing to circle the hut. It was slow, but it was heading towards him. Ryuu debated his best course of action. He snuck further into the woods, silent as death. Moriko had taught him some of her skill, and while he wasn't near as proficient as she was, he would be hard to sense among the life of the woods. He used as much of his focus as possible to mask his own intentions from the sense. After he had gone about fifteen more paces into the woods he crouched in another shadow and turned around.

The waiting was the hardest part. Ryuu could sense the shadow moving, but it was slow, deliberate. It was high too, in the trees. There was a path through the upper boughs surrounding the hut. He and Moriko trained on it often. The shadow was following the same path. Soon it would be right over the place Ryuu had first hidden.

In the dark of night, Ryuu couldn't make out anything using his sight. The moon was almost new and its faint light couldn't penetrate the trees. Without his sense he would have been blind. It felt like an eternity, but the shadow stopped above where Ryuu had first left the clearing and found cover. Ryuu squinted, trying to make out something in the trees that would tell him who was out there. His attempts were in vain. He couldn't make out anything or anyone. The shadows were too deep.

Then there was a blur of movement, the shadow dropping right where Ryuu had been hidden. Ryuu caught the glint of a blade reflected in the faint starlight. The shadow melted into the shadows surrounding the trees and Ryuu lost sight of it. It was a man, but Ryuu had never encountered anyone like this before. He felt different, darker and more dangerous than any man Ryuu had met.

Ryuu held his breath, trying to remain as silent as he could. He was hidden in the shadows of one of the giant trees, but it was a slim comfort. He didn't even have the darkness of his robes to protect him, naked as he was.

The night was perfectly still. Mosquitoes hovered around Ryuu, drinking freely of his blood. They annoyed him, but he took no action. Any movement, no matter how slight, might give him away.

The silence stretched on, moment after agonizing moment. Ryuu held the hilt of his sword lightly in his hand, ready to draw at any moment. His nerves were starting to get the better of him. His sense told him the shadow was still right in front of him in the shadow of a tree, but his other five senses told him the night was empty and peaceful. He was ready to draw and attack the man, but fear held him back. Who could feel like this to his sense? There wasn't a man he was scared of, but this creature didn't act like a man.

In the stillness he heard a soft sound, and then another. He closed his eyes and focused his ears. The sound came one more time. It was so familiar, but it was hard for him to place. Then it came to him. It sounded like sniffing. Ryuu's mind raced. Was the man trying to smell him out? Was it even possible? He gripped his sword tighter.

Sweat trickling down his face, Ryuu waited. His legs were cramping from the crouched position he had taken in a hurry. He hadn't expected to be in the position for as long as he had been.

Finally the shadow moved, but not towards Ryuu. Staying in the shadow of the tree, he sensed it climb back up to its original perch. After a few moments of waiting, it was off, heading south.

Ryuu held his stance even though his legs screamed at him, using all his senses to scan the area around their hut over and over. He shifted to a kneeling position and expanded his sense. He waited, mosquitoes making off with more and more of his life blood. But nothing came. Finally he rose, confident it was gone.

Ryuu kept calm, but his mind was racing. He didn't know why it was happening, but they were being hunted.

CHAPTER 3

Tanak looked out on the scene below him. He sat comfortably on his horse, his relaxed posture indicative of the many cycles he had spent in the saddle. Today he wore plain clothing, forgoing his usual armor for the garb of a landowner. There was no point in drawing attention to himself. He patted his horse, making small soothing noises. It was an excellent war horse, spirited and mean. Tanak loved riding it.

Below him lay two of the most important fortresses in the Three Kingdoms, that guarded the bridge that spanned the river separating Tanak's and Akira's kingdoms. Tanak and his horse stood on top of the highest point overlooking the scene. Below him, no more than a thousand paces away, was his own fortress. From his vantage point, the two fortresses were almost mirror images. Both had walls that approached the banks of the fast-moving river. Both had a gate blocking one end of the bridge. It was the most secure crossing in the Three Kingdoms. And tonight it was his target.

From his vantage point high on the hill, Tanak could see his fortress was bursting with soldiers, packed in like cattle in a small barn. There was little room to move. Turning his head, Tanak looked behind him. On the other side of the hill sat a massive encampment, the remainder of three of his armies. He had only held a single army back, just enough to make Sen think twice before seizing the moment and invading Tanak's kingdom.

It had been an impressive feat, shielding the movements of his troops. They had increased the guard at the borders, searching for any messages trickling down to the Southern Kingdom. Tanak knew his men were vigilant, but Akira's shadows were everywhere. They couldn't stop all of them. As soon as news reached Tanak that Akira had left for the Three Sisters, his armies leapt into motion. Tanak hoped he would be across the river before the message of his troop movements made it all the way down to the Three Sisters.

While his outward demeanor was calm, inside his guts were twisting and roiling. He had been the Lord of his kingdom for almost fifteen cycles and this plan was the culmination of ten cycles of planning and preparation. Tanak was confident in his planning, but war was an uncertain endeavor, and often even the best plans failed.

He had to succeed. The Western Kingdom was large, by sheer physical size the largest of the three kingdoms, but its land was poor in the metals he needed to build the economy and protect his people. Much of his kingdom was fertile plains. His people were happy, but they were also in decline. In recent cycles the trade rates between kingdoms had been brutal, and Tanak knew his people paid dearly for every resource, while the Lords of the other two kingdoms sat comfortably on their excess.

Tanak made a gentle sound and his horse trotted down towards the fortress. He rode slowly and with confidence. It would be the last time many of his subjects saw him. He knew thousands of eyes were on him at the moment. His subjects knew who he was, even if the spotters across the river didn't.

He would unite the Three Kingdoms. It had been the goal of almost every ruler since the first Kingdom had fallen. The land needed to be reunited. He could almost feel the ground pleading for reunification. They were so much stronger together. He was destined to succeed. So much groundwork had been laid, and he knew much more than Lord Akira. The end of the Southern Kingdom was at hand. He approached the second main gate of the fortress, allowing the doors to close behind him. The only way out of this fort was forward, into the Southern Kingdom.

Renzo was there to greet him, looking no different than any other foot soldier. Tanak kept himself from shaking his head. He had been working with Renzo for almost ten cycles and he still couldn't believe his good fortune. The man looked uncomfortable in a soldier's uniform, even though it fit perfectly. Tanak took a moment to enjoy his adviser's discomfort. As he dismounted he felt Renzo's strong hands guiding him safely off his horse. Tanak bridled in anger but contained himself. He knew the man was only trying to protect him. Although Tanak hated to admit it, he had seen over forty cycles, and getting off a horse wasn't as easy as it had once been. He stared into the man's eyes. Ten cycles and it looked like Renzo hadn't aged a day. Who knew what dark magics kept him going? He was a nightblade, after all.

Tanak would never forget the first time they had met. Renzo had strolled right into Tanak's palace as though it were his own home. Tanak remembered seeing him, his dark robes not quite concealing the gleam of his blade. Only the guards were allowed to wear steel in the palace. Renzo had told him a story that defied belief, but Tanak had put him to the test, and Renzo had passed every one. He was the best swordsman Tanak had ever met, and he possessed the sense of legend. He was a nightblade, a creature Tanak thought had passed from this world hundreds of cycles ago.

It was a crime punishable by death to harbor a nightblade. That decision had been one of the key provisions of the treaty which maintained the peace between the Three Kingdoms. It was death if you even knew of a nightblade and didn't report it. But Renzo told him a tale. He came from a place where nightblades still lived, a place where there were those who could see into the future. They had seen his future. He remembered Renzo's exact words.

"Lord, they saw a king ride with his armies at the head of one Great Kingdom. All were one, united as they never have been before."

Renzo had looked up at him. "Our seers know the time draws near. You are the king we have all been waiting for!"

Tanak's own seers had been saying the same for many cycles, but Tanak had a hard time believing them. Renzo's story gave further credence to his own seers. From that day forward Renzo and Tanak had planned the reunification of the Kingdom.

Ten cycles of planning had passed. Renzo had become his closest adviser and unofficial bodyguard, hidden from the entire palace in plain sight. Renzo admitted he knew no more of strategy than any other soldier, but he was a trusted confidant. More importantly, he displayed none of the sycophantic tendencies of the other advisers surrounding Tanak. They were more partners than Lord and vassal. Renzo spoke in a straightforward manner, willing to contradict Tanak when he felt Tanak was wrong. As the cycles passed Tanak found that he came to rely on Renzo's advice more and more.

The Southern Kingdom was their first target. Tanak had nothing against Akira. He was a younger ruler, but showed great potential. Depending on how the campaign turned out, Tanak even considered letting him live. If he was amenable, perhaps he could serve as some form of lower adviser. The Northern Kingdom was too hard to invade. Akira's armies were the largest and most well trained, but they didn't frighten Tanak. He had tricks up his sleeve that would decimate the Southern Kingdom. Once his conquest was complete, he expected Sen would fall in line and the Kingdom would be reborn anew.

Tanak's reveries were interrupted as two of his commanders approached. One was the commander of a covert squad acting as the tip of the spear for the invasion. The other was the commander of the initial strike force, composed of every soldier currently jammed into the fort, the spearhead. Their reports were brief. The covert team was ready to move, as was the strike force. All they needed was the order to proceed. Tanak hesitated for a moment. At his word, the treaty that had held the Three Kingdoms together for over a thousand cycles would be broken. The moment passed. He had come too far to turn around. It was his destiny. He gave the command.

Tanak climbed the wall of his fortress to overlook the scene. From his vantage point he would be able to see most of the battle, but he was still well out of arrow range. It was a quiet, moonless night, perfect for the coming attack. This date had been planned for cycles. He strained his ears to hear any sounds below him, but without luck. The only sound was that of the river crashing on its banks below. Tanak was pleased. If he couldn't hear his squad on this side, they couldn't be heard on the southern bank either. Although they had contingency plans, the success of this invasion hung in large part upon the squad of four men moving in the darkness below. Tanak's heart beat increased. If they failed tonight, Tanak wasn't certain they'd defeat the Southern Kingdom.

In the pitch darkness of the night Tanak could barely make out the barrels of flammable liquid on the bridge. There were four, two closer to his kingdom, two closer to the other bank. Each side's barrels were placed out of bow range of the other side. They were a last-ditch defense for both sides. Tanak could clearly see the small fires burning on the walls of the southern fort. Night and day, archers stood near those fires with their bows at the ready. It was the same defense they used on his side. If either kingdom attempted to use the bridge as a means to invasion, the archers could shoot the barrels and burn the bridge down. Tanak needed the bridge, so the barrels were his first obstacle.

Tanak strained all his senses, but he couldn't observe anything unusual happening below. The bridge was silent. He turned to Renzo, who was standing beside him, patient as a rock. "Tell me, what's happening down there?"

Renzo glanced at Tanak, his annoyance with Tanak's impatience clear. "Your men are just getting started. The first two have slipped underneath the bridge, and two more are following now."

Tanak wished, not for the first time, to be blessed with the sense like his adviser was. Renzo had grown up with his abilities, and Tanak felt he took them for granted. He didn't understand how much others would covet those same abilities. Tanak was hoping Renzo would give him regular updates, but Renzo was silent and focused. Frustrated, he turned back to the bridge. If Renzo could be patient, so could he. He wondered how far out Renzo's abilities extended. The bridge was several hundred paces long. Could Renzo sense all the way to the other side of the bridge? His adviser's face revealed no clue.

As time passed Tanak's impatience continued to grow. If there hadn't been hundreds of troops watching him and waiting for their next order, Tanak would have paced like a madman. He knew less time had passed than he thought. The mission wasn't easy. It was hundreds of paces across the bridge and his men were climbing underneath it. Only four men had been selected and trained. They had equipment that allowed them to claw their way underneath the bridge, but Tanak had little doubt it was a tremendous task for each of them.

His straining ears heard a splash that seemed out of place and he looked immediately to Renzo. Renzo shook his head. "One of your men fell off the bridge. He was swept away. I don't know if he lives."

Tanak swore softly to himself. The four men going across the bridge didn't wear armor, so they should be able to float, but the river was fast and dangerous. Even a strong swimmer could meet his end in the rushing water below.

The silence continued. Tanak couldn't take much more. He was a leader, unaccustomed to waiting. He considered ordering his men across the bridge. It was a desperate gamble, but better than waiting another cycle to get all the pieces into place. He had committed everything to this task. His kingdom would suffer if they didn't succeed tonight.

Renzo turned to him. "I think they've pushed over the barrels."

"You think?"

"I'm sorry. I can't be sure. I am having a hard time sensing them while surrounded by so many people. I am almost certain."

Tanak stared incredulously at Renzo. Renzo returned his stare, impassive as ever. The decision was Tanak's to make. It was his kingdom, his war.

Sometimes there was nothing to do but roll the dice and hope for the best. He raised his fist, and he felt the attention of every warrior on him. He gestured forward, and the whole fortress surged for the gate. The invasion had begun.

The gates opened silently and Tanak's men poured out. The plan had been established long ago. Messengers were sent to the armies hiding behind the hills and the entire operation leapt into motion. Tanak watched with mounting eagerness from the walls, safely out of danger.

Archers went onto the bridge first, unleashing flights of invisible arrows to rain down in the night. Tanak couldn't see them, but he could imagine the waves of arrows slicing down into the bodies of unsuspecting guards. He could hear the screams carry over the running water below. After several waves had launched Tanak saw the flickering of fires being uncovered, illuminating his archers. More waves of arrows followed, these leaving trails of flame behind them. Tanak closed his eyes but he could still see their deadly arcs burned into his memory. With any luck, the arrows would start the southern shore on fire, killing many of the men inside without having to risk the lives of his own soldiers.

As Tanak saw fire catch in the southern fortress, he heard the sound of alarm bells ringing. Everything was working better than he had hoped. The southerners were caught completely off-guard. A thousand cycles of relative peace had made them soft. Archers continued to rain fire down on the fortress, covering the advance of the infantry. There was so little retaliation it was almost a joke. A scattering of arrows was launched back at the bridge in an attempt to light it on fire, but Tanak's troops were prepared with blankets to put out any potential dangers. The bridge was far too large to be taken out by any single arrow, but Tanak's soldiers weren't taking any chances. They needed the bridge.

The battering ram went across next. It was a bloody business, and Tanak lost men as the southern fortress mounted a token resistance, but Tanak could tell it was only a matter of time. There were uncontrolled fires raging on the other shore, and resistance was scattered at best. The war began with a quiet victory.

Tanak's prediction turned out to be true. It was easier than he had dared to hope. He had expected the battle to rage almost until morning, but well before the sun rose over the horizon, Tanak's troops were taking the last of Akira's men prisoner. The garrison had been smaller than Tanak's spies had reported. Much of Akira's Fourth was spread up and down the river. Tanak wondered if he could have just sent Renzo in. He could have taken out the garrison by himself. Tanak shook his head. Better he didn't. It was still illegal to harbor a nightblade, and the fear of them was so great that even Tanak's soldiers might have turned on him if they had known. It was better for them to have this victory as the start to their campaign.

Akira's troops had a reputation of being fierce, well-trained fighters. Tanak didn't underestimate his opponent, but their easy victory here today gave his troops the sign they needed. They could stand toe-to-toe with Akira's forces, and when they did, they'd destroy them all.

Tanak slept well for the first time in many moons. When he awoke it was late morning, and he felt as refreshed as though he had slept for days. The sun was bright, beaming through all the smoke from the smoldering fortress. Tanak stood again on the walls of his fortress as he watched his troops camping on the southern side of the river. Today had been designated a day of rest. They had set their perimeter overnight. Today they would take one final deep breath before their push. Every soldier knew the plan and how ambitious it was.

Tanak spent the day in meetings with his generals. Renzo was nowhere to be found. He detested meetings. True to his namesake, he shunned the day, and he tried not to be seen around Tanak more than was necessary. Ambitious advisers were always political targets and Renzo had no desire to bring further attention to himself. However, Tanak took comfort in knowing that Renzo was always somewhere near. With Renzo as a bodyguard, Tanak felt more safe than with an entire regiment guarding him.

The three generals of his armies knew their plans well. Today's meetings were more about straightening out final details than deciding any strategy. After today they would spread out over substantial distances and getting messages to each other would be challenging. But as he looked around the room, he felt confident in the abilities of each of his generals. They all had worked together for at least ten cycles, and Tanak would trust each of them with his kingdom. Each of them had to succeed. They had the element of surprise, but Akira's troops were famous for their training. All of Akira's units cycled through actual combat at the Three Sisters, while few of Tanak's soldiers had seen true bloodshed. It wouldn't be an easy campaign.

That evening Tanak met in private with Renzo.

"What are your thoughts?"

"Last night was successful. It is a good omen. I hope you meet with such success every battle, but do not underestimate Akira. You have caught him unaware, and if you are fast you may make significant progress into his kingdom before he can react, but he is an excellent leader. If trusting to the promises of a treaty is his greatest weakness, he will be a formidable opponent."

Tanak wondered why Renzo had come to him. His respect for Akira and Sen was apparent, but he was here with Tanak. Tanak knew Renzo was trying to keep him from underestimating his opponents, but when he spoke of the other Lords he held a hint of reverence in his voice that never seemed to be present when he spoke to Tanak.

But Renzo had never led him astray, and his plans aligned with Tanak's. Tanak wasn't foolish enough to trust blindly, but he held Renzo in respect.

"What do you think Akira will do?"

Renzo shook his head. "I do not know. The question boils down to his decision about the Three Sisters. Certainly he will be concerned about the lack of an attack this spring. He won't know what to do. If he holds back an army or two to defend the pass you should be able to defeat him. He has a strong army, but not strong enough to fight a war on two fronts. Your victory is assured."

Tanak nodded his agreement. There were many pieces in motion. There was no telling how Akira would react. The other wild card was Sen. Tanak hadn't dared approach him with his plan. Sen was known for his caution, but if Akira was threatened on two fronts, it might be too much of an opportunity for even Sen to pass up. Additionally, if Tanak was successful, the Western Kingdom would be too strong for the Northern Kingdom to resist. Tanak suspected Sen would sit and wait to see how events unfolded.

Tanak knew one fact for sure. The Three Kingdoms would never be the same. They had existed in an uneasy truce for hundreds of cycles, but change was coming, and Tanak was leading it.

Tanak dismissed Renzo and collapsed onto his bed with a smile on his face. Soon, he would be King. A title the Three Kingdoms hadn't seen for a thousand cycles. And it all started with destroying Akira's kingdom.

CHAPTER 4

The sun rose on a beautiful morning. The black of evening gave way to the oranges of the burning sun, dissipating the fog hanging like a blanket over the ground. Ryuu was already up, meditating on the shadow he had encountered almost a half-moon ago. Since that night they had been vigilant, but the shadow hadn't returned. The fact they hadn't sensed anyone again was more troublesome to him than the initial contact. Was their opponent evading their sense, or had it disappeared like the morning fog? Ryuu was convinced it had been tracking him, but why had it come, and why had it disappeared? Having an enemy in front of you was one thing. A mystery was another.

Moriko had sensed the person as well, but she didn't have any answers either. Both of them were lost among possibilities.

He stood up from his meditation. There weren't any answers for him. He had imagined thousands of possibilities, but none of them seemed more realistic or probable than any other. For all the strength he possessed, he was still frustrated by what he didn't know. There were days, many days, where he wished Shigeru was still alive. There was still so much more to learn.

His adopted father had been taken from him too early. Even now he couldn't control all his abilities.

Ryuu walked back to the hut where Moriko was up and busy. He frowned. The morning was early yet. She usually slept for another watch or two. He slid the door open to reveal Moriko packing a small sack with some food. She looked up at him and tossed him a fishing spear. "It's a beautiful day," she said, "and it's about time we got out of the hut for a while."

Ryuu grinned. It sounded perfect. Somehow she always knew what he needed. Her understanding of him was deep. Getting out would distract him from the problems lingering in his mind and keep him focused on the present.

They set off for the stream that ran near the hut. Ryuu held the spear loosely in his hand. Fishing with the sense wasn't fair. When he focused he knew not just where the fish was, but where it would be. In one attempt he caught a trout as long as his forearm. It would feed both of them. He gave a quick thanks to the fish as it joined the Great Cycle, nourishing them just as one day they would nourish the planet with their own bodies. Ryuu packed the fish in the sack and they kept hiking.

He let Moriko take the lead. In the time they had spent here she had learned the woods just as well as him, if not better. She had a natural affinity for the woods and was never happier than when she was walking peacefully among the trees. Their pace was slow, and Ryuu felt the tension lift from his shoulders. He opened up his sense and everything pressed more sharply against his mind. The bird calls rang crisply through the cool late morning. Ryuu smiled. In another life this was how he had trained with Shigeru. The woods were teeming with life, and for those gifted with the sense it was almost too much to take in. Ryuu couldn't extend his senses too far, but what he could sense was beautiful.

Ryuu had become so lost in thought he almost ran into Moriko as she slowed to a stop. She naturally suppressed her aura. Most days it wasn't too much trouble. Ryuu was so attuned to her it was almost impossible for her to hide from him. But lost in thought, open to all the life in the woods, he had lost her for a few moments. He laughed at his awkwardness.

Moriko brought them to a small, secluded clearing where the trees opened up, allowing a soft bed of grass to grow in the sunlight. Ryuu lay down, stretching out as far as he could. Without a word Moriko lay down next to him on her side, her head on his outstretched arm. They lay like that for a while, and Ryuu drifted in and out of sleep. He didn't care. Life was perfect.

The afternoon wore on, and eventually Ryuu figured they should get their meal started. They had been here before and had cleared a small space for a fire. Ryuu went into the woods and collected fallen dead wood. He returned to the clearing where Moriko arranged and lit a fire. Moriko had been teaching herself how to cook over the past two cycles and had gotten better. Ryuu was still more experienced, but he knew better than to complain when someone cooked him food. She rubbed herbs on the fish and let it roast over the fire. When it came off it was perfect, and both of them dug eagerly into their food.

After dinner they sat and talked, and after their food had settled, they trained for a while. They wore their steel, but they hadn't brought wooden swords to practice with, so it was all hand-to-hand combat they trained.

As they trained, Ryuu couldn't help but think about how much stronger Moriko had become. When they had first met, Moriko had been near death. She had healed, but her combat training was nowhere near as complete as Ryuu's had been. But she was a fast learner, faster perhaps than him. As they traded blows, Ryuu realized he only had the slimmest of edges on her.

She committed to a strike she shouldn't have, putting too much force into a blow that never landed. Ryuu was behind her and had her in a hold she couldn't break or throw. He laughed, a combat high washing over him, and he kissed her on the neck. Moriko moaned softly with pleasure. She turned around as he loosened his grasp and her lips met his eagerly. With a quick motion, Ryuu disrobed her and admired her beauty. Her dark hair seemed to glimmer in the early evening sunlight. He ran his hands over the scars that covered her body, marveling both at her mental and physical strength.

Then his robes were off and they were in the grass. Moriko was a quiet and reserved woman, but her passions came out when they lay together. She pushed him down and let herself down on top of him. Ryuu opened up his sense and was lost as the two of them joined together as one.

Afterward they sat in the clearing watching the sun go down below the trees. They used their robes as blankets as it got cooler. Ryuu was moments away from drifting into peaceful oblivion when he felt it again. He cursed. The shadow was back.

Ryuu was on his feet in a moment, Moriko following his lead a heartbeat behind. He wrapped his robes around him and checked the sword at his hip. There was no point in trying to run. If Ryuu was right, the shadows could sense them already. He would stand and fight.

The shadow reached the edge of the clearing and stopped. Ryuu waited patiently, standing his ground. He had all night, and he could sense the shadow's presence high in the trees overlooking the clearing. Ryuu and Moriko were in the most defensible position around. He held his stance, still as the night air.

Ryuu wasn't expecting the shadow to split in two. He doubted his senses for a moment, but there was no time for doubt. Where there had been one shadow, now there were two, moving in opposite directions around the clearing. Ryuu turned to face one as Moriko tracked the other, turning them back to back.

Ryuu barely had time to wonder. His sense had always been precise. But somehow, he struggled to sense these shadows.

The shadows didn't give him time to puzzle out the solution. They broke from the trees simultaneously, one shadow moving straight for Moriko, the other moving for Ryuu. Within a few paces he could see the outlines of a shadow and the glint of a blade in the starlight, but he couldn't make out the distinct outline of a human. It had the approximate dimensions of a man, but its edges were blurry. There was nothing his mind could process as an arm or a leg. He shook his head, trying to clear the mist from his vision. He squinted and nothing changed.

There was a glint as a thin blade struck out from the amorphous attacker. Ryuu dove out of the way, seeing it at the last moment. He rolled to his feet, his sword drawn. He focused on his sense, pushing aside the use of his vision. The shift shocked his mind.

His assailant didn't turn to follow him. By diving out of the way, Ryuu had left Moriko's back undefended. His opponent saw the opening and was going for it. Ryuu opened his mouth to scream a warning, but he knew it was too late. She couldn't react in time, and there was no way he could recover the ground quickly enough to prevent a killing blow. His stomach sank with the knowledge Moriko would die, just like Takako.

The world snapped, and Ryuu launched himself at his original assailant. Everything was in focus. Moriko was having the same trouble Ryuu had, barely able to deflect her own assailant's blade away from a killing strike. The thin blade was cutting through her arm the moment Ryuu returned to the fight.

It didn't seem possible, but Ryuu made it just in time. He reached his own blade out to flick away the blade of his assailant, whose position in space had become as clear as day. But Ryuu was caught off guard again. His opponent sensed his attack and shifted. Ryuu had over-committed in his desperation, and the thin blade flicked at him as he sailed in front of his attacker. He felt the blade slice cleanly through his thigh, although he felt no pain. He analyzed his wound dispassionately as he came to a stop. The cut had been close to his artery. If his opponent had been a moment faster Ryuu would be bleeding to death.

This time his assailant paid full attention to him. The thin blade sliced through the air with incredible speed. His attacker's blade was a little shorter and so thin. It moved faster than Ryuu could bring his blade to bear. But every move was clear to Ryuu. With his reality snapped, he blocked or parried every strike, but he couldn't find an opening to make a counterattack. His assailant was faster even than Orochi had been.

There was a slight pause and Ryuu caught a quick breath. His opponent seemed uncertain, deciding upon his next moves. They were fighting to a draw. Ryuu remained calm. If he lost his focus, he knew he wouldn't be a match for the stranger. His attacker strode forward, and Ryuu swore his attacker grew additional arms and blades. He had never seen attacks come so fast.

Panicked, Ryuu stepped backwards, desperately blocking each strike. Finally he pushed his attacker back a pace or two, giving him just a moment to think. Ryuu redoubled his focus, and the battle resumed. Ryuu wanted to sense how Moriko was doing, but he didn't have a moment to spare. He feared the worst. He was fighting at the best of his ability to a draw. Moriko would be in trouble.

Ryuu lost track of how long their combat lasted. It seemed like forever, but he knew his sense of time when he snapped wasn't the same. His opponent was too fast and Ryuu couldn't get inside his defenses. But Ryuu was fast enough not to be killed either. They passed each other over and over again, moving as fast as thought.

It was just a sliver of a moment, but Ryuu noticed it. His attacker had become more and more violent, striking with increased strength. Ryuu deflected one strike, and it left his attacker off balance. Ryuu seized the moment and drove forward. His attacker blocked the strike, but Ryuu pushed his weight forward, pushing the attacker further off balance. In the moment his assailant tried to regain his balance, Ryuu struck with incredible speed, cutting several of his major blood vessels. His attacker dropped, but Ryuu didn't even pause.

Ryuu sprinted towards Moriko. She was on the defensive and Ryuu could tell she had been cut several times. It was only a matter of time before she made a fatal mistake. Ryuu broke in on the fight, and as soon as he arrived Moriko attacked with the last of her strength. It was decided, but still it took time. If it was possible, Moriko's opponent was even stronger and faster than Ryuu's had been. But against the two remaining nightblades in the Three Kingdoms, the tide turned. Together they swung, sliced and stabbed until Moriko's assailant fell bloody to the ground. The moment he did, Ryuu sensed the danger behind him.

He turned as the throwing knife came flying at his neck. He caught it with the side of his blade and whipped it away. His original attacker collapsed. Ryuu realized he must have used the very last of his strength to make the throw.

There was a moment of silence as Ryuu and Moriko surveyed the ground around them. Ryuu threw out his senses, but there were no more shadows. They were alone again in the clearing. Ryuu turned to Moriko just as she collapsed to the ground, blood all around her.

Ryuu was exhausted. He had yet to sleep. Too much was at stake. His first priority had been to care for Moriko. He bandaged all her cuts as well as he could with what they had with them out in the clearing. It wasn't much, but it was enough to put pressure on her deepest cuts. He hesitated but decided to take a few moments to examine the men they had killed.

There had been much to learn. The first and most obvious fact was that they weren't from the Three Kingdoms. They were taller and more muscular than any man he had ever encountered, even taller than Orochi had been, and their skin was darker than his own. Ryuu was surprised they had been so fast and agile. From the sheer size of them he wouldn't have guessed it would be possible.

Ryuu stripped their bodies of anything he found interesting. He took one of their blades and samples of their clothing and some of the jewelry they adorned themselves with. Anything that could be used to identify them. Most interesting were their cloaks. Ryuu had never seen cloaks like them, but he understood their purpose. They looked like they had been torn into tatters, but Ryuu realized the strips of cloth, fur and hide had been sewn together in a deliberate pattern. The tatters prevented opponents from seeing where strikes would come from. It was why he had struggled to distinguish their movements by sight. The cloaks had a tendency to billow and move haphazardly. It was almost impossible to guess where a strike would come from. Ryuu took one. It could be useful.

With loot in hand and Moriko draped carefully over his shoulder, Ryuu walked back to their hut. Combat had been exhausting enough. Every step he took made the cut on his thigh scream in pain. As the sun began to peek over the horizon, Ryuu's mind was ordering his body to stop, to take a break. His legs and arms and back were screaming at him, and Ryuu cursed the fact they had gone so far on their hike. But fear for Moriko's life kept him going. It wasn't long before he was covered in her blood, and he had to keep repositioning her so she wouldn't slide off his increasingly slick shoulders.

When they arrived at the hut, Ryuu stripped her of all her clothes. He tightly wrapped fresh bandages around her and made her drink water, almost forcing it down her throat. They had a poultice that he rubbed into her deeper cuts. Then came the waiting, the hardest part of all. He sat, nervous and anxious, by her side, unwilling to move in case he was needed. He considered visiting the bodies once again in the daylight, but he didn't dare leave Moriko.

It was evening when she finally opened her eyes. Ryuu made her drink more water and kept her from trying to sit up. She was far too weak, and her cuts hadn't closed yet. It was an effort for her to even speak. Ryuu made stew and served her the broth. Then she was asleep again, having said only a few words. Ryuu ate the rest of the stew and struggled against sleep.

In the middle of the night he gave in to exhaustion. He left his senses open, but nothing disturbed their slumber. Ryuu awoke in the morning refreshed, ready for the day. Moriko awoke as well, and Ryuu was excited to see she seemed to be in better condition than the day before. Together, they changed her bandages, Moriko grimacing as they came off caked in blood. She didn't complain, though. Ryuu examined each of her cuts and was grateful to see they all looked clean. He had been most worried about infection.

They spoke about what had happened. Moriko spoke softly, as if the mention of their attackers might bring them back. "Who were they?"

Ryuu shook his head. "I don't know. They were strong." He paused. "I don't think they were from the Three Kingdoms. They didn't look like anyone I've ever met."

Moriko's dark eyes were curious. "How can that be? Why would anyone outside of the Three Kingdoms want to kill us?"

Ryuu wished he knew the answer to that question. "There are many things I would like to know. Here, look at this."

Ryuu held the sword he had taken in front of Moriko and slowly turned it. He didn't want her trying to sit up and grab it for fear that her wounds might reopen.

The sword was light, but very strong. The craftsmanship and the techniques used to forge it had to be different than any technique practiced in the Three Kingdoms. Most of the blade had been painted black, another reason Ryuu had a hard time seeing it in battle. It was a straight blade, a hand's width shorter than Ryuu's own sword, not curved at all.

"Have you ever seen anything like this?" Moriko had been raised at the monasteries, so in some ways her education was better than Ryuu's.

She tried to shake her head but grimaced in pain. "No. I've never seen a blade quite like it."

Ryuu turned the blade over in his hands. "It's an interesting design. Its reach is inferior, but it's so fast that it's almost impossible to get past if it's being used for defense."

Moriko closed her eyes. "I know. If you hadn't come along, there's no way I could have lasted much longer. I couldn't break their defense."

Ryuu brushed some hair away from her face and kissed her gently on the lips. "You fought well. I was barely able to defeat them myself. I snapped again, and if I hadn't, I would have also lost."

Moriko's mouth turned up just slightly. "You're going to have to teach me how to do that."

Ryuu wished he could. For the first time since he had first met Orochi, he worried that he wasn't strong enough to face what was coming.

When the sun rose the next day, Ryuu still hadn't left Moriko's side. He hadn't gone more than a few paces from the hut the entire day. When she awoke, her voice was stronger, but she still wasn't able to sit up. When Ryuu changed her bandages, he saw most of her wounds had closed up, but just barely. She'd be on bed rest for a couple more days yet, at least. But all her cuts were clean and there was no reason she wouldn't make a full recovery. He was thankful. Moriko surviving the battle had been closer than he cared to admit. He had noticed when cleaning her wounds that some of the cuts had come very close to major blood vessels. It frightened him to know how close to death she'd come.

All morning Ryuu sat by her side, attending to her every need, which were few and far between. Moriko spent most of her time meditating, healing, and resting. In many ways she was handling her injuries better than Ryuu was. By early afternoon it was obvious she was tired of the attention. "I'll be fine. Go do something else. Get out of the hut."

"It's not just your health I'm worried about. I'm worried that if I leave they'll strike here, and there isn't anything you or I will be able to do about it."

Moriko groaned, and Ryuu was certain that if she'd been physically capable of throwing something at him she would have.

"Get out of here. Go check their bodies, see if you can find anything more useful on them. Then leave them for the wolves."

It took some coaxing on her part, but he went.

The path to the clearing was easy to follow, and the ground flew underneath Ryuu's feet. He maintained a steady trot, his senses out and aware, dedicated to not being hunted again. He was ready for the shadows, but there were none to be found. Ryuu came to the clearing, his natural curiosity overwhelming his reluctance to leave Moriko's side. The signs of the battle were all around, present even to an untrained eye. Grass was trampled and stained brown from blood. So much blood. Ryuu knew much of it was his and Moriko's. There was more blood than he would have imagined. The two of them had been lucky.

But the obvious signs of battle were not what drew his attention. His heart raced, and he drew his sword, battle instincts kicking in. He threw out his sense, overwhelmed by the stimulus he brought in. He focused but found nothing. He pushed his sense out even further, dangerous in the old woods, teeming with life as it was. It would be easy to lose his mind. Despite the flood of information coming in, Ryuu couldn't find what he was looking for. There were no shadows. But there weren't any bodies in the clearing either.

Ryuu double-checked his surroundings, but he held no doubts he was in the right clearing. All the signs of battle surrounded him. But there were no bodies, and dead people didn't move on their own. Ryuu knew they were dead. He had checked them himself.

Ryuu closed his eyes and searched his memory. He located the place where the bodies should have been. There was plenty of evidence. Impressions in the grass, pools of coagulated blood, the bodies had definitely fallen there. But they were gone.

He knelt down next to each impression, trying to create a picture of what had happened. Unfortunately, he wasn't an expert tracker, and the signs around the battlefield were too chaotic for him to decipher. Either they had walked off or they had been carried off, but Ryuu couldn't prove either guess. He supposed their bodies could have just vanished, but that was getting too far out into the realm of magic, and magic was something he didn't believe in. The battle had almost taken his and Moriko's lives, and it wasn't over.

At the thought of Moriko, Ryuu froze. If the bodies had been taken, the most logical explanation was that there were other shadows present, and she was alone and in no condition to fight them. He sheathed his sword as he took off at a dead sprint towards the hut.

CHAPTER 5

The sun rose on Akira as he completed his morning ritual of staring off into the south, waiting for something, anything to happen. He had been at the head of the pass for almost a half moon, expecting any news at all. Spring was already turning into summer this far south, and the green grass was slowly retreating against the steady onslaught of dry heat. In another moon the prairie in front of him would be brown. He supposed it was still a better color than red.

Akira didn't know what he was looking for, what he was waiting for. But he kept coming back, morning after morning. Something was happening in the south. A storm was building, and he feared its intensity. The scout's story had been unbelievable. Even once he had fully recovered, he told the story of an entire clan being decimated by a handful of warriors. The story had circulated. Akira had considered trying to halt it, but stories had a way of spreading. Like a wildfire, they would find the one gap in your defenses and blow out of proportion. Best to let it spread. Better than maintaining the appearance of secrecy.

Maybe he was searching too hard for an enemy. Like all nobility, he had been brought up in the arts of war. He thirsted for an enemy in front of him. Despite the tradition fading into legend, he still believed the purest combat was one person testing their steel against another. He despised an unknown enemy, an enemy that hid in shadows. Better the army in front of you than the assassin behind you.

His thoughts turned to Ryuu. He had been thinking about the young nightblade more often, particularly since the report of the scout. Of course the idea of nightblades was being discussed throughout the camp. It was a legend, one many considered an overblown myth. But deep down, everyone believed. It was the way they were raised, in fear of those almost too strong to die. Soldiers would scoff when the sun was up, but they'd all be silent at night, in the darkness rumored to be the domain of the nightblades. The scout's story ignited the kindling that lay dormant in the hearts of all Akira's warriors.

But Akira was one of the few people in the world who knew nightblades still existed. He had known for many cycles. First it had been Orochi, a man who kept his own secrets. Although he never said, Akira suspected Orochi had come from a haven for nightblades. The man had come well trained. Somewhere in the world the path of the nightblade was still being taught. Akira didn't know how large a haven it was, but he guessed there were at least a few dozen. After Orochi, there had been Shigeru and Ryuu, two nightblades who called the Southern Kingdom their home. If there were three, there were probably more.

He was troubled by the possibility of nightblades down in Azaria. Was that where Orochi had come from? Akira had seen Azarians, and they were physically different than his own subjects. Orochi had been large, like an Azarian, but he undoubtedly traced his ancestry back to the Kingdom. Perhaps the nightblades and the Azarians had a relationship? He shook his head. The possibilities were limitless, and he had no way of knowing what was happening. He stretched in the morning sun. There were too many problems and not enough information. He thought about trying to send a scout to find Ryuu, but dismissed the idea out of hand. Akira had given his word, and Ryuu had given his. Ryuu hadn't surfaced for over two cycles, and Akira hadn't gone looking for him.

The sun was beginning to burn brightly, and it was almost time for Akira to head back to another round of frustrating conferences with his generals. Nothing had changed. Construction on the defenses of the pass was in full swing, but it was almost time for him to head back to the Southern Kingdom. Akira had sent in another scouting party to follow the directions of the first scout. He needed more information. The scouts should be back any day, another reason Akira spent so much time on the overlook tower.

Unfortunately, it looked like the scouts would not be returning this morning. In front of him the world might as well have been empty. There wasn't even the hint of a dust trail. As he turned to head back to camp he heard the beginnings of a commotion in camp. In the few moments he was paying attention, the disturbance turned into a clamor. There was yelling and shouting and anger throughout the camp.

He didn't even have to come down from his tower to hear. When Akira heard the news, shouted from person to person as it spread through the camp like a river breaking through a dam, his stomach fell and he almost doubled over. There was no way it could be possible, but the word echoed throughout the camp, ringing in his ears like a death bell.

Invasion.

Akira strode into the command tent, trying to give off an air of command he didn't feel. He felt like he was losing his grasp on reality. The treaty had held for hundreds of cycles, and he hadn't provoked an invasion. His contact with Sen and Tanak was minimal at best. They met once a cycle, and sometimes even that gathering was canceled. Most cycles there was little for them to discuss.

He scanned the room. There was a messenger, as well as his top generals. He had requested the group be as small as possible. Rumors would start fast enough as it was, and if the news was true there needed to be some honest discussions without fear of political consequences.

"What do we know?"

Toro glanced at the messenger, who took his cue to step forward. His nervousness radiated off him as he started to stammer out his answer. Akira raised his hand for pause.

"Do you need a drink? Nobody likes giving bad news to a Lord, but you're going to need to do it, and I need every detail you have. We don't have all day."

The messenger shook his head. He closed his eyes, and Akira watched as he went through a calming exercise. The tension dropped from the messenger's shoulders. When he opened his eyes he was ready to give his report. Akira nodded his permission.

"My Lord. We've been invaded by the Western Kingdom. They took the bridge in a nighttime raid. Best intelligence says they've brought across three full-strength armies with them."

Akira's breath caught in his throat. "Three entire armies?"

"Yes, my Lord." The messenger paused for a moment to let Akira take the news in. Three armies. Tanak only had four armies total. If the report was true, Tanak was putting everything he had into the invasion. It was a do-or-die strategy. A separate part of Akira's mind praised his fellow Lord for his boldness. But the implications were apparent, and Akira worried they spelled disaster for his kingdom. Tanak wouldn't bring across three armies just to gain extra land. Three armies was a bid for the entire Southern Kingdom. It was a move that risked everything.

Akira motioned for the messenger to continue. The news wasn't good. Once they had crossed the river, the three armies had separated, each carving their own swath through the Southern Kingdom. The armies were moving fast. They were hitting key towns and garrisons but bypassing smaller ones. The Western Kingdom's intelligence was spot on. They knew exactly where to strike. If they maintained the same rate of advance they would sweep through the entire Southern Kingdom by the end of the season. Nothing like it had happened in the history of the Three Kingdoms.

Akira dismissed the messenger. He looked at his three generals. "Thoughts."

Toro was livid. "I can't believe they broke the treaty. This means war throughout the land. Many will die for Tanak's treason."

"I agree. This is tragic for all. But we need to set our pain aside and decide how we move to protect our kingdom."

Mashiro replied first. "The decision is simple. Move all our armies to intercept him. With the three armies here in the pass and the Fifth coming in from the northern border, we can crush the traitor. We destroy him here at home and then move in on the Western Kingdom. His gamble will be his end. We could reunite all the kingdoms by the end of the season."

Akira glanced at his young general. Each general around this table had been part of helping him plan their own invasion strategy of the Western Kingdom. Mashiro was right. If they could rout Tanak's men they could walk into Tanak's kingdom, a thought which had some strong appeal at this particular moment.

Makoto nodded his head in agreement. "Yes. I do not know about invading the Western Kingdom, but if we can crush his armies in our own land, he will be defenseless. And he will have broken the treaty. We could attempt to take the Western Kingdom by calling a Conclave. This invasion could become the opportunity you have been waiting for. But we need to crush them for such an undertaking. We'll need every soldier we have to secure both kingdoms."

Akira moved his gaze to Toro, and he saw Toro was thinking the same thoughts he was. "I am uncertain, my Lord. This is a grave threat to our land, but if what our scout says is true, we may have an even greater threat massing to the south."

Mashiro exploded. "We can't be jumping after ghosts! It's foolish to think an army of nightblades is massing in Azaria to attack us. We have three armies resting here when there is a clear and immediate threat in our own kingdom. We need to pay attention to the threats in front of us, not the threats that might exist in the future."

Toro also got upset. "Don't you think I know that? But it's complete folly to commit everything to one undertaking. It's the exact mistake we're contemplating exploiting in Tanak's decisions. Rash decisions today could destroy our kingdom forever. An opportunity isn't always as good as you think it might be."

"And sometimes it is," Mashiro spat back.

Akira raised his hands for silence. "We can disagree, but we can't argue here. Toro is right about one thing, and that is that we need to keep our heads about us. This will be a defining moment in our history. Our people come first. I too am worried about the unknown threat to the south."

Mashiro looked like he was about to start another tirade, but Akira held up his hand to silence further outbursts. "Let's start with the obvious decision first. Do we call up the Fifth and send them west to meet the invaders, or do we keep them on the northern border?"

Mashiro scoffed. "They'll be torn apart."

Makoto growled at his friend. "Don't underestimate them. They are soldiers, the same as the rest of us."

Akira raised his voice. "Makoto is right. They may not have the training or experience of the other armies, but our success in defending the kingdom may lie in their hands. If we commit them, they will be in the fight long before we will."

There was silence around the table as the commanders thought about their next moves. There wasn't any obvious answer to Akira's question. It all depended upon their larger strategy. Akira needed to focus their efforts. He knew he had the best military minds in the Three Kingdoms with him at this table.

Akira paused, collecting his thoughts. "I want different battle plans drawn up. Mashiro, I want you to assume we have to repel the invasion with only the Fifth and the Second."

Mashiro couldn't hide his bewilderment. "Why?"

"I haven't decided how many men we're going to commit to this. No, stop." Akira calmed Mashiro before he could explode again. "I know you want to commit everyone, but I'm not sure that's wise. If there is any one of us here who can draw up a defense with only two armies, it will be you. You're my worst case scenario. Impress me."

Akira met Mashiro's steely gaze with one of his own. Akira didn't want to send only two armies in defense of his kingdom, but it was a real possibility. He needed brilliance, and he hadn't lied to Mashiro. If any of them could come up with a plan to defeat three invading armies with only two defending, it would be him.

Mashiro nodded his acquiescence.

"Good. Makoto, I want you to do the same, but with four armies. Assume the First, Second, Third and Fifth."

"Not the Fourth?"

The Fourth was the army tasked with defending the border to the Western Kingdom. "We can't assume the Fourth is a functioning unit. You're my best case, smash-them-to-bits scenario."

Makoto nodded. Akira turned to Toro. "Toro, three armies. Assume the Second, Third, and Fifth."

Toro asked no questions. He read deeper into Akira's orders than the other two did. "Yes, my Lord."

"That's it for now. I want orders for all armies to pack up. Prepare to move light, much lighter than they did for this campaign. They'll need to move fast, essential supplies only."

Makoto spoke up. "When do we leave?"

"I don't know. I would like the scouts to be back from Azaria before we make final decisions, but I won't wait more than a day or two. Every day we lose will be harder to recover from. It'll take that long for the armies to prepare properly anyway. I want more drilling everywhere, gentlemen. Make it happen."

The three generals left the tent, orders to give and plans to create. Akira savored the small moment of silence. He still couldn't believe his kingdom was being invaded. The truth of it hadn't set in. There hadn't been a major invasion between the Three Kingdoms since the truce had originally been signed, hundreds of cycles ago. Whatever the next few cycles would bring, the Three Kingdoms would never be the same.

The sun rose, and again Akira was on the tower, looking to the south. Again, there wasn't any sign of life. The eeriness of it was not lost on him. He had been to this tower in previous cycles. Every time it had been at the height of war. The plains below had been flooded with soldiers fighting, dying, and dead. Today it seemed much like the graveyard it had always been.

He shook his head over the morbid thoughts. There was nothing for it. His father had been a pragmatic man. Akira had always been thoughtful, prone to allowing his thoughts to wander over all sorts of scenarios. He remembered his father talking with him over a game of go. Akira spent so much time thinking about possibilities that he sometimes forgot to move. He recalled the words his father spoke as though it was yesterday.

"Life is always full of limitless possibilities. You cannot prepare for them all. See what is in front of you and make the best decisions you can. It is all we can do."

Akira had lived by his father's advice, never more so than today. He had made his decision. It would be unpopular with his generals, but it felt right. He didn't have even a bit of the sense in him, but he did have a premonition the world would never be the same. It wasn't just the invasion of his kingdom. It was deeper and more menacing, and it was all tied together with the nightblades. They were elemental forces of change. They were so powerful that they changed the world just by passing through it.

Akira didn't need the sense to hear Toro climbing the steps up the tower. In the stillness of the early morning, sounds carried forever. He had asked the general to join him up here. Toro reached his side, gave a little bow, and looked out upon the plains with Akira.

He waited patiently. Akira was grateful. Toro was the longest serving general alive in all the Three Kingdoms. He had been general of the Second for many cycles, until the death of Nori. Akira had promoted him to general of the First and hadn't regretted the decision for even a moment. Toro had no desire for power, but had always been a stalwart defender of the Southern Kingdom. Akira and Toro understood their relationship. Not quite Lord and general, but not quite friends.

Akira broke the silence. "My father fought for a lifetime to see this exact sight."

"And yet you don't trust it."

"I don't. I don't think it's a trap, but something is brewing to the south."

Toro didn't respond. He continued watching thoughtfully to the south.

Akira let out a sigh. The sun wasn't even fully over the horizon and he was exhausted.

Toro spoke. "He'd be proud of you, you know. You've led this kingdom well."

"Thank you." Akira straightened his back, catching the corner of Toro's mouth turn up at the movement. He often wondered what was going on in the old man's head. Toro had served under Akira's father. They'd been friends, and in some ways, Toro saw himself as Akira's guide in life since Lord Azuma had been killed in this very pass.

"I would like you to keep the First here."

To his credit, Toro didn't hesitate. "Very well. My orders?"

"Defend the pass, on this side. Prepare for a siege lasting multiple cycles. I'm not sure we're going to be able to get supplies back to you. You may need to be on your own for a while, even if we take care of the invasion."

Akira watched Toro carefully. He saw the slight slump in the older man's shoulders, but he was a man willing to sacrifice everything. With a deep breath he straightened back up. "Very well."

Akira couldn't imagine what Toro was thinking. Toro was a proud man, proud of his realm. He would want to fight against the invasion in front of him. Not the invasion that hadn't materialized.

"Toro."

He looked up at Akira. "Yes, my Lord."

"Something is coming. I don't know what it is. Tanak we can handle. He's an enemy we know, an enemy we've studied for cycles. But there is something down there we're not ready for. Toro, I need you to use your best discretion here. When the hammer falls, I know I can trust your judgment. Do whatever you think is best or necessary to protect the realm, at all costs."

Akira let the weight of that slip onto Toro's shoulders. He needed Toro to understand he felt the true threat was here, not the invasion to the north. He wasn't being left behind, he was the point of the second front. Hell, he was the entire spear. If Akira's intuition was correct, the First wouldn't be enough to hold the pass, but it had to be. Akira hadn't lied to Toro. Toro was the only general he could trust to make the right decisions if bad became worse.

Toro simply nodded. "I understand."

Akira grinned. That at least, was taken care of. "Good, now we just need to go convince everyone else."

The tent was in an uproar, just as Akira had predicted. He sat in the middle of it, silent as curses and arguments were thrown around him. He trusted his generals, and they had developed a camaraderie that gave his command a powerful weight when he exercised it. But it also meant he had to endure the verbal disagreements. He wondered idly if it was too late to rule by fear. He imagined Tanak didn't have to listen to these types of arguments.

Nevertheless, he kept his head and tried to follow the points his commanders were making. Each of them was a brilliant strategist, and their opinions were valuable, even if they were being shouted as if they were arrows hurled at the hearts of their opponents.

Even when Akira rose his hand the commotion continued. They didn't notice him until he stood. That quieted the room.

"You each have one point to make, then the decision is final."

Mashiro spoke first. He was always the quickest. "Sir, this is a terrible mistake. We should bring everyone in to destroy Tanak. He's left himself more vulnerable than ever before. There's no threat here. Commit the First and we can take the Western Kingdom." He looked like there was more he wanted to say, but he caught Akira's warning glance and sat down.

Makoto spoke next. "I also think we should commit the First. They are our best troops, and our kingdom deserves their service at its defense. Leave the Third here, if you must, but the First will be vital."

Toro spoke last. "I do not know if I follow your logic. I admit I would want to bring my best troops in to defend my kingdom. But I trust your judgment, my Lord."

Akira nodded. He would miss Toro dearly during the campaign. Toro was always trying to act as a role model to the younger generals, showing them the proper way to disagree with a Lord. He would miss him, but it also reaffirmed his decision. The Three Sisters was vital to the continued defense of the land. He trusted Toro with it more than he could anyone else.

"I understand all your concerns. I know there will be a lot of complaints and questions about the First remaining here. But the fact of the matter is that I still believe the defense of the Three Sisters is vital to the survival of our land, and if we can't station several armies, at the least we can station our best army. It will make our job to the north more challenging, but I wouldn't make this decision if I didn't think we could do it."

That was the part he was less certain about. He had looked at the battle plans and there was no doubt in his mind they faced a tremendous battle. They were almost evenly matched in terms of strength, but Akira's troops had the advantage of defending their homeland. However, Tanak was moving fast, which would make it almost impossible to fight him on ideal terms. He could see the war going different ways, and not all of them led to victory. Akira wanted the invasion crushed by fall. Any later and Akira worried about Sen's actions. Sen was not an impulsive man, but if the other two kingdoms were over-committed, he might make a move.

Akira's orders were final. His generals didn't have to agree with him in the command tent, but as soon as they stepped outside, they would be his greatest supporters. Orders were arranged, and Akira shared one last bow with each of his generals. It would probably be the last time they would all be together for quite some time, if not forever.

Akira pushed the thought out of his mind. He needed to be the confident lord, now more than ever. Even internally he couldn't allow himself to doubt the success of their endeavor.

Akira climbed the watchtower and looked out to the south one last time. There wasn't the slightest sign the scouts, or anyone, was returning from that direction. It was as quiet as the grave. He turned to the north to watch his armies begin their trip back through the Three Sisters. He imagined he could feel the earth trembling under the power of his armies as they moved to defend their homeland against invasion.

The Southern Kingdom marched to war.

CHAPTER 6

Ryuu ran until he thought his heart would burst, but he wouldn't slow down. He couldn't slow down. The old woods flew past him as he sprinted, putting everything he had into his legs. He'd never run so far, so fast in his life. He felt as if he was drawing energy from all the living things around him. Nothing would stop him.

He burst into the clearing surrounding the hut. He threw out his sense, desperate for Moriko's presence, but he couldn't focus his mind and couldn't sense a thing. He burst into the hut and drew his sword, drawing a surprised eyebrow from Moriko. She would have sensed him coming, but she hadn't predicted him crashing through the door with a blade drawn.

"Yes?" Her voice held a hint of mirth.

He didn't answer her, instead dropping to his knees and throwing out his sense, focusing his attention and his breath. He searched far and wide around the hut, but he couldn't find any shadows. Nothing that indicated they were in danger. The only disturbance was the wake he had caused in his own haste. Beyond his actions, the world continued to go on as it always had.

When he had caught his breath and was certain they were safe, Ryuu turned to her. "The bodies are gone."

Moriko's eyes widened, and he knew she was thinking the same thoughts he was. He watched as she took the fear and overcame it. She was strong. In some ways stronger than he could ever hope to be. She put her mind to practicalities.

"So, what do we do next?"

Ryuu shrugged. "I don't know. We need to find answers."

Moriko asked the question they were both afraid to speak aloud. "Do you think Akira sent them after us?"

Ryuu thought the question over. "I've been wondering that, too. I have a hard time believing it. It's been over two cycles. If he wanted to have killed us, he would have tried something else, something sooner. And besides . . ." He hesitated, knowing how irrational he was going to sound, "I trust him. I don't think he would break his word."

Moriko studied his face. "You've met him for all of a few moments."

"Yes, but he was a good man. A hard man, yes, but good."

"We could always ask him."

Ryuu laughed at the idea, then thought about it more seriously. "It might not be a bad idea. If he is responsible, we could confront him and finish this for good. If not, he might be interested in knowing about it. If nothing else, if he is innocent, he could point us in the right direction."

Moriko was skeptical. "You know I was joking, right?" She paused and sighed. "But I don't have any better ideas, either. He's the one connection we have to power in the Three Kingdoms, and whatever sent those men has a lot of power."

They stared at each other, both in disbelief. After two cycles of peace, they'd be leaving the hut, tracking the man who had once ordered them killed. Ryuu felt like he was caught in the Great Cycle, forced to actions he wanted no part of. But he didn't see another way forward, not if they wanted to stay safe. From Moriko's look, she was thinking the same.

The matter was settled then. Ryuu didn't sleep at all that night, listening and using his sense to try to discover any more shadows. But the night was like any other. The next day, as Ryuu watched over Moriko, she asked the other question on both their minds.

"Who were they?"

Ryuu had to shake his head. "I have no idea. And that scares me more than anything."

Leaving the hut brought back a slew of unpleasant memories for Ryuu. The last time he had left the hut for a long journey, he had lost his master. As he walked side by side with Moriko, he wondered if history was doomed to repeat itself. He desperately hoped it wouldn't. He missed Shigeru and Takako every day. His grief at their partings would always be a part of him. If he lost Moriko he wasn't sure he'd have the strength to keep going.

It had been almost a half moon before Moriko had been able to move normally again. Ryuu had taken good care of her. He helped her stretch every night and do what movement she could without reopening her wounds. Her new scars were already fading into her old scars. Soon a casual observer wouldn't be able to tell the difference. Ryuu loved the scars. They were physical reminders of the pain she had endured, and they gave him strength. Sometimes when they were lying together and Moriko was relaxed, he would run his fingers up and down her back, tracing each of them.

He knew every scar was a painful memory, but her battles had made her who she was, the woman Ryuu loved. She had seen more pain than anyone Ryuu had met and had emerged from the flames stronger. He wondered sometimes in the blackness of night if he could show the same courage if it was ever demanded of him. He tried to probe every once in a while, but Moriko would tell him she hadn't felt courageous. She had just survived.

Ryuu wasn't so sure. People gave up under less. Something in her had made her keep going, something stronger than a mere survival instinct. She had a spirit he admired, a hidden fierceness he loved.

They walked slowly. Moriko was not yet at full strength, but they had to balance her recovery with their need for knowledge. She could fight if she had to. He would have liked to have waited, but he feared time was something they didn't have much of. Every instinct in his body told him they were in danger. They had to move.

Fortunately, the journey was not a hard one. Ryuu purchased a cheap horse in the nearby village. He wasn't a stallion, but he helped them keep a better pace. After they came out of the woods, they transitioned into the rolling plains which led up to the mountain range and the Three Sisters. Ryuu had decided to take a direct route, avoiding any towns or cities. At this time of the season it was likely Akira would be with the armies in the pass. They'd be able to find him without problem.

They were still two days away from the pass when Ryuu sensed a group of tremendous size. It felt like the entire city of

New Haven had doubled and moved closer to the Three Sisters. They were confused until they encountered their first groups of scouts. Ryuu and Moriko were dressed in the clothes of peasants. Their swords were hidden on their backs and the soldiers passed by as though they weren't even present.

They paused as the soldiers rode off.

"A group that size, Akira has to be moving almost all his armies," Moriko said.

Ryuu nodded his agreement.

As they stood, they could sense the entire mass of humanity moving north. At this distance Ryuu couldn't focus on individuals, but he could sense the whole. It was as if an earthworm several leagues long was crawling its way forward, contracting and expanding in sections. It felt chaotic at first, but in time Ryuu was able to sense the patterns in the movement. They were beautiful in their own way.

"Do you think they're retreating? Were they beaten in the Three Sisters?" Moriko's voice held a hint of disbelief. Everyone knew the Southern Kingdom held the entire pass. To be retreating this far north, to have lost the entire pass in just a moon or two, was almost unthinkable. It had taken Akira's father almost ten blood-soaked cycles to take the pass from the Azarians.

Ryuu shook his head. "No, a retreat would never be this orderly, especially if they were routed so badly they lost the pass so early in the season." He paused, thinking. "No, they are marching to war. Why they are heading north is beyond me."

He thought for a few moments more, but he couldn't think of any believable reasons why Akira would move so many troops.

There were many possibilities, but each seemed less likely than the last.

He looked over and saw Moriko looking seriously at the dust cloud gathering on the horizon. "I suppose we'll just have to ask him."

It was a childish joy, but Ryuu couldn't help but laugh at Akira's face when he and Moriko walked into the Lord's tent. Akira had been studying a set of maps in utter concentration. Ryuu and Moriko had made a silent entrance, barely disturbing the tent flap. They had been there a few moments before he noticed them watching him. Akira startled, his hand coming to his sword, a shout on his lips. Then Ryuu saw the recognition on his face, and he let go of his sword.

"I had increased security against this. Are they all right?"

Ryuu laughed. He saw Moriko's glare, but he enjoyed the feeling of keeping Akira on his toes. It was one of the few exercises in power he allowed himself. Moriko thought it was foolish.

"No, they are fine, doing their usual rounds."

"Then how did you get in?" Akira looked dubiously at them. Both of them were dressed as soldiers. "You didn't hurt anyone else, did you?"

"No, their path is just a bit too wide. The uniforms allowed us to get all the way to your perimeter, but there was a slight gap in their coverage. I don't think anyone but a nightblade would see it."

Akira nodded. "Why are you here?"

Ryuu's mood turned serious. "We were attacked, a little over a half moon ago. There were two of them, stronger than anyone I've ever faced before. They almost succeeded."

Akira understood the unspoken accusation. There was a hint of fear in his eyes as he took a slight step back, his hand returning to his sword. Ryuu narrowed his eyes in suspicion.

"I didn't send anyone after you. It's been over two cycles and I've kept my word. I haven't even tried to find you with messengers or couriers. I don't even know if you're still living in the Southern Kingdom."

Ryuu and Moriko exchanged glances. Ryuu was waiting for her opinion. He trusted Akira and hadn't believed it was him in the first place. But Moriko would have her own thoughts. She stared intently at Akira, allowing the weight of the silence to grow in the tent. Ryuu knew she would be probing him with the sense, trying to detect some hint of deception. Akira held his voice. Ryuu respected him for that. The Lord said his piece and was done. Few people could muster that type of courage in front of a nightblade, much less two.

Moriko looked at Ryuu and slightly nodded her head. She thought he was telling the truth. Good.

"I believe you." Ryuu watched as Akira relaxed. "We were hoping you could help us find out who sent them."

Akira looked at them helplessly. "I'd be delighted to help if I could, but I don't know if there is anything I could do. If I can't find you, I don't know how anyone else could. Rumors of your existence spread after you killed Orochi, but because you've stayed hidden they've stayed rumors."

Ryuu reached under his soldier's uniform to pull out the items he had retrieved the night of the attack. He handed them to Akira. "Do you recognize any of these?"

Akira turned the objects and insignia over in his hands, settling eventually on a piece of jewelry Ryuu had torn from one of the bodies. It was a leather necklace with what appeared to be a tooth. There was a small inscription near the root. Akira almost fell backwards in surprise. "This can't be. Where did you get this?"

Ryuu held his silence. He had no use for meaningless questions. He had already said they were attacked.

Akira glanced up at Ryuu, true fear in his eyes. "You need to tell me exactly how you got these. Don't leave out any detail."

Ryuu glanced at Moriko, who shrugged and moved to cover the entrance to the tent. They were going to be here a while.

Ryuu told the story, relating to Akira how they had been tracked and hunted in the hut. Ryuu left out any description of the place, making sure not to give any details to Akira he could track them with later. He talked about the attack itself and brought out the sword he had recovered.

As Ryuu finished his story Akira sat down on some of his traveling cushions, dazed. Moriko and Ryuu shared another look of confusion. Whatever had happened, Akira knew something that scared him more than the two nightblades in his own tent. Akira was muttering silently to himself.

Ryuu was losing his patience. If Akira knew what was going on, he needed to share his knowledge.

"Akira, out with it."

Akira looked up and shook his head. "You wouldn't believe me if I told you. I don't believe it. Ryuu, either this is the greatest prank ever pulled, or a nightmare is coming true."

Rage erupted in Ryuu, burning away his self-control. He stepped forward and effortlessly picked Akira off the ground in a single movement. Akira went for his sword but Ryuu slapped his hand away. He brought Akira's face to his own. "This is not a joke." He looked at Moriko. "She almost died, and I need answers."

Akira was shaken, both by the artifacts Ryuu had brought and by his rough handling. Ryuu almost felt a moment of sympathy. As one of the three most powerful people in the world, he probably wasn't often threatened this way.

"Okay, calm down. I'll tell you what I know."

Ryuu released Akira abruptly, and he stumbled backwards.

"When I was young I studied under my father. He believed I had a duty to know not just about the Three Kingdoms, but the world beyond the Three Kingdoms as well. We don't know much, as we've always been isolated by our geography. The only other people we've ever had regular contact with are the Azarians, and that has only been in the war in the pass. There has never been a significant amount of trade between the people."

"Anyway, the items you have there, those are Azarian. But they shouldn't even exist."

Ryuu was losing his patience again, but Akira held up his hand. "No, you need to know this."

"There is a legend in Azaria, a legend very similar to that of the nightblades and dayblades here in the Three Kingdoms. In the Azarian language they are called 'hunters,' but everything I ever learned indicated they were nothing more than legend. They don't exist. Maybe they never did. In over sixty cycles of battles in the pass, we've never encountered one, and I never believed they were real."

"The legends claimed these hunters were warriors beyond the ability of regular mortals. But they were bedtime stories used to scare young Azarians, much like the nightblades are used by our own people."

"What does this have to do with anything?"

Akira spoke, his voice a carrier for a story he didn't believe. "Legend has it that when Azarian hunters see their tenth cycle, they are sent away from their village. They go on their first hunt, armed with nothing but their bare hands and a knife. It is the first of their trials. Their prey is a large cat, considered one of the most dangerous animals in Azaria. There is only one way to pass the trial. They must return to their village with the hide of the cat over their shoulder. If they attempt to return without a hide they are killed."

Ryuu listened to every word, and Akira continued.

"If they pass, they are given a tooth from the cat to keep on their person at all times. It is to give them luck in their future endeavors. It is engraved with an inscription, just like this tooth."

Ryuu couldn't hide his disbelief. "It's a good story, but it's a long stretch between an Azarian legend and the attack on us. I don't think I've every had any contact with any Azarian." He looked at Moriko, who shook her head in the negative. She hadn't had any dealings with Azarians either.

"True, but the sword proves it. This is an Azarian design. I've seen hundreds of these on the battlefield. They are wielded by some of the elite Azarian clansmen. It's a dangerous weapon."

Ryuu was ready to blow. "But that doesn't explain anything. You've told us nothing but a legend!"

Akira looked at him wryly. "Ten cycles ago I would have said the same thing about you. But here you are. Since you've come the world has changed again."

The truth of the statement stopped Ryuu in his tracks. He had been trained to be open to all possibilities. It was foolish to dismiss something simply because he didn't believe in it. The facts were laid out in front of him. "Why are you on the move?"

Akira was surprised at the abrupt subject change. "I would have thought you knew. Everyone should know. The Southern Kingdom has been invaded by the Western Kingdom."

Ryuu couldn't hide his shock. "That's impossible."

Akira almost laughed, managing instead a harsh grunt. "So are you. But here we are, going to the first real war between kingdoms in hundreds of cycles." He stood and returned to looking at his maps.

Ryuu shared a look with Moriko. She was just as undecided as him. Silence settled in the room, and Ryuu tried to hide his disappointment. He hadn't thought Akira would be responsible, but he thought by coming here they would have a clear next step. Instead, they had only learned they had been attacked by a mythological being from a land they had never been anywhere near.

Akira turned abruptly and looked at the two of them. "Would you stay here overnight? There is more to the story, and I need to think about it. Can we meet tomorrow night?"

Ryuu nodded. He didn't have any better ideas.

Akira went to the door of his tent and called for soldiers. Two came in and almost jumped out of their uniforms when they saw Moriko and Ryuu in the tent. Akira calmed them down. "Have no fears. They are two of my best shadows." There was a hint of mirth in his eyes. "There isn't anything you could have done to stop them. They need a tent, first ring." The soldiers barked their acknowledgment and led the two nightblades to a vacant tent nearby.

Moriko looked at him with worry in her eyes. "Ryuu, what's happening? It seems like the world is going mad."

Ryuu shook his head and stared at the ceiling of the tent, wishing she didn't seem so right.

Ryuu did not sleep well. It was unnatural for him to contain his sense, but when surrounded by so many people there was little else he could do. If he let his mind wander he would be overwhelmed by the information crashing into his mind. But he didn't trust Akira so completely that he would let his guard down either. Instead, he settled for tossing and turning all night, eventually giving up in favor of meditation.

Moriko didn't seem to have the same problem. Ryuu didn't know how she did it. She was every bit as paranoid as he was, but somehow managed to sleep with no problem.

Their tent was spacious enough for Ryuu to practice his forms in the morning. By the time he was finished, Moriko was awake, watching him without a word. He laid down next to her and held her, the two of them together in silence as the sun rose. Ryuu enjoyed the feeling of his skin against hers. He was relaxed, content. It was all he wanted, to live like this forever, next to her.

Their peace was soon disturbed by a nervous messenger. The army was on the move around them and they needed to leave the tent so it could be packed up and transported. Ryuu and Moriko donned their uniforms and joined the movement, lost in the mass of soldiers. It was surreal, to be surrounded by soldiers trained to kill them. As they walked, they spoke, their voices not carrying further than their own ears, trying to understand what was happening around them.

Ryuu tried to explain himself to Moriko. "I trust Akira. He's got nothing to gain, and he's clearly got larger problems. I don't see any reason to doubt what he says. His story is too unbelievable to be a lie."

"But if it's true, what can we possibly do? I don't think hunting mythological creatures is our best plan."

Ryuu agreed. He didn't know what to do.

Moriko was lost in thought.

"What are you thinking about?"

She looked up at him. "Do you think the Azarian hunters are just nightblades?"

Ryuu shrugged. "I've never considered it. They might be. There have to be more nightblades out there. Orochi said as much. I don't see any reason why they wouldn't be down in Azaria as well."

The idea tumbled around in Ryuu's brain. He could see it happening. Orochi hadn't come from Azaria, but if there was one enclave of nightblades, it stood to reason there would be more. It was both a comforting and disturbing thought. Ryuu liked that he and Moriko weren't alone in the world, but if there were others out there with enough strength to be a threat, he and Moriko weren't as safe as he had imagined. Again, Ryuu felt like there was too much he didn't know.

Moriko seemed to be reading his thoughts. "Are you thinking about the island?"

He was. Perhaps they wouldn't have the answers he was looking for, but if there was a small enclave of nightblades in existence, they had to know more about the world than he did. But the idea of going to the island intimidated him. He had grown up knowing he was unique, the strongest warrior. But on the island, he'd be just another nightblade to them, and one that hadn't been trained properly. What if there was some sort of test he didn't know how to pass? Neither he nor Moriko had been trained formally. Ryuu's education had been closer, but was still the equivalent of being schooled at home instead of at a school. More than anything, he didn't want to fail Shigeru's memory.

When they set up camp that night they weren't any closer to answers. If anything, they only created more questions. But as Ryuu struggled to rest and calm his mind, he couldn't help but acknowledge that he felt like he had to travel to the island. It was a gut feeling, but one he was learning to trust more and more every day.

Akira summoned them to his tent well after the sun had fallen. Their tents were close enough together that Ryuu could sense the happenings in Akira's tent, and he had little doubt Akira was in conference with his generals late into the night. Only after they departed did a messenger come and usher the nightblades into Akira's tent.

The Lord of the Southern Kingdom looked like he had aged ten cycles since they had seen him the day before. Ryuu knew Akira was a man who was as hard as steel, but he was a good man, and Ryuu had let him live because he believed Akira cared about his people and their fate. He was driven by more than just power. Ryuu was convinced of it the moment he saw Akira, worn down and dispirited.

"How bad is it?"

Akira rolled his shoulders back and tried to release tension in his neck. "I don't know. Tanak has split his armies apart and they march quickly across the land. They are only hitting major cities and forts. His men are moving much faster than I would have expected. They will have control of a significant portion of the kingdom before we can even mount an effective counter-offensive."

Akira paused and rubbed his eyes with his fingers. "But honestly, that's only one part of what I'm worried about. I'm just as concerned about what happened to you. Something strange happened down in the Three Sisters this season."

The two nightblades sat down as Akira told his story. He filled them in on the barren lands to the south of the Three Sisters. He spoke of the scout's unbelievable report and his unpopular decision to leave the First to guard the pass. When he finished, Ryuu thought Akira looked like all the air had been let out of him.

A heavy silence hung in the tent. Ryuu didn't know what to make of Akira's story. It seemed unbelievable. There had been war in the pass as long as he'd been alive. But it was such an unbelievable story, it was hard to accept it as a lie. Perhaps he was telling the truth.

Akira found some of his inner steel and straightened up. "I can't believe it is a coincidence the strange events at the Three Sisters happened at the same time you were attacked. There is something afoot in Azaria and in our kingdoms, but I don't know what it is. It worries me more than Tanak. He is a dangerous opponent, but one I understand. I fear what I don't understand, the attack I can't see coming." He looked up at Ryuu, and Ryuu knew Akira wasn't just referring to the Azarians.

Neither Ryuu nor Moriko could speak. Neither had expected Akira would believe their story to be as important as he did.

Ryuu could see Akira was working up the courage to say something. Both he and Moriko waited. He respected Akira, but he didn't see any reason to make his work easier for him.

"I would like to ask the two of you to go down to Azaria and investigate what is happening."

"You have no right!" Ryuu startled at Moriko's outburst.

Akira was also startled. "I know. But I need to think about my people, and I can't fight a war on two fronts and win. My men are good, but we aren't prepared for this. I need you two to find out the truth. I'll have you carry messages to Toro, a trusted general of mine who is down in the pass. He'll support you in any way necessary."

Ryuu stood up. He could sense more than see Moriko's anger. "We'll need to talk it over. We will let you know."

Akira glanced from one of them to the other and he understood. "Please, let me know as soon as you decide. I'll leave a messenger outside your tent."

Different emotions tore at Ryuu when the sun came up the next day. His efforts at meditation were laughable and his forms were a joke. Try as he might, he couldn't focus. He believed they were doing the right thing, but it tore him up inside. He asked himself for the hundredth time if he was making the right decision. There was a part of him which spoke loudly, a part that had shouted at him over and over last night. It told him he didn't owe the Southern Kingdom anything. He should live as he please, returning to hiding with Moriko.

But there was another part of him, quiet and insistent, that rebuffed all attempts at selfishness. It was Shigeru's voice, pleading with him to use his power well. He was gifted with abilities that few people had. It would be a horrible waste if he didn't use them to help those who needed it.

Moriko did not share his sentiments. She felt strongly that they didn't owe anything to anyone. She enjoyed their time together and was just as willing to stick a sword through Akira as listen to him. Even though they fought, Ryuu saw that Moriko recognized the same truth he had. If they tried to resume their life together, they would fail. The world was crashing around them and there wasn't any place to hide from the incoming storm.

It was tempting to go back to the hut and hide. More than tempting. It was all he wanted to do. But it was wrong. He had tried to describe his feelings to Moriko last night, but he had failed. He was much better with a sword than with words. It was only an instinct, but an instinct so strong it overwhelmed him. Moriko knew it too, she was just more resistant to the idea of returning to the world again. They were warriors and war was coming for them whether they desired it or not.

Moriko argued he was letting his emotions get the best of him. He was a fool to be taken in by Akira, a man who just two cycles ago had taken away almost everything Ryuu had loved and cared for. Moriko couldn't shake her distrust completely, even after meeting him.

They had gone back and forth through the entire night. Both of them were uncertain, and their uncertainty made them volatile. Both of them wanted to run and hide, but neither of them could.

The moon had almost run the full length of the sky when their argument sputtered to a halt. A silence descended upon their tent as they both processed the consequences of their actions.

Ryuu looked up at Moriko. "Are we sure about this?"

Moriko shook her head. "No, but I don't see any other way."

Ryuu didn't either. His mind raced for alternatives, but there weren't any. They were going in different directions. They both hated the decision, but there was nothing else to be done. They had never argued the way they had last night.

Moriko would head to the south and through the Three Sisters. She would carry out Akira's request, even though she detested it. If they had been attacked by Azarians, they had to find out why. It may have been Akira's request, but they needed the information even more than he did. If they were targets, they needed to know who had ordered their deaths. If they didn't find answers, they'd never know peace. It had taken time, but Moriko had relented. She would find out what was happening and see if there was a solution. Ryuu wasn't happy about her going alone. She had almost died at the hands of a hunter and she was heading straight into the belly of the beast. He wanted to be with her to protect her, but he had his own mission.

Ryuu was going to the island Orochi and Shigeru had come from. It wasn't his first choice, but he felt he had to. If there was any place he could learn more, it was there. He didn't know what he would find. Shigeru had only spoken of it once, and Orochi had done nothing more than give him directions. He suspected he would find a small village, a small enclave of nightblades who knew more than Shigeru had. If Ryuu was going to face more hunters, he knew he would have to be stronger. It was the only solid lead they had. Perhaps they'd have information on the Azarians too. Whatever knowledge was there, both Ryuu and Moriko felt it couldn't wait any longer.

Ryuu wished Moriko could come with him. He could tell she was jealous. Both of them had a relentless desire to get stronger. But he was the logical choice. Moriko's ability to hide herself from the sense would be invaluable if she was scouting among hunters. They were heading to the opposite edges of the world, and it frightened both of them.

When there was nothing more to say, they came together with a violence that wasn't typical for the two of them. Moriko's quiet was more than skin deep, but their coming together had been more passionate than anything Ryuu had ever experienced. When they had finished, he sat at the edge of their bedroll, Moriko cuddled up against him, feeling emptied and content.

"Moriko?"

She murmured at him. She wasn't quite asleep, but wasn't fully awake either.

"I love you."

"I love you, too."

With that, she was sound asleep.

The two of them left the camp with little fanfare. Ryuu and Moriko embraced one last time in the tent before stepping outside, but there were no more words to say. The sense was strange in that way. Ryuu couldn't read Moriko's mind, no matter what some legends about nightblades claimed, but it didn't stop him from knowing exactly what she thought. It was the same for her.

They announced their decision to Akira. He wasn't pleased. Ryuu did not say where he was going, simply stating there was something else he needed to take care of. Akira gave both of them documents which would allow them to pass anywhere in the Southern Kingdom. He gave other letters to Moriko to pass along to Toro when they met. Ryuu wished Akira well in the defense of the Southern Kingdom. He did not promise aid, despite Akira's attempts to get him to do so. He trusted Akira, but he wasn't sure if it was his place to support him in war. It was exactly the sort of behavior which had led to the slaughter of the nightblades in the first place.

Ryuu and Moriko parted outside the camp. Ryuu kissed her gently and embraced her tightly. After a few moments, she turned and hopped on the horse she had been loaned by Akira. She would need the additional speed. Azaria was a huge kingdom. Scouts had never found its borders. She could have a very long journey in front of her.

It was some time before Ryuu could turn the other way and begin his own journey. He mounted his horse and took one last glance over his shoulder at Moriko as she rode away, now just a speck in the distance. Seeing her leave brought tears to his eyes, although he refused to let them fall. He hadn't told her this, but he couldn't shake the feeling that he would never see her again.

CHAPTER 7

On horseback, the journey only took a few days. Akira's armies hadn't made it that far out of the pass, and she moved much faster alone than an army did. She could have covered the ground even faster, but she wasn't an experienced rider. Horses brought back memories she would rather forget forever. She remembered when Goro, a monk from the monastery where she had been raised, had taken her from her family on horseback. It had been her first time riding. Since then she'd only ridden a handful of times, and never by choice.

So instead of covering the ground as fast as the horse was able, Moriko was content to let the horse eat up the distance at its own leisurely pace. It was still faster than walking. It gave her time to reflect.

Moriko was troubled, the frown on her face matching the overcast spring storms that occasionally wandered across the prairie of this part of the Southern Kingdom. With little natural beauty to distract her, her mind flitted quickly from thought to thought, most of them angry.

She loved Ryuu for his selflessness, but she didn't understand it either. He had grown up in isolation, away from the society that hunted their kind. It had given him an unrealistic perspective of the world. He tended to believe other people were kind and good. Moriko's own experience indicated they were scared. Scared of death, scared of hunger, scared of life itself.

She knew Shigeru had raised Ryuu to fight for something greater than himself. But he had died before Ryuu had found his cause. Listening to Ryuu's stories, Moriko decided Shigeru had expected Ryuu to bring a change to the land, but hadn't known how the change would happen. After Shigeru died, it left Ryuu with a vague dream of something greater, but no plan or goal in sight.

Moriko didn't share Ryuu's outlook or his upbringing. She had grown up in a monastery. She had seen the fear in the eyes of everyone who visited. It had always been clear to her that she wasn't a part of this society. She had known it from the moment she was torn from the arms of her mother. Moriko didn't hate or detest the people of the Southern Kingdom. She just didn't care about them.

After three days of these reflections, Moriko's mood was far less than pleasant. The horse made her legs sore in places she wasn't used to. The foothills leading up to the Three Sisters had been dry and hot, and Moriko wanted nothing more than shade and cool water. Instead, she had to deal with the regiment of soldiers stationed on the Southern Kingdom side of the Three Sisters. They were skittish, even though she knew all the correct passwords and carried letters marked with Akira's own seal.

They let her stay at their camp that night. For a single messenger, the Three Sisters would take another full day's ride.

She tossed and turned through the night, upset and unwilling to trust the soldiers who surrounded her. She knew she was attractive, but more importantly, she was a young woman in an army full of young men. Her life was frustrating enough. She didn't need to kill a soldier who couldn't control himself.

When the sun rose and ended an uneventful evening, Moriko was ready. She rode through the pass, some of her anger dissipating as she experienced the beauty of the Three Sisters. She had never been in the mountains before. Tall, jagged and impassable peaks rose thousands of paces into the air on either side of her. As she rode through the pass she could sense the men who were hidden in watch, but she had a hard time seeing them. Without the sense, she wasn't sure she would have been able to. She understood why controlling the whole pass was of such importance. A small force could hold the entire pass for a full moon if they had to, cycles maybe. Every step forward would cost the lives of dozens or more.

Moriko came upon the southern outpost of the First just as the sun was starting to touch the horizon. She danced the same dance of doubt with the guards stationed at the gates, even though they had to know she had already passed the scrutiny of their comrades on the north side of the pass. They were nervous, scared of an enemy they couldn't put a face to.

Her horse was gently taken from her, but Moriko wasn't sad to see the beast go. He had been a well-behaved horse, but Moriko was more comfortable on her own two feet. She was led without fanfare to the command tent. Akira had given her some information about Toro, but the man still gave off a powerful first impression.

He wasn't a tall man, but he seemed incredibly strong for his age. His gray hair seemed to cut like a blade, sharpening his appearance rather than weakening it. He held himself ramrod straight and Moriko saw his hands were calloused from regular handling of his sword. The man was still a warrior, proud and intelligent. Moriko felt respect for him right away.

He dismissed his guards out of the tent. "They say you bring messages bearing Lord Akira's seal?"

Moriko nodded and handed him the two letters. "The first is a general update on the status of the armies. You are to read it at your leisure. The second is about my mission. You are to read it immediately."

Toro looked at her, unable to hide his curiosity. Moriko suspected he had never seen a woman carrying swords. Since leaving Akira and Ryuu she had worn her blades openly and had attracted a fair amount of attention. Women were not allowed to carry swords in the Southern Kingdom. Many had lost their hands for less. "Who did you say you are?"

She gave him a blank look. "I didn't."

Toro frowned and opened the letter. He read it once and then once again, pausing to stare at her between readings. Moriko didn't know what the letter contained, but it clearly shocked Toro. He turned pale, his skin almost turning the color of his hair. She saw him put the letter down and reach towards his sword. She tensed up, cursing herself. For all her complaints about Ryuu being too trusting, she had let herself be led right into the heart of the most well-trained army in the Southern Kingdom. Akira had betrayed them, separated her and Ryuu with a story they had bought completely. Moriko started searching for the exits.

"You should be put to death immediately!"

Moriko heard the fear and anger in Toro's voice. She had heard that fear before. It was the fear of nightblades, embedded in even the sternest warriors. But Toro made no move to act on his words. His inaction saved his life.

"Lord Akira should not be using the likes of you." Toro's eyes narrowed. "You're not a nightblade. You're just a charlatan who has taken the Lord in."

Moriko's anger, simmering just beneath the surface, broke through.

"I don't need this, old man. If you don't believe your Lord, draw against me. You won't be the first southern general I've killed."

Understanding dawned on Toro, and he took a step back, fear overriding his anger. "The rumors are true then?"

Moriko didn't dignify the question with a response. She wasn't feeling charitable.

Toro was muttering to himself. "I had thought they were only rumors. Surely he would have told me if they were true." His anger struggled to reassert itself. "Why would he work with you if you killed Nori?"

Moriko glanced at the letter. She wasn't in any mood to repeat the story. "He thinks I can discover what's happening south of the border. I have my own reasons. Our purposes align, at least for today."

Toro sat down on a cushion. He had regained his reason and was starting to think through the implications. "Are there more of you?"

Moriko nodded.

"How many?"

Moriko stared at him. "I only need to restock my supplies and cross the border."

Toro let out just a hint of a grin, trying to master his fear. "You're not very friendly, are you?"

"It's been a long moon."

Toro nodded and thought. "Well, Lord Akira did instruct me to give you all possible assistance. Feel free to load up on any supplies you need. Other than that, there isn't much help I can offer you. I've sent out one more scouting party since the Lord left, but no one has returned. I couldn't convince another group to go even if I wanted to, which I don't. I hate to admit it, but I'm starting to share the Lord's concern about Azaria. I don't know what is happening, but I have the same feeling I get in my bones when a storm is brewing. Something is coming, something that will wash over us. I only hope the First is strong enough to hold against it."

Moriko debated. But Toro needed to know. "Have you heard about hunters before?"

"The legend?"

Moriko nodded.

Toro shook his head. "Only a very little. Some sort of Azarian bed-time story they tell their children to scare them straight."

"They are real. I fought two of them that came into the Southern Kingdom."

She let Toro digest that for a while. "What do you know about them?"

Moriko shrugged her shoulders. "Not much. Think Azarian nightblades. They are very good. It was mostly luck that I survived."

"Any weaknesses?"

"They don't fight too well without a head."

Toro looked up from the point on the floor he had been staring at. It took him a moment to realize she had told a joke. The tension seemed to drain out of him. "I'll keep that in mind."

"Whatever techniques you use against us will probably be effective against hunters. Their swords are shorter and lighter than ours, which makes them faster than us, slightly more defensive. They are also experts at stealth. Even with our abilities, they almost caught us unaware."

Toro reacted when Moriko said 'us.' She silently cursed herself. But what was done was done.

"I will keep your words in mind. Thank you."

They sat in silence for a while, Moriko studying Toro, Toro thinking through the implications of the news he had been brought. Moriko gave him credit. His whole world had essentially been turned upside down. He was taking it with a good deal of grace. She could see hints of the mind that made him a great general.

"Well, no matter, my dear. It is a problem for me to solve, and it seems like you have enough to do. I'm sure you are exhausted by now. Take rest tonight. You are welcome to leave whenever you would like."

Moriko nodded her appreciation. Toro ordered her escorted to a private tent. She was asleep as soon as she laid down on the ground.

Moriko stayed for a full day and night, not leaving camp until another day had passed. Her sense of urgency had clashed with her need for rest. Her time on the horse had left her sore and stiff, and she spent the day of rest stretching out her sore muscles. She knew she should learn to ride better, but her mind was made up. Horses were not her favorite mode of transportation.

Moriko threw out her sense as far as it would go, even though it was a pointless exercise. In the wide open plains, with so many people surrounding her, sight traveled further than her sense, and there was nothing hiding in the bushes she wouldn't have expected anyway. The plains in front of the fortress were as deserted as they looked. She had grown up in the forest and between the walls of a monastery. She wasn't used to open spaces, but even accounting for that, this space felt dead to her. It wasn't that there wasn't life. There was the usual assortment of small creatures living off the land, but they felt almost lethargic, as though their energy had been sucked from them.

When the sun rose the next morning she felt better. She found her horse again. As much as she didn't want to, Azaria was huge. If she was going to have any chance at all of making good time she would need to take a horse. Like it or not, she needed to make friends with the beast. With help from some of the stable hands she was able to load up the horse with supplies in only a few moments.

She met with Toro on her way out. She was surprised to discover there was a hint of regret in Toro's voice. His attitude towards Moriko had changed over the past day. She could tell he had started to think about the advantages of having a nightblade attached to his army. "Be careful out there."

Moriko nodded.

"Is there anything else you need?"

Moriko took a moment and thought through her supplies. She had enough food to last for a while, even longer if she hunted. If hunting was good she could stretch it out well past a full moon if she needed to. She carried her sword and a folded cloth which she could use as shelter. It was all she needed. She shook her head. "Thank you for your kindness."

"Let us know anything you find out. I am more worried by the day."

Moriko offered a short bow. It was more than she often provided, a mark of respect from her.

Toro seemed to recognize it and gave her a slightly deeper bow. Several soldiers surrounding them were surprised. Moriko held her mirth. Rumor in the camp the first day had been that she was a mistress of Toro's, but that rumor had been quickly dismissed when they found out she was heading further south. It was obvious they didn't have any idea what type of woman she was. Maybe they thought she was some sort of special whore who could succeed where soldiers had failed.

It was a problem for Toro to deal with, but she trusted he would keep her secrets. Akira had no doubt left orders as such, but even more so, Toro knew the chaos it would cause in the camp if they found out nightblades were alive and well among them. Technically, it was also punishable by death. Moriko had been impressed Akira had trusted Toro enough to even let him know. If Toro had wished, it would have been a justifiable reason for a coup.

She left the camp with little fanfare, but she could feel thousands of eyes on her as she began her journey to the south. She knew they would watch every step until she got far enough away to be hidden from sight. She was a creature of the woods, used to being able to hide within a couple of footsteps. The plains were not friendly to her. But there was little to be done. She continued onward, stopping randomly to throw out her sense. She wasn't expecting anything near the fort, and she wasn't surprised.

If there was one word Moriko would use to describe her surroundings, it would be "empty." She had grown up within woods and walls, and open spaces weren't to her liking. The spaces here were so vast, so devoid of life. It seemed like nothing could be further from the old woods she called home. As far as her eye could see there was nothing but rolling hills and grass. She had killed some small game to supplement her own food, but outside of the occasional rabbit, there was little for her to see or sense.

After only a few days she was bored of the monotony. As the days blended together, Moriko began to wonder if she was falling into madness. There was nothing here. No towns, no villages, no people out on the land. If this was Azaria, where were the Azarians? She had been riding for days without a sign of habitation.

Moriko wasn't an expert on the development of land or the running of a kingdom. She had never studied those subjects. But this she didn't understand. How did the Azarians live if they didn't farm their land? They had fought against the Southern Kingdom for hundreds of cycles. She was following a path that went more or less straight south. It wasn't a road, but it had been trampled over and over. She suspected it was the path Azarian armies took to the pass every season to attack the Southern Kingdom. Having no better options, she followed it, curious as to where it lead. But by now she should have seen something.

After a quarter-moon, Moriko was truly doubting her sanity. Every day was the same barren landscape. It was beautiful, in its own way. She would still prefer the woods to the prairie, but she was beginning to see what others saw in it. There were times when she appreciated the sensation of being alone in the world, all the land around her quiet and empty. It was just that it never ended. She had never seen such a vast emptiness. Dozens of times a day she checked her bearings against the sun to ensure she was still heading south.

She continued to follow the path, and it seemed straight, but she was beginning to doubt herself. She had never felt so lost. Days and nights blurred together.

A half-moon into her journey, she received all the excitement she could ask for. She had been riding south, lost in thought. With little to hold her attention, there was little to occupy her mind. By the time she noticed the dust rising on the horizon, it must have been visible for quite some time. Moriko shook herself awake. Her mind was so used to the unceasing monotony, she hadn't even realized her surroundings had changed.

She squinted. She wasn't sure, but it looked like three or four riders heading towards her. On the horse, she was visible from leagues away, and she cursed her lack of awareness. They were still some ways off, so she held her place, debating what to do. None of the other scouts had returned, except for the one, which meant the riders were probably hostile. But if she didn't stop to talk, there was no way of knowing.

Moriko's instinct was to turn the horse around and run, but her mission was to scout, so scout she would. She calmed her horse as the riders came galloping towards her. As they got closer Moriko saw it was four riders, each seemingly a part of their horse. She wasn't an expert, but they rode with a grace she could never hope to match.

Her sense screamed at her and she backed her horse up a few paces as an arrow fell in front of her. She glanced up, surprised. The riders were still a long ways away. There wasn't any way she should be in bow range by now. She sensed other arrows incoming and backed her horse up further as they rained down around her. So much for trying to speak with them.

Her decision made for her, Moriko turned her horse around and kicked it to a gallop, heading north. The locals were not friendly. She tried to throw out her sense, but as the horse below her bounced her around, she could barely focus. She considered herself fortunate to sense a couple of paces away. Moriko turned around, dismayed to see the riders easily gaining on her. They were much better riders than she was.

Her sense limited by her own distraction, she could only sense the arrows a moment or two before they struck. It still seemed an impossible distance, but arrows continued to fall around her. It was only a matter of time before it happened. She felt it a moment too late. She ducked her own head out of the way, but the arrow lodged itself deep in her horse's neck. The horse stumbled and started to collapse. Moriko didn't hesitate. She leapt from the saddle and tumbled across the ground as the horse fell in a heap. She got dizzily to her feet and drew her sword as the world righted itself around her.

There wasn't going to be any running from this battle.

CHAPTER 8

Before Ryuu left Akira's camp, he pulled out the faded note Orochi had given him. The directions to Orochi's island took Ryuu through the Western Kingdom, a path which seemed like a poor decision considering the two kingdoms were at war with one another. All that mattered was that he reach a port in the Northern Kingdom called Highgate. Ryuu went back into Akira's tent to ask for directions which took him through the Northern Kingdom. Akira had a clerk draft him directions while Akira himself wrote two passes for Ryuu, allowing him to travel under Akira's protection. Ryuu was grateful. He had never been out of the Southern Kingdom and didn't know what type of land or trouble he might find. Akira affixed his seal to both letters in the bottom right corner. They would mark the documents as official if Ryuu ever had to show them.

After the tasks were completed Ryuu was on his way. He rode at a steady pace, trying to balance the need to keep the horse fresh with his need to get north as quickly as possible. Time was of the essence. On horseback, if he didn't suffer any delays, it would still take him more than a half-moon to reach Highgate. He packed a minimum of provisions, trusting his skills as a hunter to feed him when necessary. Traveling light was traveling fast.

By the end of the first day Ryuu couldn't even see the dust kicked up by the rapid movement of Akira's armies marching to the northwest to do battle with Tanak's forces. Ryuu rode northeast. As he rode, the gentle rolling plains and forests of the Southern Kingdom turned into more rugged territory. It was on the fourth day of constant riding that Ryuu found the river that denoted the end of the Southern Kingdom and the beginning of the Northern Kingdom. The river wasn't wide, but its current was rapid as it crashed through the steep valleys. It was another half day before Ryuu found the bridge which would carry him over the swift currents.

Ryuu passed through the checkpoints on either side of the bridge without trouble. He had hidden his sword on his back to ensure he didn't attract attention. The guards of the Southern Kingdom accepted his pass without question. Passing through the northern checkpoint took a little longer, but he raised no suspicion. He was waved through with a minimum of conversation.

Ryuu's ride became more rugged as he went on. He had visited the mountains which bordered the Southern Kingdom while growing up, but not often. He was a child of the forest, and riding in the mountains was a novel experience for him. The trail, while well constructed, twisted and turned and rose and fell in such a way that Ryuu was sure he would have to revise his original estimated time of travel. Every day he seemed to cover less ground than he expected. He considered pushing the horse faster, but already signs of weariness were creeping into the beast's demeanor. He kept his pace while trying to hold on to his patience. A half-moon into his journey, he guessed he was halfway through the kingdom. His pace was unbearable.

Ryuu had been curious what the Northern Kingdom would be like and how it would differ from the land he had grown up in. The geography was different, more rugged and mountainous than the Southern Kingdom. But Ryuu also noticed the people were different. For one, there were fewer of them, or at least, that was what Ryuu suspected. He was on one of the well-used trade roads, but he didn't encounter many people, either travelers or villagers. Ryuu passed through or around several villages, but his sense told him none of them were overcrowded. He didn't encounter any cities with the population or energy of New Haven.

The people were clever with their agriculture, building terraced fields throughout the lush mountains, but there still wasn't enough space to grow the food needed to feed a large population. Despite his slow pace, Ryuu was fascinated to be in another kingdom. It was so similar to and yet so different from his own land.

The people Ryuu did encounter throughout the kingdom were guardsmen. Their quantity surprised him. In the Southern Kingdom there were local garrisons, but most were small and had a tendency to roam together as one unit, visiting each village in its domain perhaps twice a cycle. By and large, villages were expected to take care of themselves, with only the most serious crimes being handled by garrisons. The land was safe, but it was largely because punishments for crimes were severe and the land was prosperous enough that few resorted to banditry or other crimes.

Here in the Northern Kingdom it was different. Guardsmen were posted all over the roads and around the villages, and Ryuu spent a significant amount of time using his sense to detour around them. He often found them roaming in groups of three or five, each group affiliated with a local command. To Ryuu's southern sensibilities, it seemed like there were far more guards than were needed, but he had to admit he felt like there was a greater degree of order to the Northern Kingdom. He wasn't sure if it suited him like the freedom of the Southern Kingdom, but he could understand the appeal.

Ryuu was able to avoid any encounters until he was about a hundred leagues away from Highgate. He was riding along a typical stretch of road when he sensed them. They were high in the mountain, and Ryuu mistook them at first for wildlife. It was only as he got closer he noticed the small horse paths which led higher up the mountain. Ryuu whistled softly to himself. Anyone riding those paths would have to be a much better, or at least a much more confident rider than he was. Any mistake on those paths was punishable by death.

He caught the motion out of the corner of his eye as the five riders came charging down the path before him. Ryuu calmed his reaction with the practice of a seasoned warrior. His instinct was to try to kick his horse to speed, but he saw immediately the futility of the idea. The riders descending upon him were much more skilled than he, and the road itself was not built to carry a galloping horse and rider. Although he was trying to avoid confrontation, he was much safer standing his ground than he would be if he tried to run. Curiosity was also part of his decision. He had done nothing out of the ordinary to attract attention, and he wondered what had worked the guards into such a frenzy.

Searching the surrounding ground, he brought his horse to a small rise in the road, giving him a slight advantage in height. It didn't really matter, but there was no point in giving up any advantage, no matter how small. Then he sat and waited while his pursuit came down the mountain trails. He watched in fascination as the riders expertly navigated their horses down the winding paths in the mountain. He would have called their pace "breakneck," but each rider seemed more than comfortable in their saddle. They were having fun. Ryuu watched and sensed as they shifted their weight ever so slightly, staying always in perfect harmony with the horse. He wasn't sure of their skill as warriors, but he could testify to their amazing skill with a horse. He wondered if this was the skill of all riders in the Northern Kingdom.

As the guardsmen rode up to him the lead rider called out, "Halt!"

Ryuu looked around. He hadn't moved at all since taking the high ground.

The rider seemed to realize his mistake, a hint of embarrassment creeping over his face. He tried again. "Who goes there?"

Ryuu wasn't sure how much was safe to share. "A traveler."

"Where are you from and what is your destination?"

"I come from the Southern Kingdom, and I'm heading for Highgate."

"And what is your business?"

Ryuu didn't want to lie, but he could hardly state he was traveling to find the hidden island where nightblades supposedly lived. "My business is my own."

He said it without malice, but it rubbed the guard the wrong way. Ryuu groaned inwardly as the soldier sat up straighter in his saddle. He puffed out his chest. "Everyone's business is the business of the guards. Answer or suffer consequences."

Ryuu controlled his irritation. He was late and only wanted to complete this journey. He pulled out his documents, displaying them for all to see. "I have done no wrong and have only ridden on the roads which are open to all travelers. What is this about?"

The other four guards circled their horses around Ryuu, blocking all his exits. Their leader replied, "These are trying times, traveler, and no one matching your description has checked in at any guardhouse. It would seem by trying to avoid attention you have brought some down on yourself."

Irritated as he was, Ryuu didn't want a confrontation. "My apologies. This is my first time in your kingdom and I'm not familiar with your customs. It was not my intent to offend. I didn't realize I needed to check in."

The lead guard relaxed just a little. "Ah, I see our brothers at the border have been lax about informing our guests to our customs. No matter. Simply return with us to the last guardhouse you passed and we will get you all straightened out."

Ryuu thought back. The last guardhouse he had passed had been a full day ago. He couldn't bear the idea of backtracking and losing days of progress. He thought about showing them one of the letters signed by Lord Akira, but he wasn't sure what effect it would have. The guards were all suspicious, and he was trying to avoid attention. But he didn't see any other way out of the situation besides fighting, which he really didn't want to do.

"I'm sorry, but that is not an option." He pulled one of Akira's letters out and handed it to the leader of the guards. "I'm on a special mission from Lord Akira, and I cannot delay. I apologize for my ignorance, but I must reach Highgate as soon as possible."

The guard read the letter and tore it into pieces. "All travelers must check in. I won't fall for your foolish smuggler's tricks. Prepare to be searched."

The guards all drew their blades, and Ryuu took a quick assessment of their skills. From their balance and the way they held their blades, they had received a lot of training. They were good, but not good enough. He didn't want to fight. He lowered his voice and met eyes with the captain of the guard unit.

"I'm sorry, but I can't have you interrupt my mission. I need to go forward. Let me pass."

The guards hesitated. Ryuu couldn't guess what was in their minds, but he could sense they weren't ready to attack him yet. None of them had expected this to escalate so far, and they were nervous of a man who showed no fear in the face of five blades. The silence stretched moment after moment, but Ryuu was calm. He could take them if it came to a battle. The question was if they realized it.

He wasn't sure what convinced them. Maybe it was his lack of fear. Maybe the captain was thinking twice about tearing up a letter with Lord Akira's seal. No matter the reason, it worked.

He felt the lead guard's stance shift, and he breathed a sigh of relief. The captain had come to a decision not to fight today. Ryuu was grateful.

The guard tried to muster some of his remaining dignity as he motioned for his men to lower their swords. "Know that I will make a full report. I believe you just might be telling the truth, but if not, you will have not just one, but two kingdoms searching for you. There won't be anyplace to hide."

Ryuu hid his grin as he bowed in a gesture of respect. If they knew he was a nightblade, not just two but all three kingdoms would be hunting for him. "Thank you for your understanding. I will let Lord Akira know I was treated well in the Northern Kingdom."

The guard scoffed. "If there's even a Lord for you to go back to." He turned to his men. "Come on men, we've got bigger problems than this traveler."

Ryuu watched them depart with interest. It seemed the prevailing attitude in the Northern Kingdom was that Tanak had the upper hand. Ryuu wondered what sort of preparations the kingdom would be making. Would Sen ally with Akira, simply to keep the balance? Ryuu imagined he would almost have to. If Tanak was successful, his kingdom would be much stronger than the Northern Kingdom, and it would only be a matter of time before Sen and his orderly nation fell.

He tossed these thoughts back and forth until the riders were out of sight. Ultimately, it didn't matter to him right now what any of the kingdoms were doing. All three of them were in chaos, and he had to get to the island to find answers before events spiraled even further out of control.

Ryuu was beside himself with wonder. He had lived his entire life in the Southern Kingdom, and he had never seen the sea before. For the past day he had smelled the salt in air, a smell he had never experienced. He had spurred his horse the last few leagues to Highgate, covering the remaining distance at a fast trot. The poor beast was exhausted, but Ryuu didn't care.

Ryuu was standing on the crest of a cliff overlooking Highgate. It was by far the largest city Ryuu had ever encountered, dwarfing even New Haven, and from his viewpoint it was incredible. He could hear the hammers of the smiths ringing through the city, and the sounds of civilization were loud. Even from this distance he could hear the mass of humanity below. It was shocking after so long on the quiet roads. But Ryuu barely saw the city. He had eyes only for the sea.

The smell of the ocean had been new, but to take the fresh ocean wind straight into his face was refreshing. He looked out over the sea of blue, sparkling in the late afternoon sunlight. Even in the harbor, the waves rose high, crashing against sandy shores and wooden boats. The air was cold and crisp, even though summer was just beginning here.

Ryuu stood and stared, trying to take in the endless blue, the salt in the air, the cool wind on his face. He listened to the sound of the waves breaking on the shore, and he found there was something hypnotic in their rhythm.

Ryuu glanced at the sun and saw he wouldn't have time to get to the docks today. Orochi's note had explained the boat to the island only ever left in the morning. Ryuu shrugged. He had nothing better to do with his time but to explore the area.

His first wish was for food. Ryuu went down into the city and followed his nose, which led him to a small shop selling cooked fish from the sea. Ryuu asked the cook to prepare whatever was best. He watched with rapt attention as the cook prepared fish Ryuu had never seen before.

The food was incredible. It would have been delicious at any time, but after a full moon on the trail, the fresh fish almost brought tears to his eyes. The fish was a pink and fatty fish he had never tried, and even raw its flavor was sublime. The rice and other food were all excellent, and Ryuu washed it all down with some of the best sake he'd ever tasted. When he was done he leaned back and took in his surroundings. From everything he had observed, the port town was orderly and well maintained. He liked it here. Paying for his meal, he stood up and walked towards the shore.

When he had been younger he had heard many stories about the ocean. He knew it formed the far northern border of the Three Kingdoms. He also knew the seas were very rough, even during the summer months. Because of that, there was little trade with areas outside of the Three Kingdoms. Everyone knew the world was much larger than the Three Kingdoms, but with only a little trade from the sea and the mountains to the south and east, the Three Kingdoms were isolated from the larger world. What was known about the land outside the kingdoms was largely rumor and legend.

As a young boy, he had tried to imagine what it would be like to see water as far as the eye could see. There were stories that told of sailors who, when they reached the middle of the ocean, couldn't see any land at all. Ryuu had wondered what that must be like. To not see any land. Water was so impermanent. It didn't keep any shape. Ryuu knew about navigating by the stars and signs in the sky, but they always pointed to landmarks on the ground. To navigate with nothing but the uncaring sky to keep you company seemed a terrifying prospect.

But as Ryuu reached the shore, he felt like he could understand the desires of sailors. They were wanderers, trusting only to their own abilities to keep them alive. Ryuu felt in a way that he was like them. He had Shigeru's cabin, which he called home, but he knew he wouldn't be able to spend his entire life there. His abilities prevented him from settling the way others could. He and Moriko had tried, but their enemies had found them. Ryuu viewed it more of an inevitability than an exception. And so here he was, wandering the land as the sailors wandered the sea. They had the stars to guide him, and he had his sense, intuition, and Shigeru's wisdom, cut short as it was. Their enemies were the elements and the sea itself. Ryuu's enemy, near as he could tell, was everyone.

As his mind wandered, his body reached the shoreline, and Ryuu stood out looking at the sea and the sky and the line between the two that was barely distinguishable. He had wanted to experience the sea for so long growing up, and now here he was. At that moment he missed Moriko acutely. She wouldn't have said anything, but he knew she would be just as awestruck as he was. It was hard for him to accept, but she loved him, and she was all he needed. At that moment he thought it was a mistake to send her south. The Southern Kingdom could take care of itself. He wanted her by his side.

The waves had a hypnotic effect on him. He stared at the waves, watching as wave after wave crashed against the sand of the shore. Ryuu was surprised, but he could sense there was a power in the sea, a life just as the land itself had life. He was awed by the scale of it.

As Ryuu watched the waves crash, he could feel his body relaxing, the tension of many days of riding melting off his body.

He opened his sense and he could feel the fish off the shore, the small animals that crept along the shore line. He could feel the presence of the city at his back, but on this cool day he was alone on the beach. The sounds of the surf rolled against his eardrums, and he could feel all the patterns of life. It was almost like being in the deep old woods, so alive with life. But this was so much more rhythmic.

He couldn't even tell when it happened, but without warning something in his mind slipped. He had no better word to describe it. It wasn't the sudden snap he sometimes experienced in combat. This was much gentler, like Ryuu had somehow sidestepped the current of reality. In that moment he saw Moriko standing in a sea of her own, a sea of grass that stretched as far as the eye could see. She was walking, alone on the sea, to the south. And then the moment was gone and he was standing on the shore looking out at the ocean.

Ryuu stood as still as the rocks that bore the brunt of each wave's demise. He glanced around him and decided that no more than a few moments had passed. He didn't know what had happened. Ryuu shook his head, trying to clear the remaining fog from his memories. It was as though he had been there with her. He stood and watched the waves roll in, but no answers came to him. With one last, longing glance at the ocean, Ryuu turned his back to find nondescript lodging for the night.

Ryuu awoke before the sun the next morning, eager and nervous to begin the next stage of his journey. He ate a light breakfast at the small inn and went back to the stables. They were quiet, even the horses still asleep in the pre-dawn light. Ryuu drew his blade and went through his kata, the same exercises he did every morning. He lost himself in the movements, allowing all his attention to go to his blade and to his cuts. When he finished, he was glistening with sweat and his mind was calm. He was ready to take the next step in his journey.

He followed Orochi's directions, arriving at the docks just as the sun was starting to rise over the ocean to the east. Ryuu drank in the vision, the colors unlike any he had seen before.

He drank in the beauty for a few moments before he began his search. The docks were large, and Orochi's letter made note of the fact the ship Ryuu was looking for was rarely moored in the same place twice. Ryuu searched and searched, his impatience creeping into his positive attitude. Orochi's letter stated the ship was usually in town, but there were only two that led to and from the island, and it was sometimes possible that neither would be in harbor. If that was the case, Ryuu would have to wait until one arrived, and he wouldn't be happy about losing more time.

Ryuu almost missed the object of his search. It was a small, nondescript ship that didn't attract any attention to itself by design. What gave the ship away were the two men who seemed to be casually lying around the docks, but Ryuu sensed them. The men were wide awake and alert, a small island of calm in the hustle and bustle of the harbor in the morning. He could feel the sense emanating from both of them. They were nightblades, same as him. The shock was immediate. It was one thing to learn other nightblades existed, but to encounter them in the middle of Highgate was something else entirely.

Not having much of a plan, Ryuu decided to walk right up to them. It was direct and simple, and his impatience didn't allow for much in the way of planning. The two nightblades sensed him in unison and rose to block his way forward. Ryuu's sword was strapped to his back, still hidden from casual observation. He held himself back from reaching for it. He kept walking forward, one calm step at a time. Ryuu stopped when he was about eight paces away from them. The two nightblades held their ground, only a short stretch of planking beyond them. After that was an endless sea. Crates and barrels were stacked around them, hiding them from the view of most of the harbor.

Ryuu examined them, his breath calm and even. They both held themselves well. He set his shoulders. If it came to a fight, it would be a difficult one. He wasn't sure what to say. This was where Orochi's instructions ended.

When there were many choices, Ryuu cut straight ahead. "I seek passage to the island."

The two nightblades shared a glance. Ryuu didn't know what it signified. The one on Ryuu's left spoke. "No."

Ryuu sized up his opponents. There were others on the ship, so if he killed these two, there would still be people who probably knew the way to the island, but he would rather not start off his relationship by resorting to violence. He also felt strongly about fighting other nightblades. There were few enough of them left in the world as it was. There was no need for them to fight each other.

Both of them were strong. They were both built like Ryuu, not too tall or too large, but built with a wiry strength that would be much stronger than an opponent expected. Passerby would probably have mistaken them for down-on-their-luck seamen. Their clothes were in tatters, but Ryuu could see their sheaths almost sparkled in the early morning sun. The clothes were a disguise, but the blades would be very real.

He didn't want to fight, but it seemed he wasn't going to get to the island otherwise. Their initial response did not invite future conversation. His hand went to his blade. "Stop me."

They shared another glance and the one that had spoken held up his hand. Ryuu kept his blade sheathed, his hand ready to draw, not sure of what was coming next. The nightblade went to the boat and gave an order Ryuu couldn't understand. One of the deckhands went below and came up with a long cloth. The nightblade grabbed the package and came back to his original post. Glancing around the docks, he unwrapped the bundle and handed a wooden practice sword to his partner. He grabbed one himself and tossed another to Ryuu, who caught it with ease.

So it was to be a test, then. He didn't show it on his face, but Ryuu was glad. Facing other nightblades excited his desire for competition, but he had no desire to harm them. Orochi had been enough. He grasped the sword lightly and waited for his opponents to come to him.

He didn't have long to wait. As soon as he set his stance they came at him, their attacks synchronized perfectly. They were quick, but Ryuu also sensed them coming. He leapt towards one nightblade, throwing off their timing and entering the fray.

The blades knocked together in rapid succession. Ryuu knew he was better than either of them individually, but he wasn't sure if he was good enough to take them both on. They passed and passed each other, wooden blades searching for any opening to strike. As the battle went on all the fighters put more and more energy into their attacks until they were striking at each other with as much strength as they could muster. Ryuu was holding a defensive position, able to block their blows, but unable to land a solid strike in return.

He was falling back and he knew it. Two nightblades were more than he could handle. He let one cut brush off his practice sword, but wasn't in time to get the next one. He managed to turn enough to take the blow on his shoulder. Nothing in his shoulder collapsed beneath the blow, although he knew he would have a hard time moving it tomorrow. It wouldn't have been a killing blow with real blades, but it was the hardest he'd been hit in many cycles of training.

The pain distracted him just long enough he was a moment behind reacting to the next cut. It was coming straight for his head, strong enough to crack his skull open and leave his brains drying on the dock. The world snapped and Ryuu was in a different, more vivid world. The blow slowed down, and he had enough time to move, dodging backward erratically.

He found his balance and thrust himself back into the fight. The momentum of the battle shifted. After the snap, their moves were too slow, and he began to gain the upper hand, driving them back towards the end of the pier. It was only a sliver of time, but it was enough. Ryuu moved cleanly within the guard of one of the nightblades and thrust the hilt of his practice sword deep into the nightblade's abdomen. The man crumpled even as his partner took a desperate cut. It was a good cut, but just a fraction of a moment too early. It passed in front of Ryuu, rippling his clothes as he made his own cut. His strike was solid, knocking the other nightblade off his feet.

As each nightblade collapsed, the world sped up to its normal speed. After a few moments of groaning, each worked their way back to their feet. The one Ryuu had hit in the abdomen was using his practice sword as a crutch to stand up on. Ryuu stood ready, but the battle was over. The nightblades made a gesture with their left hand Ryuu didn't recognize. They each made a fist with their left hand and then pressed it against their abdomen. Not knowing what the gesture meant, Ryuu bowed in return. He returned the practice sword to them as all three of them caught their breath.

Ryuu waited for the nightblades to speak. He had made his case. The one who had initially spoken spoke again. "That was a good fight, if unexpected this morning. Who are you?"

A warning in the back of his mind urged caution. He remembered that Shigeru had not left the island on good terms. In fact, he had escaped a death sentence. Perhaps his heritage wouldn't be the first thing he should bring up in conversation.

"My name is Ryuu."

The two nightblades appraised him. "You are one of us." It was half a statement, half a question.

Ryuu nodded.

"But you are not one of us."

Ryuu nodded again and the two nightblades looked at each other thoughtfully.

"Why do you want to go to the island?"

Ryuu considered his answer for a moment. "There are threats against those I care about. I need to learn more so I can protect them from the dangers they face."

The leader shook his head. "If you go to the island you will never return. It is not permitted."

Ryuu wondered at that. Shigeru had escaped. That much was true. But he didn't think Orochi had. Moriko had never mentioned anything about an escape in Orochi's past. Ryuu had always assumed Orochi had been released or sent from the island. He wasn't sure if the two were lying or if there was more to the story than he realized. But he didn't feel like he had a choice. He had to go to the island. Once he was there he could worry about getting back to the Three Kingdoms.

"That's a risk I've considered. My mind is fixed."

The decision seemed to be made. "Very well. Come with us."

Ryuu was a little surprised at the efficiency. The two nightblades climbed into the ship and Ryuu followed, wary of a trap. They shouted orders in a language Ryuu didn't understand and the crew began preparations to cast off. Ryuu had expected to have to wait, but apparently the ship was ready to leave on a moment's notice. Interesting.

Ryuu had never been on a ship before, but he found that his stomach had no problems with the pitching of the boat in open seas. The stories of the north sea were legendary, and the ship wasn't large. Nevertheless, Ryuu rode it smoothly, having fun trying to keep his balance without holding on to anything. It kept him entertained long after it should have gotten boring.

Even though they flew across the sea for the entire day, Ryuu did not see the island. He did have his first chance to see what uninterrupted sea looked like. It was indescribable, blue as far as the eye could see. He rejoiced in the waves crashing against the ship and spraying him with salty mist. He licked his lips, surprised by just how salty the sea was. Now he understood what it meant to die of thirst in the middle of an ocean of water.

As the sun set, Ryuu noticed a thick cloud hanging low over the sea. Their ship was heading straight towards it, and Ryuu watched its approach with interest. He had seen low clouds, but this cloud hugged the ocean, the gray of the cloud merging with the blue water in an indistinct line. Even though he chided himself, couldn't shake the suspicion the cloud was ominous and full of evil intent, a threat to him and the crew. He glanced from face to face, but he did not see any fear in the eyes of the crew. Ominous as the cloud may be, it didn't intimidate the sailors at all.

It made him wonder, but he held his peace as the ship skipped across the waves towards the cloud bank. From a distance the cloud had looked like it was a solid wall, but he found as he approached that it was more immaterial than it first appeared. The sky darkened, and they were inside the cloud before he knew it. Ryuu watched in fascination as any way of determining distance or direction were lost. The ship did not decrease its speed at all, and the captain seemed completely unconcerned they couldn't see more than fifty paces inside the cloud. They drove straight ahead at full speed. Ryuu thought he even detected a slight relaxing of the nightblades once they entered the mist.

There was no judging time in that place. It could have been a few moments or it could have been all the remaining daylight. Ryuu did not know, even his fine-tuned senses bewildered by a new experience. He took a deep breath to calm his mind and focus on his sense. The sea surrounding them felt no different than it had before. He reminded himself that vision was only one of his senses and he shouldn't rely on it as much as he did.

The transition out of the mist was more dramatic than the transition into it. It was sudden, the last rays of sunlight streaming to their light-starved eyes. Ryuu winced, but his eyes adjusted quickly as he looked upon one of the finest sunsets he had ever seen, the sun casting deep reds upon the clouds. If he had been more superstitious he might have been reminded of blood, but he was a practical man, and saw only the beauty of colors not often found in nature.

Sight restored, he scanned his surroundings and immediately picked out their destination. It was, not surprisingly, an island, but its geography was astounding. Sheer cliffs rose out of the sea, plateauing some hundreds of paces above the surface of the ocean. Try as he might, Ryuu couldn't bring to mind any similar sight. It was still some distance off, but Ryuu didn't see any means of getting up the plateau, nor any place even safe enough to dock the boat. It was majestic and terrifying and Ryuu knew he had found the birthplace of his master. He took a deep breath as the ship approached. This island had almost killed Shigeru. He hoped it wouldn't do the same to him.

CHAPTER 9

If it would have done him any good, Akira would have torn the map to shreds. He kept thinking that if he looked at it long enough he would see something his generals had missed, some key to victory that would turn the tide of the battle. It didn't matter that he had some of the most brilliant military minds working for him. If his kingdom was in danger, it was his responsibility to save it.

The war wasn't going well, and that was the most positive statement Akira could come up with. The element of surprise had taken them in completely. He had gotten sloppy, moving so many of his forces south. If the kingdom survived, it wouldn't be a mistake he would make again.

Akira had yet to get a full army out into the field for a decisive battle. Tanak was moving too fast. Akira had never seen armies move the way Tanak's were. Tanak was practically jumping forward, hitting only essential strategic locations. Tanak's information was flawless, cycles in the preparation. He knew where the food was stored, where large garrisons were, everything needed to run the Southern Kingdom over.

Akira cursed the brilliance of the invasion. Tanak wasn't interfering much in the daily lives of Akira's people. There were almost no reports of violence or rebellion following Tanak's uprising, but Akira wasn't surprised. Although his advisers often tried to fill his head with talk of the peasants uprising in defense of their homeland, Akira knew the average peasant didn't care who was in control. So long as they were safe and unharmed, a fish could sit on the throne.

Akira was also jealous of Tanak's information network. He didn't know how they had been penetrated so deeply, but it was abundantly clear Tanak knew his kingdom almost as well as he did. The locations of the garrisons weren't hard to find out, but Tanak had hit some food storage sites whose locations had been well protected.

Already Tanak's troops covered almost half of the Southern Kingdom, and the summer was just reaching its height. If Tanak maintained this pace he would conquer the Southern Kingdom in less than an entire season. It was unheard of.

Akira resisted the temptation to slap himself. The more he stared at the maps, the more often he found himself falling into these patterns of thought. There still hadn't been a true large-scale battle yet, and while Tanak had taken half of Akira's kingdom, he had taken the sparsely populated half. All the major objectives, including New Haven, were closer to the center of Akira's kingdom, and none had fallen yet. Tanak had seen some great success, but he had yet to meet any real challenge.

He forced himself to look at the map again. Tanak's strategy, although brilliant, was straightforward in its large-scale planning. He had brought three armies across the river. Each army was

WORLD'S EDGE

slightly larger than one of Akira's. Akira's numbered about five
thousand men, a mix of calvary, archers, and infantry. Tanak's
seemed to number a little over six thousand, from the estimates
of scouts. One of Tanak's armies had driven straight south,
heading almost to the mountains which bordered the kingdom.
Once near the border they had curved east, cutting across all of
Akira's kingdom.

The other two armies had made similar moves. The largest
army, and probably the best trained, had gotten a little ways
south and was cutting east across the center of the Southern
Kingdom. The third army stayed close to the northern border on
its sweep to the east.

Akira's forces weren't so neatly arranged. The Fourth had
been utterly decimated by the invasion. It had been the army
tasked with guarding the border between Tanak and Akira, and
it had been spread thin, thinking more about garrison duty than
being on war footing. Units had been crushed, and nothing
positive had been heard, just whispers that units here and there
fought on, annoying the enemy, but little else.

Akira had left his best army with Toro at the Three Sisters.
He doubted the decision daily since he had made it, but it was too
late to change his mind now. But he heard the complaints of his
generals. With another army they would have been able to easily
defeat Tanak's forces, but as it was, it would be a challenge.

Akira was with the Second and the Third armies, moving
to finish the army crawling along the southern border of his
kingdom. Their strategy, as it stood, was to smash Tanak's
southern force with overwhelming might. If the Fifth could halt
or destroy Tanak's center army, the war would essentially be over.

An uncomfortable amount of responsibility rode on the Fifth. Akira had little doubt the Second and the Third were up to their task, but the Fifth had the most challenging battle of all. If they couldn't come through, Tanak would have a significant advantage over the Southern Kingdom. The problem was exacerbated by the knowledge the Fifth wasn't Akira's best army. They were well trained and experienced, but the Fifth was often where soldiers nearing retirement were stationed. They were responsible for guarding the border of the Northern Kingdom and often served as a training army for new recruits. Much would be demanded of them in the upcoming battle.

With one last glance at his maps, Akira made his way outside the tent. There, horses would be gathered to take him to the field of battle. The Fifth would meet Tanak's First, and Akira felt a responsibility to be there when it happened.

Akira rode with Makoto and Mashiro towards the battlefield. Usually the two generals were talkative, good company to pass the time, but this evening they were silent. Akira didn't blame them. He didn't have much desire to speak either.

The three of them were accompanied by an armed guard, but they traveled light. They were going to the battle as observers. Makoto and Mashiro would lend their expertise, but the primary reason for the visit was so that Akira could be seen by his troops. He wouldn't send these men to die without his presence.

Makoto and Mashiro weren't sure the battle could be won. As they had traveled the day before they had spoken about the odds. On paper it was one army against another, but they believed Tanak had placed his best army in the center. Their shadows hadn't given them solid information, but it was the most logical explanation. If true, it would be an uphill battle for his men, if not impossible. They held out hope they were wrong. Their men were well trained, even if the Fifth was considered the weakest army.

They reached the site of the engagement just before dawn. Already the men were up and moving, preparing for war. They had made ranks and were marching to their initial positions. Akira and his generals found their own position, up on a hilltop safely removed from combat. From their position above the field, Akira could see all the preparations for both armies. He watched in morbid interest as thousands of men formed to the lay of the land and the orders of their generals.

The battle began as the sun crested the treetops. Tanak's forces marched forward, arrows darkening the sky. From his position of safety, Akira had to admit there was a certain deadly beauty to the arc of the projectiles. His men, falling below him, wouldn't agree.

There was a part of Akira that wanted to throw it all away. He wanted to draw his sword, hold it up to bathe in the early morning light of the sun, and charge down into the fray. If he died, he wouldn't have to worry about what happened to his kingdom any more. He would have some measure of peace. But he held himself still, watching the battle progress. The kingdom depended on the outcome of this day.

By midmorning, Akira's banners had penetrated far into the enemy ranks, and Akira dared to hope. His men were performing better than anyone had expected. He glanced over at Makoto and Mashiro, who wore concerned looks. Akira squinted, trying to see what they could see. He had been trained in command, but it was the two young men to his side who possessed the experience. They didn't look pleased.

The battle took place in a low, flat valley. Akira could see the units moving almost as though he were watching pieces on a go board. Again and again he thought he saw a move a unit could make, but he held his tongue. It was tempting to try to take control of the battle, but he refrained.

As the sun rose to its zenith in the sky, the battle seemed even to Akira. Both lines were holding, but when Akira could tear his eyes away from the scene, he saw his generals seemed more and more pensive. He studied the lines, trying to understand why they might feel that way, but he saw nothing to indicate imminent defeat.

Mashiro and Makoto stood up and walked to him. "We should be leaving, my Lord."

Akira looked up at them. "Why?"

"Tanak hasn't committed all his forces. There are at least a thousand men missing, and our scouts report they are flanking the battlefield. We're turning to meet them, but unless we are given a gift by fate, this battle will be lost, and we'll be trapped if we don't move soon."

Akira shook his head. "We stay until the last possible moment. We've got fresh horses, they won't be able to pursue. Let me know."

The generals understood and issued the orders.

When the tide turned, it happened so fast Akira didn't even recognize the moment it occurred. At one moment it seemed to him his troops were doing well. They had driven well into the enemy ranks, and with a final push they could snap the line and win the day.

His optimism was completely unfounded. He never saw the moment the tide turned, but he watched as his flags were being pushed back further and further. It started slow, but by the time the sun was three-quarters of the way through the sky, his banners were losing ground dozens of paces at a time, if they weren't falling forever. Akira couldn't believe the number of men he had lost.

His heart sank. He worried that he had lost his kingdom today, but he pushed aside the thoughts. He wouldn't give in to depression. So long as he had breath in his body, he would fight for the Southern Kingdom. Tanak would never live in peace.

Akira bowed deeply to the general and commanders of the Fifth. They would never allow themselves to be captured. He had respect for each of them.

"Do you have any final requests?"

The general looked at him. "I ask only that you take care of my family, the same as you would for all the soldiers who have been lost here today."

Akira nodded. The wish would be granted.

Only one other of the commanders spoke. "Vengeance, my Lord, is all I ask." Other heads nodded around the circle.

"That I will gladly do."

Makoto looked at each of them. "Regroup if you can. Attack them wherever they go. They may destroy your army, but you can still destroy their lives."

The commanders nodded.

Akira was seized with a strong emotion that twisted his gut. These men were willing to give their lives for him. They believed in him, and he wouldn't let them down. He wanted to be a leader worthy of their belief, he just didn't know how.

He looked one last time upon the field. It was clear now that his army was being overrun. It had been a gamble in the first place, but a necessary one. They had inflicted casualties, though. It would take Tanak time to regroup.

But there was little time to be sentimental. It wouldn't be long before Tanak's army reached the place where they stood, and it was clear they had seen Akira's personal banner. The final battle would be on top of this hillside.

With one last oath of vengeance, Akira turned and went to his horse. He knew that as a symbol he was more important than an entire army, but he couldn't help but feel like he was a coward who only sent other men to die for him.

Akira cursed one final time as they rode off quickly back to the east, away from his first real defeat.

CHAPTER 10

Moriko eyed her opponents warily. The four of them were charging down, unleashing arrow after arrow. Her sense allowed her to sidestep them with little difficulty, but as they got closer it became more and more challenging. She had hoped they might run out of arrows, but when she got a closer view of their quivers, she realized she'd run out of luck long before they ran out of arrows.

Moriko kept moving from side to side, allowing arrows to pass by her harmlessly. She focused on calming her breathing and expanding her sense. She had never fought opponents on horseback before. Ryuu had taught her how, but being taught and living through the experience were very different tasks.

She thought they would charge her down, but she was wrong. Once they reached a certain distance, about forty paces away, they split off from their straight line, trotting in a circle around her. They weren't at full gallop, but they were moving quickly enough it made them hard to track.

It took Moriko a moment to figure out what they were planning. They had seen her sword, and instead of giving her a chance to defend herself, they were going to ride circles around her, shooting at her until she fell. They had no intention of giving her a fair fight.

Moriko cursed. She could dodge arrows or deflect them with her sword, but her luck was bound to run out sooner or later. She'd get tired and make a mistake, it was only a matter of time.

Moriko had throwing knives hidden in her outfit, easily accessible with a quick flick of her wrist, but she'd need them to get at least ten paces closer. Her aim was uncertain beyond thirty paces.

The archers and Moriko began an intricate and deadly dance. The archers rode around, firing at her, almost nonchalantly, while Moriko dodged and spun out of the way of arrows. She didn't draw her sword, hoping for a chance to unleash a throwing knife. She was able to sense the arrows launched behind her, but it was getting more challenging to stay unharmed.

The riders changed their pattern, making the circle more of an oval, shooting at her when they were closest to her and drawing another arrow as they pulled away. Moriko was getting less and less time to dodge, and she was grazed by at least two arrows. The ground around her was littered with missed shots. Moriko could tell the riders were getting frustrated at not being able to hit her, but their discipline held.

The moment came without warning. One of the riders, furious at being unable to hit her, rode in too close. Moriko figured he was less than twenty paces away. She drew a throwing knife, aimed, and threw. Her aim was true enough. She had been trying to strike him in the head, but the shot went low, cutting into the soldier's neck. He fell from his horse with a look of surprise on his face. His horse stood there, wondering what to do next.

Moriko leapt towards the riderless horse. She had a few options. She could grab the horse and try to escape, but her experience indicated she'd just be run down again. Instead, she went for the bow of the fallen soldier. She wasn't trained in archery, but she figured she could figure out how to nock an arrow and fire it in the general direction of a rider. If nothing else it might scare them off a bit. She dodged two arrows as they tried to bring her down from behind.

One rider yelled in a language Moriko didn't understand. She didn't know what he was saying, but she figured he'd realized what she was doing. He charged towards her.

Moriko glanced back as the horse was coming down on her. She had a knife in hand, but the horse blocked her view of the rider and she didn't think she'd have any chance of bringing down the horse itself with a knife. She sheathed it, running desperately for the bow only paces in front of her. Her sense screamed, letting her know she wouldn't make it.

Instinct and training took over. The rider was trying to ride her down by placing her on his right side, the side of his sword hand. At the last moment she leapt to the left, putting herself on the other side of the horse. She drew her blade and cut, slicing through horse and man alike. They both screamed and collapsed in one large pile on the ground. Moriko heard bones break under the force of the impact.

The final two riders veered from their own charges, deciding they had taken enough losses. They rode off until they were sitting about sixty paces away. Moriko could hear them discussing the situation, but without understanding the language she had no idea what they were saying. She waited, patient and alert. From this range there was no way they could harm her.

They didn't seem to share the same opinion. She saw them take an arrow each and dip it in a small sack hanging down the side of their horses. She wondered if they were going to use her for target practice. It seemed like a waste of good arrows. They had to realize they had no chance from where they sat. They each pulled their arrows back and Moriko realized too late what they were doing.

Moriko watched helplessly as they fired both their shots into the air. She took one last forlorn glance at the surviving horse, the horse of the rider she'd killed with the throwing knife. She wanted to run and save it, but there wasn't time. Both arrows struck in the horse's side and it collapsed to the ground. Moriko assumed they'd dipped the arrows in some sort of poison. With their final shot, the riders rode off, leaving her alone in the vast expanse of prairie.

Three horses and two bodies surrounded her. She cursed. Without a horse, she had no idea how she would survive. She was a long ways from the Three Kingdoms, and given the meager amount of game she'd killed on the way down, she wasn't sure she'd be able to kill enough to get back.

There was only one choice to make, and Moriko didn't like it. She had to keep heading south, hoping she'd find the Azarians before her supplies ran out. It was either that or die in this endless grassland.

Despair was starting to set in. Moriko had been walking south for almost another half-moon, and she had seen and sensed nothing but the occasional patrol. Whenever she encountered one she would sit in the tall grass and suppress her presence. She suspected word of her battle with the Azarians would have spread, and she had no desire to dodge arrows while Azarians used her for target practice.

Moriko didn't understand. The Azarians were a nation of people, but she couldn't find them. How could you not find a whole nation? There were more deserted areas of the Southern Kingdom, but still one would cross farmsteads. The only sign people even lived on this land was the tracks and trails which crossed the ground. If not for the tracks and the occasional scouting party, Moriko would have had no problem believing the land was hers alone.

Part of the answer had to be the size of the land. Azaria had to be much larger than the Southern Kingdom. Perhaps it was even larger than the entire Three Kingdoms. Moriko had never experienced a land so vast and untamed.

It was late morning when the mirage first appeared. At first glance it appeared to be a city, or a near approximation of a city. To Moriko's tired eyes it seemed like small mounds were rising from the ground, but in far too orderly a fashion to be natural. She paused and threw out her sense, but she felt nothing. She knew she was a long way away yet, but if it was a city, it should throw off enough energy for her to sense it. The lack of energy emanating from the mounds convinced her it was just a mirage. She glanced suspiciously at the sun. It was at the right angle to cause the sight to appear.

Regardless, the mounds were in line with the path she was following, so as the morning wore on she continued to approach them. She watched them constantly, and as the sun reached its midpoint, the mounds stopped shimmering and became solid.

Moriko panicked, ducking into the long grass. If it was a city, she would have been in sight for most of the day. Guards would be well aware of her presence by now. She sat still and calmed her mind, but still she sensed nothing from the city.

Moriko was scared. There were two possibilities she could think of. Either every person in the city knew how to suppress their presence or the city itself was empty. Moriko didn't want to consider either of them as realities. She lifted her head cautiously above the grass, scanning for signs of life, signs of movement. Gaining confidence, she sat and watched, but no matter how long she stared, her eyes couldn't make out any movement.

She loosened her sword from its sheath and moved forward. It seemed to be an empty city, but that made no sense. Perhaps it was a trap to lure in scouts like herself.

As she approached the city its size grew. The city was made of dozens upon dozens of single-story buildings. Some of them were large, but the city itself was expansive. Moriko knew she could wander the city for more than a day and not be able to explore every building.

But even with her sense extended as far as she could push it she couldn't sense a single human life. When she finally reached the first buildings, she was convinced the city was completely abandoned. She paused to examine the buildings. They were made from the long grass of the plains, woven together in a particular pattern she couldn't hope to imitate. She tested the walls. They were solid, and they would hold up against casual sword strikes. The roof was made using the same techniques.

The building would provide reliable shelter. There was no reason to abandon it.

She stepped inside the first building, sword ready to jump out of its sheath. It was barren. Clean. Spotless.

There was evidence of life. There was a fire circle with dead coals within it. But there wasn't any sign of recent habitation, or any evidence to suggest the occupants had to leave in a hurry. The dirt floor was swept clean and there wasn't a pot, pan, or utensil anywhere to be found.

With a growing sense of unease, Moriko examined a few of the other buildings. Every one was identically barren. Some of the buildings were larger than others and seemed built to be common rooms, but they, too, were meticulously cleaned.

Moriko wandered aimlessly through the city, following a path that generally led south. The buildings were evenly spaced, but the city's design didn't follow the square patterns more traditional in the Three Kingdoms. There wasn't any main street, just a number of smaller paths wandering between the buildings. Moriko thought it would be easier to march an army around the city than try to get one through it.

Halfway through the city, Moriko was starting to question her sanity. Perhaps she had been out on the plains too long. Perhaps this was some sort of dream she couldn't wake up from. A half-moon of barren plain followed by an empty city? Her mind couldn't comprehend what was happening, and she was beginning to fear what she didn't know. She had hoped there would be supplies, but every place she tried was as barren as the last. Her supplies were running low, and she worried she would die in this empty sea of grass.

When she reached the end of the city, her mind was reeling. No one. The city was as empty as the prairie that surrounded it. She found the trail heading south again easily enough. But she hesitated to take the first steps. She glanced longingly back to the north.

Moriko missed the Southern Kingdom. She ached for Ryuu's embrace and constant attention. She wanted to be back among the old woods, basking in the shade of trees that made human lifespans pale in comparison, dipping her feet in the cool stream that ran near the hut. But there was no way back, not now. The only way was forward. With an exceptional effort, she turned back to the south and scanned the ground in front of her.

She didn't camp the night in the city. She wandered south until it was shimmering in the sunset. Only then did she feel comfortable lying down for the night.

Moriko awoke the next morning to the light pressure of another on her sense. It was a delicate brush of sensation, one she doubted when she first felt it. It had been so long since she had sensed another human, she almost doubted her abilities. But the sensation was there, constant, coming closer.

Moriko's first reaction was to go back to sleep. She was laying in the tall grass and there was no way anyone could discover her. They would have to ride or walk within five paces of her to see her, and even then would only find her if they happened to look down. There were plenty of horrible things one could say about the prairie, but it was easy to hide in.

But then she sensed something she hadn't encountered since the day she left Ryuu. She felt the tendrils of the sense spreading out from the person. Down here in Azaria that could only mean one thing. There was a hunter out there.

Once the realization struck, Moriko came fully awake. She focused her sense and scanned the area all around her. As far as she could sense, she was alone with the hunter. It was both a relief and a terror. If not for Ryuu, the last hunter she had encountered would have killed her. One was dangerous enough. Moriko suppressed her presence, preparing to ambush the hunter. He was still dozens of paces away and Moriko was certain he hadn't found her yet.

Then Moriko rethought her strategy. She was out in the middle of nowhere. She hadn't seen a living soul for days, even though she had passed through a city. Her food was running dangerously low, and she had no idea which direction she should be heading. If she could get captured, it would solve a lot of her problems. It was a strategy that carried a fair amount of risk. There was no guarantee the hunter wouldn't just try to kill her. But she was becoming more and more certain she wouldn't survive in this land without help.

Moriko found a pose that allowed her to draw her sword in case of emergency, but she lay back down in the grass and pretended to be sleeping. As the hunter continued to approach her location, Moriko gradually opened up her presence. After cycles of practice, suppressing her energy had become almost as natural as breathing. Letting go of the ability was like throwing off a cloak in the biting wind. She felt bare and exposed.

As she had expected, the hunter turned towards her energy. Moriko fought off the urge to tense her body in preparation for combat. He had to think she was asleep.

Each breath passed with agonizing slowness. The hunter was nothing if not patient, and he must have suspected a trap. He got to within a few paces of her and then waited, his own sense expanding around them both, searching for anything he might have missed. Moriko forced herself to stillness, staying deep within herself. The hunter drew his sword and Moriko almost lost control. She wanted to get up, wanted to fight. But she lay there, open to attack. Her mind ran in a circle, wondering if he would go straight for a killing blow or would try to capture her. His posture gave no indication, and Moriko suspected the hunter was trying to make the same decision. She forced herself to breathe normally, wondering if she would be fast enough if he decided to strike.

When he made his move, it was smooth and controlled. Moriko opened her eyes to the touch of his steel on her neck. She suppressed the urge to laugh. He had taken the bait. She would live to fight another day. She stood up, her arms raised in a gesture of surrender as he took her blade from her. It made her feel even more naked than before, but there was nothing to do about it. As he stepped back she got her first good look at him.

He was a tall man, much thinner than the two men who had attacked her and Ryuu at their cabin. He had a lean musculature indicating plenty of strength, but not an ounce of fat on him. His hair was dark, long, and disheveled, as were his clothes. But Moriko didn't have the discipline to pay attention to the details. She only saw two characteristics. He was missing his right arm, and his left held a sword identical to the one that had almost taken her life two moons ago.

The hunter continued to search her, finding the throwing knives she had on her forearms. He searched through her sack, finding nothing of interest. Moriko was grateful his search wasn't too thorough. She had several blades strapped to her inner thighs as well. Content, the hunter stepped back and looked at her.

"You are my prisoner."

There was something off, something clawing at her attention she couldn't put her finger on. When it came to her, she felt foolish for not having recognized it earlier. "You speak our language."

"We all do."

Moriko's mind reeled. There were maybe only a few people in all the Three Kingdoms who spoke Azarian. How was it they all spoke the language of the Three Kingdoms? Her mind tried to find answers, but the hunter kept pressing the conversation forward.

"You are my prisoner."

Moriko nodded. "Yes."

"Do you promise not to try to escape? Do I have your word?"

Moriko frowned. It seemed like an odd question to ask. She promised she wouldn't try to escape. Her thoughts flashed to Ryuu for a moment. Knowing him, he'd actually follow through on his promise. But they were only words. She only planned on holding to them as long as they served her.

"Good. Let's go."

As far as captive experiences went, Moriko figured it could be a lot worse. The hunter made no attempt to bind her arms or legs. He just led the way and expected for her to follow. Moriko shrugged and followed his lead, a prisoner in a land far, far away from home.

CHAPTER 11

The island grew larger and larger. Ryuu was amazed by the size of it. When he had listened to Shigeru's story, he had pictured a smaller island. He had thought it must be small to hide from the ships that traveled these waters. There weren't many who dared the open seas, even in summer, but there were enough that Ryuu had assumed the only way the island could stay undiscovered by the Three Kingdoms was due to its small size. He realized the error of his assumption. The island was safe for two reasons. First, it was far to the north of the Three Kingdoms. They'd been sailing for over a day, and from what Ryuu understood, few traders traveled north from port. Most went east or west. Second was the geography of the island. Ryuu was stunned by the sheer height of the place. It rose, a single sheer plateau in the middle of the ocean.

Ryuu was capable of climbing. He and Shigeru had often climbed trees out in the forest, and he had grown up with no fear of heights, but he also knew that his odds of climbing up those walls without assistance were next to zero. As they got closer, Ryuu looked for a path or a landing area, but no matter how hard he squinted he wasn't able to make out a safe landing or a path to the top. For a moment, he doubted this was the island that was their destination. But when he saw the faces of the crew he knew he wasn't wrong. They were looking at their home.

They were still hundreds of paces out when the ship made a course adjustment and started to circle around the island. Ryuu figured it would only be a matter of time before he saw the harbor they were making for, but again he was wrong. As far as they traveled, nothing appeared to him. They continued to sail around while Ryuu looked for the harbor. He was looking so hard for the harbor he didn't notice they were approaching the island until he looked up for a moment and saw the island towering over him. Except for a few details, the intimidating rock face seemed the same no matter how far they sailed. Ryuu realized he didn't even know how far around the island they had come. His sense of direction was confused. He looked at the sun, only to realize it had disappeared behind heavy clouds.

The captain saw Ryuu's glance. "Storm coming in. We should be in before it hits."

Ryuu nodded, still not able to make out what they were approaching. The captain had turned straight towards the island, and Ryuu saw nothing but solid rock in front of them.

The bow of the ship rushed towards the rock and Ryuu was afraid they were going to strike the face. He glanced around, but the crew all seemed calm, and some even seemed to be having some enjoyment at his expense. He took a deep breath and focused himself. A whole crew of men wouldn't commit suicide out on the ocean just to kill him. They were taking him to the island as promised. He just had to trust them.

At the last moment, the ship turned hard and brought in its sails. It was only then, with the rock face just a handful of paces from the ship, that Ryuu saw a small cut in the rock. It was narrow, leaving only a pace or two of distance on each side of the ship as she turned in, carried by her momentum. Ryuu nodded in sudden understanding. The hole was too narrow for oars, so the ship had to build up momentum, make the turn, and glide into a hole almost invisible to all. It was only from a certain angle that the entrance could be seen. Even if it could be seen, it was too small to allow large ships. It was, in short, a perfectly defensible position, and that was if someone somehow managed to find it. Ryuu was certain it would take him days of sailing around the island, and even then he wasn't sure he'd see it. It was no wonder the nightblades had remained hidden for all these cycles.

The ship pulled into a small cave. It docked next to one other small ship, which Ryuu assumed was the only other way off this island. He took note of it, but knew it would do him little good. He was a man who had grown up in mountains and trees. He didn't know how to sail. If he had to leave in a hurry, he'd have to figure that challenge out.

The cave was lit with a number of torches, and the ship was greeted warmly by the guards who stood at the docks. Ryuu saw there was only one path out of the cave, again a very defensible position.

The nightblades Ryuu had fought on the docks joined those who were guarding the cave. Ryuu tensed. He wouldn't be able to fight four nightblades. At least, he didn't think so. Even if he snapped, he might not have enough strength and speed.

But he didn't have to worry. They had only been docked for a few moments when an older man came down the path. Ryuu was amazed. The man was old. Ryuu guessed he had seen sixty cycles, but he moved with a lithe grace that belied his age. Ryuu noticed all these facts, but they weren't what he paid attention to. Instead, he focused on the energy emanating from the man. Even the Abbot from Perseverance paled in comparison to him. The difference was this man controlled it. Ryuu knew he was looking at the strongest man he had ever seen, even if he was over sixty.

The old man was grinning from ear to ear. "My, my. What have we here? It's a pleasure to meet you, Ryuu. I'm sure you have hundreds of questions, all of which I will answer soon, but first I must insist you complete a task."

Ryuu was taken completely aback. He wasn't certain what he had been expecting, but it wasn't this. How did the old man know his name?

"What task?"

"Well, as I'm sure you know, this island is one for nightblades, and despite what you may believe, you aren't a nightblade yet. To be one, you must pass three trials. So, if you wish to stay on this island, I must insist you take the trials immediately."

"And if I refuse?"

The old man grimaced. "I'm afraid we'll have to kill you. You understand, of course. We can't allow word of this island to get out."

Ryuu was battling his emotions. Too much was happening at once. At first he was angry he was being asked to prove himself, but it was followed soon after by real fear. Shigeru hadn't finished his own training before having to escape the island. What if he wasn't really a nightblade? Ryuu shook his head, trying to clear his thoughts. He had to be. It was who he was. He had nothing to fear. "I'll take your trials."

The old man grinned. "Excellent! Your first trial is right over there." He pointed to a wall.

Ryuu looked at the old man, questions written across his face. The old man explained. "Your first trial is to climb the wall. At the top, you'll find a passage to your second trial. You'll find them to be self-explanatory."

Ryuu studied the wall again. On closer inspection, he could see it topped out with a small ledge hidden in the darkness. The wall was easily ten times as tall as Ryuu was. He shrugged. He'd grown up climbing. The wall didn't look easy, but he was sure he could manage it. He strode towards it, ready to take the first trial towards becoming a nightblade.

Ryuu approached the slab of rock. It was high, but he'd been in trees of the same height. All he needed to do was not fall. He studied the face before he began, noting the cracks and holds where he could place his fingers and toes. There weren't many holds, but there were enough. He stretched out his forearms and started climbing.

The climb began with a crack running from the floor. Ryuu stuck his hands into the crack and pressed his weight to the side, allowing him to grip the crack. His progress was slow but consistent. He kept his focus on the rock and on his body, ensuring every hold was solid before putting his full weight onto it. When he looked down, he saw he was almost half way up the wall.

He found a place where he could stand on his toes without handholds. Shaking out the tension in his hands, he looked at the last sections of wall and planned out his moves. His hands were getting sweaty against the rock, but there was nothing to be done about it. He wiped them against his robes, but they didn't stop sweating. He glanced down and saw the eyes of the nightblades watching him. They were impassive, fine with whatever outcome awaited him.

His grip was only going to get worse, so he kept climbing. The holds near the top were small, just enough for him to get his fingers over. When he finally heaved himself over the ledge, he lay there for a few moments to catch his breath. The climb had been harder than he'd expected. He glanced at his fingers, bleeding from their abuse against the rock. The skin had torn in the only places he didn't have callouses.

After a short break, Ryuu looked around. There was a cloth draped over another tunnel. His first trial had been completed, but he had two more to go. He stood up and prepared himself for whatever was next.

Ryuu pulled aside the cloth to search for a torch, but there was none. So it was to be a test in the dark. Ryuu supposed it was understandable. If it was the ability to sense you were testing, you would want to reduce the role of vision as much as possible. Ryuu entered the tunnel.

As he had expected, the path turned completely dark after a dozen paces. Ryuu felt his way along with one hand in front of his face to protect his head and one off to his side, feeling his way along the path. He let himself stay calmly alert. There was no knowing what was next, so he maintained a slow pace, wary of surprises. He imagined there weren't any prizes for finishing the fastest.

He lost time as he followed the tunnel. It was man-made, with smooth walls that could never have been created by nature. It was an unreal experience to walk through such complete blackness. He felt like he was moving, but if not for his own sensations, he would have had no evidence to support the claim. He could feel the brush of the smooth, cold rock against his fingers, but that was all. It was the first time he realized how dependent one's sense of motion was on sight.

The monotony of the hike started to lull him into complacency, and if it hadn't been for a soft breeze against his skin he might have met his end before he found any answers. The cool air refreshed his awareness, and he knew something was different about his surroundings. He stopped moving and listened, but there was no sound in the caves.

Ryuu threw out his sense, searching for more information. Someone was above him, at least twenty paces up. Ryuu focused and sensed the pull of a bow. He cursed silently to himself and threw himself forward. He tried to land in a smooth roll, but he couldn't see the ground and he smashed into it with his shoulder. Behind him, he heard the soft hiss of an arrow as it passed where he had been, then clattering against the rock. He drew his blade, his body primed for action. But the person above him was gone, walking away through some passage high above him. Ryuu guessed he'd just passed the second trial, leaving one last. Holding his hands out, he traced the shape of the room until he came to another smooth passage. He followed it.

Ryuu found the same technique of keeping one hand above him and one hand following a wall served him well. Again, he lost his sense of direction. He could feel the ground was angled upwards, but beyond that slight piece of information he could have been walking in a void.

He paused on occasion to take a deep breath and throw out his sense, but every time it came back with nothing. In the Three Kingdoms, the darkness had been his friend. He could sense what others couldn't see, but in here it felt more malicious. Was this the way his opponents felt when they knew he was near? He knew he'd welcome the first light he saw.

Doubt was starting to creep into Ryuu's mind when he sensed a shift in the air. It wasn't much, but any sensation at all in these tunnels was significant to him. He threw out his senses and waited. He decided he was in another large room. It was impossible to say any more with any confidence. He moved forward cautiously, straining his sense to see if he could feel anything that would lend him a clue to what was next.

Ryuu was surprised to sense a blade spinning towards him. He hadn't sensed anyone in the room with him. It wasn't thrown fast, but it was spinning rapidly, aimed right at Ryuu's chest. He moved to the side as it went spinning past him. It clattered as it struck the rock behind him.

Clatter? Ryuu realized it was a practice sword that had been thrown at him. His sense was strained, but he couldn't sense anything else coming at him, or anyone else in the room with him. After a couple of breaths had passed, Ryuu searched the ground behind him and picked the sword up. He had a suspicion he'd be using it for the next trial.

If he couldn't sense the person throwing the sword, there was only one logical explanation. He had thought Orochi's skills unique on the island, but apparently others possessed the ability to suppress their presence as well. They were in for a surprise. He'd been living with Moriko for two cycles. Now that he knew what he was looking for, he wouldn't be surprised again. Ryuu found another passage and followed it, knowing the end was near.

It was obvious to his heightened senses when he reached the final room. He had been in the darkness long enough that he was beginning to understand it. This room was different than the ones he'd been in before. Here there was a strong breeze, and although it was still pitch black, Ryuu felt like he must be getting closer to the surface.

Ryuu found a place to stand his ground and halted. He knew if a challenge was going to occur, it would happen in its own time. So he stood and focused his senses, trying to understand the space around him. He was trying to sense someone who could suppress their power like Moriko. It was challenging in the room. Typically, Ryuu sensed Moriko as a shadow. Everywhere they went was teeming with life, from the bugs and the grass below them to the birds above them. Moriko's ability cast a slight shadow, and if you knew what you were looking for, it was easy to find. But this cave wasn't teeming with life, so there wasn't any shadow to cast. It was probably why he hadn't sensed his opponent yet. When everything is darkness, a shadow hides well.

Ryuu's mind raced. If he couldn't sense his opponent he suspected he'd fail the next trial. There had to be a way to sense him. When the idea struck, it almost knocked Ryuu back with its brilliance.

Moriko had been trying to teach Ryuu how to suppress his presence, just like Orochi had taught her. He had never mastered it like Moriko, but he understood the idea. But if one could suppress their presence, it followed that one could expand their presence as well. The Abbot at Perseverance had done it, so it should be possible. Ryuu thought back to the Abbot to try to remember how it had felt to him.

When he thought he had it, Ryuu tried to expand his presence. It seemed like it was working, but it was tough to tell. He kept pushing and pushing, putting more mental effort into every attempt.

He felt the faint stirrings of a shadow near him. His idea had worked! He brought his attention to bear, but it disappeared. Frowning, Ryuu focused again on expanding his presence, and again he could just make out a shadow near him. He wrapped his hands around his practice sword in preparation.

Ryuu decided to let his opponent know the game was up. "I know you're there."

Ryuu registered the shock from his opponent. He was so focused that when the attack came it was as if he had been struck by lightning. The sudden sensory input was far beyond what he had gotten used to. He had been prepared, though, so he moved out of the way while he gathered his wits. He could barely sense the second attack. It was as if the intruder had suppressed his intent instantly. Moriko couldn't do that.

The battle between the two was pitched. Ryuu wasn't sure his attacker wasn't carrying steel, so was hesitant at first, attempting to deflect cuts he would have preferred to block. But the sound of wood on wood reassured him, and he threw himself into the battle.

The battle went back and forth. Ryuu figured he was better with the sword, but his opponent kept trying to blind his sense by alternating bright, intent strikes with strikes where his intent was hidden. Ryuu had never encountered any strategy like it, and it prevented him from getting the upper hand against his opponent.

But as the fight wore on, Ryuu's opponent's abilities started to deteriorate. His opponent wasn't able to switch from one type of strike to the next as quickly, and Ryuu gained the ability to sense the attacks with more and more clarity. Ryuu stayed on the defensive. He knew if he kept himself safe, his opponent would wear out to a point when Ryuu could strike with little risk.

The moment was longer in coming than he expected. Every time he felt like he was just about ready to strike, his opponent would seem to find another reserve of energy and attack with renewed vigor, and Ryuu would find himself on the defensive again.

The outcome, however, was inevitable. Barring a lucky strike, his opponent couldn't outlast Ryuu. Ryuu could sense enough to know where the blows were coming and was able to keep one step in front of his opponent.

When the moment came, Ryuu felt like a door had opened in front of him. In frustration, his opponent had struck out with too much force and lost his balance. It was only a matter of a moment, but Ryuu had sensed the moment coming and was prepared for it. He thrust violently, catching his opponent in the stomach.

Ryuu was surprised when the gasp of pain was female. He had been fighting in complete darkness. There was no way to tell if his opponent had been man or woman. But he had assumed he was fighting a man. The blows he had deflected were strong. Moriko was the only woman he knew capable of striking with such force.

He chastised himself. He was on an island where there were other nightblades, other women who were as strong as he and Moriko. Hopefully stronger. It was why he had come here in the first place.

Ryuu's thoughts were swept away by the wave of light that flashed all around him. Ryuu blinked away the tears at the sudden brightness. He looked down at his opponent. The woman was really a girl, a cycle or two younger than Ryuu. Her eyes shone with a bright intensity, but she was grinning through the pain. She was attractive, strong and capable. She looked up at him with a mixture of respect and nervousness.

He smiled and extended his hand. It had been an excellent fight. She looked at it, hesitating, before returning his smile and placing her hand in his. He helped her up, surprised by her weight. She was small, but Ryuu could sense the strong muscles covered by the flowing robes.

He took a moment to look around him. The room he was in was large, a perfectly flat surface contained inside a hemisphere of smoothly carved rock. The room must have taken ages to make, and Ryuu was impressed by the skill of those on the island. As he watched, a perfectly smooth section of rock developed a crack, and the crack opened to reveal a door the older man from below walked through.

Again, Ryuu was struck by the power of this man. It was something beyond what Ryuu understood. It was a power deep and bottomless, but contained, like a well with no bottom. When Ryuu looked into the man's eyes he knew the man held a knowledge and wisdom about the world that Ryuu could only dream of trying to obtain. His eyes sparkled with a hidden mirth as he looked Ryuu over.

"Well done, Ryuu."

The voice was soft but commanding. Not even knowing the man, Ryuu found himself bowing deeply to him in a gesture of respect. As he came back up he saw the man looking at him again, studying him in a way that made Ryuu feel naked, but still strangely comfortable. It was difficult to describe. It was almost as though he was being observed by a parent.

Ryuu didn't know what to say, so he decided to stay silent, observing everything happening around him. A few nightblades trickled into the room behind the old man, but no one seemed to have any hostile intent. Most just seemed curious to see him.

Ryuu returned his gaze to the old man. "How do you know my name?"

The old man tilted his head and looked at Ryuu as though he expected Ryuu to figure out his own question. Ryuu thought about it for a moment. There were a couple of possible explanations, but only one was likely. "Orochi wrote to you."

The old man nodded. "My name is Tenchi, and I am the leader of the last of the blades. I formally welcome you to our island, Ryuu, adopted son of Shigeru. It is my great pleasure to officially bestow on you the rank of nightblade."

Something was close to breaking in Ryuu. After all these cycles, was it possible he had found a place to call home? A place where he would be welcomed for who he was? He contained his emotion. "Thank you. It is an honor to be here." He didn't know what else to say, so he said nothing.

Tenchi seemed to understand. He turned to the assembled group of nightblades. "Brothers and sisters, please join me in welcoming our new brother." He turned back to Ryuu and bowed deeply, the other nightblades following suit.

Ryuu held back tears. He was home. He was a nightblade.

CHAPTER 12

"Well," said Lord Tanak, "what do you think?"

Renzo stood with Tanak on the same hill Lord Akira had stood so foolishly on the day before. Renzo had wanted to disappear into the battle and assassinate Akira, but Tanak hadn't allowed him, wanting him nearby for protection in case the battle turned against them.

It had been the first large-scale battle Renzo had ever observed, and he'd been impressed by the generals who commanded such large groups of men. It was barely contained chaos, but the commanders brought some semblance of order to the nightmare below. Renzo had tried to use his sense to gather more information about the battle, but he was overwhelmed by the information coming into his mind.

Renzo came back to the present. "It was well fought, my Lord. It only serves to strengthen my belief in our seers. A great victory is nothing more than a matter of time."

Tanak grinned from ear to ear at the statement. Renzo was disgusted. Everyone in the Three Kingdoms was weak, but Tanak was pathetic. He was weak because he thought he was great.

There were no seers on the island, no one who dared predict the future. Even the old fool Tenchi knew the future was still unwritten. But Tanak believed so much in himself, he believed in seers of the future. It was an abomination, although it had made a fair number of charlatans in the Western Kingdom rich. It was profitable to predict success for the Lord.

"I am glad to hear it. I know you wished to enter the fray, but I am grateful for your protection."

Renzo hid his thoughts. Tanak wasn't grateful; he was terrified of death. He would have collapsed into a blubbering pile of terror if he hadn't known Renzo was nearby. In Renzo's eyes, he wasn't fit to lead, but it was because of his weakness he was the perfect tool.

Tanak continued. "What do you think Akira will do now?"

Renzo was wondering the same question. Akira was a competent leader of his kingdom. Weaker than Sen, in Renzo's estimation, but still competent. Akira's First had never come up from the pass, even though there weren't any reports of battle. His Fourth was a disorganized mess and his Fifth had just been shattered. Tanak's First had taken substantial losses, and they were fighting at less than half strength. Tanak's armies were slightly larger than Akira's, and Renzo's best guess had Tanak with almost half again as many soldiers left. He tried to put himself in Akira's position, but the truth was, he had no idea. He was a killer, not a commander.

Renzo's primary concern was that they hadn't done as thorough of a job destroying Akira's armies as he had hoped. While they couldn't mount an organized resistance, they were loyal to Lord Akira, and they could harass supply lines.

Renzo answered honestly. "I don't know. But he won't take this without fighting back."

Tanak nodded. "I think you're right, old friend." He walked away, and Renzo shook his head. Allies they might be for now. Friends they definitely weren't.

Two days had passed, and little had occurred to improve Renzo's mood. Tanak had decided to celebrate with his men after the victory. He ordered that two days be spent reorganizing the troops. His argument was that it would give his men a chance to relax, to rejoice and get to know the new soldiers in their units.

It all sounded fine to Renzo, but time was Akira's friend more than it was theirs. They needed to keep jumping forward, pushing before Akira could organize his troops. Rest was fine, but ultimate victory required more of the men. It would require sacrifice. But still, Tanak was the ruler, and there was little Renzo could do to force the issue.

His fears regarding Akira's left-over troops were proving to be well-founded. Though Tanak and his men were supposed to be at rest, they were attacked over and over. Nothing major. Nothing even substantial. But every soldier they lost here was a soldier who couldn't push deeper into the Southern Kingdom.

Renzo spent the evening in his tent meditating while the revels happened without him. His tent was small and bare, and many commented on Tanak's closest adviser and how he kept little for himself. Renzo traveled and lived simply. His life was dedicated to one purpose, a purpose not even Tanak had ever guessed at. His life was dedicated to forcing the blades to take their place in the Three Kingdoms once again.

His meditation was interrupted by a clamor of activity outside, the shouts of men in battle. Renzo furrowed his brow. It wasn't the sound of men in friendly competition around a campfire. It was the sound of men at war. Renzo allowed his sense to expand. Here in the camp, he usually kept it close to him. But a battle was being waged outside, about a hundred paces away from his own tent, right next to Tanak's.

Renzo reached for his sword, but hesitated. His blood burned with the desire to fight, but he had to hold here if he could. If there was even a rumor that Tanak had a nightblade in his army, their entire situation could change. He prepared, covering himself in cloth, leaving only his eyes uncovered. If he did have to fight, he couldn't be recognized. All the while he kept his sense on the battle.

It was hard to tell with so many people, but Tanak guessed it was almost a hundred men attacking, a group of incredible size considering they were so near the heart of Tanak's camp.

The battle moved closer to Tanak's tent. Too many of his honor guard were drunk or ill-prepared for combat. It would be only moments before Tanak himself was involved. Renzo had no love for Tanak, but he was necessary to Renzo's plans. He stepped out of his tent and took a moment to survey the scene. The soldiers from the south had stolen uniforms from Tanak's men. Renzo assumed they'd raided the dead on the battlefields. It was how they had managed to get so close without drawing suspicion. Dishonorable, but effective.

It was all the information Renzo needed. He drew his blade, felt the energy of the night surround him, and he moved.

To Renzo, killing the soldiers from the south was as easy as drawing breath. Their strikes were weak, slow, and Renzo could sense them coming far before they were a danger to him. There was a moment when Renzo felt some measure of disgust at the work he was called to do. It wasn't that he had to kill so many men, but that the men he had to kill were so weak. They didn't deserve to hold a sword. If they were stronger, if they could truly fight for themselves, he wouldn't be needed.

Soldier after soldier fell to Renzo's blade. His ears filled with the screams of battle, but the longer he worked, the fewer screams he heard. Out of the corner of his eye, he saw that Tanak had left his tent. His armor was on haphazardly, and his eyes were bleary. He did not shout orders or give commands, but gazed upon the battlefield with a look of disbelief on his face. It was as though he could not understand what was happening right in front of him, Renzo swore to himself. The man was so blinded by his own vision of greatness, he didn't realize he was just as fallible and as mortal as the person standing next to him.

What was more of a problem for Renzo was that Tanak was standing outside his tent, open to attack from any who saw him, and there were plenty of soldiers from the south who had seen him. There weren't many left, maybe ten to fifteen, but those remaining attacked with a renewed vigor when they saw their target in the flesh, Renzo understood. For the soldiers who were attacking, this had never been a mission they planned on returning from.

Renzo brought his attention back to the moment, and his blade sang its song as it drank the blood of one victim after the next. In a moment, he was by Tanak's side, defending him from the last few remaining warriors. The Lord of the Western Kingdom didn't even draw his blade. Renzo didn't know if it was due to disbelief or to fear, but it didn't matter. Either way, the man was pathetic.

The last attacker fell to Renzo's blade. Renzo examined himself quickly and saw that one of the warriors had managed a small cut on his arm. He was disappointed in himself, but he pushed it aside as he looked at Tanak. Although he had yet to come to his senses, Tanak seemed otherwise unharmed. Renzo didn't bother asking him if he was fine, but stole out of the camp so he wouldn't be noticed.

CHAPTER 13

Like Moriko, the hunter who had captured her seemed to prefer silence over empty conversation. Moriko had hoped for a while that the hunter would have a horse, but that was seeming less and less likely the further they walked. He seemed to be on foot as well. Moriko would have been content with the silence, but she was here to gather information.

"What is your name?"

The hunter turned back and looked at her over his shoulder. He seemed to be deciding whether or not to speak to her. "My name is Kalden." After a long pause he asked, "What is yours?"

"Moriko."

She could see him saying her name silently, learning the combination of sounds. She hoped it would start a longer conversation, but Kalden turned around and kept walking, content with the level of discourse. Moriko allowed the silence to continue for a few hundred paces before she decided to try again. "Are you a hunter?"

Kalden didn't respond for a long time, and Moriko wondered if he was avoiding the question, or if something had been lost in translation.

"I am a goner."

Moriko frowned. "Goner. What's a goner?"

He searched for the words. "I am gone from the clan. I am not allowed to return."

Understanding dawned on Moriko. "You're an outcast?"

He nodded. "Yes, that is the word."

"Why?"

He glanced at his arm. "It is a long story."

With that, Kalden set his shoulders, and Moriko understood the conversation was over. She had hit a sore point and wouldn't get anything more from him for a while. Even though they'd only exchanged a few words, there was a lot for Moriko to think about. Until she learned more, there was nothing to do but keep following him to see where this journey led.

As the sun set, they settled to make camp for the night. Moriko wasn't sure how it would work, but Kalden went about setting out his camp gear as if she was a traveling companion and not a prisoner. He seemed to take her word at face value. Moriko set out her own equipment. When they were both done, they sat and ate Kalden's food and watched the sun set. As they ate, they studied each other in silence. Moriko was surprised when it was Kalden who broke the silence.

"You speak little. I thought you would speak more."

Moriko was startled. It was about the last thing she'd expected to hear.

"Why?"

"Our leader, he says your people speak much but don't fight much. You seem different. You don't speak much. I don't know how much you fight."

Moriko decided there was an opportunity to break through the ice between them.

"Why didn't you kill me, back there when you caught me sleeping?"

Kalden was silent for a moment, and Moriko wondered if she'd pushed too hard again. But then he spoke. "With you, I might be able to get back to the clan. They might let me return if I bring you with me."

"Kalden, why are you an outcast? Does it have something to do with your arm?"

He looked up, searching her face for some sign of deceit. There was none. She was genuinely curious about his arm. Moriko had watched with fascination throughout the day as he had completed tasks one-handed. She realized how much she had taken having two arms for granted. It was clear he hadn't been trained to survive with one arm, but he still managed to live remarkably well.

"I lost it long ago. My kind, we are special. We are called the demon-kind. Do you know?"

Moriko nodded. "We call your kind hunters." She assumed they were talking about the same thing.

"It is a good description, although it does not describe how terrified our clans are of us. They say we are not natural. We see things, understand things no one else can. You too, I think, can do this."

Moriko nodded again. There wasn't any need to insult his intelligence. She had been using her sense when she was captured. He would have felt it and known immediately the type of person he was dealing with.

"That is news. Our leader says your people don't have demon-kind. That you have hunted and killed them all."

Moriko shrugged. "It is mostly true. There are very few of us left."

"Why do you hunt and kill your strongest people? Here we are feared, but we are not killed by our clans."

She shook her head. "I don't know. Fear, probably. Fear of what they don't know."

Kalden thought on her answer for a moment. "When we are young, we are given a test. There is a creature we must hunt, a wild creature that kills many of us. We are to go with only a knife and kill such a creature. If we fail, we are killed by the demon-kind. All demon-kind must be strong, otherwise we are useless."

"I had seen ten suns. Like all demon-kind, I was sent out with my knife. I was proud. Excited. I found one of the creatures, but I was not good enough. It knew I was coming. I did not hide, did not hunt well enough. It attacked and we fought. It bit deep into my arm, but I stabbed it, again and again, until it died. I then took it one handed back to the people."

Moriko imagined the story. She remembered Akira saying something about the hunt each potential hunter had to take. Sure enough, Kalden wore a necklace with the tooth on it. So it was more than a legend. She admired Kalden then. She knew little about the creature he had killed, but if it was a trial, she assumed it would be dangerous. To make the kill while still bleeding, then drag the creature back home. It was impressive. It was a strength worthy of a nightblade, or a hunter.

"What happened next?" She didn't have to feign her curiosity.

"The demon-kind were undecided. It happens, sometimes. The kill is made, but the man is wounded. It happened with me, it has happened with others. After two days, the arm was bad. It was red and big. They took the arm and waited to see if I would live. No more was given. I lived, but I couldn't be demon-kind, not with only one arm. Because I killed, I wasn't killed, but I was not demon-kind."

Moriko was able to fill in the blanks. He had succeeded in his trial, but there wasn't any place in their culture for weakness, so he couldn't take part in it either. He occupied some place in the middle. Not an outcast, but not part of society either.

Kalden's story, rather than answering any questions for her, had piqued her interest for more information. But he seemed to be done telling stories for the day. Maybe he realized he had said too much, given away a bit of information about their society. She knew she wouldn't get anything out of him for the rest of the night.

As they lay down to rest, Moriko started to worry. Kalden's story, simple as it was, had touched her. He was a man who had triumphed over adversity, but whose life had been horrible nevertheless. In some ways, it had resembled her own. For the first time, she wasn't sure she'd be able to kill him if it became necessary.

The next morning, Moriko awoke to Kalden practicing his forms. Moriko was surprised, memories of Ryuu running through her mind. How many mornings had she woken up to watch him practicing his forms? It gave her a weird sense of déjà vu she couldn't quite shake.

Moriko watched Kalden's practice with interest. She had been captured without a fight, so she had never seen his fighting style, and she had never seen the fighting style of a one-armed man. Again, she was impressed by his movements. Although he had not been trained in one-armed combat, he moved with a surprising grace. Moriko was certain she would beat him in a fight, but she was just as certain he would be a dangerous opponent to many of the swordsmen in the Three Kingdoms.

When he was finished, he and Moriko packed up their gear and set out for another day of hiking. Moriko noticed they had turned from their southern course to one heading more towards the west. She decided to try her luck with more questions as they walked.

"May I ask where we are going?"

Kalden answered, "We are going to the Gathering."

It was an answer without any usefulness. "What's the Gathering?"

Kalden just grinned at her, excitement evident on his face. "You will see."

They hiked for another day and camped another night. Despite her repeated attempts, Moriko was unable to gather any more useful information from her captor. He continued to be content to make the journey largely in silence. Moriko weighed her options. She could escape if she wanted to, but she still hadn't learned anything worth taking back to the Three Kingdoms. Her transportation situation hadn't improved, either. She didn't see any other better options than continuing to follow him.

The following day seemed as though it would also be uneventful, until the sun started to set. They had been walking all day without rest. As usual, it passed in silence. Moriko was doing her best to contain her growing frustration. Every step they took was another step further from the Three Kingdoms. The further from home she got, the more she wanted to return. She hadn't expected she would miss it so much.

As had often been the case on this journey, she saw them far before she sensed them, twin pillars of dust on the horizon. Her first instinct was to hide, but then she remembered she was a prisoner. The patrol was coming from the west, the direction they were heading.

It didn't take long for the twin pillars of dust to resolve themselves into two riders who rode straight for them. Moriko had to admit they didn't look friendly. She had expected Kalden would be greeted with a little more respect, but it seemed his status as an outcast, even an outcast hunter, didn't buy him anything in Azarian culture.

The two guards couldn't have been a more mismatched pair. One was a large bear of a man, the other a small wisp. The large one was in charge, but as Moriko watched the two, she decided it was the small one who was a more dangerous opponent. He was wary and well balanced on his horse.

The big man spoke, his voice thundering even though they were only paces apart. "What do you think you're doing?"

Kalden set his shoulders. If nothing else, he did not lack for courage. "I bring a prisoner to my clan."

The big man laughed. "Do you have any idea who she is?"

Kalden looked back at Moriko. "I assume she is a messenger or a scout of some sort."

The big man laughed again. "I don't know how a one-armed hunter like you managed to capture her, but this woman is one of those who he wanted killed."

Moriko's mind raced. Whoever this 'he' was, he was the one responsible for sending hunters after her and Ryuu. And somehow he had known Moriko was coming. Her life was in danger.

She watched as understanding dawned in Kalden's face. His eyes went wide, and Moriko knew she only had moments to act. She had four blades, two knives strapped to each thigh, Kalden hadn't found. With one motion, she reached down with both hands and launched two of them at the men on horseback. If they got away a whole search would be launched for her. Her aim with her right hand was true. The blade embedded itself deep into the neck of the big guard, and he began to fall off his horse. Her aim with her left was not as accurate. The knife embedded itself in the left shoulder of the thin man, an injury he seemed to brush aside as he drew his sword. Moriko turned as Kalden drew his blade against her.

Moriko pushed down the fear she felt when she saw that short blade pointed at her once again. The night her and Ryuu were attacked flashed in her mind. There was no need to worry. This battle was hers. Like putting a cloak of shadows back on, she suppressed her presence once again and moved in. Kalden, who had gotten used to her presence, found himself befuddled at the sudden lack of energy emanating from her. He was relying on his own sense-ability and lost track of her. She seized the moment, getting behind him and cutting his throat with one of her remaining blades.

As he dropped, she grabbed her own sword from his belt and drew it, its weight in her hands a welcome reassurance. The thin man looked like he was about to charge, but decided at the last moment it wasn't in his best interest. He turned his horse around, but he didn't have time to escape.

Moriko threw the knife in her hand, already covered in Kalden's blood. It struck the guard's neck, and he too fell off his horse.

Moriko surveyed the scene around her. The two guards were dead, and she couldn't care less, but it was different with Kalden. He'd been a hunter, yes, but she couldn't shake the feeling he deserved better. Azarian culture seemed strict and merciless. Yet he'd fought to survive. He didn't deserve this ending, killed by one who had promised not to harm him.

It was then that all the rage, despair, and frustration boiled to the surface, and Moriko fell to her knees, tears streaming from her eyes. They had almost had peace. For two cycles, they had convinced themselves, but now it was all gone. She didn't think she would ever lie next to Ryuu again, watching the stars as they slowly turned overhead.

Here she was, in the middle of Azaria, with no way home that she could see. She was more leagues from home than she could count. It was all wrong. She knelt there and wept until there was nothing left.

When she was done, something had changed. She felt colder inside, like all the weakness had been burned from her body, leaving only cold steel behind. She stood up and faced the west. The Gathering was there, and she thought it was time for her to pay it a visit.

CHAPTER 14

Tenchi and Ryuu walked together from the caves where Ryuu had taken his trials. Ryuu was filled with so many questions that he didn't know where to begin. Tenchi saw his indecision and spoke first, breaking Ryuu's nervous tension.

"You remind me of him, you know."

Ryuu glanced at Tenchi. The comment struck a chord with him. He missed his adopted father more than he admitted.

"You're wiser than he was though."

Ryuu almost reached for his sword. Shigeru had saved his life in more ways than one. He wouldn't stand for anyone dishonoring his memory.

Tenchi held up his hand. "I mean no insult. I only knew Shigeru as a young man, and he hadn't seen much of the world. I believe you have seen and experienced much more than he had at the same age. As a result, you have more wisdom than he did. You hold your tongue when you're uncertain of what to say. It's a distinct sign of wisdom, in my experience."

They walked in silence for a few paces, Ryuu trying to decide which question to ask first. Each than ran through his mind seemed more imperative than the last. Tenchi broke his train of thought.

"I apologize for the trials, but it was necessary for us to know. Your performance on the docks was impressive, but you could have been an extremely talented swordsman. There was no way you could have passed those tests without possessing a well-developed mastery of the sense." Tenchi grinned. "I should confess, I made the tests harder for you. I wouldn't have sent Rei in for a regular trial, but I wanted to see the extent of your skills." He indicated the girl Ryuu had fought in the final chamber.

"Every nightblade has to complete the trials?"

Tenchi nodded. "Yes. For each of us to wear the black, they must pass these trials. I am impressed by your performance, though. Rei's surprise when you sensed her was a delight to observe."

Ryuu finally found the voice to start asking questions. "How is it you know so much about me and my skills?"

"Orochi wrote a detailed letter to me. I assume it was just before you and he met for the final time. I was surprised when I received the letter. Orochi, like Shigeru, was not of the community. Shigeru, I suspect you know, was under a sentence of death when he escaped. Orochi wasn't given our blessing, but we couldn't stop him without killing him, and there are too few of us as it is. I heard from Orochi once when he left but hadn't heard from him since. His letter arriving out of the blue was quite the occurrence."

"Orochi told me what occurred between the three of you. He confessed to killing Shigeru and spoke at length about you. He looked forward to your battle, but indicated there was a chance he wouldn't survive. But he felt honor-bound to finish the job he had promised. He mentioned that if he were to fall, he would leave you directions to the island. That was two cycles ago. And now you are here. I assume you managed to defeat Orochi, and that he is dead. I mourn his loss but respect his decisions."

Ryuu nodded. "He fought honorably to the end, but I didn't realize it until it was too late."

"Orochi was, despite his faults, a good man. We mourn the loss of two of our own. It is a tragedy they came to the ends they did. We had all hoped that at the end they would come to peace."

"I hope they have found it."

Tenchi stopped and studied Ryuu. "There is one last question I must ask, as your arrival comes at a challenging moment for the island. What is your intent?"

Ryuu had been prepared for this question, but in the presence of the power he was experiencing he hesitated. He had worked up all number of phrases to make his mission seem more palatable to the nightblades of the island, but he felt like Tenchi deserved his full honesty.

"I came for strength, and I came for answers."

Tenchi looked at him silently, waiting for him to elaborate.

"There is something moving, an energy no one in the Three Kingdoms understands. The Azarians hunt me, though I have done no wrong against them. They possess warriors of strength equal to mine. There are rumors of civil war in Azaria, and civil war is consuming the Three Kingdoms for the first time in a thousand cycles. The world is changing, and I'm afraid no one is strong enough to withstand its power."

Tenchi was silent, so Ryuu rushed forward, trying to get all the information in as quickly as he could.

"In the Three Kingdoms there is no information about the Azarians and their hunters. I had hoped the records here on the island might be more complete. I also hoped to seek training here. There is too much I don't know, and I can't protect those I love without greater strength."

Ryuu took a deep breath. He had said all he had to say. He met Tenchi's level gaze.

"And what if I were to tell you that you could never leave this island again?"

"I would do everything I could to escape when my mission here is complete."

Tenchi smiled. "I appreciate your candor. I am undecided about you. There is something greater at work that I don't understand. In this I agree with you. But we are not of the world anymore, and your desire to play a role in the events transpiring in the Three Kingdoms are of great concern. I will not guarantee you passage back to your homeland, but you are welcome here."

Ryuu didn't feel like he had a choice. He had known what he was getting into when he stepped on the ship.

"Thank you."

Tenchi motioned for Ryuu to follow him and together they continued up the tunnel. Ryuu could sense the life above him, but decided to hold his questions.

"How much do you know about us?"

"Very little. Shigeru only mentioned the island the evening before his death, and Orochi and I never really spoke. I know there are other nightblades here, and I know this is where both of them grew up and trained. I assume the training Shigeru gave me originated here. Other than that, I know little else."

"We came here after the Great Purge. It has been almost one thousand cycles since we cut ourselves off from the rest of the Three Kingdoms, and a lot has happened in that time. In some ways, there are some similarities here to your monastic systems. We train daily and value knowledge and experience above all else. Daily we make progress in learning more about the world and the sense we are gifted with. I would argue our warriors today are more capable than those of legend."

Ryuu nodded as he took all the information in. "I have many questions for you. I have only been here a little while, but I've already experienced techniques I didn't think were possible just yesterday."

"I expect you have. You must remember your training was probably very haphazard. Shigeru was one of our best students and strongest swordsmen, so that bodes well for you, but mastery of the sense is a skill developed with time and patience. Our older men may not be as physically strong as our younger ones, but they would still win most duels because of a greater understanding of the sense. Shigeru was gifted, but he was forced to escape the island before he learned some of his most valuable lessons. It was a shame. I had hoped, perhaps, that he would have been my successor."

Ryuu hung on to every word. He had grown up with Shigeru, but Shigeru had been a very private man, and Ryuu knew little about his history. It wasn't his priority, but he was hoping he might learn more about the man he called father during his stay here.

As they walked, Ryuu realized even the final chamber of his trial was far from the surface of the island. They climbed and climbed, eventually reaching a narrow stairwell that curved around and up. The higher they got, the more life Ryuu was able to sense. He didn't understand it. There must be much more life on the island than he had assumed. It wasn't the same as entering a city, but it wasn't that different either.

When they reached the surface Ryuu almost fell to his knees. The light was blinding, but despite the tears that ran down his face, Ryuu saw something he had never expected to see. They had come up on a small rise which gave them a commanding view of the area around them. Tenchi grinned at Ryuu's reaction, having clearly expected it.

Below him stretched not a small village, but a well-inhabited area, stretching wide and covering the entire plateau as far as the eye could see. Everywhere below him were people moving back and forth, all dressed in the traditional robes of the nightblades. There weren't just a few hundred. There were a few thousand. Ryuu had found an island with enough strength to change the history of the Three Kingdoms.

Tenchi led Ryuu to a small unoccupied hut. "I do not know what conditions you have grown up in, but here we believe in modest living. There is little here, but it will provide all the shelter and warmth you need."

Ryuu chuckled to himself when he saw the building. It was a small hut almost identical to the one he had grown up in with Shigeru. Apparently his adopted father hadn't quite been able to leave the comforts of his own upbringing behind. "It is perfect and more than enough. I thank you for the hospitality."

"It is no problem. As you can imagine, getting a visitor from the outside is very, very rare. I imagine word of your arrival has already spread throughout the community. Being the leader of this bunch, I can say I'm usually the last to hear of events of importance."

Ryuu grinned at Tenchi's self-depreciating sense of humor. He didn't underestimate the man. Tenchi's attitude might have been flippant, but his power belied his mask. Underneath the surface there was a man who had been born and raised on the island, one who probably knew more about the sense than anyone else alive. He was the man who could fill in the gaps in Ryuu's training.

"I will leave you to rest. You have had an exhausting journey, and there is still much in front of you, if my instincts are any indication. Will you dine with me and the rest of the leadership of the island tonight? Until then, I will place an escort at your door. You are not under guard and are free to travel wherever you like. However, you come at a rather delicate time. I can explain more to you later, but for now you should get your rest."

Questions darted through Ryuu's head, but the trials had taken more out of him than he was willing to admit. He was exhausted, and the idea of a day of rest appealed to him. "I'd like that very much, thank you."

A few moments later, a young woman appeared at the door right next to Tenchi. Ryuu recognized her as the opponent he had fought for his third challenge. She was even more attractive in the daylight.

"You have already met Rei. She will stay outside your door until this evening, keeping away unwanted company. If you want for anything, please let her know and she will assist you. I'll come this evening before sundown to bring you to the supper."

It hadn't occurred to Ryuu how much of a celebrity he would be on the island. He'd never had anyone guard his door. Ryuu doubted the sincerity of the gesture for a moment, but he was too tired to provide much of an argument.

Ryuu lay down on the mat provided for his bed. He had intended to think through recent events, but he was asleep the moment his head hit the floor.

When he awoke, the sun was high in the sky, well past the mid-point of the day. He reached back in his memory. He had gotten to the hut sometime during the early morning, meaning he had slept about half the day. It didn't sound like much, but he awoke feeling like a new man. He didn't have any idea what he was in for, but he felt more prepared for it now than he had this morning.

He stepped outside to see Rei sitting in the sun, meditating. She didn't look at him but spoke warmly.

"Good morning."

Ryuu laughed, her relaxed demeanor putting him at ease. "Good afternoon, I think you mean."

She looked up at him, and Ryuu could tell that she was studying him with the same intent a scholar would study a difficult passage. It only lasted a moment, then it was gone, replaced by her bubbly demeanor. "Is there anything I can do for you?"

"Honestly, I was wondering if there was some place I could clean up. I've been on the road for almost a moon now, and I've not had a chance to bathe in ages."

Rei grinned and nodded. "We do! Follow me."

She got up nimbly and Ryuu reminded himself not to underestimate her. Her personality made her seem like a young, naive girl, but Ryuu had fought her. She had skills that would end most anyone who fought against her.

As they walked through the town, Ryuu was surprised to find how normal everything seemed to be. He wasn't sure what he had been expecting, but it wasn't the scenes of daily life that surrounded him. Women were carrying water to the houses, young boys were out playing. They passed several community places where larger numbers were gathered. Ryuu saw one clearing where school appeared to be in session. He was surprised to see both boys and girls sitting and learning side by side.

In the Three Kingdoms, only the richest women were educated. Moriko had learned to read in the monastery, but she was more the exception than the rule. Ryuu faced a moment of sadness as he thought about Moriko. He was worried about her. The further he traveled from her, the more certain he was they had made a mistake in separating. They should have stayed together. They could have stayed here, in a place where they were welcomed instead of hunted.

A little further on, Ryuu found a small square where both boys and girls were practicing their swordsmanship. Ryuu paused to watch. Their skill level was far beyond that of their Three Kingdoms peers. Ryuu noticed that the drills they were doing were the same as those he had practiced with Shigeru. A small pang of regret struck Ryuu. He missed Shigeru.

They continued on, Rei taking the time to let Ryuu take everything in. He was shocked by the numbers of people he saw. He wasn't sure of any way of estimating how many people were on the island, but it numbered well into the thousands. If both men and women were trained, he was in the center of a military force stronger than anything the Three Kingdoms had ever seen in its entire history. Why hadn't Shigeru told him about this? He had grown up thinking his kind was almost extinct.

"This is amazing. I never thought I would live to see so many blades. There's so many of you. Of us."

His comment seemed to be exactly what Rei was waiting for. Ryuu could tell she was bursting with questions for him, she had been trying to be patient and give him time to adjust to the island. She couldn't hold herself back any longer.

"So it's true? In the Three Kingdoms the nightblades are hunted? Why?"

"Yes, we are hunted. I've only ever known of four. Myself, Shigeru, Orochi, and Moriko. They hunt us because they believe we are a danger to the Three Kingdoms."

"In our classes they say we are hunted because the people in the Three Kingdoms are afraid of our skills."

Ryuu nodded. "That's true. With so few nightblades left, there is more legend than truth left about us in the kingdoms."

"Were you hunted?"

Ryuu thought back to Orochi tracking him and Shigeru across the Southern Kingdom. "Yes. Yes, I was."

Rei saw it wasn't something he wanted to talk about, so she switched subjects. "What is it like in the Three Kingdoms?"

Ryuu shrugged. It seemed hard to describe his entire upbringing in a few sentences. "It seems a lot like here. Most people go about their lives every day, just doing the best they can. It's all the same, but with way more space and far fewer nightblades."

"Have you fought in any wars?"

He shook his head. "No. I've fought multiple opponents, but I've never been part of a war. I don't think I ever want to."

They continued on in silence for a few steps, but Rei's questions soon came bubbling up again. Ryuu answered them as best he could, always keeping an eye on his surroundings. His presence was being noticed everywhere they went. Most people didn't seem to care one way or another, but there were some who took a prolonged interest in him. Ryuu could almost smell the politics, knowing it would be a necessary evil in a community this size. He contained his sigh. He didn't want to become a pawn in some petty political struggle he didn't understand.

Fortunately, Rei's presence seemed to deter anyone who was too curious about him. He wondered what it was about this girl, who seemed so insignificant, that kept others away. In his usual manner, Ryuu decided to ask.

Rei's easygoing demeanor dropped for just a moment and Ryuu saw there was much more to this girl than he had initially thought. It wasn't that her behavior was a disguise, but it was camouflage of a sort. It hid a very quick and intelligent mind.

"I am one of Tenchi's top students. There are those who think I am being groomed to take over as elder when Tenchi rejoins the

Great Cycle. I'm not convinced it's true, but he and I are close. His policies aren't popular with all the people here, which is why you're drawing even more attention than an outsider usually would."

"But why not approach anyway?"

Rei barked a quick laugh. "Remember our fight back in the caves?"

Ryuu did remember. She had been a difficult opponent, particularly in the dark. Ryuu had never met anyone who could use their presence as a weapon.

"You're the first person who's successfully defeated me in over a cycle. So, yes, they'll stay away until it's proper to come forward at the dinner tonight."

Ryuu nodded. It was fair enough.

"Also, I'm going to want to know how you beat me one of these days."

"With pleasure."

With that they turned to a private bath house. It overlooked the sea, a gorgeous view. Rei pointed. "There you go. There will be warm water inside."

Ryuu grinned. It was the first thing he had looked forward to in a very long time.

Ryuu was certain he had never felt as refreshed as he did after his bath. He felt as though he had shed whole layers of dirt and grime from his skin. He and Rei walked back, Ryuu answering question after question. Her curiosity seemed to be boundless as she pestered him with her rapid-fire questions. She reminded him a little of himself back when he had been a few cycles younger. He was still curious, he just wasn't as forthcoming with his questions as she was with hers.

In fact, he wished he had time to get some of his questions in edgewise. He wondered if part of Rei's incessant questioning was an attempt to delay any conversation about the island. The more they walked and talked, the more Ryuu was convinced it was at least a part of the role she was playing. He tried to relax. He was in a rush, but his answers wouldn't all come in the next day or two. Even if he didn't like it, he would be here a while. Instead, he kept his senses open to the island, trying to soak in all the information he could.

When they got back to his own hut, Rei left him at the door.

"You're welcome to come in if you like. I could answer more of your questions."

He could see a hint of temptation in her face, but she shook her head. "No, I need to stay out here so you can have some privacy. I'm sure there's still a lot on your mind, and dinner won't be long from now. I'll have plenty of time to annoy you with my questions later."

He went inside, not entirely disappointed she wasn't coming in. She was right. He still hadn't had enough time to process the last few days, or the last moon, if he was being honest with himself. He made himself comfortable and let his thoughts drift.

It didn't seem like long at all before there was movement outside his door. He roused himself from his meditative daze and stood up to greet Tenchi as he came in the door.

"I trust you have found everything to your satisfaction?"

Ryuu bowed. "You have been very generous, both with your time and your resources. Thank you."

Tenchi grinned. It seemed to be the permanent expression on his face. "Rei told me she kept you very busy with questions about the Three Kingdoms. Please forgive her if she offends. She is very curious about what happens beyond this island."

"It was no problem. It must be difficult to spend one's entire life caged in by the sea. I suppose it also prevents a guest from asking difficult questions."

Tenchi's grin turned mischievous. So Ryuu's guess had been correct.

"There is much to be discussed. I've mentioned before that your arrival comes at a delicate time. Your arrival will force our community to make a decision, and I fear we aren't ready for it. I asked Rei to keep you distracted not because there are secrets here, but because I wanted to have the first opportunity to speak with you about us."

Ryuu found that he wanted to trust Tenchi. The man was open and friendly and kind, but Ryuu's rational mind kept his guard up. This was most likely the man who had sentenced Shigeru to death. No one here was quite as they appeared. Ryuu reminded himself not to trust too easily.

"We have some time before dinner. I'd like to speak to you about the situation here, but please, ask your questions first. You've waited patiently."

Ryuu's mind spun. There were so many questions, it was hard to know where to start. "What is all of this? I never expected to find more than a handful of nightblades."

"Someday I will show you the long history, which is written and must be memorized by all. But first, I must answer your question with a question. What is taught about the Great War in the Three Kingdoms?"

"That the nightblades tore apart the Kingdom with their feuding and greed. After the war, relations couldn't be mended, leading to the political system that has held for the past thousand cycles."

Tenchi ran his hands thoughtfully through his white beard. "It seems the legends haven't changed much then. The truth is more complicated, as the truth often is. Here on the island, we have a complete account of the time, which you are welcome to read. In short, the nightblades and the dayblades were instrumental in the downfall of the Kingdom. We weren't the only reason, but we aren't without blame. After the war, there were still thousands of blades left alive. Those who took a vow never to get involved in the politics of the kingdoms became the ancestors of the monastic system you are familiar with. The system was made of both nightblades and dayblades, but the healing arts of the dayblades were better tolerated by the Three Kingdoms. They attempted to create a standardized curriculum attainable by all blades, a curriculum which ignored much of what we hold true."

Ryuu was curious. He had always wondered how the monasteries had started. "What do you mean?"

"The sense reveals itself in different ways to different people. You've seen a number of different abilities in your time, and despite your strength, you are unable to learn them."

Ryuu thought about Moriko's ability to hide her presence. He could match it to some degree, but Tenchi was right, despite his other abilities, hers was beyond him.

Tenchi saw that Ryuu understood. "The problem with a common curriculum with the sense is that it must be the lowest common ability, which is quite low. Because of this shared curriculum, the abilities of the monks in the monasteries has degraded to the level you know it to be. They've strayed too far from the paths which grant true power."

Ryuu nodded. He didn't know about the heritage of the monasteries, but he knew his strength was much greater than that of the monks. Now he had an idea why.

"Other factions were exiled. A large contingent ended up here, almost a thousand people when all was said and done, close enough to the Three Kingdoms we never really lost touch, but far enough away and hidden enough that we haven't been discovered. Other blades elected to stay in the kingdoms and were killed. Other factions have spread out throughout the world, although we only know of a few that still survive and attempt to communicate. Most have been lost for good."

"However, we've done well on the island. The plateau provides enough land, and the sea enough food, for us to support a bit over three thousand people comfortably. We've been at this population now for hundreds of cycles, dedicated to only one purpose, strengthening our abilities in the sense. It's the tradition you yourself were trained in, even if you didn't know it."

Ryuu took in all the information with rapt attention. Every word was news to him.

"What happened between Shigeru and Orochi? Shigeru said they had a feud which ended in a young girl dying at his blade."

"He didn't lie to you. The elders knew about the feud, but underestimated how serious it had become. The death of the young girl was not intentional. That was clear. But our laws, our values, are strict and unbendable. We must never repeat the failings of our ancestors. I loved Shigeru almost as a son, and his skill set him apart from others his age. But there can be no leniency. I was the one who sentenced him to death by exposure."

"What happened to Orochi?"

"He was a more complicated case. He had broken some of our rules, but the punishments were not as strict. But he was always different after that night. He had never been a happy child, but he became hostile and prone to violent outbursts. Six moons after the incident, he managed to escape the island by forging my signature and gaining admittance to the boat going to the mainland."

"Why do you sail to the mainland at all? You've been exiled and seem happy here."

Tenchi stood up. "That's a good question, and one I can answer as we walk to dinner. It plays a role in what is coming."

They both stepped out of the door. With a nod from Tenchi, Rei led them on.

"Ever since the Great War, we have been divided about our purpose here. Politics come and go, but each of us is raised with a love for our homelands. We all know where we come from, even though most of us have never touched the ground we want to call home. Our ancestors were trying to escape. We now debate whether we should go back."

The news was surprising to Ryuu, but he supposed it was understandable, with as many nightblades as were on the island. With the military might surrounding him, they could take the Three Kingdoms by force if they chose.

"Mostly we stay connected to trade and to gather what news we can, even though we've never established a significant network of spies and informants. We have a general idea of what is happening in the Three Kingdoms, but that is all. We keep the boat because we aren't willing to sever the tie completely."

"How does this affect me?"

"I am the leader of this island, but I hardly rule with an iron fist. I've been able to reserve your time for the first day you've been here, but that will end tonight. Tonight you will meet the leader of another faction on the island, a political group whose membership is becoming quite large. If the trend continues, they will be in the majority by this time in the next cycle."

"What's the argument?"

"There is one faction that believes the proper role for us is to remain on the island. It is the faction I lead. I believe we should lie here, apart from the Three Kingdoms. I am not convinced our power is meant for the Three Kingdoms. As much as I want to return, I think we would only do more harm than good. The second faction, the one which is growing in power, believes we should make a triumphant return to the Three Kingdoms, using force if necessary."

Ryuu tried to judge all the implications in his mind, but there were too many for him to wrap his mind around. "You want me to support you?"

Tenchi laughed. "Of course I want you to support me, but I won't attempt to coerce you more than you would expect. Someday later I will explain my reasoning to you, but for now I'd simply ask you keep an open mind and resist pledging your support to either side. I don't know what your personal thoughts are on the matter, but I would ask that you recognize that as an outsider, your opinion will carry more authority than others'. Please use the responsibility wisely. Much may rest on your shoulders."

Ryuu couldn't help but like Tenchi. Even if he was an excellent politician, Ryuu thought the old man believed in what he was saying. He thought of Akira. The best and most dangerous leaders were the true believers.

Ryuu's thoughts were cut short as they reached the large building where dinner would be served. Ryuu had no problem identifying it. It was filled with the energy of dozens of people, and Ryuu knew it was his turn to step into the political spotlight.

Tenchi ushered him in without fanfare, but Ryuu could still tell he caused quite a stir by his arrival. The island was small enough that everyone knew everyone, so an outsider stuck out from the crowd. To his host's credit, everyone was very polite. He had worried he would be mobbed, but people circulated easily and Ryuu was introduced to people one at a time, each person having enough time to introduce themselves. Ryuu was able to remember most names, but it wasn't just the people in front of him that interested him. It was the crowd.

Tenchi had warned him about the tension among the island's population, but it was nowhere to be seen in this room. Everyone seemed to mingle freely, and Ryuu couldn't identify any distinct cliques. The atmosphere was more family dinner than political showdown.

There were nine long tables spread throughout the hall, three rows of three. Ryuu was seated next to Tenchi at the table in the center of the hall. They were joined by another eight, men and women alike. As Tenchi sat down, so did all the others. Conversations ended as people made their way to seats. Ryuu noted each table had ten people, for a total of ninety present. Tenchi had said tonight's meal would be held among the leadership of the island, so ninety people ruled over three thousand. Ryuu wished he understood government better.

Tenchi introduced Ryuu to all the people at their table, even though Ryuu had already been introduced to many of them. Ryuu's attention was immediately drawn to a small woman just a few cycles older than him named Shika. She was quiet, but very attentive, and she seemed to draw people's attention to her whenever she spoke. He knew he was making a host of assumptions, but he knew she was the leader of Tenchi's opposition. It was something about the body language and the effortless way she attracted people to her. She was a natural leader, even though she was quiet. She radiated power and confidence.

Once food was served, the volume of the room increased. People were busy speaking to one another, and at Ryuu's table almost all conversation was directed at him. People were eager to hear news of the Three Kingdoms, even if Ryuu didn't feel qualified to give it. He was hardly versed in the current affairs of the region, and really only knew what Akira had told him before he left. But he recognized he was still more familiar with the Three Kingdoms than anyone at the table and tried to answer questions as honestly as he could.

As he gave his answers, he watched Shika studying him. He felt that she could read him like a book. He wondered what Shika was thinking, what was going on in her mind. His wondering was put to rest as she asked him directly.

"What do you think would be the reaction of the Three Kingdoms if they learned about this island?"

Ryuu paused. He felt like he had walked right in front of an archery target, and Shika was holding the bow.

Ryuu couldn't bring himself to lie. If his information was going to influence the decisions on this island, they needed to have accurate information.

"I don't know, but if I had to guess, I would guess the reaction would be panic and fear. The prevailing attitude in the Three Kingdoms is that the nightblades and dayblades are a menace. Every child grows up in fear that if they are naughty, a nightblade is going to come for their head. It's hard to shake hundreds of cycles of tradition."

"But Lord Akira knows you, and your relationship isn't based on fear."

Ryuu considered her point. He supposed she was right. Maybe it was mutual respect? Ryuu had never thought about it much.

"What would you say if I told you that people in the Three Kingdoms don't fear us because we're nightblades, but because they don't know us? That if they were exposed to us, they'd come to realize we're just as human as them? People only fear us because we have become myths they tell at night around the fire."

Ryuu was frozen on the spot. "Maybe? I really don't know. I suppose it's possible."

Shika turned up the corner of her mouth, and Ryuu felt like he had just given her what she wanted.

The rest of the meal went smoothly, but Ryuu continued to replay his answers in his head. He knew he'd have a lot to think on. The meal went late into the night, but everyone was polite, kind, and welcoming. Ryuu had never felt like he could be so open with people. When your biggest secret wasn't secret, life was much simpler. As people filed out of the building, Shika came up to him.

"Ryuu, I would be happy to talk to you more in a private setting. Please come see me when you get the chance."

Ryuu forced a grin. "I'd be happy to."

As Shika left Ryuu looked at Tenchi. Tenchi was stroking his beard, lost in thought.

"She's the opposition, isn't she?"

Tenchi nodded, saying nothing. He looked like he had lost a battle, and Ryuu felt like he was responsible.

CHAPTER 15

Akira wandered around his camp, lost in a state of shock. His men bowed respectfully as he passed, but Akira thought he could see the doubt in their eyes, the same doubt that enveloped him. They had known throwing the Fifth into battle against a larger enemy would be a gamble, but it had been necessary. They needed to stop the advance of Tanak's troops. Akira realized now that he had thought fate would be on his side, that something would happen to save his kingdom.

It wasn't so much the death of his men that shocked him. It was the loss to Tanak's forces. Akira had been Lord of the Southern Kingdom now for over ten cycles, and never had his forces been defeated in battle. He had thought he would never see the day, foolish as the belief now was.

Different gambles ran through his mind. He thought about calling the First up from the pass. Toro's latest report was more of the same, an army prepared to fight with nothing but empty prairie in front of them. Akira thought back to his time in the pass. At the time, leaving the First had seemed to be a brilliant plan, but now that he had the benefit of time and space, he was regretting it. If no attack was coming this cycle, Akira could use those men up north with him.

He thought about bringing either the Second or the Third north and finishing the work the Fifth had started. Though the Fifth was no more, they had hurt Tanak, and reports filtering in said Tanak had taken a few days to reorganize and regroup. If they attacked now, they could crush Tanak's center forces. But Makoto and Mashiro had warned him against it. They would fight, here in the south, before they moved north. They considered their two armies as one now, a force strong enough to walk through and cleanse the Southern Kingdom of this western scourge.

There were times he considered surrendering. His people deserved to live, and if there was no way to protect his kingdom, the honorable action would be to surrender and allow his people to live in peace. Life under Tanak wouldn't be too different for most of the people who had nothing to do with government. Court politics would be a little more deadly, but Akira found he didn't find the idea as reprehensible as he would have expected.

But Akira couldn't shake his belief the Southern Kingdom was meant for something more. This war was far from over, though they had lost the first major engagement. He believed he was a good leader, the leader the kingdom needed. He wouldn't give up yet.

When he returned to his command tent, there was a messenger waiting there, almost ready to pass out from exhaustion. Akira straightened his back. He was still a Lord of the Three Kingdoms, and his men needed him.

When Akira let the messenger into his tent, the messenger's demeanor changed. He went from exhausted to alert in a moment. Akira was startled by the transformation. "Sir, I come from the shadows."

Akira's ears perked up. His shadows were his spies, sent to gather information from the other Kingdoms. Rarely did one show up in person.

"Report."

"There have been happenings in the enemy camp, my Lord. This past night Lord Tanak's tent was attacked by almost a hundred men who wore the uniforms of the Western Kingdom."

Akira's eyes shot up. "A coup?"

"No, my Lord. It was a large group of men from the Fifth who had come together. They had stripped uniforms from the dead in the battlefield. With the uniforms they were able to sneak close to Tanak's command tent. When they were finally discovered, battle broke out within a dozen paces of Tanak's personal quarters."

Akira was on edge. "What happened?"

"They were slaughtered, my Lord."

Akira was surprised. He had thought, hoped, for a moment that his men had killed Tanak. But why come to report something ultimately so meaningless?

"How were they slaughtered if they got so close?"

The spy hesitated, as though he wasn't sure Akira would believe his report. "Sir, I believe there is a nightblade with Tanak."

Akira was glad he was already sitting. Had Ryuu betrayed him? He pushed the possibility away from his mind. Not Ryuu. The young nightblade certainly had enough reasons to hate

Akira, but Akira believed that if Ryuu wanted him dead, he would already be dead. He didn't believe Ryuu trusted him, or even liked him, but Akira trusted Ryuu. If it wasn't Ryuu, that meant there was another nightblade in the Three Kingdoms. That made five Akira knew about in the past two cycles. It meant there were probably more. It was inconceivable that nightblades would be coming out of the woodwork like this without purpose.

"Explain."

"Sir, our troops were doing well. They were only moments away from fighting directly with Tanak. Then a single swordsman, dressed all in black, attacked our troops. I've never seen anything like it. He passed through them like he was made of water, cutting them all down as he passed. He must have taken out thirty or forty men by himself in the space of a few moments. It was terrifying. I've seen excellent swords in my life, but I've never seen anyone so capable of taking human life away so quickly. It was almost meaningless to him."

Akira's mind was racing. More nightblades? The consequences were far-reaching.

Akira looked up and noticed the shadow wasn't finished.

"Yes?"

"Sir, I think I know who their nightblade is."

Akira was surprised again.

"I was able to follow the nightblade for a time after the battle, and I saw him speak briefly with Tanak before departing. It reminded me of someone else. I wasn't able to follow the man after the conversation, but it came to me later. His stance, his posture, his height and build, all point to the nightblade being one of Tanak's chief advisers. A man named Renzo. The man escaped into the night, but I checked Renzo's tent right after and it was empty."

Akira considered the accusation. It would be a reasonable plan for Tanak. Akira had hidden Orochi in his court under the thin disguise of being an assassin. It had been the truth, but not the whole truth. He had thought it clever. Orochi's role had been an open secret, but because everyone felt privileged to know it, they didn't probe any deeper to find out he was a nightblade as well. An adviser was another role Akira could have used, but he didn't have the time to set the cover up. Akira suspected Renzo had been with Tanak for some time.

"Thank you. Do you have anything else, anything that can't be refuted?"

The spy shook his head. "There was no evidence for me to collect. But I only speak it to you because I am as sure as a man can be."

"Thank you. Is there anything else?"

"No, my Lord."

"You have done a great service. You will be rewarded. Thank you."

The spy bowed low and departed from the tent while Akira pondered the news. If Akira could prove Tanak had a nightblade, he could change the course of this war without more of his men having to die. There was only one way to make the spectacle and the news big enough, but if it worked, it would change everything, the course of the entire war. Perhaps even the entire history of the kingdom. Akira had to call in his advisers to consult. They had a day full of planning ahead of them. For the first time since the defeat of the Fifth, Akira felt hope racing through his heart. He was going to call a Conclave, the first in six hundred cycles.

CHAPTER 16

It had been a difficult decision, but Moriko left the horses behind. Although she craved the greater speed they afforded her, she suspected she was getting closer to the answers she had been seeking. A horse would attract attention. She could hide easily in the tall prairie grass. She had taken plenty of food from Kalden and the guards who had confronted them, enough to last her days without hunting. Although she couldn't say why she was so certain this stage of her journey was almost over, she knew her wandering was almost over.

Moriko continued wandering west, the direction the two guards had ridden from. There was a new peace in her heart that hadn't been there earlier. Nothing would stand in her way.

After another day of walking Moriko's tenacity was rewarded. She felt a presence pressing against her sense she had thought at times she'd never feel again. It was the feeling of a city. The tension melted from her shoulders. She was surprised at how worked up she had become about the strangeness of the land. There were plenty of signs of camps and trails through the prairie, but she hadn't found any people, and she'd been wandering the land for over a moon.

To her frayed senses, it felt as if someone was building a larger and larger fire the closer she got to it. What started off as a bright pinprick of energy grew and grew until Moriko felt her sense would be overwhelmed by the sheer number of people in front of her.

The plains in this area were more geographically varied. They rolled like waves that had been frozen in time and turned to dirt. Her going became more difficult as she was forced to go up hills and back down the other side. Her ability to see diminished from endless leagues to whatever was behind the next hill. Moriko's legs, sore from walking for over a moon, screamed curses at her every time she went up and over another rise.

Soon she dared go no further in the daylight. Moriko could sense people for as far as her sense could extend, and patrols roamed the area frequently. None seem to be gifted with the sense, but she would make better progress at night when she didn't have to hide half the time.

Once night fell, sneaking up on the city was not a hard task. Though there were plenty of patrols, the grass was high and the space to guard was enormous. She was able to find a ridge that overlooked the city. When she did, she rubbed her eyes because she couldn't believe what she saw. The valley, which was leagues long and at least a league wide, was covered with people. Hundreds, thousands of fires dotted the landscape. If she hadn't been in danger, she might have called them beautiful.

But what Moriko saw was not a city. Instead, it was the largest gathering of camps she had ever seen. There wasn't a single permanent building anywhere in the camp. She corrected herself. There was one permanent structure near the middle of the encampment. It was a small raised platform, flat and featureless, but from it, a speaker could be seen the entire width and breadth of the valley.

She scanned back and forth down the valley, soaking in all the knowledge she could. There were thousands upon thousands of people down there, and Moriko was sure she heard the voices of women and children carry up to her ears. It was a city for all intents and purposes, just without permanent lodging. As she scanned, she began to notice patterns. She could see where the city was divided, clear lines between camps. Some were larger than others, some by a significant amount. She figured even the smallest camp held at least a hundred members.

In the darkness and with the distance she could not make out any other details. She was too far away for the sense to do her any good, either. At this distance, everyone was blended into one enormous outpouring of energy, too much for her to separate and analyze.

Moriko debated her choices. She would have to go down into the Gathering. As much as it pained her to admit it, there weren't any other options. She had made it further than any scout, but she still didn't know what was happening. She didn't know why they'd been attacked. In a perfect world, she would have taken a day to rest, but someone in this Gathering knew Moriko was out here. She worried he would send more hunters. Better to be in the camp now.

The moon was well on its way across the sky by the time Moriko worked her way down into the camp. The guards had been staggered in such a way that it took her much longer than she expected to sneak down the hillside. When she got closer to the camp, she stopped to observe the scene below her.

Most of the habitations seemed to be made of cloth and leather, wrapped around frames of different shapes. Some were more conical, while others were more spherical. She figured the tents could hold four or five people in some of the smaller ones, and maybe twenty to thirty in some of the larger ones. From the people walking in and out of each of the units, it seemed like each one served many purposes. Women, children, and warriors came and left from each door.

The scene below was largely one of celebration. Women were speaking to one another in tongues Moriko didn't recognize, and children played freely with one another. At first, Moriko believed there seemed to be little concern for safety, but as she watched more closely she saw her assumption was false.

She noticed it first with the youth. While at first glance they seemed to be given leeway to play wherever they wished, Moriko saw that in several instances that wasn't true. Youth would argue with one another about where they would play, and although she couldn't understand the words they were using, their body language was easy to interpret. The youth were only allowed to play a certain distance away from camp. Once they reached their limit, they were afraid of their mothers finding out if they went too far. Moriko almost laughed as she saw one young man give in to the peer pressure of his friends, leaving his designated area. It wasn't long before he was caught and brought back by his ear, protesting his innocence the entire way.

What seemed a haphazard assortment of tents was anything but. There were patterns in the tents, and Moriko could guess at the meaning behind some of them. Some were organized to protect a central tent, others to create small community spaces that offered a semblance of privacy. Although the Gathering was enormous, Moriko could see it was composed of hundreds of smaller tribes. She felt like she could make some educated guesses about each tribe just by studying the designs of their camps.

All of it was interesting, but none of it gave her the answers she sought. She had hoped to hide in the crowd, but once she saw how the tribes were organized, she realized it would be impossible. Few wandered from camp to camp, and no matter where she entered, she would be immediately recognized as an outsider. She realized that if she was going to get closer, she'd have to get captured again. She studied the camps in her vicinity, wondering if one would be better than the others.

Moriko's gaze settled on one of the larger camps at the perimeter of the Gathering. The people there all seemed cheerful and well-organized. She didn't see some of the signs of dysfunction she saw in other camps. It seemed as good as any. She crept as close as she could, and when sneaking was no longer an option, she stood up and entered the camp, hoping she was making the right decision.

It didn't take Moriko any time at all to draw attention to herself. As soon as she entered the camp, she was spotted by children playing among the tents. Their shouts brought the attention of their mothers, who screamed their surprise. Moriko moved forward calmly, her hands held high. The first warrior to reach her was a young man, barely the age of adulthood. There was an unnatural eagerness in his eyes, and he didn't stop to question her as he lunged forward with his sword. Moriko saw it was a short blade, even shorter than those of the hunters she had encountered in the forest. It was more a long knife.

The young man was no hunter. His moves were obvious well in advance, and she easily knocked the blade off track with one hand while slamming her palm into his face. She wasn't out to make enemies, but she wasn't going to allow herself to be attacked either. His nose broke with a satisfying crunch and he was down on the ground in tears. She raised her hands again and looked at the young man with pity. The boy had probably been hoping for some story to woo the women with. She had wrecked that dream, probably for some time, given the new shape of his nose.

Next to the scene were two more young men who weren't any more cautious. They saw their friend on the ground, and Moriko worried they weren't getting off on the right foot here. They weren't armed, but they charged her anyway. In a few moments each of them joined their friend on the ground, gasping for air.

The next group that approached was a group of seasoned warriors. Moriko hadn't moved since fighting the young men. She had cleared a space, but she figured it was smartest not to work her way further into the camp until she'd actually spoken with someone. The warriors strode into the space where Moriko was standing, scattering women and children out of their way. Their leader was a bear of a man, at least two heads taller than Moriko. He looked at the scene she had caused and laughed. He said something in Azarian, but Moriko shrugged her shoulders. "I do not speak your language."

The man was surprised, but recovered quickly. "It seems you have taught the young men here a lesson. I thank you."

Moriko nodded, but the man wasn't done.

"However, you will not do so well against me." The man came after her, blade steady.

Moriko didn't want to keep fighting, but it seemed she had no choice. More than anything, she didn't want to have to draw her blade. In her mind, all was fair when it came to fists and fighting, but if you drew a blade, you drew it to kill. But the man attacking her was good. Very good. Moriko had to give up ground, and the man didn't give her any openings she could exploit without her own blade. If she drew, the fight would be over in a moment, but it was the last action she was willing to take.

The Azarian's blade got closer and closer, and then Moriko snapped. She had never experienced the sensation before, but it was immediately apparent to her what had happened. When it came to her, it was so easy. She knew exactly what had happened and knew how to find the ability without problem again. The blade that had once been such a danger to her was now almost a joke. The openings were as easy to find as a mountain in the plains. Her actions were smooth and controlled, and she delivered a series of blows that staggered the man.

Her opponent stumbled back and Moriko's world returned to normal. She studied her own hand as thought seeing it for the first time. So this was what Ryuu had been experiencing. The world had been so sharp, so clear. Moriko was addicted to the sensation, to the power.

The bear in front of her wasn't done. He caught his breath and moved forward, his actions cautious and controlled. Moriko didn't sense any openings, but then she pushed herself to snap again and there they were, as clear as day. She allowed herself to drop back to normal perception, and the openings disappeared. Her opponent almost caught her. She snapped again and delivered one tremendous blow after another.

In her opponent's defense, he fought with incredible tenacity. He took punch after punch and kick after kick and still kept coming at her. Finally he made a last desperate attempt to cut her. He was the most off-balance he'd ever been. Moriko leapt out of the way and delivered a powerful roundhouse kick to the side of his face that laid him flat in the dirt. He tried to get back up and couldn't, finally giving up in a sitting position.

Moriko shifted back to her normal perception. She was surprised to find the man was laughing, even though blood was streaming down his face.

"I never thought I would see the day I was bested by a woman. At least, not in a fair fight. Tell me, what is your name?"

"Moriko."

"Moriko. It is a strange name. But your strength is incredible."

He stopped laughing and stood slowly back up, a deadly calm on his face.

"So, Moriko, who are you?"

Moriko's mind raced. She hadn't thought through much of a plan. "I'm here as a messenger to speak with your leaders."

The large man scrutinized her. "You are a strange messenger, but I suppose these are strange times." He stopped to consider the facts. "Very well, do you consent to be bound?"

Moriko wasn't in the mood. "I am a messenger from a Lord. For what it is worth, you have my word I will not strike anyone else while I am here in camp. Unless I am attacked first."

The man laughed again. He seemed the type that found much enjoyment in all that life had to offer. "You are a bold woman. Had I met you at an earlier age, I would have taken you as my wife. I like you."

He shouted orders in Azarian and men moved to action. Moriko was impressed by how quickly the camp returned to normal. Even the children went back to playing now that the action was done.

"Very well, I will take you to my clan leader. He will then decide your fate."

Moriko nodded. It was as good as she felt like she was going to get.

"Thank you."

With that, the man led her off deeper into the camp. Moriko's plan had worked. She was now a captive of the Azarians.

It was a short walk to the clan leader's tent, sitting at the center of the circle of tents Moriko had identified as this particular clan's. She kept her eyes, ears and sense open to everything happening around her. Any small detail might be a useful key to the puzzle of the Azarians.

The Gathering seemed to be a time of significant cheer among the people. Women crossed boundaries between clans to speak with one another, and although Moriko couldn't understand what they were saying, the sound of women exchanging news and gossip sounded the same, no matter where one traveled. Children ran underfoot, cautious of the men but otherwise carefree.

Moriko decided the Gathering was primarily a time of peace, although she assumed with any group this size there would be inter-tribal tensions. It was amazing to her such a large group could exist in one place at all. She'd have to ask how long the event lasted. She smiled as she saw the day-to-day lives of the Azarians. If not for the tents and the physical appearance of the people, she could have been in any city in the Southern Kingdom.

The tent they brought her to was larger than those around it and decorated more extravagantly. Most tents seemed to be made of unadorned leather, but this one was decorated with garish designs made with some sort of red ink or chalk. Moriko entered, accompanied by the man she had fought. He had cleaned off his face a little, but it was still obvious he had been in a fight. Apparently that wasn't anything he was ashamed of, even though he'd lost.

As soon as they stepped into the tent, the first person Moriko noticed was an older man. He had seen maybe fifty cycles. Despite his age, he still looked to be in peak physical condition. He moved well and his eyes were bright. He was a man who commanded respect, and Moriko had no doubt she was face to face with the leader of this clan. The man she had fought spoke rapidly in Azarian, and Moriko couldn't make out any of it. She had hoped she might be able to pick out some individual words, but everything came across as gibberish to her. She couldn't tell if the two men were having an argument or a conversation, so she stood silently, ready for whatever would happen next.

In time the matter seemed to be settled, and the man who had brought Moriko to the tent backed out of it, leaving her alone with his clan leader. Moriko was mildly surprised. She was still wearing her sword, and the man who had left knew she was capable of violence. She realized he must have taken her earlier promise at face value. Interesting. Her mind flashed back to Kalden, who had also taken her word at face value. She pushed aside the little pang of regret she felt.

The clan leader looked her over, a process she bore with as much grace as she could muster. This was her first chance at learning something useful to bring back to the Three Kingdoms. Already she had been gone much longer than she had anticipated. She would be lucky to make it back before the leaves finished falling.

"My name is Dorjee. I greet you, Moriko." There was no smile on his face. She sighed inwardly. Perhaps it had been too much to expect a warm welcome.

"Thank you, Dorjee."

"You gave Lobsang there quite a fight, and quite a story to go with it. Is it true?"

Moriko admired the man's simplicity. She wondered if she lied if he would believe her without question.

"It is true. I have come from the kingdoms of the north to speak with your leader."

He rose an eyebrow. "You stand before the leader of the Gathering you see before you."

Moriko studied Dorjee for a moment. She hadn't encountered any duplicity in Azarians yet, but that didn't mean it didn't exist. She didn't believe him, but wondered if it would be appropriate to call out his lie. Perhaps it would be rude, but the Azarians seemed to value honesty. "No, I don't."

Dorjee let the silence hang in the air for a moment, but Moriko could see from his face she had made the right choice in calling out his lie.

"You are right, of course. What is the message you bring?"

"I am sorry, but that message is only for the leader of the clans."

"But if your message is negative, it may be my people that suffer. Surely you can be reasonable."

"No harm will come to your people due to my message."

"You cannot promise that."

"No, but my message is one of friendship." Moriko's mind was racing. She had no idea what her "message" would be, but she hoped Lord Akira would back her up. She'd have to figure it out when the time came.

Dorjee paused and thought. Moriko could almost see the thoughts running through his mind. She imagined it would be something of a coup for him to bring her to whoever the clan leader was. Her suspicions proved to be correct.

"Fine. I will lead you to our clan Lord, although I should warn you it will probably cost you your life."

Moriko nodded. She was trapped in a current of events she couldn't control. All she could do was hold on and keep her wits about her. Ryuu would throw a fit when he found out she had walked straight into the Gathering and requested an audience with their leader. She didn't care. It was the quickest way to her destination, and for the first time, she had a clear picture of what she was capable of.

Dorjee said, "You will spend some time here in the camp with my men. They will tell you what you need to know. It may take several days for me to find a way to gain an audience. Until then, do I have your word you are not here to spy or harm my clan?"

Moriko thought for a moment. The tribe seemed to value honesty. "I will give my word I will not bring harm to your people while I am here, and that I shall follow whatever instructions I am given, so long as they don't endanger me or my mission."

"Good enough. I will speak to you when I can."

Moriko nodded and stepped out of the tent, where Lobsang was waiting patiently for her. She was surrounded by thousands of Azarians. She hoped she knew what she was doing. A single mistake now would cost her her life.

CHAPTER 17

In the time since he had come to the island, Ryuu had settled into the daily patterns of life. He had requested what training the island had to offer, and his request had been granted. Every morning he and the other nightblades trained in physical combat. They would break for a light lunch, and then they would mix with dayblades and train in different mental aspects of the sense. It was most often guided meditations, and Ryuu's more impulsive nature strained against the discipline of the afternoons. He recognized the importance of what he was learning, but it was difficult for him to calm his mind with so much happening.

In the evenings, Ryuu sometimes questioned why he had come to the island. Once the shock of discovering such a large enclave of blades had worn off, he'd slipped into a new type of routine. Yes, he was learning, but he didn't feel he was learning the skills he had come to learn. More than anything, he had come to gain strength, but there was little here anyone seemed able to teach him. They were strong warriors, better than any swordsman in the Three Kingdoms, but when Ryuu snapped, they all fell to his practice blade. He had hoped to learn why he snapped and if it could be controlled, but none of his instruction addressed his problem. It was all general combat training, old news to Ryuu.

The difference between them was that Ryuu had been in real combat. He had killed, and most of the nightblades he trained against had only trained with wooden swords. It seemed like a subtle difference, but it was a difference that changed the dynamics of their practice matches. Ryuu struck harder and didn't have any rules. He struck exposed flesh, understanding that if he didn't, he would hesitate in an actual battle. It was the manner in which Shigeru had trained him, and it was the manner he held to everyday. The people he fought against practiced almost as an academic exercise. They didn't train as though they would see real combat. Ryuu trained to fight because his life depended upon it.

This morning started out the same as all the rest. Ryuu was paired against two nightblades who were to practice coordinating their attacks. Although it wasn't said aloud, it was obvious Ryuu's job was to prove again that he could fight multiple nightblades. The idea was simple. Disrupt their attacks and take out the weaker opponent as soon as possible. If you let them coordinate, you deserved to get beaten. Ryuu held his wooden practice blade in a comfortable grip. He wasn't worried about the two opponents in front of him.

The two nightblades moved in, each taller and older than Ryuu. They had more experience in training, but neither had seen real combat. He had observed each of them in the past, and he knew what they were capable of. They didn't have a chance. They came in at him, perfectly synchronized with one another. If Ryuu had remained in place, it would have been hard to stop them, but he drifted towards the one on his right, forcing the one on his left to adjust. Ryuu kept moving, deflecting a hastily aimed strike from the nightblade on the right.

He sensed the one on the left attempting to get in position. He had to act quickly, before his opponent succeeded. The nightblade on the right was off-balance from his strike being deflected, and Ryuu stepped inside his guard. Ryuu drove the hilt of his sword into the gut of his off-balance opponent. It wasn't enough to do more than stun him, but it was enough time for Ryuu to rip the sword from his hands. He grabbed his opponent's hilt and twisted, snapping it out of his opponent's hand and taking it for his own. He turned to meet the incoming strike from the nightblade who had started on his left and smashed it aside. If Ryuu had only had one blade, it would have left him terribly open, but he kept turning and followed with a strike from his new second blade. The nightblade saw it coming, but couldn't react in time. Ryuu felt the wooden sword smash against his opponent with a satisfying crunch.

He turned to the second nightblade, who was recovering and trying to decide what to do without a sword. Ryuu looked into his eyes and saw a man who knew he couldn't get past Ryuu's defenses. He bowed, and Ryuu returned it in equal measure. Another day and he had taught these isolated nightblades something new once again. He tossed the stolen wooden sword back to the nightblade. He hadn't even snapped. Ryuu looked around at the assembled nightblades and was surprised to sense Tenchi in the crowd. It wasn't often he attended training sessions.

Tenchi seemed thoughtful, but he pointed to a nightblade who had been hovering on the fringes of the crowd. The nightblade would be the oldest Ryuu had fought since coming to the island. Until this point, he had only fought nightblades about his age or younger. As the older nightblade worked his way to the center of the circle, Tenchi spoke.

"Ryuu, you come to us with great strength, and in terms of pure swordsmanship, you are probably the best on the island right now. I thank you, for you have reminded our young nightblades they still have much to learn. But a fight with a sword is not always won by the individual with the greatest skill with the sword. There is always more. As you have taught our young students a lesson, now one of our more experienced warriors will teach you one as well. It seems like a fair trade," Tenchi smiled, his mirth obvious, "and it is a lesson many of our young nightblades are excited to observe."

Ryuu examined his opponent. He had probably seen forty cycles, and he looked strong, but Ryuu couldn't see anything about him to fear. He was far less intimidating in stature than Orochi. Ryuu tried to remind himself not to underestimate his opponents, but he had yet to be impressed by anyone he had fought. There was no reason why this should be any different.

They bowed to each other, and the older nightblade waited patiently for Ryuu to come to him. Ryuu sighed. He preferred not striking the first blow, but his patience was thin. He was beginning to wonder if there was anything related to combat he would learn on the island. Approaching with caution, he struck several times, but each time his blow was turned away easily by the nightblade he faced. Good. Ryuu knew he was fighting someone with some skill then. He increased the speed and complexity of his attacks, and their wooden blades began an intricate dance in the air, snapping into each other with quick cracks that echoed throughout the island.

In the background, he knew they were attracting a crowd. Ryuu had to admit it was the most impressive fight he had been in since coming to the island. They passed each other multiple times, neither one getting the opening they were looking for. Ryuu was starting to sweat. He kept attacking with more power and more speed, but every time it was as though the nightblade he was facing was a step ahead of him.

Ryuu was caught off-guard when the nightblade switched from defending himself to attacking. Ryuu gave up ground slowly and intentionally. He was able to keep up, but he felt himself slipping more and more behind in the battle. It would only be a couple of moments before he broke under the onslaught.

He felt the snap coming, and when it did, the tide of the battle turned again. Ryuu went on the offensive, but even with the world moving in slow motion, the nightblade in front of him kept up. The momentum of the battle turned over and over again in the space of a heartbeat, and Ryuu fought against his own surprise. He'd never been matched when he snapped. Even the hunters who had almost killed him and Moriko had eventually fallen under his increased speed and strength and foresight. But this nightblade kept matching Ryuu, no matter how fast or how hard he struck. Ryuu felt like he was being played with, like the nightblade was teasing his strength.

Ryuu was right. In front of him, the nightblade exploded into action. Ryuu's mind was flooded with an impossible amount of information. There was no way anyone could move as fast as the man in front of him was moving. For the first time in many cycles, Ryuu didn't know how to meet an attacker. He retreated backwards, taking a few glancing blows and deflecting some at the last possible moment.

It was inconceivable, and his mind could barely keep up, much less his body. He was on the retreat, stumbling over himself to get out of the way. When the nightblade finally slipped his defense, it was dramatic, a strike coming in Ryuu had no hope of blocking. He could sense it, but even snapped he couldn't block in time. The sword struck Ryuu's left forearm with tremendous force, and Ryuu felt the bones of his arm crack as he dropped his wooden blade.

Time and pain and sensation all came rushing back to Ryuu with tremendous force, and he almost fainted from the noise of pain which permeated all his thoughts. He had never broken a bone before, much less two. His heart sank and filled with rage. He was a warrior, and a warrior with only one good arm was no use at all. Everything he was had been taken away in a moment.

Ryuu watched in mute horror as he tried to flex his left wrist and hand, all to no avail. The pain in his arm was intense, a fire burning, centered in his arm. But the physical pain was dwarfed by his mental anguish. If he couldn't fight, if he wasn't a nightblade, what else was there for him? It had been all he had known since he had been five and Shigeru had rescued him.

The crowd had dispersed. They had been entertained by the fight, but now that their champion had demonstrated his superiority, there was little left to interest them. Ryuu didn't understand. Couldn't they see they had destroyed him? How could they walk away as if nothing had happened? His rage swallowed his despair whole.

Tenchi came near and Ryuu looked up at him with hatred. Tenchi was the man responsible. He may not have swung the sword, but he had given the command. Ryuu looked at Tenchi and saw nothing but a slight mirth, inflaming his rage all the more. He could barely control himself. "Look what you've done to me! I'll never swing a sword again!" The words came out in an angry whisper.

Tenchi's look changed from humored to surprised. "I'm sorry, Ryuu, I'd forgotten that you didn't grow up on this island. Some days it seems like you've been here forever." He motioned to another blade to approach. Ryuu glanced at the young man. He seemed no different than anyone else, and he wondered what Tenchi was hiding from him.

"Ryuu, give him your arm."

Despite his anger, Tenchi's calm voice and command wrung obedience out of him. Without question he raised his arm to show it to the young blade. The man frowned and glanced at Tenchi. "It's a bad break. Should we give him some drugs?"

Tenchi looked at Ryuu. "This young man is going to heal your arm. If you like, I can have a liquid prepared which will help numb the pain. The healing process is quite intense. I might recommend it to you."

Ryuu glared at Tenchi. "I'll be fine."

Tenchi shrugged his shoulders. The mirth had returned to his eyes. "It's your decision. But don't say I didn't warn you."

Ryuu was distracted by his anger at Tenchi, and he didn't even feel the warmth spreading through his arm right away. The young man was brushing Ryuu's arm rapidly, barely touching it with his right hand. Ryuu couldn't understand what he was feeling. His arm was warm, and with a sudden motion, the young man jerked on Ryuu's arm in a precise motion. Ryuu could feel the bones snapping back into place and he screamed out in surprise. Tears streamed down his face as he fought to control his reaction. The young man clasped Ryuu's arm with an unbreakable grip, sending spikes of pain up and down Ryuu's spine. But as he grasped, Ryuu could feel something happening, something he couldn't understand. The warmth permeated his arm again, mixing blinding pain with surprising serenity.

Ryuu tried to keep his focus. Everything became a blur as his sense became internal. What he experienced was indescribable. He could sense his arm coming back together as though nothing had happened, as though time was somehow being turned backwards. Ryuu could feel the young man grasping his arm, and he could tell it was the will of the young man creating the change in his arm. And then his sense got tangled up in the young man's will, and Ryuu felt his entire body fill with the lightness of the sun. He felt at peace for the first time since Shigeru had died. He didn't even realize how distraught he'd been.

Ryuu drifted further and further, the tendrils of his sense filling with light and order. He understood. He was locked in the will of the young man grasping his arm. Dayblade. The word came unbidden to his mind, but he knew what he was experiencing. Ryuu had known about them, met plenty of them around the island, but he hadn't placed any stock in their abilities. Ryuu understood the young man's focus, but at the same time he was lost. Everything became an unbearable brightness and his world went white.

When Ryuu came to, he knew days had passed. He also knew he wasn't alone. He sat up and realized with a start that his arm didn't hurt at all. It moved through its full range of motion without a problem. It was as good as it had ever been. He looked down at his arm in astonishment. He could have sworn it had been broken. Had he dreamed the entire event?

Tenchi was there, looking over him with an air of concern. Ryuu wondered for a moment about the government of the island. Tenchi was the head of all blades, but he rarely had much to do. Ryuu had expected that the head of the island would be much busier.

Tenchi glanced at him. "I believe I owe you an apology. Please, there is some fresh water on the table beside you. Drink slowly."

Ryuu didn't need to be told twice. He sipped at the water, resisting the strong urge to gulp it all down at once.

"How long have I been out?"

"A little over a day."

Ryuu nodded. Not as bad as he had expected.

"He was a dayblade, wasn't he?"

"Yes. I apologize. I forget that in the Three Kingdoms there are no dayblades. You thought your injury more debilitating than we do here. It is my oversight. I forget not everyone has grown up knowing the truth of what we are capable of."

Ryuu nodded. He understood now why people hadn't seemed to care when his arm was broken.

"Do you know how he did it? He told me you turned your senses onto him. You should know, it made his job much harder."

Ryuu shook his head. "It was as though he was bringing order back to my body. I don't know how else to explain it."

"You're not that far off. You're familiar with the lines of force that run through the world?"

Tenchi's tone indicated he believed it to be a rhetorical question. He was surprised when Ryuu shook his head no.

Tenchi sighed. "For one so talented, it's surprising how little you know. It's not your fault. Shigeru left before he could tie the pieces of his training together."

Ryuu held his tongue. The only reason Shigeru had to leave was because he had been hung from a cross to die, an order Tenchi had given.

"Let's start with a basic question. What is the sense?"

"It's a heightened state of awareness. It's the ability to gather more information from the world than anyone else can."

"Yes, but how does it work?"

Ryuu started to speak and then closed his mouth. He realized he didn't know.

Tenchi shook his head in disbelief. "All that power, and you really have no idea what it is? It's amazing that you've lived as long as you have."

Ryuu ignored the well-meaning sarcasm as Tenchi launched into his explanation.

"The world is filled with energy, the energy of all living things. You possess the energy, ants possess the energy, the trees possess the energy. This I'm sure you know. You're right in saying the sense is a heightened state of awareness. What we call the sense is in fact two different abilities coming together. First, it's a full and complete understanding of the world around you. It's the five senses all humans possess developed much further than usual. There is some debate on the topic, but I personally believe that anyone, with proper training and dedication, can achieve this aspect of the sense. I don't think it's limited to those who are considered sense-gifted."

Tenchi checked to see if Ryuu was still following. He was, with rapt attention. He felt like he was finally starting to get to the heart of the secrets he had come all the way to the island for.

"The second ability, and the one that truly defines us, is the ability to sense this energy in all living things. It's a sixth sense of a sort, but it allows us to know where someone is even when we can't see them. There are those who believe it is also accessible to everyone, it just takes extreme amounts of training. I'm open to the idea, though I've never seen anyone develop the sense without an inborn aptitude."

"Put these two abilities together, and you have the sense. It allows nightblades to know where their opponent is going to strike a moment before it happens and it allows dayblades to mend broken bones."

Ryuu was confused. "How is that possible? Those seem like two very different activities."

Tenchi nodded. "They are, but not by as much as you might think. The energy in the earth is collected and funneled. For right now I'll ask you to trust me on this. Understand there exist what we call lines of force, the channels through which energy seems to pass across the planet."

Ryuu didn't believe Tenchi, but he let him continue.

"Just as these lines pass through the Earth, they also pass through you. When a bone is broken, the lines are interrupted, broken. Dayblades have the ability to bring these lines of energy running through your body back into order. What this means in practice is that bones heal in moments instead of moons."

"That seems unbelievable."

"Perhaps, but you've experienced your own bone healing. How can you doubt what you've lived through? But maybe a demonstration is in order. There is a way to demonstrate the lines of force concept. Given your stunt when you were healed, I think we could do it together. Perhaps it will allow you to believe the same exists in your body. Is there anyone back in the Three Kingdoms you would like to sense?"

Ryuu's mind jumped to Moriko. He missed her every day. "There is."

"Good, then come over here. Can you duplicate what you did with the dayblade?"

Ryuu dug through his memories and nodded. Tenchi asked him to stand behind him and put his hand on Tenchi's shoulder. Tenchi reached down and put his hand against the ground. He looked up at Ryuu. "We do this together. I'll show you the way, but you need to find the person."

Ryuu didn't even have time to nod. He had focused his sense on Tenchi, and as soon as they were connected Ryuu felt his sense torn away. It spread out and out, and Ryuu could feel the earth pulsing beneath him. There was a sense of tremendous speed, of tremendous distance covered. Ryuu shook off his shock to keep himself linked with Tenchi. He searched for Moriko, knowing how she would feel. It was as though he was looking for a drop of water in a sea of energy, but something in his will did the work for him. He got closer and closer until he sensed her. She was in a strange, barren land, angry and hungry but not alone.

It was just a moment, but Ryuu knew everything. He knew she had been wandering south trying to find the Azarians. She had seen battle and had found them, tens of thousands of them at least. She was surrounded by them, a rabbit surrounded by wolves. But she was alive, and as near as he could tell, physically fine.

And just like that the distance receded underneath him, and he was back in a hut, sweating over Tenchi, trying not to throw up from the disorientation.

Tenchi looked at him with his quiet humor. "I didn't know there was another nightblade out there as well. So much has been happening I haven't been paying attention to. How long have you known her?"

"Two cycles. She was Orochi's disciple."

Tenchi stroked his chin thoughtfully. "Now, that is interesting."

He seemed to shake off his train of thought and turned to Ryuu. "I hope the concept has been validated."

Ryuu was stunned. He thought he could pull off the same feat now that he had done it with Tenchi, but he would wait until Tenchi was gone. Ryuu still didn't fully trust the nightblades and didn't want to show off all his abilities, even the new ones. Pieces settled into place, raising even more questions for Ryuu.

"If you could do this, why didn't you find Shigeru?"

Tenchi glanced at him. "Who says I didn't find Shigeru? I was the one who made the decision to leave him alone. After he escaped from the island he had nothing, and his life was meaningless. It was the best punishment that could have happened. Although, I admit to forgetting about him after a time. He kept our secrets well. If I had known about you, we might have come after him."

Tenchi stood up. "From now on, I'll train you directly, as often as possible." The leader of the island seemed to have something else on his mind. Had he sensed something Ryuu had missed? He walked out of the hut. "Get your rest. You're going to need it."

Ryuu agreed, lost in his own thoughts. Moriko was in the heart of the Azarian camp. He wondered what she was up to, a world away.

As Tenchi left, Ryuu felt another presence at the door of his hut. He groaned. It was Shika, calling for him at a late hour. He didn't want to see her, not now. If he met with her, he wanted it to be when he was fresh and ready to deal with politics.

There was a three-way conversation outside his door. Tenchi, Shika, and Rei were trying to have a quiet argument. Tenchi was telling Shika that Ryuu was exhausted, and it wasn't a good time for visitors. Shika was insisting she'd only be a moment.

Their bickering made Ryuu sick. There had to be a better way to spend their time. He struggled to his feet and to the door. His appearance silenced the argument.

"It's okay, Tenchi. She can come in. If she causes me too much trouble, I'll just have Rei kick her out for me."

Tenchi didn't look so certain, but conceded defeat.

Ryuu gestured Shika in.

"So, to what do I owe the pleasure?"

Shika looked torn, and Ryuu was surprised. He had only met her at the supper, but there she had been a dynamic and forceful presence. He had expected the same here.

"There's a few reasons. First, I wanted to see how your healing had gone. Rumor has it you interfered with the dayblade's efforts."

Ryuu smiled gently. "Apparently I did." He flexed his left hand. There was some residual soreness, but everything was working well. He was still amazed at the healing.

"There aren't many nightblades who could do that."

Ryuu shrugged his shoulders. "It wasn't something I meant to do. I'm still not quite sure how it happened, but Tenchi seems to have a more clear idea."

Shika nodded. "He and I may disagree, but there isn't any doubt he's got more knowledge and wisdom about our skills than anyone else alive. You are fortunate to train with him."

Ryuu heard the respect in Shika's voice. "Shika, if I may, why do you disagree with Tenchi if you think so highly of him?"

She sighed. "It's sometimes hard to explain, and I regret the trouble it's caused on the island. If you asked me logically, should nightblades stay on the island or return to the Three Kingdoms, I wouldn't know which way to answer. Up until this cycle, the Three Kingdoms have gotten on well enough without us. I can't explain why I feel so passionate, but I am. It's time for the nightblades to return home. I've felt it now for a while, this desire getting stronger every cycle. And now you're here, and I can't even think straight, I want to return to the Three Kingdoms so badly. And I'm not the only one. There are others too, lots of us."

Ryuu was polite enough to shut his open mouth. It wasn't the explanation he'd expected, not even close.

Shika's outburst had put her in a thoughtful mood, and she didn't speak for some time. Ryuu shifted uncomfortably, not sure what to say to her.

She looked up at him. "I'm sorry, I didn't come here to talk politics with you. That can wait until you're in better health. Do you mind if I ask Rei to come in here?"

He shook his head. "If you can get her to come in, but she's pretty vigilant about that door."

Shika smiled, as though she had a secret Ryuu didn't understand. She poked her head out the door and said a few words to Rei. In a moment both women were inside the hut. Ryuu realized he was alone with two beautiful, strong women. He started thinking of Moriko.

Shika's voice was low. "Ryuu, I want you to be careful."

Ryuu smiled. "There's no need for the dramatics. It's just a broken arm, and now I know it can be healed."

Rei shook her head. "That's not what she's talking about, Ryuu." She turned to Shika. "What's happened?"

"He's had men on the ships lately. Two or three every time."

Rei lost her smile, and Ryuu knew he was seeing the warrior underneath. "You don't think he'd dare?"

"I want to think he wouldn't, but it makes me nervous."

Rei nodded and the two women turned to Ryuu, who was lost as to what was going on.

"What are you two talking about?"

Rei looked to Shika for an explanation. "I don't want to say too much, Ryuu, but I am worried for your safety. Please be cautious, and whatever you do, bring Rei with you wherever you go."

"Even here on the island?"

Shika nodded. "Even here on the island."

Questions were running like rabbits through Ryuu's mind, but he couldn't catch any of them. Shika stood up and dismissed herself. Ryuu wanted her to wait, wanted her to explain, but he knew she wouldn't say more. She left, leaving behind more questions than comfort.

Rei was about to follow Shika out, but Ryuu stopped her.

"Rei, I thought you were Tenchi's prize student. But you seem quite close to Shika."

Rei paused for a moment as she considered. "I have nothing but respect for Tenchi, and I'm not sure he's wrong, but I know what Shika speaks of. I feel it too, the burning desire to go home. And anyway, we're all blades here. We need to stay together if we're going to survive."

CHAPTER 18

The war was going better than Renzo had hoped. There had been large deviations from his original plan, but the critical pieces continued to move forward. What was important was that Renzo's campaign was working its way through the Southern Kingdom, making more progress every day. Every league they covered was one more step towards Renzo's ultimate goal.

And now Akira had called a Conclave. Renzo was curious, wondering what trick Akira had up his sleeve. Renzo hadn't even known what a Conclave was until Tanak had told him. A mandatory time for the three Lords to meet, only to be called in times of the most dire crisis. Tanak had given him all the details. They each smelled a plot, but neither had any idea what it could be. Tanak had ordered his armies forward while he left with his honor guard to the Northern Kingdom, host of the Conclave.

They had been on the road for a few days now, almost half-way to their destination. At first, Renzo's mind had circled the possibilities, but there was no guessing what Akira was up to. He had settled back into his daily routine, ready for anything.

Tonight they camped at the border of the Western Kingdom and the Northern Kingdom. Tomorrow they would cross the river which divided the lands, but for tonight they stayed in Tanak's territory. Renzo sat in his tent, allowing his sense to roam far and wide, far beyond the bounds of the camp. He was curious about the movement of Akira's troops, curious what old Sen was doing. Renzo prided himself on keeping track of all that happened in the Three Kingdoms. Knowledge was power, and it would bring him success in his endeavors.

He sensed them then, a beacon burning in the empty fields north of the encampment. Renzo sighed. There shouldn't be any reason for them to be here, but they were calling for him.

Renzo dressed himself in the garb of a soldier of the Western Kingdom. He did not want to be noticed as Tanak's adviser. The uniform would allow him to move freely through the camp and out of it. He put on his swords and fingered them gently. Perhaps they would drink blood again tonight.

The journey out of the camp was uneventful. Renzo had the papers in case he ever got stopped, but the men were still lax, even after the attack that had almost claimed Tanak's life. Renzo made a mental note of it. He would have to bring the subject up again, even though they had already discussed it several times. Tanak needed to live, at least for a few more moons.

Once he was out in the field, Renzo took a moment to meditate and extend his sense. Now that he was away from the crush of people he was surrounded by day in and day out, he had the chance to sense his surroundings more clearly. He focused first on his guests, ensuring they had come alone. When he was certain he was safe, and they were alone, he stood back up and walked towards them.

It was a dark night, the sort of night his guests seemed to prefer. The moon was near-full, but its light was blocked by a thick layer of clouds. They were clothed all in black, and if Renzo hadn't already known they were there, it would have been easy for them to ambush him. Renzo was on his guard. They might work together, but he certainly didn't trust them.

Renzo heard, rather than saw, one of their short, painted blades hum through the night. He almost drew his blade, but his sense told him he wasn't in danger. One of them just seemed bored and was practicing. The sword was sheathed as Renzo approached.

"About time."

Renzo glanced at the speaker. He had never met this one before. "You don't have the right. Getting away from camp takes time. And your people still haven't reached the pass. You can't pass judgment on me for being late."

The two glanced at each other. The one on Renzo's right spoke. "There have been. . . complications."

A silence stretched between them. Renzo suppressed his frustration, but his time was precious. "Why have you summoned me here?"

"It's about the boy."

Renzo shook his head. They continued to use the diminutive term, even though the "boy" had killed two of them already. He was a man grown, although Renzo suspected he was still coming fully into his power. "I've already told you where you could find them."

"And he defeated those who we sent."

Renzo stared daggers at the two men. He knew that, of course, but he kept his abilities secret. Better they underestimate him. They expected him to be scared of them, but he wasn't. He had assessed their skill and found them wanting. He was the strongest on the island, and he was by far the strongest here. "That's your problem."

"No, that's our problem, and He isn't happy. Now He really wants the boy dead, but the boy has gone beyond our sight."

Renzo already knew all of this. He had sensed the battle, sensed the two of them go to Lord Akira. He couldn't track her, but Renzo knew where Ryuu had gone, and Renzo assumed she was with him.

"So what do you want from me?"

"We know that you know where he is. Tell us."

"No. I've already told you he was dangerous, and I told you where he was once. That was the deal. You don't need to worry about him now, he's gone far away."

One of the two men stepped closer to Renzo. "I don't think you understand. First, this was business. Now, it's personal. If you don't give us what we want, the deal is off."

Renzo stepped back, not because he was scared, but because he was surprised. "What do you mean?"

"Was I not being clear enough? He wants the boy dead, and it has become very important to him. Give Him the boy or it's off. All of it."

Renzo thought quickly. He hadn't expected the situation to escalate so far. One nightblade wasn't that much of a threat. Even alive, there was no way Ryuu could stop the pieces in motion.

Renzo frowned. It was a betrayal further than he cared to go, but he was committed. When he had started this journey, he had promised himself he would go as far as was necessary, no matter the cost. His hesitation lasted only a moment. Getting people onto the island would be a challenge, but one he had already thought through.

"Fine. It will be done."

Renzo started describing what they would have to do, his disdain for his actions melting as he went deeper into his betrayal.

CHAPTER 19

The man she had fought, the one who reminded her of a bear, remained by her side for the rest of her first day in the Gathering. His name was Lobsang, and Moriko couldn't help but be entertained by him. He was open with her and answered most of her questions without guile. While she had seen firsthand his skill with a blade, in person he was the type of man who seemed to find joy everywhere he went. His laugh was loud and frequent, and after a day with him, Moriko found herself more relaxed and at ease than she had any right to be. She tried to remind herself she was in the middle of a Gathering of the Southern Kingdom's greatest enemy, but it was hard to be serious about it when children were clambering up this mountain of a man, trying to pull his long hair.

Lobsang was not the leader of the clan, but Moriko gathered that he was well respected. He had multiple wives, whom he introduced to her at his earliest possible convenience. She asked him about the young men she had injured when they first met, and Lobsang laughed again. They were young men who had earned some small regard in a small horse raid that Moriko learned were common among the clans. It was a way for the young men to gain combat experience. The warriors who were more experienced had chalked the young men's success to luck, but the young men's egos had grown. They had been a terrible nuisance, but clan rules prevented them from receiving the discipline many of the warriors felt they deserved. Then Moriko had come from nowhere and taken care of it for the clan. All of them had been beaten by a single woman. They wouldn't be able to live down the shame for many moons. Lobsang was overjoyed and didn't make any effort to hide it. He told Moriko they were considering adopting her into the clan just to take care of proud young men. Moriko couldn't tell if he was joking or not.

Moriko was fascinated by everything she saw. She estimated the clan she had stumbled upon had about five hundred members in approximately eighty of the portable structures. They had a large number of horses, and although Moriko wasn't an expert, even her unpracticed eye could tell they were mounts of uncommon grace. People moved among the tents, laughing and doing chores. Everyone seemed happy, but Moriko felt an underlying tension, subtle but ever present.

Moriko had dozens of questions about their day-to-day life, and as she spoke with Lobsang, she started to develop a more complete picture of Azarian life. The People, as they called themselves, were a tribal, nomadic people. They moved across the land, following herds of animals that roamed the plains. Their lives were hard, filled with leagues of travel and a constant struggle for survival, but Dorjee sounded like a competent leader. The clan had grown under his leadership, and the people were more content than at any time in the elders' memory. But

Lobsang said times were getting tougher. It was getting more and more difficult to find food. The herds were becoming scarce. It sounded like he would say more, but then he studied Moriko and held his tongue. She decided not to push. Lobsang had been very open with her, and she didn't want to endanger that, not now.

The children were active and happy, and Moriko felt like this place was a home for them. When she asked about the Gathering, she found out it was a meeting of all the clans that happened every cycle during the summer moon. It was a time to make marriage alliances, settle disputes, and trade news with other clans. The idea seemed brilliant to Moriko. An annual meeting kept the blood fresh in all the clans, and it was a good way to maintain clan alliances. Again, Moriko felt there was something about the Gathering that Lobsang wouldn't speak about, but she kept her peace.

The Gathering wasn't the only subject Lobsang was silent on. He didn't bring up anything about the hunters, and Moriko was careful not to ask. She didn't want to raise any suspicions. His silence on the subject was indicative of something. If the scout's report to Lord Akira was true, hunters were killing off clans, and there was no way it wouldn't be news at the Gathering. Moriko was content to let it be a mystery for today. She enjoyed Lobsang's company and didn't want to drive off the big man by being too nosy.

Moriko's barrage of questions ended when they came to a large tent. Most of the structures they had passed were plain, with only one or two markings on them, but his one was bare leather, not a symbol to be found anywhere. Lobsang's grin had faded. "Moriko, you are a strange messenger, but you seem honest."

The words stuck needles into Moriko. Her memory flashed to Kalden, his throat cut, astonishment fading to death in his eyes. Lobsang misjudged her.

He continued, oblivious to Moriko's inner torment. "If you want to know more about our clan, more about the People, you must look in here."

"What is it?"

"It is," Lobsang struggled to find the word in Moriko's language, "a death home."

Moriko was shocked. She hadn't expected to go from playing children to a death home. But Lobsang was right. She was curious. She stepped into the tent without hesitation.

Moriko had expected it would be filled with corpses, but she was wrong. Inside were the old, the sick, the young and injured. There were a few people wandering among them, caring for them, but most fought against death alone. She turned to Lobsang, who had followed her into the shelter. "Why do you call it the death home? These people aren't dead."

Moriko's gaze settled on a young man, no older than she was. He had cut his arm, and it had gotten infected. She shook her head. With the proper care they could have prevented the infection. At best, he'd have to lose his arm, the way Kalden had.

Lobsang spoke softly. "No, they aren't dead, but they are fighting their final battle. They must live or die on their strength alone. If they aren't able to keep up with us when the Gathering breaks, they will be left behind."

Moriko considered herself a strong woman. She had seen death, been tortured. But this pulled at her. This was wrong. "Why show me this?"

"Because this place defines our clan. Defines all the People. Survival and strength are everything. If you aren't a benefit to the clan, your life is forfeit. You would grieve over what you see here, but we do not. They do not. Life is hard, with no room for weakness. If you can understand this, you can understand us."

Lobsang led her out of the tent. Moriko gave one last look at the barren tent before she followed him, her mind racing to explain what she had just seen. She didn't understand.

It was surprising to Moriko how quickly she fell into the daily patterns the clans held to. She had thought when she first came into the Gathering she'd be able to get to the leader of the clans with little difficulty, but her assumption had been foolish. Clan politics were so complex she didn't have a hope of learning all the intricacies in the time she had. Lobsang and Dorjee tried to explain what they were doing to get her an audience with the head of the clans, but she lost track of their plotting moments after they started speaking. She trusted them and they were making efforts, slow as they were.

Although the vast network of clan politics set her head spinning, there were some basics she understood. Dorjee and his clan, the Red Hawks, were on the perimeter of the Gathering for a reason. Clans fought for position closest to the center of the Gathering, and they were accorded honor based on how close they were to the elevated platform Moriko had seen coming down into the valley. Most cycles the Red Hawks were close to the center of the Gathering, but this time, Dorjee hadn't even made the attempt. They'd hunted late and were one of the last clans to arrive. Moriko gathered that there was some sort of disagreement between Dorjee and the Azarian leadership, but no one would speak to her about it. Not even the older women, who gossiped all day, would say a word about it. They were much more concerned about how strong of a man Moriko was with.

Moriko had been informally adopted into the clan, and while she waited for a chance to speak to the Azarian leadership, she fell into their daily lives. They were up before the sun, no matter how late they had stayed awake to celebrate the night before. Moriko struggled at first to find her place in the clan. She slept with a group of unmarried women, and they talked constantly. As a deference to her, they spoke in her language as much as possible, although sometimes they became overwhelmed with passion and slipped back into Azarian. They were all kind to her, but it was the event of the year for them, and Moriko wasn't given to much talk. She bore their questions with as much grace as she could manage, but her interests were a world away from theirs.

The Gathering was the most important event of the year for many women. Those Moriko lived with were of marrying age, and it was expected several would be married to men outside the clan. It was a source of endless speculation. They were strong and beautiful, but they weren't warriors like Moriko. Every morning she itched to work her way through her combat practice, but a close eye was kept on her every day. She didn't want to draw more attention to herself.

The women she stayed with were industrious. They quilted and repaired clothing and cooked. Moriko alternated between looking down on their habits and being jealous of their skills. Their fingers moved with a dexterity and grace she couldn't match. She could repair clothes to some extent, but she was a horrible cook. Ryuu was much better. In the monastery, she had always been fed. She had never had to develop skills beyond boiling rice.

When boredom overwhelmed her, she wandered through the tents, being careful to stay within Red Hawk territory. She wanted to go hunting, but she needed to hide her ability with the sense, and she was worthless without it. The only reason she ever got food was because she knew where the food was going to be. The only person she was a danger to with a bow was herself.

It was with the children that she found her place. She had never been much around children, but she naturally gravitated to the Red Hawk youth. They asked questions, but their questions were innocent, like how old she was and how many messages she'd delivered. She played frequently with them and got to know them well. They were strong and active, and after a day with them, she felt as though she had run for leagues without stopping. No other adults tended to them often, except for the occasional mother who would come in and yell at them for making mischief.

Almost a full moon passed in this manner. She talked with the women, she talked with Dorjee and Lobsang, and she talked some more. She had never talked so much in her life. It wasn't that she was happy, but there was a contentment in the clan that was hard to resist. A part of her knew it couldn't last forever. The Gathering was reaching its peak, and action had to be taken soon.

On the last day of the Gathering, Lobsang came to see her. The grin on his face was contagious, and Moriko wondered if they'd finally been successful in garnering an audience for her. She asked, and he shook his head. "I am sorry. Dorjee doesn't have many friends close to the center of the Gathering right now. You will have to decide what to do, but the clans aren't separating. We'll stay together and march north."

Moriko didn't have to ask what that meant. Her heart dropped at the thought of so many thousands of Azarians heading towards the pass.

"Will you keep trying?"

Lobsang nodded. "Dorjee believes you when you say you come with offers of peace. Perhaps it's not too late yet. He'll keep trying."

Moriko frowned. She could put off her decision for a few days, perhaps, but if they didn't make progress soon, she'd have to try something else. She still didn't know why the hunters had come after her and Ryuu. "Well, if you're not grinning from ear to ear because you have good news for me, why are you here?"

Lobsang laughed. Moriko listened. She loved how he laughed from his belly, getting his entire body into it.

"We are having a contest as a clan this afternoon. Perhaps you'd like to join?"

Moriko glanced sideways at the man who seemed more bear than human. It was hard to tell if he was joking or not, but she was pretty sure he was joking. She smiled. "No thanks, I'd like for all your young men to have a chance this time."

Lobsang roared with laughter. Moriko worried for a moment he would actually blow over one of the tents with his hearty laugh. Despite herself, she grinned. It was hard to remember that she was among enemies and not friends here. She had been watched closely, yes, but that was hardly unexpected. She had been treated with a kindness she hadn't expected.

"I thought you would say so. I've seen the way you watch our warriors. You may be a messenger, but I know the sword you carry isn't for decoration. Dorjee has insisted you participate."

Moriko considered it. In the time she'd spent with the Red Hawks, she had decided Dorjee was a pacifist. At the least, he eschewed violence when other options were still available. What would he gain from having her fight? Did he expect her to win? There was no way of knowing. But the idea of stretching her muscles was more tempting than she cared to admit, and it seemed rude to deny Dorjee after he'd opened up his clan to her.

"Fine. I'll participate."

Lobsang grinned. "Excellent. I'll let everyone know. We'll be starting after lunch."

When Lobsang had told her there would be a contest, he seemed to have understated just how big a deal the contest was going to be. The entire clan had gathered for the display, the first time Moriko had seen everyone together. Although Lobsang hadn't mentioned it, the event was clearly the final celebration of the Gathering for the Red Hawks.

Moriko found Lobsang in the crowd and worked her way towards him. "What exactly did I agree to?"

Lobsang chuckled. "It is a tournament we hold at the end of every Gathering. There are three events. Archery, mounted archery, and the blade. Each event has a winner, and the person who has the highest score after all three events wins."

Moriko shook her head. "And I'm expected to compete in all three?"

"Yes!"

With that, Lobsang was carried off by a crowd of people wanting his attention. Moriko was left alone trying to decide what to do. The only event she had a chance in was the sword, but it would be rude to deny Dorjee his request.

The first event was archery. Moriko was able to watch several rounds of archers go before her, and she tried to study their style. They were good. At fifty paces, their arrows always landed near the center of the targets. She supposed that in the plains their aim needed to be excellent.

When Moriko's name was called, she stepped forward with several other archers, realizing too late that she was the only one without a bow. Everyone else had brought their own. There was a chuckle in the audience and Moriko fought the impulse to turn red. A bow was given to her, and she tried to mimic the style of the archers she'd watched.

She shot five arrows and was pleased with the result. Three of them managed to stick into the target, the other two missed by just a little. It wasn't near as good as even the youth who were competing, but she felt it an impressive display for her first time. Some of the children she'd befriended even clapped for her. She gave them an exaggerated bow.

When the standings were released for the archery competition, Moriko was in dead last. She didn't mind. It was no more than she'd expected.

Next came the mounted archery. Again the warriors of the clan displayed their prowess with bow in hand. Moriko couldn't even imagine hitting the targets they hit as a matter of course. Despite herself, she was impressed.

When Moriko's turn came, she shook her head. Riding a horse was bad enough. She didn't dare try to shoot while riding. It would have been irresponsible and dangerous to bystanders. A murmur went up from the crowd. It was one thing to take a trial and fail it, but they considered it another not to try at all. Moriko brushed aside her irritation. It was the right decision.

When the names were read, again Moriko's name was in last. She'd have to win the sword competition to even get halfway up the ranks.

It was late afternoon when the sword competition began. Based on her standing at the bottom of the list, Moriko was the first to compete, against the highest ranked Red Hawk so far. She wondered how they were going to run the competition, and was relieved when wooden swords were given to each combatant. Moriko studied hers. It was smaller and lighter than even the wooden practice swords she was used to. She tried a few swings and cuts with it to get a feel for it.

Her opponent was first in the ranks, but not because of his swordsmanship. His archery might have been unmatched, but his strikes were obvious. Moriko parried his blows easily, the light practice sword moving through the air with incredible speed. It was over in two passes, the young man down on the ground with blood pouring from a broken nose. There were hoots and hollers from the crowd at the leading champion being defeated by the outsider woman.

Moriko watched the rest of the first round with interest. She had seen some of their training, but she hadn't seen any combat.

After a few matches, it was clear to her the Azarians, even those who weren't hunters, were dangerous opponents. Their youths were as well trained as many Three Kingdoms soldiers, and their adults even more so. She began to understand why the Azarian threat kept Akira awake at night.

In time her turn came again. Half the field had been eliminated. Her second battle was more intense, and she had to rely on her sense to defeat her opponent. He had seen about twenty-five cycles and was a smart fighter. His defense was nearly impenetrable, and it was only when he over-committed to a strike that she was able to beat him.

As the skill level of the fighters rose, so did Moriko's interest in the tournament. Some of the second round fights were incredible.

The last of the second round fights horrified her. It was two young men, both younger than her. The fight had drawn on, and the two youths had resorted to attempting to overpower each other. Their blades were coming together with tremendous force. Moriko feared one would break under the pressure. They clashed and clashed again, and finally, one of the blades broke. To his credit, the boy whose blade broke didn't even hesitate. He spun under the guard of his shocked opponent and made another cut. With a practice sword it would have injured the boy's shoulder, but with the broken, jagged edge it cut through skin near the armpit of the boy.

There wasn't a sound from the audience. The fight was over, one boy's arm hanging limply from his side. He was taken to the dead house. Moriko was in shock. The boy couldn't have seen more than sixteen cycles. The cut was bad. But with herbs and treatment he had a good chance. There was no need to send him to the dead house. She pushed her away across to Lobsang. "I can try to save the boy."

Lobsang turned and looked at her. "I know what you are trying to do, but the boy must survive on his own. We will close the wound and do our best to keep it clean, but it's his job to live or die. Not yours."

Moriko almost cursed in frustration. It was a meaningless death, if it came to that. The third round started and she was up again, and she took her frustration out on her opponent. As soon as the match started, she snapped and time slowed down. Her strikes were quick, efficient, and brutal. The Red Hawk she faced was down on the ground, unconscious. The crowd was hushed. They had never seen her move so fast. Moriko glared at Lobsang, but he just kept grinning. It seemed nothing got under his skin.

Her turns came more and more quickly as the number of competitors decreased. Her fourth round was against one of the young men she had fought when first entering the camp. He was more cautious this time, but Moriko was still furious, and she snapped and brought him down with a not-too-gentle groin shot.

Her fifth opponent was an older man with reflexes like a cat. Moriko fought him without snapping, her sense enough warning against his blows. The fight took longer than she expected, but it was a good one. The old man's style was a wonder to behold. It was as though she was watching water with a sword, his moves were so smooth.

Moriko's final match of the day was against Lobsang. She had been watching him fight the entire time, and she realized he hadn't been using all his skill the first time they met. He was an incredible swordsman. He was fast and strong, and his size allowed one to underestimate him easily. He moved with uncommon grace, especially for one so large.

They squared off against each other. Moriko wouldn't allow herself to snap. To sense was natural, she wouldn't be able to avoid that in combat, but she could avoid snapping. It seemed a more fair fight to her.

Their battle began with a flash. Lobsang's strikes were quick, and he came out swinging. Moriko lost ground immediately. She'd gotten used to combat escalating in intensity, but Lobsang meant to end this right away. She blocked and parried and ended up diving away from a cut that got inside her guard. He was fast.

Moriko rolled to her feet, but Lobsang didn't give her any time to recover. Moriko was amazed. Lobsang was nearly as good as the hunters, nearly as good as a nightblade. She met his attack with all her energy, their swords dancing in the evening light. For a man so fast and so strong, he never made a mistake. He was always perfectly balanced, but he had so much mass behind his strikes, they kept forcing Moriko backwards.

Her only advantage was that Lobsang was getting tired. It took energy to move so much bulk around, and he was running out. If she held out long enough, she'd be able to press her own attack. Lobsang knew it too, and redoubled his attacks with a ferocity Moriko could hardly match.

Even knowing where the strikes would be coming from, it was all Moriko could do to keep herself from getting hit. She was fully focused on the battle, her world no larger than the two blades dancing and striking.

Then her sense picked up something she hadn't felt for a long time. Someone else was using the sense. Someone close. Moriko immediately cut herself off from the sense, swearing to herself. She'd been using the sense to fight. Anyone sense-gifted would know who she was. Anyone like a hunter.

Without her sense, Moriko was no match for Lobsang's skill. She couldn't tell where Lobsang was going to strike, and in three moves he was inside her guard. His blow to her stomach flattened her. Not only was he fast, he was strong. She crumpled to the ground, more worried about a hunter nearby than the pain to her gut.

As she lay on the ground, she felt the tendrils of someone else's sense. It was a cold presence. They knew who she was, and thanks to Lobsang, moving was going to hurt for a day or two. She never should have agreed to the contest. Being rude was the least of her worries.

A cheer went up from the crowd. They had seen a fine battle, and all were excited. It was a worthwhile end to the Gathering for them. Moriko was swarmed by Red Hawks congratulating her on a great fight. She tried to scan the crowd. There they were, two hunters speaking to Dorjee. One was staring at her with curiosity in his eyes. She could only see them in fits and starts as the crowd crushed around her, but it looked like they were arguing. One was pointing angrily at her. Moriko's heart sank, but Dorjee stayed calm.

It didn't take long for the hunters to leave, but Moriko wondered what was in store for her now that the hunters knew where she was.

CHAPTER 20

The captain of the ship *Destiny* lived for the feel of salt air on his face. Like all the inhabitants of the island, he had been saddened to hear the Three Kingdoms had descended into war, but there was an upside, and that was that he got to sail more often. He glanced west at the sun, about to set on the horizon. Nothing beat a sunset at sea.

Usually there was little need to sail back and forth from the Three Kingdoms. There were goods to be traded and foods to be purchased, but it amounted to only a handful of trips every cycle. But with war, Tenchi wanted goods and foods stockpiled on the island, and he wanted news. So the two ships were at sea much more frequently than usual. Though his crew complained, the captain was happy. Unlike most people he knew, he was only content when the ship was rocking underneath his feet. He had no stomach for dry land.

They were riding low in the water, but he didn't worry. He prided himself on predicting weather, and he predicted the last leg of the journey would be a calm one. Already they were over halfway to the island. The winds were light, and they weren't making as good as time as he wanted, but they'd be in dock before the sun rose again. Although he'd be glad to see his wife back on the island, he was already looking forward to his next journey.

His attention was distracted by one of the men, Hikaru. The captain had sailed with him a few times. They didn't always have the same crew, but it ended up being most of the same people working the ships. Most were content to stay on the island. Hikaru had been acting strange on this journey. He was often the clown of the ship, acting silly and having fun, but on this trip, he was serious and pensive. The captain supposed they were all a little on edge. He'd never seen the island as divided as it was now. It was the war, he supposed, making them reconsider their decision to stay on the island.

Now Hikaru was meditating, but he was throwing off a tremendous amount of energy. It was almost blinding to the captain's sense.

"Hey, Hikaru," the captain called.

Hikaru opened his eyes and the energy dissipated. "Yes?"

"You're releasing a lot of energy!"

Hikaru gave the captain a boyish grin, and for a moment, the captain saw the same man he'd journeyed with before. "Sorry, sir, but I just feel like I need to practice right now, what with everything going on. Do you need me to stop?"

The captain thought for a moment. He respected the sentiment. All of them could use more training.

"No, but if we go fishing, I'll need you to stop. I'm not sure any of us could sense anything right now. I'll let you know if it happens."

"Thanks, captain."

The captain shook his head. It was good to see the younger generation taking their studies seriously. There wasn't much need for the sense out here on the seas. Sight carried further than the sense for most people here. He scanned the horizon. There were two ships on the horizon, one to the southwest and one to the southeast. The one to the southwest had been with them for a while, but the captain didn't think much of it. They had a long night of sailing ahead of them yet. If he could see the ship's light when they were near the island, he wouldn't dock. The secrecy of the island was paramount, and as captain, it was his responsibility to ensure no one found their small bay. But for now, there were a dozen reasons why the ship would be in sight. He pushed the thought out of his mind.

The captain was inspired by Hikaru's behavior, and in a moment of determination, went down to his cabin and began to meditate. He didn't come up until evening. There wasn't much moon to see by, but the stars were clear and their destination was approaching.

The captain scanned the horizon and wasn't surprised to see it was clear in all directions. There were few ships that sailed this far north, so being observed was rarely a problem. The uninterrupted blackness of the ocean stretched as far as he could see was. They were almost home.

Ryuu's days seemed to pass by too quickly for him to keep track of. There was a part of him that knew he was spending more time on the island than he had planned, but there was so much to learn, and Tenchi seemed intent on drowning him with knowledge. He no longer trained with nightblades in his age range, and there were few lessons in combat. Tenchi had decided there was little of swordsmanship left for Ryuu to work on.

Instead, most of his days were focused on developing his skill with the sense. He worked with Tenchi or the older nightblades. It was special treatment, but Ryuu didn't care. He was learning faster than the nightblades who worked together in a group. In the space of a few days, he felt had learned more than he had learned over the course of several cycles with Shigeru.

Ryuu was astounded by how much Shigeru hadn't known or hadn't taught him. He didn't blame his former master. Shigeru would have been too young when he left the island. Ryuu sometimes wondered how strong Shigeru would have become had he had the chance to stay on the island. So much had happened because of Shigeru's exile.

One afternoon, Ryuu learned the secret he had come to the island to learn. Ryuu went to Tenchi's, as he always did after lunch. When he entered, both Tenchi and the nightblade who had broken his arm were in the room. Tenchi motioned for him to sit.

"Today you are going to work on a new skill, Ryuu. You will work on aligning your new knowledge of the sense with your combat ability. Your other instructors and I have noted how quickly you seem to pick up new skills, and we believe you are ready for this. Know however, this skill is usually not taught until an individual has seen at least thirty cycles. You may not be able to master it."

Ryuu nodded. He would learn how he had been beaten, and he thirsted for the knowledge. Finally, he would have the strength he had come to the island for.

"Do you remember what I taught you about dayblades and how they fix bone and illness?"

Ryuu nodded again. He had been over it several times. The idea made sense to him, but the actual ability seemed well beyond his grasp.

"Good. The idea is the same as what you will learn today. A dayblade not only senses the energy which moves through all things, they also manipulate that energy to achieve desired effects, like mending a bone at an accelerated rate. Nightblades, at least some of them, are capable of manipulating the same energy to lend power to their own movements."

None of this was surprising to Ryuu. He had gathered as much on his own from everything he had learned. What he needed to know was how.

"In essence, a nightblade can tap into this energy. Their mind is quicker, their cuts are a little faster, and they are a little stronger. Essentially, a nightblade becomes as strong as the degree to which he or she can manipulate the energy that surrounds them."

Ryuu saw what Tenchi was getting at. He wasn't beaten earlier because he was a weaker sword. He was beaten because the nightblade sitting calmly across from him was able to manipulate this energy better than he could.

"You already do this when you 'snap,' as you call it. The difference is it isn't intentional for you, and you lack control. It's an instinctive reaction to you being in danger. If you learn this technique, you can control it, and when you control it, you have the ability to make this energy work for you even more. Come, lay your hand on me and we will attempt this together."

Ryuu stood up and walked over, resting his hand on Tenchi's shoulder. He focused his sense on Tenchi, and he could feel Tenchi's will as it went to work. Ryuu first sensed Tenchi focusing his own sense, feeling out and understanding the energy around him. Then Tenchi seemed to insert his will into the energy, and Ryuu felt his own body come alive with a feeling of power and understanding. The action was almost impossible to describe, but Ryuu couldn't deny the extra power he felt. Tenchi let go of the energy and the power disappeared.

"Do you think you can do it on your own?"

"I'm not sure. But I'll try."

Ryuu hadn't told Tenchi he had been practicing long distance sensing every night after his formal training was over. Every night he had searched for Moriko, and he had even found her a few times. He didn't have the ease with the technique that Tenchi possessed, but Ryuu was confident that with time and practice, he could be equally skilled.

The evening trainings came in handy as he reached out his own sense, trying to understand the flow of energy surrounding him. He found it and inserted his will as he had felt Tenchi insert his, feeling immediately the power that came into him. Ryuu stood up, flexing his hands, amazed at how he felt. He saw Tenchi nod and the nightblade across from him leapt to his feet in an attack of blinding power. Ryuu was surprised, but his instincts took over and his will warped the energy around him. His sword was resting in the corner, but he was able to sidestep the swing and deliver his fist right into the nightblade's stomach.

He didn't think he had hit too hard, but the nightblade went sprawling backward, tumbling over his head before coming to a not-gentle stop along the wall. He coughed up blood, and Ryuu felt the power leave him as he lost his focus.

Tenchi had a stunned look on his face, but he called for a dayblade, who came rushing in moments later. Ryuu registered it and realized that Tenchi had expected someone to get hurt.

Tenchi looked at Ryuu with a mixture of awe and fear in his face. "Practice, Ryuu. He will be fine, but you should rest and practice. Let this skill become second nature to you."

They sailed in the dark. Not of the seas, they trusted their lives to the smugglers who brought them across with promises of riches untold. Their ship was crewed by eight, all vicious-looking men with gold and death in their eyes.

The smugglers didn't need any light, practiced as they were sailing through the dark. Their two passengers didn't either. The beacon they followed was as bright as fire, and as easy to track as smoke on the plains.

They reached the island before the sun rose. The beacon on the ship had stopped shining, but another beacon directed them to a hidden passage, not the bay their target had sailed into, but a depression in the rock covered with painted leathers, a lifeboat for an emergency no one expected to occur.

The two killed the eight then. It was nothing to them, though the eight were surprised to be killed by only two. The two climbed out of the ship and followed their guide up the dark and hidden ways. Already they could sense their prey. The island was filled with strength, but one stood out among the rest. He would be easy to find.

They climbed upward in the dark, their hunt drawing to a close.

CHAPTER 21

Akira's decision to call a Conclave had been controversial. He didn't dare trust any besides Makoto and Mashiro with his plans, and even their approval had been begrudging. If his plan was going to work, Tanak needed to be taken by surprise.

The Conclave was a measure inserted into the treaty which governed the Three Kingdoms, designed as a way for the three Lords to seek reunification should the day ever come. Akira hadn't been sure the treaty and the Conclave would still be honored. Tanak had ripped the treaty to shreds with his invasion. Fortunately, the power of the Conclave still drew them all together. For the chance, Akira was grateful.

A Conclave was a right granted to each Lord of the Three Kingdoms. When called, all Lords were required to assemble. Each was to appear with no more than one hundred soldiers, the number which had become the size of each Lord's honor guard. The purpose of the Conclave was to bring the kingdoms together. In the thousand cycles the treaty had stood, only one Conclave had been called, about six hundred cycles ago. There had been a great famine at the time, and the Three Kingdoms had come together to save their people. The records said that after the famine had passed, there had been hope the Kingdom could be rebuilt, but the Lords at the time couldn't agree to terms, and life and politics had returned to normal.

Now a second Conclave would be held, and Akira was certain Tanak would lose his throne.

Though the Conclave had been called, it hadn't halted Tanak's advance. He continued to drive deeper into the Southern Kingdom, and the second significant battle of the campaign would happen soon. It might already be happening. Akira had felt guilty, abandoning his men as they went to war for him, but he could do little of practical use in the battle. Makoto and Mashiro would be fine without him. His troops would be fine without him.

The Second and the Third would meet Tanak's Second in battle. Akira's forces needed an overwhelming victory. If Makoto and Mashiro could pull it off, there would still be a chance to save the kingdom if it came to war. Akira hoped his work here at the Conclave would prevent more violence. If he could depose Tanak, the invasion would fall apart. In his imagination, Akira even saw some paths which led to reunification. He hoped it could be true.

Their caravan followed a trail that curved around a mountain. As they came upon the city of Stonekeep, Akira was struck again by the sheer brilliance of the Northern Kingdom. The Northern Kingdom was the least populous of the Three Kingdoms, largely because of the geography. Even though there were fewer opponents, Akira felt sorry for the general tasked with trying to conquer the territory. In all his planning, Akira had never thought to take the Northern Kingdom by force. Their army was small compared to his, but the land here would give the northern soldiers an insurmountable advantage. They had been in the kingdom for days now and Akira had the opportunity to watch the mounted riders and scouts who ranged far and wide over the land. Even the least skilled of them could control their mounts over terrain the best of Akira's riders would think twice about. A small group of northern riders would be a match for any regiment of Akira's in this terrain.

When Stonekeep came into view, Akira stopped his horse to take in all the details. The capital of the Northern Kingdom was perfectly positioned, the most defensible position Akira had ever seen. It wasn't a large city. It sat high in a valley, the trail they were on the only entrance. The trail dipped down into the valley and worked its way back up, edged by a precipitous drop on one side and sheer cliffs on the other. Akira wasn't even certain there was space on the path to bring up a battering ram.

His eyes moved up the trail to the wall. From his current position Akira could see that the wall was both tall and wide. It was an engineering marvel. Akira scanned it carefully, but he couldn't see any way to attack the wall without tremendous loss of life. He wasn't sure the wall could ever be taken by military means.

Beyond the wall was the city, a tightly packed maze of narrow corridors. Like the surrounding mountains, Akira suspected it was easily navigated by those familiar with the area, but a nightmare for those new to the passageways. Akira shook his head. Even if an army was to somehow breach the wall, their blood would make slick the roads of the city.

A siege wouldn't work either. Akira saw that above the city were terraced fields, currently full of a bountiful crop. A river came down from the top of the mountain, and even this late in the season, it crashed down the valley, strong and clear. It wouldn't dry up, no matter how long the siege lasted. In short, Akira wasn't sure it would be possible to conquer the city. It had been many cycles since Akira had last visited, but the place instilled a sense of awe in him every time he saw it.

Akira waved one of their escorts to him. The man, a young officer in Sen's army, rode over with an easy grace.

"Yes, Lord?"

"What is behind the valley which contains the city?" Akira asked, pointing to the crest of the valley.

The officer chuckled. "Many leagues of mountains. There are few of us that dare to venture in there. The mountains are too steep and too high even for our mounts to carry us."

Akira chuckled. It really was the perfect place to keep a city. He admired Sen's ancestors. It was the safest place he could imagine to hold a Conclave.

As soon as they were in the city, Akira was led to Sen's palace. It was small and compact, fitting for a city in which everything was smaller than Akira was used to. From the outside it barely looked a palace, but once inside there was no doubt. The space was warm and decorated lavishly with fabrics and scents Akira couldn't place. Most of the outside trade of the Three Kingdoms came through the Northern Kingdom, and through Highgate in particular.

Sen stood up to greet him, his bow deep. Akira bowed to an equal depth. He was impressed by Sen's vitality. He had seen fifty-six cycles this summer, but he still moved with the grace of a warrior. There was strength in those bones, and his eyes were lit with an intelligence that couldn't be hidden.

Akira had always looked up to Sen. They had been introduced when Akira was young, and his father and Sen had been as close as two rulers of the Three Kingdoms could be. Sen ruled his kingdom well and his people were content. He had ruled for over forty cycles, close to a record for any Lord of the Three Kingdoms in history. The man was wise and benevolent, but Akira had to remind himself that he was dealing with another Lord. To Sen, the needs of the Northern Kingdom would always come first.

Sen had granted the location for this meeting, but Akira didn't make the assumption he was dealing with an ally. As Lord, Sen had the interests of his Kingdom first, and no bond of friendship or respect would change that.

Sen, as host, spoke first. "Welcome, Lord Akira." He smiled and moved forward to hug Akira.

Akira let down his guard a little. They were Lords first, but friends too. "Thank you, Lord Sen."

They sat down on comfortable cushions while beautiful women brought them tea. Akira couldn't help but let his eyes wander. He had been with his armies too long and hadn't given women any attention for many moons. The women who served Sen were strong, and Akira suspected they were trained as guards in addition to serving staff. Akira found their obvious lithe strength appealing. It made him think of Ryuu's partner, Moriko. He would never tell Ryuu, but he found her attractive. She was strong, and Akira loved that. He wondered if there were other nightblade women he might find.

Akira caught Sen's slight smile, and he knew Sen had caught him glancing. He returned Sen's smile and sipped at his tea. The quality was excellent. They sat in companionable silence and enjoyed the drink.

It was Sen who broke the silence, which surprised Akira. He had expected to be the more impatient of the two.

"You come in difficult times."

Memories came flooding back to Akira. Sen was a traditionalist, a man who rarely said what he meant. He was subtle in a way Akira couldn't manage.

"Yes."

"It is a historic occasion, a Conclave called after six hundred cycles."

Akira tried to grasp Sen's meaning. Did he think Akira had been rash?

It was difficult to overstate the importance of the Conclave. The Three Kingdoms had been formed in the hope that one day they would be unified again as one Kingdom. Akira wondered for the first time if he had gone too far. He was less interested in reunification and more interested in trapping Tanak. Perhaps he was taking the wrong action. Akira thought carefully, an effect Sen always had on him.

"The treaty has never been broken, not for almost a thousand cycles."

"And you have been building up the strongest army the Three Kingdoms has ever seen, along with trade policies that have hurt the Western Kingdom."

Akira processed this. Sen had realized his intentions, then. But Akira hadn't acted on them. Tanak had broken the treaty, not him.

Akira wanted to tell Sen his plan. He wanted to let Sen know about Tanak's collusion with a nightblade, but he couldn't bring himself to trust. Everything depended on surprise.

Sen spoke again. "Have you considered, really, what you are going to do here? Are you prepared to do whatever is necessary?"

What was Sen referring to? Akira wished the old man wasn't so cryptic. Did he mean reunification, or did he have some idea what Akira was planning? There wasn't any way it was possible. Sen would have to be a mind reader.

Akira decided to change his tactics. "I worry the Three Kingdoms will be under threat from the Azarians soon."

Sen's eyes took in Akira, trying to decide if Akira was attempting to fool him. Akira noticed. So Sen hadn't been expecting that news.

Sen stroked his beard, long and white on his face. "The Southern Kingdom has been under the threat of Azarian attack for over sixty cycles. You have held the pass well."

His inference was clear. Sen didn't consider the Azarians a threat, not to his kingdom, at least. They were far removed from the Three Sisters here.

"They have hunters. They've been in my kingdom."

Even Sen wasn't able to hide his surprise. He was well educated and would know of the legends of the hunters. Their presence changed everything.

"You have evidence?"

Akira nodded. "Weapons and jewelry."

"Hardly a convincing argument."

"You know I wouldn't lie about this."

Sen shook his head. "Once, maybe. We haven't seen each other in many cycles, and I don't see your motives anymore."

Akira was hurt. It was surprising to him to learn how much Sen's approval meant to him. It was a childish emotion, left from his days spent on Sen's lap. He wanted the old man to trust him.

"Tanak won't just endanger my kingdom. If I'm right about the Azarians, we're all at risk."

Sen nodded. "You've given me much to think about."

Akira took Sen's hint. The meeting was over. "Thank you for hosting this Conclave. It is a kindness." Akira wasn't being polite. Sen would be the deciding factor in the meetings to come.

As Akira stood to bow out, Sen smiled at him, a weary smile. "It is good to see you again, Lord Akira." Akira looked at Sen and knew it wasn't just polite talk either. Sen meant it. Akira's heart was light as he left the audience.

Akira hardly slept that night. Over and over, he thought about how he should proceed. Sen's tone haunted him, made him wonder if he was abusing his power as a Lord.

Tanak wouldn't know what Akira was planning, but he had come because of the solemnity of the Conclave. Any other attempt to meet would have been rebuffed, and Akira admitted he would do the same if he was in Tanak's place. Akira knew the war wasn't over, but he couldn't deny Tanak's forces had momentum, and if they weren't stopped, his kingdom's days would be numbered. Akira wondered what Sen would do if the Southern Kingdom fell. He knew the old man's wish for reunification was strong. Would he give up his kingdom? Akira had to admit he could see it happening. Perhaps he wanted Akira to fall.

Akira's strategy wasn't complex. The power of the Conclave was that it was public. It was required by the treaty. He would reveal knowledge of Tanak's nightblade. Akira knew Renzo was in the city with Tanak. He would be tested by the monks, and it would be public that Tanak had worked with a nightblade. Tanak's rule would be broken, and Stonekeep would mark his grave.

Akira wasn't sure what would happen after, but he hoped there could be talk of reunification. There would be chaos, but perhaps out of the chaos the Kingdom would emerge. Akira had to hope. It made the sacrifice of his people worth it.

When the morning came, Akira dressed in simple robes of the finest fabric he possessed. He wanted his appearance to be noble but not lavish. He walked with quiet, determined steps towards the dining hall, where the Conclave would be held.

When he opened the door, he surveyed the room before stepping in. As the one who had called the Conclave, tradition demanded he be the last to arrive. He saw Sen and Tanak seated around a small round table. His anger rose when he saw Tanak, the man who had broken the treaty and killed thousands of his men. He bowed, which was matched evenly by both Tanak and Sen. Around the room he could hear the pens of the nine scribes sitting around the Conclave, writing everything they observed.

The Conclave was public, but the founders had believed it should not be directly observed. Logic demanded an audience that would not be swayed by the arguments of the Lords. It would be a recipe for violence. Instead, three scribes from each kingdom transcribed the meeting, and the accounts would be bound together in a book to be spread throughout the Three Kingdoms. This method would ensure the complete proceedings were documented for all.

Akira took a deep breath and took a seat at the table. Sen served the tea himself and tasted it first to prove it wasn't poisoned. It was a kind gesture, but one that meant little to Akira. None of them would try anything of the sort at a Conclave. If any of them were to die mysteriously here, chaos wouldn't begin to describe the consequences.

Sen began. "We are here today because Lord Akira has called a Conclave, a chance for the three Lords to discuss the events that have moved the Three Kingdoms, and perhaps finally bring peace to us all."

Akira nodded. It was well spoken. It told the truth and hinted at reunification. The scribes wrote faster.

Sen continued. "Lord Akira, why have you called this Conclave?"

It was the moment Akira had been waiting for since the spy had come to his tent almost a moon ago. "I come to the Conclave today to announce the treaty has been broken." He paused and glanced around the table.

Sen was watching him with rapt attention and Tanak looked like he thought he had wasted his time by coming. Tanak spoke up, disgust evident in his voice.

"Of course the treaty has been broken. It's not like my invasion of your land is a secret here."

Akira looked at Tanak with hatred in his eyes. He suppressed the desire to grin. "I don't speak of your invasion, but of your cooperation with nightblades."

Akira took in the reactions of both Tanak and Sen. Sen was surprised at the twist, but Tanak looked afraid. He tried to hide his reaction, but Akira could see the fear in his eyes. Akira had him. "I would like to call your adviser Renzo to the Conclave, along with three monks, one from each kingdom."

Tanak's eyes widened, and Akira tasted the victory on his lips.

Sen glanced at the soldiers stationed around the perimeter. "Make it so."

The three rulers sat in awkward silence as Akira's wish was granted. Akira risked a smile at Tanak. The Lord of the Western Kingdom was fidgeting back and forth, barely able to sit still. Akira savored the moment. Perhaps Tanak's fall would bring some peace to all the men who had perished in this invasion.

Renzo was brought in first to join the small group in the dining room. He looked inquisitively at Tanak. Tanak replied. "Lord Akira believes you are a nightblade. You are to be tested by the monks."

Akira replied. "I think it only fair all of us be tested in the room, so there is no room for error or accusations of bias."

Renzo bowed to Akira. "It is a wise decision, Lord."

Akira studied Renzo carefully. The man wore loose robes which hid his body well. He was tall, but Akira couldn't tell by looking at him he was a nightblade. But a warning went off in his head. Renzo didn't seem concerned at all. Could he hide his ability? Akira had heard it was a skill Ryuu's partner, Moriko, possessed, but he also remembered hearing the skill was rare. Ryuu had also said the monks would be able to sense anyone's skill when they touched a person. There was no way to hide from a monk's touch. Akira relaxed. Perhaps Renzo could contain his emotions better than Tanak, but he would be found out. Akira would ensure it.

Three monks came in. Akira recognized one as being the one who traveled with his own party. Akira tried to remember his name, but couldn't. He did remember the monk had been at Perseverance when Ryuu had killed their Abbot. That was good. He would have no love lost for a nightblade. The other two he didn't recognize, but it made no difference.

Sen motioned to Akira to proceed.

"To all of you, thank you for being here. The Three Kingdoms requires your assistance. Would you please test everyone in this room to see if anyone here is sense-gifted? Do not speak your results, but test us all, by touch if you would. When you are done, we will have a guard escort you out so you can't speak to anyone."

Akira had thought the test through carefully. There had to be no collusion possible, none at all, not for a test this important.

The three Lords waited as the monks each walked around and tested every person in the room. They tested the Lords, the guards, even the scribes. No one was spared, and Akira made sure all three monks tested Renzo. He smiled, his victory almost complete.

Afterwards, the three monks left and were summoned back in one at a time. Akira couldn't wait. He called in the monk from the Western Kingdom first. If one would lie, it would be him. The monasteries were supposed to stay out of political affairs, but Akira knew it wasn't as true as it should have been.

Akira asked the question. "Sir, is anyone in here sense-gifted?"

The monk spoke without hesitation. "No, Lord."

Akira nodded, allowing himself to remain expressionless. So the western monasteries were cooperating with Tanak. It was a problem to be dealt with later. He called in the second monk, the one from the Northern Kingdom, and repeated the question.

The second monk also spoke without hesitation. "No, Lord."

Akira glanced at Sen, who was watching the proceedings with interest. He couldn't read Sen at all. Had he stumbled onto a conspiracy?

Akira dismissed the monk with a wave of his hand. It wouldn't look good to have only the monk from the Southern Kingdom speak against Renzo, but Akira could beg for another test.

The monk from Perseverance came in, and for the third time, Akira asked the question.

"No, my Lord. No one here is sense-gifted."

The floor fell out from under Akira. He couldn't believe what he was hearing. Renzo was a nightblade, but none of the monks sensed him. His head spun as he checked his facts. What was happening? He couldn't process everything fast enough. He could hear Tanak speaking, but everything was jumbled in his head. When he was finally able to focus, the monk was gone and Tanak was denouncing the proceedings. "I didn't come here to be accused of cooperating with nightblades! I came here to speak about reunification."

Akira tried to wrap his head around where Tanak was going.

Tanak continued. "Let's not mince words while we are here. This is a Conclave, and the people have been hoping for a reunification for almost a thousand cycles. We have all been trying to figure out a way to force reunification. Each of us have desired the title of King. Do either of you deny it?"

Akira couldn't, but he was surprised that Sen didn't speak out. Every assumption he had made was wrong.

Akira's misery wasn't over. Tanak continued. "I propose we discuss the reunification of the Three Kingdoms. It has been almost a thousand cycles, and the time has come."

He couldn't recover fast enough for his thoughts to catch up to reality. One Kingdom?

"With my invasion, I recognize the balance of power has changed forever. There is no going back to the borders of the Three Kingdoms, so our only question here today is to decide how we want to move forward. We all want reunification, so why not make it happen right here, right now?"

If Akira hadn't been sitting he would have collapsed. He could see where this was going. Everything he had worked for, everything he had lived for, had been a failure. He straightened his back with a strong effort of will.

Tanak's monologue continued. "I now control over half of the Three Kingdoms. It makes sense for me to become first King."

Akira heard the words as though he were underwater. He knew they were being said, but he couldn't think fast enough around this. His kingdom, his people, had been victimized by this man, and he was brazen enough to ask for the crown? This wasn't justice, but a crime of the highest order. It sparked a bright, intense fire in his stomach that brought him back to focus.

Akira looked to Sen for support. Sen would recognize the unjustness of the action.

Sen returned his gaze calmly before responding to Tanak. Akira felt his spirits lift. He could trust Sen.

"As Lord of the Northern Kingdom, I would be willing to abdicate, conditionally, to re-create the Kingdom."

Akira felt like he would throw up. Sen's words hit him like a punch to the stomach, and he almost doubled up in pain. Tanak and Sen had to have been allies all along. How had he missed it?

His anger flared again at the betrayal he felt. "I will not abdicate to a man who has invaded my kingdom and killed my people. It will never happen."

Tanak looked to speak, but Sen held up his hand, and the older Lord commanded respect.

"Lord Akira, I urge you to consider. I recognize the anger and emotion you must feel, but think about your people, think about all our people. You yourself have indicated the threats your land faces. Although it is not what you have envisioned, the outcome remains the same. We can be one Kingdom again."

Akira couldn't believe that Sen would turn the Azarian threat against him in this way. No swords were allowed at the Conclave, and this was for the best. He would have murdered the Lords in his anger.

Tanak spoke next, focusing Akira's anger on him. "Lord Akira, you would have a place at my side. You have managed your kingdom well and your people are content and well fed. I would welcome your advice."

Akira raged. He would never advise a man like Tanak. He was about to speak when Sen's voice cut through the anger clouding his mind.

"I see our discussion here will be ruled by emotion, not by logic. I propose we delay this discussion until tomorrow morning, when we have all had the benefit of a good night's sleep."

Tanak agreed, and the meeting was over. The two Lords bowed out of the room, and Akira was left alone with his anger and confusion.

That evening, Akira was still trying to process what had happened. Sen had been right. He needed time to think through the events of the day. His shadow had been so sure Renzo was a nightblade. But he had been tested by three monks, and Akira had designed the test himself. He could come up with all types of conspiracy theories, but the simpler explanation was that Renzo wasn't a nightblade. But Tanak had looked so worried. There was something else happening, something he didn't understand.

Akira forced the thoughts out of his mind. He had larger problems than proving Tanak had a nightblade as an adviser. He was being asked to give up his kingdom. Sen was willing to abdicate, leaving the decision entirely on Akira's shoulders. Akira still couldn't believe what had transpired. He thought he had come to the Conclave knowing what to expect, prepared for anything they might try, but he had been wrong.

His thoughts went round and round as he tried to figure out what was true. He didn't know who was allied with whom or what forces were arrayed against him. Perhaps he should abdicate to Tanak, watch as the dreams of so many Lords before him were realized. It would end the war.

Akira's thoughts were interrupted when there was a knock on the door. It was a messenger. Akira couldn't contain his nervousness when he realized what the message was. The day had become so chaotic, he had forgotten entirely about the battle being fought to the south. It was a message from Makoto. The Second and the Third had crushed Tanak's Second army in battle. Their results had been everything Akira needed to hear. Casualties had been light, but they had eliminated Tanak's Second as a functioning unit. It was beautiful news.

The letter went on to say Makoto and Mashiro were bringing their forces north and east, to meet with Tanak's Third and the remnants of the First. Tanak still had the advantage in men and material, but Makoto and Mashiro were hoping to get to the foothills in the eastern half of the kingdom before Tanak's troops. They could set up a defensible position and fight from high ground. If they were successful, they could end the invasion.

The letter brought a hope to Akira he hadn't felt before. Perhaps they could turn the invasion around, defeat it with nothing but their own strength. His soldiers were the best in the Three Kingdoms. They could handle whatever was thrown at them.

Akira's mind was decided. His men were fighting and dying for their kingdom. He couldn't throw their sacrifice away. It would dishonor their memory. Perhaps reunification was at hand, but it wouldn't come about because of violence. It would come around due to diplomacy. Akira was confident. He drafted his own message to send back to his generals, urging them forward, telling them he would be with them soon.

That night, Akira slept well. He would protect his people, never giving them a ruler they didn't deserve. His course was open and obvious to him.

The next morning the three Lords met again. Akira could see Tanak had received news of the battle also. He didn't look like he'd slept as well as Akira. Good. Their bargaining positions would be much more even today.

Sen opened up the discussion. "Lord Akira, have you thought more about the offer Lord Tanak has made?"

"Yes. I have given it serious consideration." Akira spoke for the benefit of the scribes. His words would go down in history. "I believe more than anything our three kingdoms need to reunite once again. It's the dream we have all shared, and my feelings have never changed. At one time, I entertained dreams like Lord Tanak, that perhaps the kingdoms could be reunited through violence. Now, though, I see that reunification through violence is never possible. Some scars never heal."

Both Sen and Tanak looked like they wanted to interrupt Akira, but he kept his speech moving forward, not giving them a chance to interject. These words would go out to all the people.

"We have all received news today of the battle in my kingdom. More life has been lost, but Tanak's armies are weaker now than they've ever been. A kingdom can't be taken from people in violence, but it can be given in trust."

Akira looked directly at Tanak. "Lord Tanak, I can't surrender my kingdom, not after the violence you have visited on my people. I can't trust their welfare to your care, not right now. But like you all, I want reunification. Lord Tanak, pull back your forces beyond the river. I will order all my units to grant you safe passage back to the Western Kingdom. Then let us meet back here again and decide the fate of our people. All our people. If you do this, I will give you my word I will consider granting you the crown you seek. But it must be done in peace."

Sen looked to Tanak. It was a reasonable offer, and Akira didn't lie. If the terms of the treaty were good enough for the people of the Southern Kingdom, Akira would consider giving up his throne. The thought pained him, but he would do it for the people of the Three Kingdoms.

There was silence around the table as Tanak considered the offer. Slowly, he shook his head.

"I'm sorry, but I came here to bring about reunification. Not in the future, but now. If you hope to delay the process so your troops can recover, I won't allow it. If you won't see reason today, I don't see how you will see reason in the future. I will not ask my troops to retreat."

Sen looked back at Akira. "Lord Akira, will you relent?"

Akira shook his head. He would destroy Tanak if the war continued. He believed it, though he was sorry the Conclave had to end this way. "I'm sorry, but I won't negotiate with the man who has invaded my kingdom and killed my people. Any treaty signed here today wouldn't last."

Akira looked to Sen, and Sen seemed more unhappy than Akira had ever seen him. Akira's heart went out to his fellow Lord, but he couldn't relent. He believed in what he was saying. Any treaty that came out of talks today would be met with resistance from his people. It wouldn't be a peace that could last.

Sen took a long look at each of the other Lords, but neither backed down. "Well, it appears we have come to an impasse. Thank you both for coming. I would have liked to have seen reunification happen, but perhaps we three aren't strong enough to make it work. This Conclave is concluded."

With that, the three Lords of the kingdoms stood up and bowed to one another. Akira left the room first, to return to his kingdom engulfed in war.

CHAPTER 22

Ryuu stretched his muscles. It had been another long day of training, but he was beginning to understand the technique Tenchi was teaching him. He could snap his mind on command now, and he was learning how to move faster every day. His growth was worth the pain he went through.

His entire body hurt. His back and shoulders were sore from a full day of swinging a sword, and much of the rest of his body was covered with bruises. Tenchi could move fast for an old man, and Ryuu suspected the leader of the island was still holding back. But then again, so was he.

Ryuu was rubbing his shoulder when he sensed Rei come up behind him. He turned to look at her face, practically glowing with excitement. "Yes?"

"You're walking the wrong way for food."

"Not tonight, Rei. I'm exhausted and all I want to do is sleep."

Rei's look of disappointment couldn't be matched. She was a voracious eater, and if Ryuu skipped a meal, it meant she did too.

Ryuu found it silly. He was more than capable of taking care of himself, and he didn't think the island held any real dangers for him, despite Shika's cryptic warning.

"Rei, I'll be fine. Go grab a meal, then if you want to camp out outside my place, go for it. I'm just going to fall asleep anyway."

Rei looked torn, but her desire for food won out over her typical discipline. "Don't worry, I'll be right back."

Ryuu watched her go. He hadn't been completely truthful. He would search for Moriko, the same as he did every night. But then he'd fall asleep.

Ryuu looked up at the stars, burning bright above him. He had grown up with the stars and always found them comforting. Whatever they were, they were far, far away, and just watching them made Ryuu feel small. Perhaps he was strange, he thought, but the idea of being small and insignificant comforted him, made his problems seem less pressing. He wondered if Moriko was looking at the same night sky tonight.

It was the thought of her that saved his life. Some correlation in his mind, but as he thought of Moriko, he sensed something was off. Shadows were nearby, two of them.

Ryuu frowned. They felt familiar, but strange. Why did they seem familiar? He placed them just a moment before it was too late. Hunters, like the ones that had come for him at Shigeru's hut. He didn't question how they had gotten on the island. He trusted his sense. They were here.

Ryuu drew his blade as the shadows detached from the walls of nearby huts. He had been right. They were hunters. He felt a pang of nervousness as he saw their short blades, and he remembered how he had almost lost Moriko. His rational mind was screaming questions, but he shut it off as he dropped into a combat stance.

His mind snapped and he found the energy flowing through and around him. As the hunters took their first steps, Ryuu fell into the flow of energy, moving to meet their attacks.

They came from each side, their short blades darker than the night. Ryuu shifted, leaping towards the hunter on his right. Isolate and defeat, just as he'd drilled over and over here on the island. Their blades met, the hunter just getting his blade up in time. The strength of Ryuu's attack sent him scrambling backwards, trying desperately to keep his balance.

Ryuu wasn't going to let him stand, but the second hunter moved faster than Ryuu expected. He was the dangerous one. Ryuu could sense him, a malevolent shadow. He turned and met the attack, blades dancing against each other. This hunter's attacks felt random and uncontrolled, challenging Ryuu's sense of proper swordsmanship. The hunter attacked with big, powerful swings not suited to his short sword, masking them with remarkable agility.

It took Ryuu a moment to adjust to the new style. It was designed to confuse opponents with the sense, make them doubt what they were sensing was real. Ryuu trusted his sense and tried to strike, but the agile hunter melted away from each attack.

Then the first hunter was up again and Ryuu was on the defensive. He had taken on two nightblades before, but these two were a different order of deadly. They had blood on their hands.

Ryuu dove out of the way of two cuts, rolling to his feet and gaining just a moment of freedom. The agile hunter leapt into the air, ready to bring his sword slicing down on Ryuu's head.

The other hunter came in from the side, attempting to strike at the same time.

The smart move would have been to move back and dodge, but they would be expecting it. Ryuu stepped forward at the last moment, his cut a hair faster than the agile hunter's. Ryuu felt the first hunter's sword graze his back, but his own sword slid through the hunter like he was cutting water. The agile hunter fell to the ground in two pieces while Ryuu focused his attention on the second hunter.

It was over in three moves. The hunter was balanced well, but Ryuu was too fast and too strong. Ryuu's first cut opened the hunter's belly, the second his neck. He dropped to the ground, not long for this world.

Events sped up to normal speed again. Ryuu sensed the commotion his battle had caused. With the energy he'd been putting out, he assumed he'd alerted the entire island. It was Shika who was first to him, blade drawn. Ryuu had never realized she was so fast.

"I saw the end of the battle. Where's Rei?"

"I sent her off to get a bite to eat."

Fury erupted on Shika's face. "How dare she leave you! I warned her something like this would happen."

Ryuu quieted her. "It was my idea. She'll feel bad enough as it is."

Shika turned to the assembled crowd. "Somebody clean up this mess, and somebody find Tenchi." She turned to Ryuu. "This has gone too far. It's time we settle this once and for all."

Ryuu, Tenchi, Shika, and Rei were sitting around Ryuu's hut. The tension was so thick, Ryuu was afraid someone was going to choke on the air before they had a chance to make their point.

Tenchi glared at Shika. "Our island has stood safe for over a thousand cycles, and now this. Were you involved?"

Shika looked liked she'd been expecting the question. "No."

Ryuu understood. His death would have brought the political battle to its final stage. If the blades weren't safe here, there was no reason for them not to go back to the Three Kingdoms. Shika would win, but would she have killed him? She had been the first to show up. Ryuu didn't know. He didn't know anyone here well enough. All he knew is that he wanted to trust them all.

Ryuu tried to turn the questioning in a direction that didn't bring Tenchi and Shika nose-to-nose. "They had to have come through the harbor. Is everyone fine down there?"

Tenchi shifted his glare from Shika to Ryuu. "Everyone's fine, and most everyone down there is loyal. They didn't come through the bay. I've had my men searching every ship."

"Why?"

"Because this island is splitting up, and I've been worried for some time that someone would try breaking the rules we've lived by for so many cycles." He glared at Shika.

Shika's voice was soft. "That's not fair, Tenchi. We may disagree, but I'd never break the rules which govern us. It's not the right way."

Ryuu was trying to keep up. "If they didn't use the bay, how did they get here? There's no way to climb those cliffs."

Rei spoke quietly. "There are other ways up, ways that have been hidden well. No one searching could have found them."

Tenchi elaborated. "We don't just have the two ships. There are many boats scattered around the island. Long ago it was decided we needed enough transportation to get off the island in case of emergency. There are boats down near the water, well disguised and covered and only checked occasionally. They would be next to impossible to find. The only way they could have used one of those passages was if we were betrayed."

There was a sound of footsteps at the doorway. Tenchi looked out and saw a messenger. "Yes?"

"Sir, we've found two things. First is this note. It was on the body of one of the hunters. Second, we found the boat they came in on. Smuggling vessel. They killed the entire crew. It looks like they came up through one of the emergency ship tunnels."

Tenchi nodded and dismissed the man. He unfolded the note. Three words were written on it. "War is coming."

"Cryptic enough," Tenchi remarked.

Ryuu caught a glance from Shika. He wanted to speak out, to let Tenchi know Shika had predicted the attack, but her glance told him to be silent. He swore to himself. Politics couldn't ruin this island. It was too great a treasure. People needed to start trusting each other.

"Tenchi, Shika warned me I might be in danger. I don't think she's behind the attack."

Shika looked like she was willing to finish the job the hunters had failed at, but Tenchi fixed his stare on her.

"What do you know, Shika?"

She looked as though she was about to be torn in two. She deflated, all the pride knocked out of her. "I think it was Renzo, sir."

Tenchi stroked his beard. "You have proof?"

Shika shook her head. "He is actively plotting with Lord Tanak, sir. He's raised a militant faction among my own supporters."

Tenchi stood up. "I see."

Tenchi paced the small hut, back and forth, and Ryuu worried he'd wear a hole in the ground. They all sat in perfect stillness, afraid to incur the wrath of the old man.

When he stopped, he was grinning the same grin he always seemed to have on his face. "Well, this is a problem that will take me a little while to solve. Ryuu, I'm glad you survived. It was an impressive display you put on for the rest of us."

Ryuu wasn't sure how to respond. "Thank you."

Tenchi turned to Shika. "Shika, there's much we must talk about, and much I need to think on. Let us meet again, soon, and let's be honest with one another. The time for our disagreements has passed. We're in more dangerous waters now, and I'll need everyone's help."

Tenchi led the other nightblades out into the evening coolness. As he was leaving, he turned to Ryuu. "Be careful, Ryuu. I know you can take care of yourself, but a storm is coming, and I don't know if any of us are prepared for it. Be safe."

Ryuu nodded, and Tenchi left, leaving Ryuu alone with his thoughts.

Two days later, Tenchi, Shika, Rei, and Ryuu were in conference again. Ryuu had barely seen Tenchi since the attack.

Today he looked haggard and worn. For the first time since they had met, Ryuu thought Tenchi was showing his age. He had the look of a man who had a distaste for everything he did.

"Thank you all for coming. I've been doing a lot of thinking since Ryuu was attacked. It's obvious our island is divided, now more so than ever, but I never thought it would get this far. Shika and I may disagree, but we both want what we believe is best for the blades."

Tenchi paused for a moment. "Today we need to be honest with one another. Shika, I haven't dug any deeper into your theory, but you seem to know things I don't. Will you share them with me?"

Shika nodded. Ryuu could see she'd come to her decision before the meeting had started.

"About two cycles ago, Renzo sent me a letter, asking me to join forces with him. He outlined his plan and asked me to support him and be his other half here on the island."

Ryuu looked up. Two cycles ago he had killed Orochi in battle. Was it a coincidence? Or were the two somehow related? Had Orochi been preventing Renzo's plans? His mind spun, but he kept his silence.

"What was his plan?"

Shika shook her head. "His letter wasn't specific. He didn't trust me completely, but he said he knew the Three Kingdoms would soon be involved in civil war, and his dream was that the war would provide sufficient motivation to bring the blades back to the Three Kingdoms."

"Why didn't you tell me?"

Shika met Tenchi's questioning look straight on. "I didn't like his plan. It relied on spreading chaos in the Three Kingdoms and would cost many lives. But at the same time, I wasn't sure he was wrong. I refused, but I've tried to keep an eye on his actions ever since."

"What do you mean?"

"I've worked hard to figure out who his people on the island are. I've been watching them to ensure they didn't try anything foolish."

"But you didn't prevent the attack on Ryuu's life."

Shika bowed her head. "I never thought Renzo would give anyone the location of the island. He's a believer, in his own way. I never thought he'd try to recruit outsiders. Truth is, I was blindsided as much as anyone here. I thought he'd try something with another nightblade. It was why I've had Rei sitting watch for these few moons."

Tenchi nodded. "And here I thought it was just because she liked him."

Ryuu's gaze darted over to Rei, who was blushing. Perhaps Tenchi's guess hadn't been that far off either.

Everyone sat around in a moment of silence. Ryuu looked from face to face, and each of them seemed deep in thought. But he still felt he was missing part of the story. He raised his hand and spoke when Tenchi addressed him.

"Why is Renzo in the Three Kingdoms, anyway?"

Shika was the one who answered. "The practice can actually be traced back to your master, Shigeru. After he escaped from the island, it was only a matter of time before Orochi followed him. Orochi was young and obsessed with power when he landed in the Three Kingdoms. We're not sure how it happened, but he eventually worked his way into service with Lord Akira. While we didn't condone his actions, it presented an opportunity and a challenge for us."

Tenchi picked up where Shika left off. "Orochi gave us valuable information, information that helped shape our path here on the island. It was useful for him to be stationed so close to Akira, but it also created a shift in the balance of power in the Three Kingdoms. I feared if one kingdom had a nightblade, the power would shift in the kingdoms altogether. The council at the time, led by me, made the decision to send two other nightblades, one to Tanak and one to Sen."

Ryuu was shocked. It had been surprising enough when he had discovered Akira was in league with a nightblade, but to know each Lord was advised by a nightblade, it was almost too much to handle. It was information that would send the Three Kingdoms into uprising if it became public. All because of his master. He stopped to consider the man he'd thought a father in a new light.

Rei asked the most important question. "So what do we do?"

Tenchi frowned. "I've been thinking, considering what I would do if Shika's theory was true. I don't like it, but I believe we need to assassinate Renzo."

Ryuu heard the intake of breath from around the room. Rei spoke first. "You'd order the death of a nightblade?"

Tenchi looked as though he'd just lost a loved one. It was hard to meet his gaze. "If I need to in order to protect this island and the people, yes, I would."

Shika laughed. "Are you forgetting Renzo is the best sword this island has? You've always said you were stronger, but no one alive has seen you fight. Are you going to take him on yourself?"

Tenchi smiled. "There's not been one worth drawing a blade against. But, you're right. He was the best sword, but my plan was to send Ryuu. I believe he's stronger than Renzo."

Shika took in Ryuu at a glance. "I won't deny he's good. But you think he's that good?"

"I hope so."

Ryuu was getting frustrated. It was annoying to be talked about as if he wasn't even present. He had opinions too, and he refused to be part of the politics on the island. He had come here to learn how to protect himself and Moriko, not become an assassin. When Akira had offered him the position, he had refused, and he didn't see any reason his answer should change just because it was Tenchi who was asking. "What if I don't want to kill him?"

Tenchi fixed him with a stare. "Then you give up your only hope of bringing peace to the Three Kingdoms."

Ryuu was angry, starting to see red in the corners of his vision. How dare Tenchi try to pin peace in the Three Kingdoms on an assassination! Takako had been right, just before she was killed. Violence only led to more violence.

Tenchi looked around the faces of the room and sighed. "This is what it means to lead this island. Think on that, if any of you want the job. If you can come up with another idea, bring it to me. Take a few days and think it over, but I don't see any other path forward."

CHAPTER 23

It had been over two moons since Moriko had left the comfort and relative security of the Three Kingdoms. She had probably seen more of Azaria than any living citizen of the Three Kingdoms. And now she was coming home, only now she was at the tail of an advancing army. Not quite the homecoming she'd been hoping for, but she was traveling north, and that was a small comfort. She'd have to take action soon, but was worried what the consequences would be.

They had been traveling for five days now. After the Gathering had broken, all the clans had started to head north together. It would be the largest invasion force the Three Kingdoms had ever seen. She had to get ahead of them and warn Toro as soon as she could, but she still didn't know why she and Ryuu had been attacked by hunters, or even how they'd been found. Until she had more information, she didn't want to leave. And their leader knew where she was now. She wasn't sure she'd have a chance escaping.

After the hunters had met with Dorjee, Moriko had worried she'd be taken by them. But they had left, and Dorjee hadn't been pleased. Their conversation afterwards, in Dorjee's tent, had been tense.

"You did not tell me you were demon-kind." His whole attitude towards her had become cold.

"What does it matter who I am?"

"I never would have let you come into the clan if I had known."

"You let me in because you saw strength and a chance for peace, no matter how slim. None of that has changed."

"He will never listen to your proposal!"

"Who is He? I've been with you for over a moon now, and still I know nothing about your people. You march to war against my land, but I don't know why." Moriko's frustration was getting the better of her. "All I want is to meet with your leader and speak with him. Why can't this happen?"

Dorjee was about to retort, but it was Lobsang who spoke up, his deep, calm voice easing some of the tension in the room.

"This clan wishes for peace. When you came, we hoped there would be a chance. But events have come too far, and if you are demon-kind, there is no chance for peace. Dorjee won't admit it, because he's a stubborn man, but he cares for you and doesn't want to see you come to harm."

Moriko glanced from one to the other. Lobsang was telling the truth of it. "I have nothing to fear from your leader."

Lobsang shook his head, sadly. "I know you were holding back when we fought, and I would have fallen to you otherwise, but your best is far less than His. You've never seen a fighter like Him."

"I've seen strong fighters."

"If you'd seen one like Him, you'd fear Him." He turned to Dorjee. "Sir?"

Dorjee nodded and spoke softly, the anger gone from his voice, replaced by sorrow. "There is some I can tell you, some which will help you understand."

He gestured for Moriko to sit down.

"The People have never had a ruler, not like you in the Three Kingdoms. Each clan is led as they see fit, and at the Gathering each summer, councils of the leaders get together to make any decisions that must be made. It has been this way for as long as our stories go back. But last summer, it all changed when He came."

"He has no name. None of his kind do. You call them hunters in your language, and you are more right than you know. They have always been a breed apart. They are important, called on in times of crisis. The demon-kind can gather food where none can be found. They can fight off enemies our own clans cannot. But they never lead. They are servants to the clans, set apart. But He has other plans."

"You have heard times are tough. Times have always been tough, but game is disappearing. There is no longer enough food in this land to feed us. The demon-kind are called on more and more to feed clans. Many of us have worried for many cycles, but there is little we can do."

"Last summer He came forward and told us He was taking charge, that He had a plan to save the clans. He said He was the ruler and we must do as He said. Those who disagreed with Him at that first campfire were killed by his own sword. Some clans rebelled, but they were wiped off the face of the planet, man, woman, and child. He leads the demon-kind, and the demon-kind are the strongest of us all. It is that strength that draws us to Him."

"This spring the last of the rebelling clans was wiped out. Here, at the Gathering we just left, He told us His plan. We march north to take over a new land, a land where the people have gone soft, have forgotten how to fight. We have always sent our young men to the pass to build their strength, but He means to take over your land and make it our own."

Moriko understood, everything falling into place.

"He will kill you, as soon as He meets you. But it is out of our hands. His scouts have found you, and He will summon you when He is ready."

For a while, Moriko thought the summons might never come. Dorjee said she should be grateful for every day of life. She contemplated escape, but somehow He knew she had been on her way south. Perhaps escape was out of the question. She worried she would bring retribution down on the Red Hawks, but she was more worried she wouldn't be able to get away at all. So she spent her days with the clan on the move. Dorjee had no wish to be part of the hostilities, so they were near the end of the column.

Moriko was amazed by how much ground they covered every day. The clans moved fast. Every day they covered between seven and ten leagues. She didn't know much of anything about marching large groups, but she had never imagined they'd be able to cover so much ground. They were making much better time than she'd made alone on foot. At this rate, they'd be at the Three Sisters before the pass closed up for the winter.

Five days passed, and no summons came. Dorjee had been kind enough to lend her a horse, and Lobsang took her under his wing. He taught her how to ride better, and after five days, riding had almost become pleasurable to her. Almost.

On the evening of the sixth day, the summons came. Moriko suppressed her fear. She had been rehearsing for this moment for a long time. They were to come to His campfire when the moon was high.

As the sun began to set, Moriko joined the Red Hawks for their evening meal. They all gathered around a campfire and ate as the men and women told stories. Moriko still didn't understand a word they were saying, but she did understand the look of contentment on the faces of everyone around her. It seemed such a striking contrast to the reason she was here. This was home for these people, and they had shared it with her. She was grateful.

The sun went down and the moon started to rise. As it approached its zenith, Dorjee came to her and escorted her further forward along the column. Almost immediately, Moriko noticed a difference in the camps as she went deeper in. Other clans were not as content as the Red Hawks. Many clans sat around cooking fires silently, and Moriko sensed a deep tension among the people. The closer they got to their destination, the greater the difference seemed to be.

Dorjee confirmed her suspicions. "Be aware, there is much tension among the People. My clan is happy, but we have distanced ourselves from the events that surround us. There is no love lost between my clan and the demon-kind. Walk gently for both of us."

Moriko nodded.

It wasn't hard to pick out their destination. The fire there burned much larger than anywhere else in camp, and Moriko glanced away to keep up some of her night vision. There was a large circle gathered there, all men. Moriko wondered momentarily if it had been a mistake to send her instead of Ryuu. The Azarians were less patriarchal than the Three Kingdoms, but it was still clear men ruled here.

She pushed the thoughts aside as they entered the circle. Moriko glanced around as she became the center of attention. Before her arrival, quiet conversation had filtered through the night, but now many silent eyes were on her. She took in all the information she could. The men here were all very strong, and she saw everyone's body was covered with the scars that signified a life full of battle. But here they all wore the tooth. She was surrounded by hunters. There were more of them than she could have imagined.

Moriko didn't have any difficulty identifying the leader. He sat on a low bench, the same as any other man, but there was something about him. He drew power into himself, and Moriko could sense him much more strongly than any of the other men in the circle. She had never felt such strength. Even the Abbot of Perseverance would have quailed under this power. There was no doubt he was the leader, and her suspicion was confirmed when Dorjee addressed him, in Moriko's language for her benefit.

"My Lord, I bring one who would see you."

The leader looked at both of them and replied in the same language. "Dorjee, why do you bring a woman into my circle. If I wanted a whore, I would have taken one of your wives!"

Moriko could sense the tension building in the Red Hawk chief, but he suppressed it as the hunters around them laughed. "You have summoned her, my Lord, and she has come. She is a warrior from the kingdoms above."

The man stood up and laughed. "She may be a warrior by your standards, but to use the word in this circle is a disgrace. I should have your head."

Dorjee bowed low. "I do as you request, my Lord."

It pained Moriko to see such a great leader humbled before a bully, but the leader's attention was now on her.

"So you are the one I sent my men to kill. I don't see how they failed. The one you travel with must be very strong."

Moriko suppressed her anger. She found the cold steel inside her and embraced it. She looked directly at the leader and said nothing.

The challenge was clear, and the leader nodded his appreciation. "Dorjee says you are a messenger, so what is your message?"

Moriko had lived with the lie so long, it rolled smoothly off her tongue. "My Lord wishes for peace between our great kingdoms and asks for your intentions."

The man laughed again, and Moriko could see on his face the incredible disdain he had for the Southern Kingdom and for her. "It figures they would send a woman. They are tired of their men dying under our blades!"

There was another round of laughter after the comment, but Moriko felt nothing. She studied the leader. Something about him wasn't right. She didn't sense him in quite the same way she sensed everyone else. He stepped forward, and his grace and strength were apparent.

"You ask what my intentions are? My intentions are simple. I am going to conquer your lands and make all of you slaves. You are weak and you disgust me."

Moriko felt like she needed to retort before this became a campaign speech. "There is much strength in the Southern Kingdom, and if you attack, all Three Kingdoms will join against you."

The leader waved his hand dismissively. "You were once a strong people, many, many cycles ago. But no more. You have hunted and killed all your strongest warriors, and now your lands are weak, filled with people who have no concept of the power they can't access anymore. Any society that makes its strongest warriors its greatest enemy deserves death at my hands."

Moriko understood with a start the man was talking about the nightblades. The Azarians knew that all the nightblades in the Three Kingdoms had been killed. The next connection was obvious. They had to have spies in the Three Kingdoms. This had been planned.

"Who are you?"

The leader glared at her. "I am nameless, like all my brethren. Our identity is unimportant. What is important is our will to serve the People."

The silence felt ominous. "Is that to be your message to my Lord then?"

Nameless gave her an icy stare. "I think your body on a stake at the front of our column will be enough message." He raised his voice so that all could hear. "Tomorrow there shall be an execution!"

Moriko's blood went cold as the cheers went up all around her.

CHAPTER 24

Ryuu had been on the island for far longer than he'd planned. It had been foolish to think he could make the trip as quickly as he had first believed. He could spend his entire life here learning more about the sense and the powers it granted.

He was angry. Angry at Tenchi and Shika for their politics, angry at fate for always threatening to take away everything he loved. His only desire from the day he'd killed Orochi had been to live in peace, to be undisturbed. He ached for the beauty of a day spent in the garden, pulling weeds. It shouldn't be this hard. He was falling in love with the island just as it seemed to be falling apart.

Every day he spent here, he wanted to spend another. It pained him that politics were slowly ripping the island in two, but there was so much here that he loved. More than anything, he felt comfortable here. He felt like this was a place where he could find peace. It made it that much more difficult when his dreams were shattered by hunters and politics.

Ryuu had never considered how much tension he and Moriko lived under every day in the Three Kingdoms. He would have said most of their days were normal, but here on the island he realized how wrong he had been. In the Three Kingdoms there was always the knowledge pressing on their thoughts, that if they were to be themselves, to show their skills and talents in public, they would be hunted like criminals. Ryuu hadn't spent much time being hunted in his life, but the knowledge had always been there, an undercurrent of fear that scarred every daily action.

He hadn't realized it until he came here. On the island, he was a nightblade, and nobody cared. He couldn't get over how beautiful that lack of fear could be.

Beyond that, he was in a position where he was respected. He wasn't sure he was as important to the island as Tenchi believed, but he did feel like he was somebody here. He was now the top swordsman he knew of. Every day he was under the personal tutelage of Tenchi, the most knowledgeable man on the island. He didn't let his position get to his head, but he couldn't help but feel a twinge of pride at what he had accomplished. If Moriko were here, he thought they could throw off all the concerns of the world.

And all of it was being destroyed by the events to the south. Every night after training was over, he returned to his hut and continued his training alone. He practiced flowing into the sense, increasing the power and speed of every strike. After he was physically exhausted he trained mentally, extending his sense throughout the Three Kingdoms. His progress was slow, but continual.

Ryuu could sense the Three Kingdoms at war. He felt the Northern Kingdom, massing its armies against the borders, prepared for whatever might happen next. He could sense the

Southern Kingdom driven backwards a step at a time and knew that unless something changed, the Southern Kingdom wouldn't last the summer. Then he pushed further south, into Azaria, to check on Moriko. She was still among the Azarians, in the heart of it all, but now they were moving north, all of them. She was indistinct among the masses - only Ryuu's familiarity with her allowed him to sense her at all. From what he could sense, she was fine, but worry gnawed away at his confidence.

After checking on the war and on Moriko, Ryuu laid awake and considered all the developments until he fell asleep. He thought about Tenchi's proposal and his anger grew. The old man had no right to ask him to assassinate another nightblade. Yes, there were thousands on the island, but in Ryuu's mind, they were still in danger, and he didn't want to kill another nightblade if he could help it. He'd rather not kill at all.

But there was always another voice in his head, a voice Ryuu had come to recognize as Shigeru's. It was the voice telling him to think through all the angles, to think about what it meant to have the power and strength of a nightblade. It was a small and persistent voice that told him he had a responsibility to the Three Kingdoms, that all the blades did, whether the Three Kingdoms accepted them or not. Ryuu hated that voice, but he couldn't rid himself of it either.

And so most nights Ryuu passed out from exhaustion, angry and undecided.

For Ryuu, the night started like any other. His day had been full of training and he practiced on his own in the evening. He settled down to meditate and expand his sense, filling his mind with all the information it could handle. He moved through the armies and events of the Three Kingdoms easily and focused on Moriko. It was her world that interested him most. He worried about her every day, though he knew she was capable of defending herself.

His mind searched for her, struggling to identify her in the sea of people she was surrounded by. She was closer to the center of the mass than she had ever been before. After sensing her every night, he understood something different was happening. He focused his attention, trying to pick out more details, sweat forming on his brow.

Here he was at his limit. Tenchi told him with practice he'd be able to resolve the sense down to an individual level, but tonight he couldn't do any more than focus on groups. The only reason he could find Moriko was because he was so used to her presence. Sweat dripped as he tried to use brute force to no effect. He lost the trance-like state necessary to maintain the contact with the sense. Ryuu cursed. He had the feeling that something was happening, but he didn't know what.

Ryuu stood up and stretched his tired limbs. He'd try again, but he wanted to be in the best shape possible. He stretched in various angles, paying particular attention to the parts of his body that were especially tight. Then he drank some water and sat back down.

Again his mind rode upon the streams of the sense that ran throughout the world. He flew south, moving as fast as he was comfortable. Now that he knew where to look, finding Moriko didn't take as much time as it had on his first attempt of the evening. He stayed calm and searched for details about Moriko's surroundings.

She was surrounded by thousands of people. Beyond that, there wasn't much that Ryuu felt he could discern. He kept a calm focus, trying to discover something, anything that would give him a clue what Moriko was up to. A little knowledge was worse than complete ignorance.

As he watched, he felt the presence of another, strong beyond belief. Ryuu tried to focus on the energy, but his skills weren't sufficient. Wherever Moriko had found herself, she was facing someone of incredible power. The source of power was greater than that of the Abbot of Perseverance, greater even than Tenchi. A hint of fear flirted across Ryuu's mind. If Moriko was up against that, she didn't have a chance. He wouldn't have a chance against that kind of power.

Ryuu held the connection as long as he could, long enough to sense Moriko being taken away from the source of power. In a moment of clarity, he sensed that she was bound, half dragged, half carried to a tent in the camp. The clarity faded and Ryuu was left with the vague impression of Moriko moving through the camp.

Ryuu broke away from the sense. He knew enough. Moriko was in danger, critical danger. He was a world away from her, but there wasn't anything that would stop him. He stood up, only to find his legs wouldn't support him. Sensing at that distance for so long had taken more out of him than he realized. He tried to stand again, only to fall to the ground, passed out.

Ryuu woke up to Rei standing over him, a concerned look on her otherwise happy face. He tried to grin it off, but there wasn't any fooling her.

"What's wrong?"

Ryuu sat up. He glanced outside, and from the shadows, he saw he had slept past mid-day. He wondered how long she had been by his side.

"It's Moriko. She's scouting the Kingdom south of the Three Kingdoms and is in danger. I'm worried for her."

Rei raised an eyebrow. "What is she doing in Azaria?"

Ryuu glanced at her and debated his options. He liked Rei a lot, but he still didn't know who to trust on this island. "It's a long story. Do you know where Tenchi is?"

She nodded. "Yes, he's with the council right now. Nothing urgent, just day-to-day matters."

"Can I speak to him?"

"Certainly."

Rei gave him one last look that Ryuu couldn't decipher as she stepped out. He tried to decide what he would say to Tenchi when he got to the hut. It was time for him to leave the island.

It was some time before Tenchi arrived at Ryuu's hut. Ryuu felt like he was ready to pace a track into his floor. When Tenchi arrived, Ryuu could tell Rei had already filled him in.

"Moriko is in trouble?"

Ryuu nodded.

"Tell me."

Ryuu related what he had sensed. Tenchi paused him every so often to ask a question, but the story was short of telling. He spent most of the time trying to describe the massive power he'd sensed.

Tenchi waved his hand as Ryuu attempted another half-formed explanation. "I know, I've been sensing him for a while now. Get on with it."

Ryuu tried to contain his surprise and failed. What else was Tenchi not telling him?

As Ryuu finished telling his story, Shika came into the hut and sat down. Ryuu had been so distracted he hadn't sensed her approach. She listened to the end of his story, asking just a question or two to get caught up. Shika hadn't known about Moriko, so there was some more explaining required.

When Ryuu finished the story the four of them sat around quietly, each with their thoughts. Ryuu wasn't sure of the best thing to say, so he didn't speak. Silence was his best council.

Tenchi spoke first. "Shika, what are your thoughts?"

She didn't reply right away, taking the time to gather her response, testing it in her mind before loosing it on the world. "Ryuu needs to leave the island. This is the first I've heard of Moriko, but if she is a nightblade, she deserves our protection the same as any other, whether or not she's grown up on the island. Ryuu could even take others if he wished."

If Ryuu hadn't been so serious about Moriko, he would have laughed. Shika would stop at nothing to have a greater presence in the Three Kingdoms.

Tenchi looked at Rei expectantly. She just nodded. Ryuu didn't know what she was agreeing with or what passed between them.

Tenchi then turned to Ryuu. "What are your desires?"

"I love her. Nothing could stop me from going to her."

"Even if she is at least a moon away, under the best of conditions?"

"Yes." Ryuu didn't mean to put as much force into it as he did, but his passion got the better of him. He couldn't rest with Moriko in danger.

Tenchi looked at all the young warriors around him and sighed deeply. "Very well. The tide is already out today, but tomorrow you may depart the island. Rei, you are to go with him, and you alone."

He held up a hand to still three different objections. "Shika, any more is too many. Rei, you are welcome back if you so decide. Ryuu, you can't leave any earlier, no matter how much you wish. We can't change the requirements for sailing off the island."

He continued. "The plan comes at a price. Tonight we shall gather the blades for a display of strength. Ryuu, your first duel is with Shika. If you manage to defeat her, you must then fight me. Regardless of the outcome, you may still leave tomorrow."

There were outbursts all around, but Tenchi rode the waves of outcry without losing his composure.

Tenchi waved his hand at the women. "Depart. I need to speak to Ryuu in private. Rei, make sure we are not bothered or overheard."

Shika looked like she was going to kill someone, but she bowed and left, Rei following right behind her.

Tenchi held Ryuu's gaze in his own. "You have had time to consider your options. Will you kill Renzo?"

Ryuu shook his head. "I won't. Violence will only beget more violence. It's a lesson I should have learned a long time ago."

Tenchi's gaze never left Ryuu. He was silent.

"Thank you, for allowing me to leave. I have been here over two moons, and I still feel like I know nothing."

For just a moment, Ryuu saw Tenchi's friendly exterior drop, and he got a glimpse of the steel that made Tenchi the leader he was. "That's because you don't."

It was just a moment and the Tenchi Ryuu knew returned. "Sometimes we can't fight the tide, and this is one of those times. I only hope we will survive this storm. Sometimes I wish you had never come, or that I'd never let you on the island."

Ryuu was surprised. "What do you mean?"

Tenchi replied. "Ryuu, for all your strength, you still lack the control necessary to take right action. You bounce around from crisis to crisis, only acting once tragedy is at your doorstep. If you wish to become more, you need to grow up. Until you do, you're a danger to us all."

Ryuu glanced up angrily. "That's not true!"

Tenchi continued as if Ryuu had never spoken. "Your rescue of Takako was ill-informed. Shigeru should have stopped you. It was not wrong, wanting to save an innocent life, but every action is a pebble dropped in a pond, reverberating out far beyond the pebble itself. How many people died because of your decision to save one life, a life that was ended prematurely anyway?"

Ryuu was silent, anger burning inside of him. He had come to peace with his decision, convinced it was the right action to take. Tenchi's words cracked the shell of his conviction.

"I am sorry. If I had more time, I would be more gentle, but again you have brought this pressure upon yourself. Again you go off to rescue a woman you care for, but at what cost? You will go galloping through the Three Kingdoms, heedless of all the danger around you. Your odds of rescuing her in time are slim to none, and the hunters are not to be trifled with. They are in every way as strong as we are. Their lore may be different, but their strength is no less substantial."

"Your journey is a threat to this island and the Three Kingdoms, especially given your general ability to find trouble. You realize Renzo can sense at a distance, too. If he senses you coming down through the Three Kingdoms, he may come to finish the job, and despite your strength, I'm not sure you can beat him. He has experience on his side. You risk all for nothing."

Ryuu couldn't contain himself. "But at least I'm doing something, something more than hiding away from everything!"

Tenchi shook his head. "You are foolish. You are making the same assumption Shika and Rei are, despite my warnings. We aren't on this island hiding or waiting. We are preparing."

Ryuu's confusion was apparent. He didn't bother to hide his disbelief.

"Someday I will tell you what happened when the Kingdom broke up. We aren't the demons legend has made us out to be, but we aren't without blame. It was our responsibility to keep the Kingdom in order, but we forgot. We let power go to our heads. For better or for worse, the Three Kingdoms have survived without major problems for a thousand cycles, but again I feel we have been the catalyst for war, especially now that I know Renzo is involved with the invasion. Perhaps they are better off without us."

Ryuu considered Tenchi's words. He had never heard the old man so worked up.

"For a thousand cycles we have prepared. We have learned, we have kept true to the old knowledge while developing it further. We have studied history and politics so the mistakes of the past won't be repeated. Surely you've seen how even Shika and I, though we disagree, can work together so openly?"

Ryuu had to admit that he had.

"That isn't by chance. We aren't waiting. We are preparing for the day we are needed in the Three Kingdoms once again, if that day ever comes."

"Then why let me go at all?"

"Because not letting you go would become a much greater issue. Knowing your impulses, I suspect you would try to escape, and Shika would support you in an attempt to force the issue. Sometimes it is best to know when to bend. I'm hoping that sending Rei will temper your impulses, and it will be good for her to experience the Three Kingdoms herself."

It seemed as though Tenchi had thought of everything. "Why the duels tonight? Shika seemed upset about that."

Tenchi grinned his old mischievous grin. "I thought that was pretty good myself. There's been rumors spreading around the island since you arrived. 'Leader' is a bit of a misleading title, but she's been trying to win my position for some time. We aren't governed by strength alone, but we aren't foolish enough to dismiss the usefulness of a strong, experienced warrior. The skills transfer well to leadership. Shika is mad because you'll beat her. She's very good, but I think you're better. Then you'll fight me and lose."

Ryuu raised an eyebrow. "Are you telling me to lose on purpose?"

Tenchi laughed. "Oh, no. I hope you give me everything you've got. I'll still beat you. You'll be allowed to leave the island, but it will quell dissension for at least a few moons, giving the situation time to develop."

Tenchi got up and left. "I'm not going to stop you, even though I should. Just know this. You need to think about your decisions more clearly." With that he left, leaving Ryuu confused, but more ready than ever to duel with the leader of the island.

Ryuu was excited for the evening. He wasn't sure if he was the best nightblade on the island, but he looked forward to finding out. A duel was something solid in front of him, something he could handle. It was black and white, life and death. It was simple. He was curious to see if Shika or Tenchi had the skill to beat him in a duel.

Apparently he wasn't the only one. When the sun fell a great dinner was held, and all were invited to the amphitheater, a natural bowl with a flat bottom near the northwest corner of the island. Ryuu had never been there before, and as he was escorted to the front, he was amazed to see so many people in one place. He knew that over three thousand blades lived on the island, but it was another thing altogether to see three thousand dark-robed individuals gathered in one place. Ryuu thought of the power in the space and was in awe that the island had remained a secret for as long as it had.

Some entertainment had been arranged, individuals who specialized in exotic weaponry, some dayblades who had learned a fluid style of dance. Ryuu watched with rapt attention. None of the weapons styles would be useful in a fight, but the beauty of them was undeniable. He was also fascinated by the dancers, most of whom were female. Rei leaned over and explained there were some dayblades who believed that by moving their bodies in the same patterns that lead to healing, miraculous results could be achieved. Ryuu had seen dancers at Madame's in New Haven, but those were dancers who danced to entice customers. This was altogether different, a power and sensuality combined into a feeling more powerful than either alone.

Ryuu didn't see any miracles, but he was impressed by the style. It was fluid and graceful. At first glance the movements seemed random, but the more Ryuu watched, the more he felt like there was a deeper pattern, a deeper meaning than what was present at first glance. He gently opened up his sense and was almost blinded by the beauty.

There was a deep energy radiating from the dancers, a power that seemed to flow around them, shaped by them. He didn't have the words to describe what he was seeing. In the end, he didn't try. Instead, he sat and watched, taking it all in without trying to understand it. When it ended, he felt as though a void had opened up in him. Glancing around, he found he wasn't the only one who felt that way. Rei said it was rare to see such a performance from the dayblades.

Then he was up, introduced to the entire crowd. Ryuu was sure that by now, everyone knew who he was, but tradition still dictated life on the island. Tenchi gave a brief account, leaving out Ryuu's involvement in the affairs of the Three Kingdoms. Tenchi concluded by saying Ryuu should be considered an adopted member of the island, and in unison three thousand heads made a short bow in his direction. Ryuu was overwhelmed, but didn't have time to process what had happened. It was time for his duel.

Any nervousness Ryuu held dissipated like the morning mist as he stood against Shika. Politics, consequences, these weren't concepts that came to him easily. Combat was something he understood, something he excelled at.

As soon as the duel began, Shika struck like a cobra, her quick thrusts coming at Ryuu with blinding speed. He had been prepared, but not for the duel to start with such ferocity. He managed to block her first few attacks but was sent backwards faster than he could recover. Every time he thought he'd have a moment to gather his wits, she was on him again.

Ryuu cursed himself. He had gotten used to a certain type of duel, a duel where the opponents tested each other first, trying to gauge the other's abilities. He had been foolish. Shika knew his abilities. She had watched him fight others over and over, though he had never seen her draw a blade even in practice. She was going for the quick win, trying to catch him off guard before he could bring his full strength to bear.

Without thought, Ryuu fell into a state of relaxation, dropping the stress of combat like a heavy burden he would no longer carry. His mind emptied and his body fell into the natural rhythms of the world. He felt the flow of energy strengthen his limbs and sharpen his mind and Shika wasn't moving as fast as she once had.

Shika was quick, but Ryuu had matched her for speed. He could sense, more than he could observe, the interest of all the spectators who were watching. It was a treat to see two warriors of such ability fighting each other. Ryuu had guessed Shika was capable, but he hadn't any idea just how capable until this evening.

With speed being equal, the contest came down to a matter of skill and technique. Ryuu had thought he'd be her superior in skill, but wasn't so sure any more.

It came down to a single cut, one move that left Shika slightly off balance. Ryuu quickly moved inside her guard, the first opening she had given him. Shika tried to back away but

Ryuu pursued her with relentless determination, pushing her backwards. The momentum of the fight had turned in his favor. She blocked his cuts, but was falling further behind. They both knew it was only a matter of time.

Shika committed to a last effort, a strong overhead cut that would have broken Ryuu's head or shoulder, but she was too slow. Ryuu sensed the strike coming and moved in, striking her across the chest with his own wooden blade before she could defend herself. If he'd had a real blade in hand, she would have been opened up.

As it was, the blow knocked her off her feet and rolling across the grass. The world returned to normal and Ryuu came over to Shika's aid. She was slowly getting back to her feet, winded, but no permanent damage. Tenchi signaled for a dayblade, but Shika waved them away.

"I'm fine. Only my pride is hurt." Even as she said it, she gratefully accepted Ryuu's hand.

As she stood, a round of applause rippled through the amphitheater, a sound Ryuu had never heard before. He had listened to the tromp of hooves and the guttural cheers of men in battle, but never this polite clapping on such a scale. He wondered what the assembled nightblades thought of the demonstration they had just witnessed.

He didn't have too much time to think about it. Just as the applause ended, an eager silence descended over the crowd. Ryuu studied Tenchi. Tenchi had expected he would beat Shika, but still seemed confident he'd have no problem defeating Ryuu. He wondered what tricks the old man had up his sleeve. He didn't seem the type to boast needlessly.

The entire island felt as though it was holding its breath. Ryuu didn't make the same mistake again. He emptied his mind and slipped entirely into the flow of the world as the duel was announced.

Tenchi didn't seem to be interested in attacking. They each stepped closer until only two paces separated them, but neither moved, each on their guard. Tenchi was as immovable as a stone. In combat, Ryuu might have waited, but this was a duel with wooden swords. He grew impatient and attacked.

He came in with a low cut, moving up and across Tenchi's body. It was easily deflected, but then the battle began in earnest. Ryuu wasn't surprised that Tenchi was incredibly fast. The old man matched Ryuu in speed. Ryuu tried different techniques, always staying just a hair ahead of Tenchi's counter-strikes.

They passed and passed, but Ryuu kept waiting for Tenchi's tricks. He kept his guard close, not allowing Tenchi a moment to attack. Despite his best efforts, Tenchi turned the tide and Ryuu had to disengage or get beaten. They kept their distance, both looking for any opening.

What happened next, Ryuu couldn't explain. Tenchi attacked, but it was as if he was attacking everywhere at once. Ryuu's sense screamed at him, and he sensed all the cuts coming at him, but another part of his mind was shouting just as loudly that such an attack wasn't physically possible. No one could make eight cuts at one time. It was impossible.

Ryuu didn't know where to block. He couldn't block eight simultaneous cuts. Ryuu did what came first to him, he jumped into the air as far as he could. He leapt above the attack, coming down with an attack of his own. Tenchi easily dodged it and the battle resumed.

Ryuu could feel the excitement radiating off the assembled nightblades. They had seen and sensed everything that had just happened. Ryuu's mind was racing to catch up with an attack that wasn't humanly possible. It didn't seem like he was the only one. He could hear the low murmur going up through the assembly.

They split apart and came together again, Tenchi repeating the same attack. Ryuu tried to focus, find the truth of what was happening, but he couldn't. In desperation, he dove to his right, rolling out of the way, barely dodging the attack.

How? How could one man strike in eight places at once? There was always an explanation, Ryuu just had to find it. It had to be a trick of some sort, a deception of the sense. But Ryuu couldn't let his sense drop. He'd be hit in an instant. He reached out, quieting his mind, focusing on Tenchi's movements.

Tenchi struck again, the same impossible attack reaching out to pummel Ryuu. He didn't dodge but kept himself centered, focusing, searching for any information he could use to defeat the attack. A person could only strike in one place at a time. There could only be one real attack, he just had to find it.

At the last moment, Ryuu felt something. One strike, slightly different than the others. More substantial. Ryuu took the chance and blocked just that cut. His block was slow, but he connected with Tenchi's wooden sword.

There was a gasp from the crowd as they realized what had happened. Ryuu felt a surge of pride. He could beat Tenchi and his tricks.

But then he saw Tenchi's smile and realized he was deluding himself. Tenchi launched himself into a series of cuts, each showing multiple possibilities. Ryuu's mind reeled, unable to focus. Some attacks would have two possibilities, some four. Ryuu dodged and blocked, but he blocked empty air as often as he blocked Tenchi's strikes. The hits came with increasing rapidity, and Ryuu knew he had lost. Unbalanced, Tenchi delivered a series of blows which knocked Ryuu off his feet and eating grass. He tried to move, but Tenchi's wooden blade was resting at the back of his neck. A killing stroke for sure.

Ryuu swore and then laughed. His body felt stronger than it ever had before, but there was still more to learn. When Tenchi heard him laugh he relaxed his own posture. Ryuu flipped over onto his back and gladly accepted Tenchi's outstretched hand. He brushed himself off and shook his head. "I've never seen anything like that before."

Tenchi was about to reply, but was drowned out by the cheering that erupted from the audience. Ryuu looked up, surprised. In the heat of the combat he had forgotten there were thousands of people watching. It was almost enough to make him blush.

Ryuu had never seen Tenchi's grin wider. He waited for the cheering to subside a little and then leaned over to Ryuu. "I had forgotten how much fun a real challenge can be. You are stronger than I expected. It was well fought."

"You'll have to show me that technique some time. I imagine it isn't much good against those that can't sense."

"It isn't. But if you're fighting someone without the sense you'll never need it. I'll teach you when you return."

Ryuu caught and held Tenchi's eyes. He was an impressive man. Of that there wasn't any doubt. He was as strong as steel but also knew enough to bend when the pressure was too great. He possessed an integrity Ryuu admired. Ryuu wasn't sure where his life would take him, but he knew he wanted to come back to the island. This was where he belonged.

CHAPTER 25

Renzo was on horseback, galloping across the Southern Kingdom. He had gotten used to riding horses, something he had never been able to do growing up on the island. It was one of the small pleasures of the Three Kingdoms he delighted in. Even though he had spent almost every morning and afternoon of the past two moons in the saddle, it still never got old. He loved the feel of the wind in his hair, the sensation of speed as they flew through the grass.

He had made a mistake. In retrospect, he should not have allowed the hunters to go to the island. He had underestimated Ryuu's abilities once again. The young man was gifted, strong. But all the attack had accomplished was to give away Renzo's plans. He was sure of it. They couldn't come to any other conclusion. When he had approached Shika, he hadn't been surprised when she turned him down, although he had hoped they could work together. They both felt the pressing need to bring the nightblades back to the Three Kingdoms, but Renzo didn't think she had the courage to go as far as was necessary. Change wouldn't happen unless the blades were pushed. Renzo wished that it could be different, but it wasn't.

The hunters on the island would have forced her hand. Shika would have told Tenchi about his approach. Renzo had trusted her enough at the time. Their methods may have been different, but they had the same goals, and she had told him she wouldn't speak to Tenchi about it. But he suspected he had gone too far. She wouldn't protect him after this. Renzo wondered what the old man would do, if he would send assassins.

Every evening Renzo extended his sense, sacrificing sleep to learn all he could about what was happening on the island. He had sensed the battle between Ryuu and the hunters. He had known it had failed the moment it was over. Every night he returned, wondering what would happen. For a while, he had thought perhaps everything would continue as usual. Days passed and nothing seemed different. But then he sensed Ryuu leaving the island. He tracked the young nightblade for two days, wondering if the boy was coming for him.

Two days of tracking, and Renzo was increasingly certain Ryuu hadn't been sent to assassinate him. The boy was making a beeline through the Northern Kingdom, racing to where the Southern Kingdom troops were. Renzo made up his mind. He begged leave of Tanak for a few days. There was only one place Ryuu would go, and it would be straight to Akira. Renzo didn't know what Tenchi or Ryuu hoped to accomplish, but he couldn't let their plans come to fruition. Even though he had failed, Akira had shown himself as a dangerous and cunning opponent at the Conclave. Public opinion supported Akira and the words he had said. The people wished for peace. Tenchi was no fool either.

Renzo couldn't let them cooperate, not when his plans were so close to fruition. The Three Kingdoms were on the brink of complete chaos. It would only take another small push and it would all be over.

And so here he was, on a horse in the Southern Kingdom, riding to intercept Ryuu. It was time to put these games to an end. Ryuu had to die. Then Akira. And then his plan would be complete. He kicked his horse to go faster, riding towards Ryuu's end.

CHAPTER 26

Moriko was in shock. She wasn't sure what she had expected, but it hadn't been a quick death sentence. They hadn't even listened to a word she said.

She glanced around and saw that many of the hunters around the fire were on the edge of their seats. They were expecting her to try to run for it. She didn't have the time to process everything. Escaping under the spotlight wasn't going to be an option.

She kept her courage and bowed. It was mock respect, and their nameless leader understood. "I am sorry to hear it, but I am not sure you will live to regret it." The threat sounded hollow, even to her. She had her throwing knives and her sword but decided against using them. Nameless was on his guard, and she wouldn't be able to surprise him. Better to wait for later.

A group of warriors came up to her, and she submitted to being bound, her wrists behind her back and her ankles given a pace of leeway. She could shamble along, but that was it. A leather strap was tied around her neck and she was led roughly away from the campfire. She offered no resistance. Better for them to think her meek. It wasn't much, but it might give her the opportunity to make an escape later.

She was brought to a large tent and thrown inside. The strap around her neck was tied to an upright support at such a height she had to remain straight to prevent being choked. She admired the cruel simplicity of it. Her blade was taken from her and placed off to the side of the tent, taunting her with its closeness. She tried to reach her knives but couldn't. She forced herself to take slow breaths and think. Her will was as sharp as her blade, and there was no way she'd let them execute her.

It didn't seem like much time had passed when she heard an angry conversation outside the tent. She had fallen into a meditative state to stay completely upright, but she jerked herself aware when she heard one of the voices outside. It was the voice of Dorjee. There were two voices arguing, but then Dorjee burst through the tent, trailed by the two guards. He was carrying a small pack, which he tossed into the corner of the tent. He drew his sword and sliced through the leather strap around her neck, close to the upper support.

The sudden release would have brought her to her knees, but Dorjee's fist was in her gut before she could fall. He might have been older, but he could still hit. Moriko had just taken her first full gasp of air in some time, but his fist drove all the precious breath out of her lungs. She collapsed over his fist and fell to the ground, unable to protect herself or process what was happening.

While she was on the ground, Dorjee kicked her over and over, shots to her legs and chest. She was gasping for air but nothing seemed to come into her lungs except the dust from the ground. He lifted her up and a small knife appeared, as if by magic, in his hand. He cut her left arm, blood flowing freely from the wound. A few more blows and a slap to the face sent her crashing to the ground, blood all over her. Dorjee had gotten some on his hands. Finally, he stood her up and rammed his fist one last time into her gut. He didn't let her fall, but kept her limp weight supported on his fist. He grabbed her hair and pulled her face to his and whispered "Not all of us look for war." Then he let her drop heavily on the ground.

She felt the tension tighten around her neck as Dorjee bound that leather strap to the one tying her wrists together. She was still in shock as his agile hands worked on her bonds. It didn't even occur to her to struggle. When he was done, he shared a laugh with the guards as they all walked out of the tent.

It took Moriko some time to gather her wits. The first thing she noticed was that the strap around her throat was loose. It had seemed tight at first, but it had quickly slipped until it was almost meaningless. Then she noticed the straps around her wrists were also coming undone.

Moriko looked around and saw that the small pack Dorjee had come in with was still in the tent, apparently forgotten. But she knew better. She smiled to herself. It was perhaps the first time she found use in political maneuvering.

Moriko was patient. There was no rush, but she was eager to see what Dorjee had left for her. She waited until she figured the moon was past its peak. The camp all around her was quiet, only the soft laughter of drunk couples breaking the silence of the prairie. Moriko undid the straps at her wrists and then made short work of the straps around her throat and feet. Silently, she walked over to the pack and opened it up.

All her belongings were in the pack, as well as Azarian clothes and food. It was all she needed to escape.

Moriko thought about trying to cut a hole in the hide, but she wanted blood. The guards outside the tent never knew what happened, their throats slit from behind. She dragged them into the tent and left them.

The experience of getting though the camp was horrible. She was dressed as one of the Azarians, but she still did not want to draw any attention to herself, so she tried to avoid being seen. She moved from tent to tent, using her sense to tell when people were nearby. She stayed out of sight as often as she could, and when she had to be seen, she made it look like she was in a hurry to get from one place to another.

The worst was when she was in between the tents of different clans. At night, these spaces were no-man's land, and she had to ensure she wasn't seen as she crossed through each of them. There was usually a fair amount of open space between the clan's tents, and every one was a complete and utter nightmare. She kept turning around, expecting to find a hunter behind her.

By the time she reached the edge of the camps, Moriko was exhausted. She wanted to stop and rest, but there wasn't any time. If they could find her at a distance, her only friend was more distance, more time. She found an unguarded horse and cut it free. There were outriders, but as she passed them at a distance she waved, just another scout on a mission. They waved in return, and she was free of the camp. She rode as hard as she could, knowing the hunters would soon be behind her.

When the sun rose, Moriko was exhausted, but the rising of the sun led to a new outlook. She had succeeded. She knew who had sent the hunters, knew they could find her at distance. Most important, she knew what was in store for the Three Kingdoms. Now all she had to do was get back in time. Even though the journey would be long and treacherous, she felt calm and confident. The prairie stretched as fas as the eye could see, and she was free.

She rode through the day and through the first night. When the sun rose on the second day of her escape, she allowed herself and the horse a break. She laid in the grass and fell asleep before her head hit the ground.

When she woke up, the sun was high overhead. She didn't bother trying to throw out her sense. Instead, she found a rise in the land and looked in every direction. There was no pursuit. She didn't question her good fortune. Perhaps Nameless didn't care she'd escaped? She knew it wasn't true, but it was the best explanation she had.

Moriko traveled by night and day. She slept as little as possible, seeking only to put as much distance between her and the People as she could. It was the end of summer and the days were hot. Often she had to get off her horse and walk beside it. But she stopped as little as possible. She knew she was covering ground much faster than she had going south. Now she had a purpose.

A half-moon passed, and Moriko knew she was close to the Southern Kingdom. She had found the foothills of the mountains, and now all she had to do was ride east until she found the Three Sisters. A handful of days, no more. It was just as well. She had been eating sparingly and hunting as much as possible, but even so, she was at the end of her food. In a few days she'd have to kill the horse and eat it.

When they came, they came from the mountains. Moriko was surprised. She had been looking to the south, but Nameless must have had birds sent to an outpost. There was only one place she would go. Moriko didn't hesitate. If she could see them, they would have seen her too. She dropped off the horse and sliced its throat open. Raw horsemeat wasn't her idea of a good meal, but she'd need the energy, and she couldn't hide on horseback. When they dropped into a depression she ran, heading south. She figured it was the last direction they'd expect her to go. She ran and ran, staying low, squatting in the grass when the dust came over the depression.

Moriko sat high enough that she could see them as they crested the horizon, but low enough only the sharpest eye could have seen her. When they came over the horizon, she knew they were hunters. Nameless didn't have so much disdain that he'd sent only regular warriors. There were five of them. The number seemed off to Moriko, but she couldn't put her finger on why. They rode easily on horseback, but they didn't follow any recognizable search pattern. They moved organically, covering the ground with the confidence of men who knew they could sense all the life around them.

Moriko didn't press her luck. She burrowed into the ground where she was as far as she could go. Evening was coming. It didn't feel like enough, but it was all the cover she was going to find. She would have to wait for evening. The only thing that kept her alive was her ability to hide herself from the sense.

That evening was one of the worst of her life. The hunters rode to and fro, not seeming to follow any pattern Moriko could follow or anticipate. Even though their movements seemed random, they covered the entire area, going back and forth multiple times. Eventually they gave up for the evening, setting up camp about two hundred paces from Moriko's hiding spot.

She spent the evening giving them a wide berth and walking north and east. She pushed as far as she dared, but as soon as the sun began to peek over the horizon, she dug in again. As the day rose, the hunters were on her trail again. They covered the ground around her, and Moriko wondered if they were playing with her. Perhaps they were able to track her, simply toying with her to keep themselves entertained. She forced herself to sleep, though she feared she'd wake up with a hunter standing above her.

Moriko slept fitfully, hunters sometimes passing within two dozen paces of her. When evening came they set up camp near her again, challenging her to work her way around them again. Between the lack of sleep and the fear, she was starting to lose touch with reality. If she didn't make a move soon, she wouldn't be in any condition to fight them.

Moriko could have gone around the camp again, but she suspected the result would be the same. She had either been lucky so far, or they were playing with her. Either way, she couldn't expect to reach the Three Kingdoms with the pursuit. She'd have to attack them. Fortunately, there was only a sliver of moon in the sky. Darkness would be her friend.

Moriko allowed herself to sleep for a while. She was exhausted from spending all day in fear and needed the rest. When she came to again, the moon was low in the western sky. It was maybe a watch or two until dawn would break. It was a good time to strike. The night had been quiet. If she was fortunate, they wouldn't expect her.

She glanced up through the long grass and saw their campfire still burning. She wasn't sure, but she thought she could make out the shadow of the hunter on watch. Once she got closer she'd be able to sense them clearly.

Moriko crawled through the grass, her lithe body trying not even to disturb the grass. Her tongue was dry, fear threatening to ruin her movement. Two hunters had almost killed her and Ryuu. Who was she to think she could attack five and live to tell about it? Terror stopped her in her tracks. She didn't see any other way, but this would get her killed just as surely.

She went deep inside of herself, focusing on her breath, focusing on her presence. There wasn't any way they could sense her. They would wake when she killed the first, but she could better the odds considerably if she could get one or two before they could act. It was as good a plan as any, and if she died, at least she would go out fighting.

Moriko resumed her crawl. She stopped ten paces away from the hunter she could now sense on watch. He was making a sound it took her a moment to identify. It was sniffing. The hunter was sniffing the air and was alarmed. Moriko hesitated. How was that even possible?

Off in the distance, something flashed brightly against Moriko's sense. She resisted the urge to spin around, knowing she wouldn't see anything in the dark. What had that been? It was as if someone strong had existed there for just a moment and then disappeared. She didn't have time to consider the question. Whatever it had been woke up the hunters in front of her, and there was a cry of alarm from the hunter on watch.

Moriko didn't panic. She sank even further into the ground, ready to spring at a moment's notice. But she knew she had gone from the hunter to the hunted.

The hunters all came to attention in just a few moments. The man on watch growled out something Moriko couldn't hear, but she could sense them forming a line and spreading out from their camp.

The line came Moriko's direction. She was in the grass, but two hunters would pass only a few paces from her. She stayed, still as a rock, as deep inside herself as was possible. The hunters were not quick. They moved deliberately, and Moriko was certain she'd be found. Terror held her in place as much as her will.

The line approached her, came even with her, and passed. Moriko's legs were burning, but she didn't dare move a single muscle. She took a shallow breath, hoping beyond hope they'd passed her for good. Then she heard the sniffing sound again. How could they possibly smell her? She couldn't smell anything besides prairie out here.

One of the hunters who had passed right next to her turned, curious about something. Moriko held her breath again, but she feared it wouldn't matter. She would be found. It was only a matter of time.

They took a step towards her, and something in her snapped. The fear erupted into anger, and it consumed her. She was more angry than she had ever been in her life. Even when she had been beaten at the monastery, she hadn't been this angry. She had worked so hard and had gotten so far, she wasn't going to give up now, not when she was only a few days away from the pass. If sneaking didn't work, there was always killing. She jumped to her feet, sword drawn in one smooth, arcing motion that took off the head of the hunter who had stopped only a pace away. One more step and she made another cut, killing a second hunter before they had time to react.

She thought about diving into the grass, but everyone was too close. Hiding was no longer an option. Too angry to give up, Moriko stood up defiantly, a lone nightblade in a circle of three hunters. She glanced around in surprise. Now that she was seeing them for the first time up close she saw they were boys. Two of them couldn't have seen more than sixteen cycles, although the third was a man older than Moriko. She cursed. She was being run to ground by hunters on a training run. They hadn't even had enough respect for her to send mature, seasoned warriors. Her joy at killing the first two diminished, but she didn't hesitate. She'd kill them all before the night was over.

The first boy attacked. He was unreasonably fast, but Moriko snapped and the world slowed down. She moved with grace and power, evading his cuts and returning hers in kind. They passed and passed, but Moriko wasn't given an opportunity to gain the upper hand. The other boy and the man moved in, and the battle was joined.

Even snapped and in the darkness, it was all Moriko could do to keep up with the strikes of the three hunters. She had thought it would be easy to defeat the boys, but each cut from them snapped that illusion in half. They were young, fast, and strong. What they lacked in experience they made up in enthusiasm, and any time Moriko sensed an opening, the older hunter was always there, blocking her strikes.

It was only Moriko's talent for hiding her presence that kept her alive. In the darkness of the night, the hunters couldn't sense what she was doing and were forced to rely on their sight. Moriko knew if she could have just a moment alone with any one of them the fight would be over.

She wasn't the only person getting frustrated. One of the boys struck at her with incredible force. She deflected the cut and moved inside his guard. She could sense the more experienced hunter coming to the boy's rescue. Moriko couldn't let it happen, not this time. She drove her elbow into the boy's stomach, knocking the wind out of him. Bending her legs, Moriko got underneath him and pushed forward, trying to get the two of them away from the center of the fight. The older hunter pursued and Moriko knew she only had a few moments before they were caught. The boy tried to stay on his feet, dizzied from the hits he'd taken. He'd regain his balance in a moment.

In the moment she had, Moriko let go of her sword with her left hand. The boy felt the shift and moved to strike, but in the one heartbeat, Moriko grabbed a throwing knife from her hip and stabbed it into his gut. Once, twice, five times, as fast as she could punch him with it.

Then the moment was over and the older hunter was upon them. Moriko stopped and turned. She let go of the knife and tried to bring her hand to her blade, but there wasn't enough time. The hunter's strike landed with tremendous force, knocking the blade straight out of Moriko's hands. It spun into the ground and Moriko was grabbing for a second knife. She felt the hunter's sword cut into her left shoulder, but she had no idea how deep it was. Despite the pain, Moriko grabbed a second knife with her left hand and thrust it under the hunter's chin.

As the hunter fell, Moriko sensed the attack of the final boy. He leapt in the air, certain of his killing strike. Moriko couldn't use her left arm, but she grabbed the blade from the older hunter and leapt at the boy. He wasn't expecting her attack, not realizing his master was dead. Moriko's cut was clean and the boy landed in a heap on the ground.

Moriko stood up just in time to sense the first young man pull her knife from his stomach and throw it at her. It was a weak throw, and Moriko caught it easily. She studied the young man, impressed by his courage. He was clearly dying, but hadn't given up. Moriko retrieved her sword and ended his life with one clean cut. It was what he deserved.

When her world snapped back into order, Moriko was standing over the bodies of all the hunters that had been after her. She smiled. It didn't matter to her that they were boys. She had won. She stared down at her sword, disgusted at the sight of blood on it. With a quick motion, she snapped it off the blade and found a clean piece of cloth from one of the hunters. She ripped it off his dead body and used it to clean her sword. She tossed the used rag onto the ground and looked around. The power of her blade was intoxicating. She had killed five hunters on her own. She hadn't even realized how strong she'd become.

Her sword taken care of, Moriko looked to her shoulder. She realized, as she looked down, that she had been cut several times. She examined her body. None of them were fatal. The shoulder was the worst, but even that cut had been more shallow than she'd thought. A day or two and it should be fine.

She looked around. She could see the camp of the hunters a little ways away. There would be plenty of food there. There were horses too. From here it was a sprint to the Three Sisters, and all that mattered was speed. Moriko was free. She started walking back to the camp, eager to eat.

When the shadow came up in front of her, she was too surprised to even react. She hadn't sensed anything at all. He was a giant of a man, and in the moment she had, Moriko flashed back to her memories of the other hunters she had faced back in the Three Kingdoms. This man was like them. She knew what had been off about five hunters. They always traveled in pairs. She wasn't given any time to rejoice about her discovery. His fist moved with inhuman speed, and Moriko's world went instantly black.

CHAPTER 27

The morning after the duel, Ryuu and Rei left the island without much fanfare. Many people had approached Ryuu after the fight, either to introduce themselves or to say goodbye. Ryuu had met a lot of blades, and remembered a few names, but he was saddened he didn't have the time to know them better. Most of his time had been spent with Tenchi or in training. Far too little of it had been spent getting to know the other inhabitants of the island, the thousands of others who shared his gift.

Tenchi and Shika were at the docks to bid them farewell. Ryuu thanked Tenchi sincerely for all the guidance. He still felt like there was much more on the island to learn, more secrets he hadn't uncovered, but he was called south. Moriko needed him.

His parting words with Shika were short. She wished him well.

"Like Tenchi, I also hope you return to us. But when you do, I won't let you defeat me again."

With a final wave they were off, Ryuu relaxing into the back of the ship for the trip back to the Three Kingdoms. He took one last glance at the island as they sailed away, but then pushed the memories out of his mind. It was time to move forward. He laid back and closed his eyes. Good rest would be hard to find once they were on the road.

They arrived at the Three Kingdoms without incident. Ryuu had spent almost all his time resting and relaxing, giving his body the break it needed after a season of grueling training. Rei was a different story altogether. She was excited by everything she saw and experienced. When Ryuu wasn't sleeping, he was busy answering more questions than he thought possible for a single person to have. Many of the questions were easy to answer, questions about the day-to-day behavior of those who lived in the kingdoms. But there was much he didn't know about history, politics or culture. Rei made him realize how much he didn't know about the Three Kingdoms. He had grown up in relative isolation.

They docked and Ryuu found the Southern Kingdom's embassy in Highgate. Flashing his letter from Lord Akira, he borrowed horses and supplies for the journey back. They wasted no time, Ryuu pushing them out of the city as soon as they had supplies. The disappointment on Rei's face was obvious, but Ryuu couldn't care less. He was here for one purpose only, to get back to Moriko. There would be time for Rei to be a tourist later in life. They rode hard for the first few days, maintaining the fastest pace the horses could keep up.

Eventually, Ryuu had to slow the pace, even though it pained him to do so. The horses were getting tired too fast. They kept moving at the fastest sustainable pace, but Ryuu wanted to do nothing more than to kick his horse into a full gallop until it collapsed from exhaustion. They were returning much faster than Ryuu had left, but it still wasn't fast enough for him. Tenchi's assessment of a full moon of travel didn't seem to be as far off as Ryuu had hoped.

Rei's stream of questions was constant, and Ryuu was grateful. Her enthusiasm kept him moving forward, kept him optimistic. It was hard to be around her and not wonder at the simple majesty of new places. Occasionally, Ryuu was able to insert one of his own questions, like one that had been bothering him the entire time he was on the island.

"If you agree with Shika so much about nightblades returning to the Three Kingdoms, why does Tenchi devote so much attention to you?"

Rei paused to consider the question, as though she had never thought of it. "It's not that I agree or disagree with either one of them. When you think about it, both of them want to return to the Three Kingdoms. Every blade wants to come back. Something about this land calls us home. They only disagree as to the timing."

Her answer gave Ryuu pause. He hadn't ever thought of it in that way. Her answer reminded him he still had a lot to learn about the blades. They viewed the world in a manner fundamentally different than he did.

The leagues passed under foot and hoof. There was conversation when possible, but there was also prolonged periods of silence, silence Ryuu appreciated. It wasn't that he didn't want to speak with Rei, but he had a lot on his mind, and travel was one of the few times he had to make decisions, to think his plans through. Tenchi's words to him before the duel had gotten under his skin. He'd never been talked down to like that, and it affected him more than he cared to admit.

When he wasn't answering Rei's questions, there was only one question running through his mind over and over again. What should he do next?

He had left the island with a clear purpose, to rescue Moriko, no matter what obstacles he faced. But as they traveled further south, his mind was filled with doubts, no longer as certain as he had been when he had first sensed her in danger.

Tenchi had been the spark. He had made Ryuu question his decisions, his motivations. His heart kept shouting that he needed to go rescue Moriko, but his mind kept whispering that he needed to think it through. The debate raged viciously in his mind, racking him with indecision.

His mind was a giant scale, weighing his feelings. He loved Moriko, and he had sworn to himself he would protect her. He felt responsible for the trouble she had found. If it hadn't been for him, she never would have agreed to go down to Azaria to scout. A part of him was convinced that if he had gotten her into this, it was his responsibility to get her out.

But there were whispers of discontent within his mind, a whisper that said he wasn't thinking clearly. The armies of the Southern Kingdom were being decimated, forced to retreat over and over again. He could influence the course of events there, but not if he traveled to Azaria to save Moriko. It was a choice between the Southern Kingdom and the woman he loved.

Ryuu didn't believe he could single-handedly change the course of a war, but he was certain he could save lives. If the Azarians were plotting to invade the kingdom, as his sense told him was happening, every life he saved would be a life that could stand against a much greater threat than the petty civil war currently raging. He worried saving Moriko would doom the kingdom.

During the ride, he often reflected on his conversations with Shigeru after Takako had been kidnapped. He had been adamant that he should rescue her. He had believed if it was in his power to save even one person, it was his responsibility to do so. Shigeru had seen the error of the thought, had suspected Ryuu's actions would have consequences far beyond what Ryuu could anticipate. He had warned Ryuu against it, but he had gone along in the end, sentencing himself to death. Ryuu wondered sometimes if Shigeru had somehow guessed how events would unfold, if he had gone forward knowing what was in store for him. Why had he allowed Ryuu to take the risk? It was a question Ryuu would never know the answer to.

Either way, Ryuu's decision had gotten Shigeru killed. Ryuu had accepted that responsibility. Was he making the same decision again, the same mistake? The first time he had sacrificed everything to go after one person. Now he was considering sacrificing the entire kingdom to save Moriko. The Great Cycle turned again, and Ryuu was as lost as when he'd been a child.

Every night Ryuu put his hands to the ground and threw out his sense, hoping he would gather some small piece of information that would make his path clear, make it so there was only one rational choice.

But every night the story was the same. The battle for the Southern Kingdom was coming to its inevitable conclusion. All of Akira's armies were retreating to the same point, and all of Tanak's armies were pursuing them. It would come down to a final battle in the eastern foothills. Terrain would be an advantage for the southern army, but the western army had more numbers. It would be a difficult victory for either side.

At the same time, Moriko was being hunted. He could sense her alone on the prairie, men circling around her, trying to find her. She was on the move, but it seemed like a small miracle she wasn't caught every evening when Ryuu threw out his sense. He kept expecting to sense her captured or dead. Every evening he breathed a deep sigh of relief when neither was true.

Ryuu had kept all his worries secret, but Rei wasn't fooled. There was no way for him to hide the complete distraction he was suffering from. She pestered him with questions until he broke down and told her the debate running through his mind.

She sat and listened to him explain both sides of his reasoning. She let him prattle on for longer than she should have, allowing him to reiterate several of his points. He concluded by shaking his head in misery. "I just don't know."

Rei laughed, her attitude reminding him a little of Tenchi. "Ryuu, you are a fool. If what you say is true, what you've sensed is accurate, Moriko doesn't need rescuing. If anything, the men who are chasing her need the help."

"They're very dangerous." Ryuu was about to warn her about underestimating them, but she interrupted.

"And you can't seem to see she is just as dangerous. If training against her allowed you to defeat me in the dark, I would bet she's one of the most dangerous nightblades in her own right. Don't let your own strength deceive you. Men," she scoffed, "always thinking they need to rescue us. It's women who are always rescuing the men."

Rei could see he was still disturbed, so she didn't say anything more on the subject, letting Ryuu ponder her words and their wisdom.

Ryuu still hadn't reached a decision, but either way, they kept moving south, making good time. Rei had never seen any geography other than that of the island, so the jagged and broken terrain of the Northern Kingdom was a delight to her, even though it slowed them down. They were riding through a crack in the ground, one of many that seemed to tear apart the landscape of the Northern Kingdom. It was as though the earth itself was splitting in half, sheer rock on either side of them, the path in front of them only wide enough for a single horse at a time. Ryuu rode in the lead, Rei behind.

He sensed the presence above them, tracking them ten paces above their path along the western ridge of rock. Ryuu brought his horse to a halt, Rei following suit behind him. They exchanged a glance and Rei shrugged her shoulders. Ryuu dismounted. He suspected an ambush, and he fought better off his horse than on. He could only sense one person. If a bandit was hoping to take them by surprise, he would be receiving his own soon enough. They waited. Then Ryuu felt the tendrils of the sense emanating from the person above. If he hadn't been so distracted by thoughts of Moriko, he would have noticed a long time ago. The warrior was strong.

The day was bright and sunny, one of the glory days near the end of summer. A shadow detached itself from the rocks above and dropped down in front of Ryuu, about ten paces away. Ryuu noted the grace with which the shadow moved. The landing was soft and controlled, indicating considerable strength and skill. He had a suspicion about who he was about to meet.

Rei confirmed it. "Renzo." She dismounted and stepped to Ryuu's side.

Renzo bowed. "It's been a long time, Rei."

Ryuu could sense Rei tense. "What are you doing here?"

"It's none of your concern. I'm here to kill the boy. Stay out of my way. We'll talk when I'm done."

Rei stepped forward, blocking Ryuu with her body. "I can't let you kill him."

Renzo stood up straighter, staring at Rei. "You would fight me for him?"

Rei nodded.

Renzo considered for a moment, then lowered his center of gravity, preparing to strike. Ryuu held his blade, prepared to draw. Rei's shoulders slumped, as though she had hoped to stop him without a fight. For a moment they stood there, a tableau on the edge of violence.

"I'll give you one last warning, Rei. You know your tricks won't work on me. I don't want to hurt you, but I will to get to him. He has to die."

Renzo twitched, and Ryuu fell into his combat trance, finding the energy surrounding him and dropping into it. He could sense Renzo's attack coming. Renzo's speed was unbelievable, but Rei was there, drawing her blade and in his way.

Ryuu watched, horrified at being unable to do anything fast enough to change the outcome. Rei flashed her energy, trying to blind Renzo's sense, but it was no use. She didn't have the power to surpass Renzo's will and skill with the sense. Renzo ducked underneath her weak cut and drove his fist into her stomach. She collapsed and Renzo drew against Ryuu.

Steel met steel in the narrow confines of the crevice. The crack was narrow, and both Renzo and Ryuu had to be careful not to have their strikes blocked by the rock walls surrounding them. They cut and spun around one another, their cuts and blocks forced close to their bodies by the tight space.

It was Renzo who took to the walls. He used the walls as vertical ground for a moment at a time, adding an extra dimension to the fight. He would push off and strike from above, then bounce off the other wall and strike from the other direction. Ryuu had never fought in a crevice like this, never seen anyone use walls to plant and kick off of. His sense and his reflexes kept him alive, but Renzo had the upper hand as steel flashed closer and closer to him.

Rei struggled back to her feet. Ryuu wanted to shout at her, tell her to stay down, but he didn't have the time to give a warning. He couldn't tear his attention from Renzo, not even for a moment. Renzo's strikes were coming from all different directions, directions no fighter on flat ground would have to consider.

Ryuu took to the walls. He wasn't as experienced as Renzo, but he was young and agile, and the dance of swords was bright in the light of the sun.

Ryuu could sense Rei looking for an opening, but she didn't have the power and speed of the two nightblades in combat.

Ryuu could sense it wasn't going to stop her though. She was determined to stop their fight.

She thought she saw an opening and leapt for it. Both Ryuu and Renzo sensed the approach. Ryuu stepped back, giving ground in the hope she'd have space to pass through their battle safely. Renzo tried to cut at Ryuu as he retreated, coming just a hair's width away from cutting Rei's neck. He stepped back as well, torn between his desire to kill Ryuu and his desire to leave Rei unharmed.

Rei attacked Renzo, but she was too slow. Renzo struck her twice with the flat part of his blade, but she kept on coming. Finally, his fist landed against her cheek in a blow that sent her reeling backwards.

Renzo shouted a curse. Ryuu held his stance, waiting to see what would happen. Renzo wasn't faster than him, but his experience was greater. Ryuu wasn't sure he'd win in a straight fight, but in this tiny space, Rei would continue to get between them, and Renzo clearly didn't want to kill her. Renzo seemed torn between attacking and walking away. He stood up and sheathed his sword.

"It's not over, Ryuu. Your days, and Lord Akira's, are numbered." He bent over Rei, ignoring her feeble attempts to slap him away. "If you get in my way again, I will kill you."

With a final glance, Renzo turned and walked away, leaving a confused Ryuu to care for Rei's injuries.

That evening, Ryuu came to a decision. He wouldn't go after Moriko, as much as he wanted to. She was getting closer to the Southern Kingdom, but Ryuu also felt the hunters coming down out of the mountains to intercept her. Either way, he was still a half-moon of travel away, no matter how fast he rode. As he looked on Rei sleeping, her words ran through his mind. He knew Moriko had gotten stronger, could sense she had somehow changed, somehow grown.

He could do more good if he stayed in the Southern Kingdom, helping Akira decide what was next. He needed to protect Akira. If he didn't, Renzo would kill him and the Three Kingdoms would descend into chaos. Ryuu could still sense the Azarians moving north, although he wasn't sure they'd get to the pass before it snowed. He wasn't sure they were an invasion force either, but he couldn't imagine what else they would be.

Akira's need was greater, and the odds of Ryuu getting to Moriko in time were slim. His decision angered him, but it was right. He held back his tears of frustration, hoping Moriko would survive.

His decision made, the rest of the journey passed quickly. Ryuu appreciated not being torn apart by indecision. He liked having a path laid out in front of him, a straight way forward.

His letter from Akira opened many doors. At the border of the Northern and Southern Kingdom they were given fresh horses, and they pushed them as hard as the beasts could go. Ryuu wasn't familiar with the eastern side of the Southern Kingdom, but the paths were worn and well marked. Ryuu worried they might run into some western troops, but none had made it that far yet.

When they reached the main encampment they were directed to a supply tent near Akira's command tent. Ryuu was becoming familiar with the routine. Akira would see them at night. He was the ruler of an entire kingdom at war. Ryuu had to remind himself he was fortunate to see Akira with the ease he did.

Ryuu took the time to relax. Rei was fascinated by everything around her, and he could feel her throwing out her sense in an effort to learn more of what was happening. There were more people here than on the whole of the island. He smiled to himself and laid his head down on the ground, intending only to rest his eyes. Instead, he fell asleep.

He awoke to Rei moving towards him. Despite his time of relative safety on the island, Ryuu never lost his ability to use the sense while he was sleeping. It wasn't foolproof, but it was much better than sleeping without knowing what was happening around him. Rei startled at how quickly he came awake.

"I'm sorry. The sun has gone down, and I figured you would want to be awake to go meet the Lord of the Southern Kingdom."

Ryuu shook the sleep from his eyes. "You're probably right. I should clean up." His eyes took in Rei, her dirty hair and face and clothes. It was remarkable you could still see her beauty through all the grime. "You probably should too, although we'll have to have water brought here. Akira won't want us wandering around camp."

Rei raised an eyebrow. "I'm not shy."

Ryuu poked his head outside the tent and asked the guard to bring them water. Ryuu could never fault the efficiency of Akira's troops. Water was in their tent almost as soon as Ryuu stepped back into the tent. There wasn't any doubt Akira had some of the best trained troops in the Three Kingdoms.

Rei shed her clothes without hesitation, and Ryuu couldn't help but let his eyes be drawn to her. Like Moriko, she was lithe and strong, but unlike Moriko, her body wasn't covered in scars. It was a work of flawless perfection. It didn't help that Rei seemed to be flaunting it at him. A fierce desire awoke in him, and it occurred to him that Moriko was a very long ways away. He knew Rei liked him, but he believed she liked the power he represented more than she liked him.

He pushed the thoughts out of his mind and splashed water over his face, scrubbing away the dirt that he could. He soaked his hair and wiped every nook and cranny he could find. It was cold, but he felt better than he had in almost half a moon. Being clean made the rest of life much more bearable.

The summons came just as they were finishing. They both dried themselves, changed into cleaner clothes, and followed their escort to Akira's tent. It wasn't hard to find, being the largest tent in the center of the ring.

The first thing Ryuu noticed in the tent was Akira. When he had left the Lord, Akira had looked like the weight of the world was on his shoulders. Now, Akira stood tall and straight, determined. His kingdom was on the brink of annihilation, but he stood firm. Akira looked noble. Ryuu felt a surge of respect for the man. Akira was a leader, a man who would inspire others. Ryuu might defeat him in combat, but Ryuu wasn't sure that made him the stronger person.

Rei drew up short in a deep bow, catching the eye of Akira. Ryuu stifled the urge to laugh. He had been deliberate about not showing Akira too much respect, no matter how he felt. He wanted his position to be clear.

A hint of a grin broke out on Akira's face. "Ryuu, every time I see you, you seem to be in the company of some new beautiful woman. My father warned me I would be cursed with beautiful women as the Lord of the Kingdom, but I think your gifts have brought you better women than I had ever dreamed of."

Rei blushed, and Ryuu could see she was pleased by the compliment.

A quick thought passed through Ryuu's mind. He hadn't ever heard of Akira with any women, or any men for that matter. His life seemed dedicated to the kingdom. Ryuu glanced over at Rei and extended his sense. It only took him a moment to understand. She liked him.

"Akira."

Rei looked shocked at the cavalier attitude with which Ryuu dealt with the Lord.

Akira saw her discomfort and waved it away. "You can stop bowing. Do not worry. Ryuu and I have a unique relationship, and I don't hold to titles with him, though I don't think I'm bold enough to call him my friend yet."

Ryuu provided the introductions. "Akira, this is Rei, Rei, Akira."

Rei jaw almost dropped. It was obvious she didn't believe either of them.

Akira couldn't help but poke more fun at her. "Didn't he tell you that the first time we met he held my own blade to my throat and threatened to kill me?"

Rei's eyes seemed to roll back in her head, and Akira just laughed.

"Thank you, Ryuu, for if nothing else, you have brought me a little joy today."

Ryuu nodded. "How goes the campaign?"

Akira looked down at the maps spread below him. Ryuu could see the figurines representing troops scattered across the maps, but they did nothing but confirm what he already knew through his sense. The final battle would be upon them soon. Probably within a quarter moon, depending on how fast the troops reached their position.

"Tanak's forces move in for the kill. We have the high ground and much better position, but they outnumber us almost two to one at this point. It will be a bloody battle."

Akira looked up. "I have many questions for you, Ryuu. I suspect from the way Rei holds herself, she is every bit as dangerous as she is gorgeous. Someday I would like to hear your story, but for now my only question is why you are here."

"I've come to help."

Akira almost leapt with excitement. "Does that mean you'll fight for us?"

Ryuu shook his head. "Not in the way you hope. If I was to enter the battle, dozens, if not hundreds, would fall to my blade. I don't know if I could live with that decision, and I won't do it."

"Then how will you help, if not to lend me your steel?"

Ryuu held up two fingers. "I'll do two things for you. The first is that I can use the sense to tell where people are." He pointed at Akira's map. "Between your intelligence and my sense, I can give you the most accurate information about enemy troop movements. It will give you a distinct advantage. Second, there is a nightblade in Tanak's camp. His name is Renzo."

Akira laughed, and Ryuu stopped, surprised.

"Renzo is not a nightblade. Trust me on that one. The monks tested him right in front of me."

Ryuu glanced at Rei quizzically. Rei spoke up. "We grew up together, my Lord, and I can assure you, he is a nightblade."

Ryuu and Akira both paused as they considered the implications. Either Renzo had fooled the monks somehow, or the monks were involved. It opened up doors that Ryuu was afraid to open, worried he'd find nightmares on the other side. He pushed the thoughts aside. Whatever had happened, it didn't change Ryuu's attitude.

Ryuu spoke into the silence. "Don't worry, Akira. I'll kill him for you."

CHAPTER 28

When Moriko woke up, she was tied to a horse, so tight there was no chance of her moving, much less falling off. It was enough to rekindle Moriko's dislike of the beasts. She tested her movement, and the answer was disappointing. Her bindings had no slack at all. The final hunter wasn't taking any chances.

Moriko hurt. The cuts she'd received from the battle had crusted over. She'd hoped to clean them. Her head throbbed where she'd been struck. She'd seen the hunter's fist, but it felt like she'd been hit by a tree. Every jostle of the horse made her want to both throw up and kill someone.

They were traveling east, much to Moriko's surprise. By her reckoning, they were actually getting closer to the Three Sisters. All she had to do was escape, but that was going to be impossible. Even after she awoke, the hunter didn't untie her. He'd stop every couple of watches to give her some water and check that her bindings were still tight. The one evening they camped, he staked her to the ground so she still couldn't move a muscle. He had watched her kill his brethren and wasn't going to give her a chance to move.

She sensed him before she could see him, tied to the horse as she was. There were several of them, but he stood out among them all. Nameless. His power was beyond belief. There wasn't any mistaking him. She went limp as they got closer.

When they entered camp, the hunter who had captured Moriko cut her bindings. She didn't entertain any thoughts of escaping. She counted ten hunters in the circle around them, plus Nameless.

Nameless stood in front of her, and once again Moriko was surprised by the effortless strength and grace with which he carried himself. It was the first time she had seen the chief of the Azarians in full daylight, and she was impressed by what she saw. In the heat of the day he wore only a loose tunic and leggings. He was a tall man, a head and more above Moriko. At first glance he appeared heavy-set, but Moriko realized it was an illusion. He was a large man, but there wasn't any fat on his body. His arms were bigger than Moriko's thighs.

In a way, Nameless reminded her a bit of Orochi. Both of them were intimidating, both larger than average. But Orochi had been possessed by a calm Nameless did not possess. Orochi had been focused on control. Nameless was focused on strength and power, barely contained in his massive body. He paced up and down, and even when he stood still he was tapping his foot and scanning the horizon. Nameless would never know peace, but he knew power.

The hunter who had captured her gave what Moriko assumed was a short report. They spoke in Azarian, and Moriko couldn't pick up a hint of what they were saying. She stood as still as possible, focusing on her breathing, trying to get her mind to think of any way to get as far away from Nameless as possible. Try as she might, she couldn't get coherent thoughts through her mind.

Nameless turned to her after he had finished speaking with the hunter. "This man claims you fought with a skill they were not prepared for. He says you killed four of the young men who were sent to retrieve you and their mentor. They were young, but they were blooded. I am not one to doubt my men, but his story defies belief. Is it true?"

Moriko nodded. She saw no reason to deny what had happened. She was also too afraid to speak. His power was awesome, burning into her sense like she was standing too close to a fire.

Nameless paced back and forth, and if Moriko could guess, she figured he was deciding what to do. He spoke. "I did not know the Three Kingdoms had warriors of your skill. Let me tell you a story. Once, some time ago, I sent two of our hunters to kill two warriors in the Three Kingdoms. Hunters, you see, always hunt in pairs. One to track and one to kill. I sent only two, because why would I have need to send four? Four of my men could destroy an army of yours. Even two seemed too many, but it was the fewest I could send, and I knew that by killing these two warriors, no one would have the slightest chance of standing in my way. And then one of them appears at my Gathering with an offer of peace."

Nameless paused, and Moriko wondered where this was going. "They all said that of the two, it was the man who was stronger, the one who can cut the wind with his blade. But now I think they lied, or were deceived. I think it is you who is the dangerous one."

Moriko felt a perverse pride at being honored by her enemy. But she didn't know how to respond.

He smiled. "You are a brave warrior, and I will grant you a warrior's end. Tomorrow morning we shall duel." His judgment pronounced, he turned to go back into his tent. There were looks of shock around the circle of hunters.

Moriko was also surprised. "Why not just kill me?"

"You are the strongest warrior of the Southern Kingdom. I am the strongest warrior of my people. When we meet tomorrow morning, it will be as though the war has already begun. If you win, you can save the Three Kingdoms. If you lose, it will be a good omen for my army. It is the way a warrior should die."

Moriko understood then he was honoring her. She bowed slightly to him in response to his offer.

He turned his head as he was lifting the flap of his tent. "Tonight, all your bindings will be cut. No one will guard your tent. You are welcome to try to escape. But if you do, my hunters will pursue you with a fury you haven't yet experienced. You will die a coward. No more boys, now that I know your skill. If you stay, you will be fed and well rested. You must be at your best tomorrow. When the sun rises, you will fall before me in battle and I will take your head in one clean cut. You should be honored. I have not drawn my sword for some time in combat."

Nameless went into his tent without another word. Moriko's mind was racing. Neither option sounded appealing. Either way, it sounded like tomorrow morning was the last sunrise she would ever see.

The evening crawled along, content to take its time. Moriko was fine with it. She was convinced she was going to die the next day. She'd give him everything she got, but his power was beyond her comprehension. It was more than anyone should possess. It was too much. She knew she was going to die, and there was a lot to think about.

There was a part of her that was angry. She and Ryuu had never asked to be brought into this conflict. If they'd been left alone, they would have stayed away from it all. Moriko didn't want any part of politics or war. All she wanted was to live and be left alone, but fate kept wrapping her in its cruel embrace. As fascinating as Azaria was, it wasn't anything compared to a quiet night looking at the stars with Ryuu.

She was angry at him too. She knew they had made the decision together, but how could he have let her go? What happened to him after they separated? She wondered if he'd ever made it to the island, and if he did, what he had found there.

With the thoughts of Ryuu came sorrow. She'd never get to find out what he had discovered on the island, or if the island existed at all. She'd never be held by him again.

But she was strong. Stronger than she'd ever been. Maybe even stronger than Ryuu. She had killed five hunters on her own in the prairie. Perhaps the Azarians were right. Maybe it was all about strength. Strength was the ability to exert your will on the world.

Moriko sat through the evening, thoughts rushing through her head. Every time she tried to hold one, it slipped away, draining through her mental grasp. But as the evening began to fade, she felt at ease. Her life had been far from perfect, but it had held beautiful moments too. Tomorrow she would fight with everything she had, and if she lost, so be it. She was ready.

Stepping from the tent, Moriko was greeted by a blood-red morning sky. She shook her head gently. It seemed appropriate, considering what lay in store. She would miss Ryuu.

Moriko went through her morning routine, holding herself back. It was the first time she practiced since she had met Kalden over a moon ago. It was freeing. The muscles in her body remembered every move, every strike, and she moved with a practiced grace. Her shoulder was sore where it had been cut, but it was functional. She ached in a dozen different places. It had been a hard moon. But she was as ready as she'd get.

She sensed Nameless behind her, but she paid him no mind until she was finished. When she was done, she turned around to look at him. The appreciation was evident in his eyes.

"Among our people, women fight as our men do, but never have I seen a woman with such skill. Your practice is beautiful."

Moriko lowered her eyes at the comment. She wished she wasn't so proud of the approval she received. "Thank you."

"Are you prepared?"

A simple question, but one that spelled her death. She nodded, not trusting herself to speak with dignity. The fear was catching in her throat.

"Very well." Nameless barked something out in Azarian, and all the hunters gathered around her, forming a loose circle about twenty paces wide. They were evenly spaced out, and although Moriko knew they were only observers in this battle, they were alert and ready to prevent her escape.

Moriko drew her sword and took in a deep breath. As Nameless drew his own blade, Moriko felt her mind settle. Cycles of training took over. Everything external fell away, her focus on his body and the point of his blade. She was terrified, but she no longer felt it. Her fear had been locked in a cage, an observer like the hunters around her. She didn't suppress her presence. Although she knew Nameless would be aware of her ability, if she could utilize it in a key moment of their battle, it might turn the tide in her favor.

Nameless, confident, didn't hesitate to come in for the first cuts. Moriko deflected them easily, knowing they were tests. Nameless wanted to know her strength. She feinted, but Nameless didn't buy it. He slapped it away almost carelessly.

They retreated a pace. Nameless judged her for a moment and leapt to the attack. This time he wasn't testing. His cuts were true and fast, and it took Moriko all her skill to block them. She was moving backwards, giving him ground, approaching the edge of the circle. Moriko focused her thoughts and snapped, Nameless' blade slowed down, her own cuts came faster. The tide of the battle turned, and Moriko dared to hope that she could win this fight. Back and back they moved, passing each other with speed Moriko had once only dreamed of.

Nameless unleashed a flurry of cuts that drove Moriko backwards, but as soon as she had a moment of freedom she launched herself at him, low. She was much smaller than him, and although he was fast, she wanted to bring the fight down to the ground. Her blade flashed at his shins, ankles, and thighs, and Nameless was forced to give up ground, even faster than Moriko had lost it. His blocks were awkward as he tried to protect parts of his body he wasn't used to having attacked.

Moriko drove Nameless to the edge of the circle with her low cuts. Without room to maneuver, he leapt in the air, and Moriko's heart leapt with joy. Once you committed to an attack in the air, you were easy to defeat. Once committed, it was hard to change your angle of attack, and a quick opponent would make short work of you.

But Nameless didn't attack. He kept his sword low, using the energy from his jump to strongly deflect one of her strikes. She struck hard to stay on the offensive, but he'd gained the smallest opening, and his sword snapped forward with power Moriko wasn't prepared for. She tumbled backwards, rolling to her feet before he could take advantage of his strike.

They met again in the center of the circle, and again Nameless gained the upper hand. It wasn't much, but every cut of his was just a little faster, each deflection a little stronger. It was barely enough to notice, but in a battle this close even the width of a hair could make all the difference.

They broke apart, and Moriko took the opportunity to study him. She was pleased to see he was cut, more than once. She was sure she was bleeding too, but she couldn't feel it. The silence from the surrounding hunters was appreciative. He came again, faster than before. Moriko couldn't believe his speed. How could a man so large move so fast? She had never faced anyone so quick and so strong.

Moriko gave up ground again, and no matter what techniques she tried, she couldn't regain control of the battle. She pulled out her last trick. In between strikes she went inside of herself, focusing all her energy. It was hard to suppress her presence while in the middle of combat, but sometimes she could make it work.

It worked this time. Nameless, stripped of his ability to see where she was going to be, faltered and was driven back. Again, Moriko thought she could win. The point of her blade found his flesh before he could block. It wasn't fatal, but it had to hurt. She moved like the night, invisible and deadly. She felt strong. There was no warning for what happened next.

Nameless exploded, his body and limbs a blur of speed. Moriko, invisible as she was to his sense, couldn't move fast enough to defend herself. She blocked one cut after the other, barely getting his sword away from her body. Even with all her skills, it was everything she could do just to stay alive. She could sense his blows coming, but even with the sense, she wasn't physically fast enough to block what was happening to her. She couldn't believe it. The whole advantage of the sense was to know what your opponent would do before they acted. Nameless was just too fast.

Moriko's defense could only last so long. Finally, she found herself out of position, and Nameless' giant foot found her exposed stomach. Moriko tumbled backwards, rolling painfully back to her feet. She tried to stand up but doubled over in pain. She felt like her guts had been wrapped around her spine. Slowly, she struggled back up to standing. She had no hope of winning after a blow like that. Her body would never physically react quick enough.

Moriko's eyes darted around, searching for some option, some escape. Nameless approached her, confident in his victory. Moriko didn't see any escape, but she did see admiration in the eyes of the hunters. At least she'd made a show of her death. And she thought she'd been so close. She'd never expected he had such a reserve left. She considered her options. She could let him inside her guard, try to kill him after he'd gotten in his fatal blow. It was a technique Ryuu had taught her, the last technique he had learned from his master, Shigeru. Unfortunately, she didn't think she'd be fast enough. With his speed, he'd have plenty of time to dodge or block.

She settled into her stance. If the outcome wasn't in question, all that was left to do was all she could. With her ability to disguise her movements, attacking was the best defense. She darted forward with all the speed she had left. For a few passes it was even, but she couldn't maintain her previous effort. Her attacks slowed, and finally she gave Nameless a moment of freedom. In that fraction of a moment, he switched onto the offensive, and Moriko was driven back, cut after cut appearing on her skin.

Anger swept over her. To have figured out so much of her powers, and to die at this man's hands, was infuriating. She was as good as Ryuu, but it wasn't good enough.

It was only a matter of time. She kept his blade mostly away from her, but she left herself open to his brutal fist, which sent her crashing down to the ground again. Before she could get up, his booted foot was in her stomach, kicking her up into the air and back into the ground. She dropped her sword as she slammed into the earth, choking on dust and blood.

He spoke loudly in Azarian. Moriko managed to open her eyes, just a squint through the pain, to see him pointing at her, gesticulating wildly. She cursed. There was some laughter as Nameless picked her up by her hair. Another solid punch sent her folded down onto the ground, every hint of air shoved violently out of her lungs.

Moriko reached out and grabbed her sword before his foot caught her again. She managed to hold on to it, but it was a meaningless victory. She didn't have the speed or strength to use it. Moriko went deep inside herself as Nameless continued his beating. He had promised her a clean death, but it was forgotten in his passion to demonstrate the weakness of the Three Kingdoms.

Her mind flashed back to the monastery she had grown up in. There she had been whipped nearly to death. Her body would always bear the scars of that experience. This was worse. But inside herself, she tried to push away the pain. Her world was blackness and stars, and at the center was one small pinprick of light. The light that refused to give up, the light that burned wi

She couldn't open her eyes, but her sense was alive and well. She was kicked around like a dog, finally falling near the edge of the circle. She could sense all eyes on her, the wind blowing through the tall grass, the horses about twenty paces away.

She stayed deep within, focusing on her desire to live. There couldn't be any intention. Nothing that would give herself away. He came towards her. He was wary, but he couldn't sense her. All his instincts, all his training, told him he was approaching a woman who might as well have been dead.

Inside, Moriko was focusing on her last piece of energy, the ember that wouldn't die. She stoked it into a raging furnace, contained within the steel walls of her will.

Moriko sensed him step next to her and bring his foot back for the kick. In that moment, when his foot came back, and he was balanced precariously, she struck. She cut down with her sword from above her head. It was a fast strike that he just managed to dodge. Moriko had hoped to cut off a foot, but if she couldn't, so be it. He was still off balance.

She twisted and lunged from her position on the ground, feeling her sword pierce the flesh of his stomach. Only then did she dare to open her eyes. It wasn't necessarily a mortal wound, but it was deep. She pulled out her sword, twisting as she did.

What happened next happened fast. The hunters had been lax, sure of their leader's victory. She broke out of the circle. It was only a matter of moments, but it gave her the lead on her captors. She ran to the horses, slicing through their ties with one stroke of her sword. She leapt on a horse, awkwardly got her feet into position, and kicked it into motion, yelling at the other horses as she did.

As she galloped away, she risked a small glance back. Confusion reigned behind her. Several of the hunters were kneeling next to Nameless, trying to make sure his wounds weren't fatal. She hoped he would die, but couldn't bring herself to believe it. He was too strong, and the blade hadn't cut deeply enough for it to be fatal. She'd missed the vital organs.

Other hunters were working on gathering their horses. Moriko had succeeded in spooking them, but not much. They were being rounded up quickly and efficiently. She hadn't bought herself much time, but they didn't seem to be in too much of a hurry to come chasing after her. She thought for a moment that she might get away, but then she remembered that she had become a symbol to the hunters, an omen for their invasion.

It wasn't that they weren't going to chase her. They were hunters. They didn't need to hurry after their prey.

CHAPTER 29

The next few days were busy ones for both Ryuu and Rei. For Ryuu, the focus was on training. He wasn't sure he was better than Renzo. In their short confrontation, Ryuu had felt evenly matched with him, but Renzo's experience gave him an edge. Ryuu had been lucky that Rei had been with him and Renzo had been unwilling to kill her. If not for her, he might not be alive.

So Ryuu trained from the time the sun came up to the time it went down. They cleared out their supply tent, unwilling to let anyone in camp observe their training. With wooden blades they came at each other time and time again, but Ryuu wasn't getting stronger, not enough.

It was Rei who had the idea on the third day of their training. "You know Tenchi's attack from back on the island, the one you couldn't block?"

Ryuu nodded.

"You could try to teach yourself that one. I know for a fact Renzo doesn't know it, and it may give you the edge you need to beat him."

"How could you know that?"

"Because I asked around after your duel with Tenchi. I'd never seen the attack, so I asked some of the other elders who trained with Tenchi and Renzo. No one had ever seen it. You're the first person to have drawn it out of him."

Ryuu nodded. It was a good idea, although he wasn't sure how he would go about learning it. He started by trying to piece together what he did know of the technique. It was only good against people who were sense-gifted, so it had something to do with intent and action. Somehow, Tenchi had intended to strike in all directions. It had thrown off Ryuu's sense, but only one of the strikes was the real strike.

He and Rei practiced, over and over. All around them the camp prepared for war. The men drilled, and the sound of practice swords filled the air. There was a nervousness and a fear in the air pushing Ryuu to train more diligently. He struck and Rei told him how she had sensed his attack. Over and over they repeated the process, neither of them willing to give up, even though Ryuu's progress was incremental at best.

At night, Akira summoned the two of them, and they stayed up late and talked. Ryuu told him about the Azarians moving north, but mostly they just talked. Ryuu came to realize that Akira used them to bounce ideas off of. He trusted their opinions. Mostly Ryuu realized Akira just wanted to spend time with Rei. Ryuu thought it had become a strange world.

Rei didn't train with the same intensity Ryuu did. The battle was not her own, and she was considering leaving before the final battle was joined. Ryuu was disappointed, but he understood.

He had gotten used to Rei's companionship, and he was grateful she had raised his spirits.

At night though, when Rei thought Ryuu was asleep, she would leave the tent and go to visit Akira. The first night Ryuu sensed what the two of them did. He was surprised that he wasn't surprised. A nightblade and a Lord. That was breaking the treaty in just about every way. There was a pang of jealousy, but Ryuu pushed it aside. Rei was an adult and could do as she pleased. As attractive as she was, Ryuu was still in love with Moriko.

After the first night he didn't try to sense her when she left. It seemed rude. One morning she came back after he was awake again, and their eyes met. He knew where she'd been, and she knew that he knew, but they never spoke of it. There wasn't any need, and Ryuu didn't judge. So long as she trained with him, helping him develop Tenchi's technique, he was content.

For Ryuu, it was strange how quiet his life was when all around him the world was spinning out of control. His last few days had been a constant cycle of training and rest, preparation for his inevitable confrontation with Renzo. Rei told Ryuu that sometimes it felt like there were multiple attacks coming, just like Tenchi's attack. It wasn't much, but it would have to be enough. As Ryuu looked out on the scene before him, he was sure he wouldn't have much longer to practice. He had been in the calm before the storm, but the storm was coming, and it was looking to break them all.

Ryuu stood on top of a ridgeline looking down at the valley below. Below him sat both of Tanak's armies, spread out for a league in either direction. Behind him sat Akira's own armies, victors in their previous engagement, but much smaller than the camp below. Between them were rolling hills. Akira's men held the higher ground, but there were so many of Tanak's men. Ryuu had never been able to look down on a camp like this, and he was astounded by the sight.

Tanak's camp was a city unto itself. The smoke from the fires was oppressive, the wind blowing it into Akira's camps. The sound of men and horses carried clear to Ryuu's ears, and it was loud, even at this distance. Ryuu glanced behind him and measured the size of Akira's camp. It was smaller, but still large. He couldn't imagine what it would be like when these two armies met.

Ryuu had fought multiple opponents in his life, but he'd never been a part of organized warfare. He had a new respect for Mashiro and Makoto. There wasn't any way he could manage or lead an army to victory. It was a skill beyond his grasp. He held on to his sword. Killing was his talent.

Ryuu didn't want the battle to happen. He knew there was no way the battle would be anything less than devastating for both sides, but both sides were set. Ryuu had suggested Akira propose a duel for the kingdoms. Ryuu would fight for the Southern Kingdom. He had little doubt Renzo would fight for the Western Kingdom. Akira had considered it for a moment and then laughed. He said it was tempting, but he wasn't going to trust the fate of his kingdom to a single duel.

Everything Ryuu saw screamed waste. He thought back to the last time he had tried using his sense at a distance, remembering the experience of the Azarian army moving north. He wanted to shout at Akira, let him know that army, with the power at the heart of it, was the real enemy. Both he and Rei had tried, but Akira wouldn't change his plans. They had held the pass for many cycles, and he wasn't worried. He believed Toro could hold the pass without a problem.

Ryuu wanted to share in Akira's belief, but every time he sensed the Azarians, he couldn't help but think there was something more at play here. Akira had dismissed his notions.

Ryuu sighed and turned to go back to his tent. The battle would begin tomorrow, and the valley would be bathed in blood.

That night, he and Rei were summoned to Akira's tent. Ryuu wasn't surprised. He assumed Akira would want to discuss their plans for the upcoming battle.

When they entered, Ryuu saw Akira was in conference with his two generals. He and Rei waited quietly while they finished their final details. The two generals left, giving the two nightblades a look Ryuu couldn't place. It was somewhere between anger and disgust.

Akira ushered them in. He looked tired, but his back was straight and he spoke with authority. "It's good to see both of you." The comment seemed to be directed more at Rei than at Ryuu, but he shrugged it off.

"I've asked you here because I'd like your advice."

The three of them sat down. Ryuu was intrigued. It wasn't like Akira to ask for advice, not from him.

"There's been news from the pass."

Ryuu started. Ever since he'd made the decision to meet up with Akira instead of traveling further south, he had been far less diligent about tracking Moriko in the evenings. Part of it was that he was exhausted after his days of training. Another part was that he wanted to stay focused on the problems in front of him, but the biggest part was that he was scared. He wasn't going to save Moriko, and he feared that one day he would try to sense her and she'd be gone. It was easier not to know.

"Is it Moriko?" He dared to hope she had made it back safely.

Akira shook his head. "I'm sorry, Ryuu. She traveled into Azaria, but we never heard from her again."

Ryuu's head dropped. Tonight, if he got the chance, he would search for her. He had to know.

Akira continued. "I received a letter from Toro today. Ryuu, your abilities did not lie to you. There is a tremendous mass of Azarians moving north to the pass. Toro's scouts found them just a few days ago. There are more Azarians marching north than both Tanak and I have in the valley right now."

"What are you going to do?"

Akira paced back and forth. "My first instinct is to fight this battle and decimate Tanak. Then I can form up all the men from both kingdoms and press them into the pass. We should be able to hold it until the snow comes, at least. Then maybe I can speak with Sen and we can cooperate. We've never faced a force this large, this strong before. We'll need all the help we can get."

Ryuu shook his head. "If you fight here, you'll decimate both your own troops and Tanak's. You won't have many people left over to move down to the pass. You know that."

Akira shrugged. "So what do you propose?"

"Surrender."

Akira's blade came out and cut towards Ryuu. He sensed it coming and stepped out of the way. Akira slashed wildly, but he never came close to Ryuu. His anger spent, he stared daggers into Ryuu. "Don't ever tell me to surrender my kingdom!"

Ryuu stepped right into his face. Akira raised his blade, but Ryuu knocked it from his hands. He slapped Akira hard across the face. He heard Rei gasp behind him. "Don't be foolish! You're not just talking about too many Azarians. They're going to have hunters in that pack. Maybe not many, but enough to make their numbers seem even more powerful. The only way these kingdoms will have any chance at all is if you work with the other Lords, not fight against them. Swallow your foolish pride and surrender your kingdom so you can save it."

Akira stepped back as Ryuu released him. After the shock of what had happened had passed, he smiled. "You certainly don't feel the need to be on my good side, do you?"

Ryuu didn't dignify the question with a response.

A silence stretched between the three of them. Ryuu didn't know what else to say. If Akira didn't want to listen to his advice, there was little else he could do. When tomorrow's battle came, he would try to save as many lives as possible.

Ryuu was just about to offer Akira encouragement when he sensed it. Rei sensed it too. They shared a glance with one another, surprise in their eyes. Akira saw them share the glance. "What is it?"

Ryuu looked at Akira. "It's Renzo. He's calling for me."

Akira looked from one nightblade to the other. He spoke to Rei. "You can do that?"

Rei replied. "He's being a bit dramatic. Renzo is acting as a beacon, throwing out his energy so anyone sense-gifted knows where he is. However, in this situation, Ryuu is right. Renzo is calling for him."

Akira turned Ryuu's question back on him. "What are you going to do?"

Ryuu's answer was certain. "Just what I told you I would do. I'm going to kill him."

CHAPTER 30

Moriko rode without stopping. She had no food or water, but they were far less immediate concerns than the pursuit she was confident would follow. They might not have rushed after her, but they would come. After what she had done, the hunters would hunt, and there was no place she could hide. They could afford to let their prey have a little space.

She rode hard to the north and east. She didn't know why Nameless and his crew of hunters had been so close to the Three Sisters, but she was grateful. At most, she figured the pass was two or three days hard riding.

It was late afternoon when she saw them behind her. They were still a long ways away, but they were gaining. She wasn't surprised. They knew how to manage their mounts much better than she did.

It had become a race between her and the hunters. Her biggest problem was that she didn't know how far away from the pass she was. She turned more towards the foothills, hoping to find some terrain that would give her an advantage. She didn't think she was close enough to the outpost to outrun the hunters, and she didn't want another battle in the open plains. If she was going to fight again, she needed help. Her eyes wandered constantly through the foothills and to the pursuing hunters.

As the sun began to set, Moriko became desperate. She was already riding in hilly, rolling terrain. She was close to the mountains, but her horse was exhausted. Moriko had no grain, nothing to sustain the beast. To make matters worse, she was being cut off. As soon as the hunters had seen her riding in the foothills they split into two groups. One group kept following her, driving her across the foothills. The other group cut across the prairie, taking advantage of the flat land to gain speed and cut her off.

As near as she could tell, there were four of them hunting her. She was impressed. Nameless' speech echoed in her mind. No reason to send more than two. More than two had never been needed. But today he had sent four. Four for one, and these weren't children. These were hunters who traveled personally with Nameless. From a nightblade's perspective, four opponents didn't seem like many, but she knew that four of Nameless' personal honor guard would make short work of her. She rode harder.

Night had fallen and Moriko was trapped. The two hunters who had cut across the prairie were in front of her, blocking off her path to the fort. Two were behind her, pursuing her trail with a determination that was impressive and depressing all at the same time. Moriko had three options. She could head deeper into the mountains, trusting herself to increasingly difficult terrain. She could escape out into the plains and try to out-run her opponents, or she could stop and fight.

Fighting was out of the question. She was exhausted, her vision blurring at the edges. She was dehydrated and hungry and wounded. Taking on any one of the hunters would be near suicide unless she had some advantage. Taking on all four was a guarantee of an early death. The prairie to the south was also a poor option. The hunters had already demonstrated they were faster than her on their horses. She might prolong the inevitable, but out on the plains, her end would be certain.

So she turned towards the mountains, not sure what she was looking for, but hoping something would change the situation. She rode hard, kicking her horse one final time. It too was exhausted, but it only had a little further to go. The terrain was getting rocky and narrow, with sheer cliffs rising on every side. Her ride was almost over.

Moriko searched for any advantage. Her heart was pounding. She could feel the hunters behind her, drawing the net ever tighter. There wasn't any choice. She chose a valley and rode for it. She was committed. There wasn't any way back. It wasn't long before the horse was moving slower than she could. She got off, debated for a moment, and tied the horse to a tree. If she came back this way, she wanted a form of transportation.

She moved up the valley as fast as the terrain would allow. The ground was rocky and uneven, and the moon was no more than a sliver, providing little but shadows to guide her way through the unfamiliar area.

Moriko stopped. She'd covered maybe half a league, but there was something off. She examined her surroundings. One shadow in particular was darker than the surrounding shadows. Curious, Moriko moved towards it. The shadow revealed itself as a cave, a gaping blackness her sight had no chance of piercing. She threw out her sense. There was nothing in the cave, but the hunters were just a few hundred paces behind her. She didn't have any better ideas, so she went in.

Immediately she was swallowed by darkness. She was not a child of the mountains any more than she was a child of the plains. She had experienced darkness in the deep woods of her youth, but never like this. This darkness was real, a presence she could feel brush against her skin.

Moriko swallowed her fear and walked further into the darkness, all her senses searching for information. She moved slowly, her hands running along the edge of the wall. She tried to reach for another wall, or a ceiling, but found nothing. The cave, or cave system, was big.

As her mind stopped trying to see, her sense took over, and Moriko discovered she could sense the shape of the cave. It was faint, but life grew even here. Bats, awake, hung alert on the ceiling, listening to see if she was a threat or not. Along the walls, lichen grew from trickles of water in the rock. It was not much, but it was something, and in the darkness, even the faintest of lights give hope.

Her feelings weren't precise, but she had a decent understanding of the shape of the cave. Behind her a light flared and was quickly extinguished with a quick mutter in Azarian. Moriko didn't know what was said, but she could guess. They trusted their sense more than they trusted their sight in the caves. She understood. Sight was unreliable. Light cast shadows that hid dangers. The sense never lied.

But, her heart quickened, it could be fooled. Here she could be their doom. She allowed her presence to seep gently from her, as though she was trying to control it but failing. They should be able to track her, but it wouldn't be easy. If it was too easy, they might guess it was a trap. She moved deeper into the caves, delighted they continued on without end.

The hunters followed her further under the mountain. She suppressed her excitement. Focus was essential. She had the advantage, but she couldn't underestimate her opponents. These were the most dangerous men she had ever encountered. Moriko moved as quickly as she dared, trusting to her sense of the caves. When she reached a branch, she made her move.

In her mind, the memory of the hunters sniffing the air for her was imprinted deeply. Perhaps it wasn't only the sense they possessed, but a heightened set of senses in general. She stripped off her clothes, tossing them down one branch of the cave. She then suppressed her presence completely and went a few paces down the other branch, hiding herself in a depression along the wall.

There was no way to track time in the caves, but it felt like it was only a few moments later when she heard and sensed the four hunters at the branch. She measured out her breathing, keeping it as silent as the grave. She went deep within herself, keeping everything inside. If they sensed anything, the trap would be ruined. She heard a sniffing sound from up the caves.

There was a moment's pause. Then, without a word, they split up into two teams of two. Moriko cursed silently to herself. She had hoped they would all follow the scent of her clothes.

Moriko didn't have time to move, so she froze where she was, keeping her focus as tight as she could. She sensed the first hunter walk less than a pace in front of her. She couldn't see him at all in the perfect darkness. It seemed inconceivable that he couldn't sense her, but he kept walking in front of her, slowly, unsure of his place in the cave.

His partner stepped in front of her as well, but stopped just a pace or two past her hiding place. Moriko held her breath. She heard him sniff softly and knew he suspected something. Keeping her focus tight within, she moved slowly, her blade in front of her. The hunter was perfectly clear to her sense, and she thrust once, killing him with one strike.

Even if the hunter had been suspicious, he hadn't been ready. The blade went in and out and he fell to the ground with a dull thud, causing his partner to turn around in surprise. Down the other branch, Moriko could sense the other hunters noticing the death of the fourth.

There wasn't time to think, and Moriko's combat instincts took over. She stepped over the dead body and stabbed out again. The other hunter knew Moriko was somewhere close, but with no sight and no sense of her, there was nothing he could do. Moriko's blade passed right behind his guard without touching it, killing him as quickly as his partner.

Behind her she heard the soft commotion of the other two hunters as they realized what was happening. They were coming back to where the cave had branched in two. Trusting her sense, Moriko took off deeper into the caves. In the darkness she would move faster, their caution for their lives slowing them down. She let her presence seep out of her again, both to draw her hunters deeper into the caves, but also to relax her own mind. Suppressing her presence as far as she did was mentally exhausting.

Naked and in the dark, Moriko felt an understanding of her own power rush over her. Here, she was the hunter and they were the hunted. Another four hunters would meet their end. Despite her exhaustion, despite her injuries, she had never felt so strong, so deadly. She wanted to kill.

The hunters behind her didn't have her confidence. They moved slowly and deliberately towards her presence, but they moved with caution. She moved with determination.

As the footfalls became quieter behind her, Moriko realized she was in a large cavern. It was as good as place as any for her final stand. She felt like she had become everything a nightblade could be. She was deadly, silent, and undetectable. A flood of confidence rushed through her veins. She was everything that Orochi had taught her and so much more. She breathed in the darkness, taking its power for herself.

The hunters came into the room, moving slowly. She had suppressed her presence again and was as silent as the bodies of their friends back up the path. They didn't have any clue where she was. She could almost feel their fear.

Moriko reached out with her sword, deliberate and sure. With a single thrust she took the life of the third hunter. She grinned viciously. That made the count eight and a half hunters dead by her sword, two by Ryuu's. He'd be jealous.

She heard the sound of flint on steel, throwing sparks onto a torch. The cavern illuminated in an instant, blinding both Moriko and the final pursuer. The flame and the movement was enough to frighten the bats too, and they beat furiously against the air to escape the light.

Between the light and the bats, both Moriko and the hunter were disoriented. They had both been in the darkness long enough that the light hurt their eyes. Moriko closed hers, trusting to her sense. Her opponent was tall, much bigger and stronger than she was. Her confidence was high, though, and he couldn't see well and didn't trust his sense. She wished, just for a moment, that she could face Nameless in a dark cave. He'd be dead on the ground in just a moment and all this would be over.

The hunter moved in, his sword moving quickly where he thought Moriko was. He had seen the battle between her and Nameless. He knew what she was capable of, knew the best way to defeat her was to keep moving, keep attacking and rely on speed and strength.

For Moriko, the outcome was never in question. The hunter's sight was imperfect as it struggled to adjust to the light, and her sense of him was flawless. With a series of cuts she broke through his guard and he fell silently, as dead as his other companions. The enormity of what she had accomplished hit her and she fell to her knees. By herself she had killed four hunters. Not children, freshly blooded. Hunters of Nameless' honor guard. No one alive had accomplished anything similar. She bowed her head and soaked in the darkness.

Moriko didn't know how much time had passed in the caves, but when she opened her eyes, the torch had gone out. She eventually stood up and worked her way towards the entrance of the cave. When she found the first branch, she went and gathered her clothes. She was surprised by how exhausted she was. It was all she could do to stay on her feet.

When she came out of the cave, she took a deep breath of fresh air. She felt like she was born again. She stumbled down to where she had left her horse. The hunters had conveniently left their mounts tied up right next to hers. She found food, both for herself and for the horse. There were also skins of water. Moriko helped herself to as much as she could carry.

From here, it shouldn't be too much of a ride to the fort. By the time tomorrow ended, her mission would be over.

CHAPTER 31

Ryuu and Rei moved through the night, shadows cast long by the rising full moon. Renzo had decided on an interesting location for their meeting. He was standing alone, dark robes snapping lightly in the breeze, right in between the camps for the two armies. They would be fighting on tomorrow's battleground. It seemed fitting, though conspicuous, in Ryuu's mind.

They stopped ten paces apart. Ryuu was relaxed and alert. He'd fought Renzo before, and he was prepared for the battle. He had no doubt he'd emerge as the victor.

Renzo looked to Rei first. "I had hoped not to see you again."

Rei's anger was apparent. "I can't let you stay on this path. Do you know how much chaos you've caused?"

Renzo nodded. "And there is much more to come."

Rei's anger flickered into confusion. "How could you do this?"

"Rei, you know the blades need to come back to this land. You've been traveling a while now in this land. You've seen the weakness, the fear in which they live. They aren't like us. They aren't strong enough. I'd hoped Shika would see reason, but she's been influenced far too much by that sentimental fool."

Ryuu knew Renzo was speaking of Tenchi.

Renzo's gaze traveled to Ryuu. "And you, you are strong, too. You have the strength to make a difference in this world, and you already have. But with all that strength, you don't step forward and seize the power you deserve. This land needs our protection."

"I agree," Ryuu said, "but not this way. You can't tear apart the land you're trying to protect."

Renzo laughed. "Were you ever forced to clean a house when you were young? You take everything out, organize it, and then put it back where it belongs. When you're done, everything is clean, but there is a time, right after you've taken it all apart, that it looks worse than when it started. This is no different. Yes, the Three Kingdoms is a disaster right now, but it will be much stronger in the end."

Ryuu shook his head. "But you are talking about people's lives, not items in a house."

Renzo shrugged. "We disagree. I didn't come here to persuade you, though I hoped you might understand. I will detest having to kill you."

Ryuu sensed Rei's intent a moment before she moved. He tried to stop her, but she was too fast. He turned to Renzo and was amazed by how fast the man slipped into the energy surrounding him. Ryuu followed suit, trying to catch Rei before it was too late.

A set of three throwing blades sprung into existence in Renzo's left hand. He threw them all at Ryuu, forcing Ryuu off his line. It gave Renzo the moment he needed.

Rei was strong and fast, but not enough of either to be a match for Renzo. She suppressed her presence, but not as well as

Moriko could. Ryuu could still sense her movements as clear as day, and he expected Renzo could, too.

Rei cut twice, once high, once low, but Renzo stepped away from each of them. Ryuu was running to the battle as fast as he could, trying to get there before Renzo could counter-attack. He was too late.

Renzo's sword blurred in the moonlight, and Rei couldn't react fast enough. She got in front of the first cut, but the second cut sliced deep, cutting through her arm and back. Her sword arm went limp, and as she tried to move, she collapsed, blood starting to drip onto the ground in front of her.

Ryuu barely registered it as he reached Renzo, just a few moments too late. Their swords met in the dark of the night, the sound of steel carrying through the empty space between the camps. Ryuu wondered if this battle was being watched. The moon provided light, but it would be hard to make them out as more than shadows from either of the camps.

Two passes and they were evenly matched. Ryuu went for low strikes, hoping to find a hole in Renzo's defense. Renzo blocked the strikes with little difficulty. He seemed to float between Ryuu's cuts, slippery as an eel. He moved from strike to strike without effort, his cuts whip-like through the night.

They broke apart, each taking a moment to catch their breath. Ryuu felt more alive than he had in several cycles. Renzo was strong, maybe even stronger than he was. He found the idea of facing a stronger opponent thrilling. His blood raced and the world around him became more vivid.

They didn't speak, for there was nothing to be said. Ryuu had accepted Tenchi's mission, and Renzo had gone much too far.

He had lost all hope for redemption the moment his blade cut through Rei's flesh, and he seemed to recognize it as well.

Renzo drew a second, shorter blade. It was a traditional blade, one Ryuu hadn't seen used in combat before. Shigeru had always taught him a second blade was meaningless. All encounters would be decided by the skill with one blade. Ryuu had found it to be true thus far.

But Renzo stood firm, perfectly balanced, ready for a strike from any angle. Ryuu attacked, his blade searching for an opening in Renzo's defense. There was none. Every time he approached, he was driven back by the second blade. Renzo blocked with one and cut with the other, moves blurring together with blinding speed and accuracy. Ryuu couldn't get close to him.

Ryuu came in again, focusing his mind, trying to bring all the energy he could to bear. He lost his balance for a moment and Renzo's blade sliced through his back. It wasn't deep, but it was the same type of cut that had left Rei twitching on the ground. Ryuu paused his attack and considered his options. Renzo resumed his stance, perfect and prepared for anything Ryuu might try.

Ryuu cursed to himself. This wasn't going anywhere. Time to try the trick Tenchi had used on him. He focused his attention, playing through his actions in his mind. Fortunately, Renzo seemed more than willing to give him all the time he needed, confident in his dominance.

Ryuu slid into his attack, stepping forward. The trick was to intend to strike in multiple places at once. Ryuu struck, and Renzo blocked a strike that never came. Ryuu struck Renzo's second blade, knocking it out of his hand with the force of the cut. Renzo switched his stance and again the two nightblades met in a flurry of strikes and counter-strikes, neither gaining the advantage on the other.

They split apart again, each of them looking to gather their energy. Ryuu was getting tired. He was putting everything he had into every attack, and still he'd just barely been able to cut Renzo. Renzo looked more uncertain than he had when the battle had first been joined. It was something, at least.

As they caught their breath, Renzo spoke. "I've never seen that attack before. Is it Tenchi's secret technique?"

Ryuu nodded. Renzo laughed uncontrollably, and Ryuu understood. His blood was rushing through his body. Everything was vivid and he struggled to contain his emotions. "I'd always wondered what that technique was. He spoke about it all the time."

Ryuu settled back into his combat stance. He didn't have many advantages over Renzo, but youth was one of them. Renzo had seen more than twenty more cycles than Ryuu, and Ryuu hoped he'd tire more quickly.

Ryuu charged forward again, his mind focused and clear. Their blades met twice and Renzo sprinted uphill, trying to gain the upper ground. Ryuu sprinted after him, trying to attack Renzo's lower body while parrying attacks meant for his upper body. Renzo stopped running and the battle continued, the ground uneven and the grass slippery with night dew. Ryuu struck again with Tenchi's attack, managing to cut Renzo again before he was able to recover. Then Ryuu slipped, and Renzo scored a cut across his chest before Ryuu could get up to block in time.

He didn't want to keep using Tenchi's attack. Every time he did, it gave Renzo a chance to understand it better. He risked the attack one more time, this time cutting deep into Renzo's leg. Renzo howled in frustration, finding a reserve of energy Ryuu wasn't expecting.

Renzo came at him, his blade almost impossible to track, even for Ryuu. Ryuu found himself scrambling backwards, slipping and falling on the slick grass. Finally, Ryuu dove downhill. He didn't want to give up vertical ground, but he saw little option. Renzo wasn't giving him any openings at all, and Renzo's blade was cutting closer and closer. Ryuu rolled, the cut on his back screaming in pain, but when he tried to come to his feet he couldn't. The slope was steep and slippery, and he couldn't find purchase for his feet with his momentum. Renzo recognized his predicament and sprinted down the hill after him, sword low for the killing cut.

Ryuu panicked, almost losing the flow of energy that surrounded him. He was slowing down, but he wasn't sure it was fast enough. His feet kept scrambling for something to stop him.

When his right foot hit the rock, Ryuu felt something in his ankle give way under the force. His body compressed as he managed to stop his momentum. Ryuu ignored the pain and sprang forward, right at Renzo. His stomach sank. If his ankle was hurt, he only had one chance to end this. If it went further, Renzo would wear him down and finish him. Ryuu focused his mind, his intent to make all nine cuts at once. It all came down to one strike.

Time slowed even further, a moment stretching into forever. Then steel met steel, and Ryuu was past Renzo. It couldn't be.

Renzo had blocked the strike.

Ryuu landed on his left foot, his good foot, uphill from Renzo. He turned and launched himself back down the hill at Renzo. He knew it was hopeless, but he had to fight until the end. The battle wasn't over until his breath left his body for the Great Cycle.

He didn't believe what he saw. Renzo's defense was open, his back turned to Ryuu. Renzo was starting to turn, but he was too slow. Ryuu put all his strength into his final cut, a clean strike through Renzo's spine. Ryuu didn't trust landing on his right leg, electing to fall hard onto the hillside and slide to a stop twenty paces down the hill. His whole body hurt, but when he looked up the hillside, Renzo's body wasn't moving. He had to be sure.

Slowly, Ryuu managed to get back to his feet. He sheathed his sword and used the scabbard in place of his injured right foot. It felt like it took him forever to reach Renzo's body, but when he did, he could see why Renzo wasn't moving. Renzo's spine had been severed, and he was bleeding out. Already his eyes were starting to glaze over. Renzo turned his eyes towards Ryuu and smiled, a vicious grin made worse by the blood dripping from it. "I blocked his attack."

Ryuu understood. He had blocked Tenchi's secret attack, but hadn't recovered from his success quickly enough. It had only been a moment, but a moment was all Ryuu had needed. Ryuu was moved to pity. It was hard to see someone who relied on their physical skill have their gift taken from them. "Yes, you did. You're the strongest I've faced. May you find peace in the Great Cycle."

Renzo laughed, then grimaced in pain. He struggled to make the words. "Not the strongest."

It was all he could do before he gave up the effort. Ryuu sat with him for his final moments, waiting until he felt Renzo's energy depart and merge with the energy surrounding him. He had rejoined the Great Cycle.

After Renzo died, Ryuu started working his way back towards where Rei lay. He could sense her energy getting weaker. He moved as fast as he could, which wasn't very fast on his bad ankle. The moon was well on its way down the sky by the time he got to her. It wouldn't be long now before the armies began forming up for battle. When that happened, the place they were was the last place anyone in the Three Kingdoms would want to be.

Rei's injuries were serious. She was unconscious and bleeding profusely. Ryuu sized up the situation, and it wasn't pretty. He was having a hard time moving, but if she didn't receive care soon, she was going to die. They weren't too far away from Akira's camp, but Rei was down near the bottom of the valley, and Akira's camp was a climb up. Ryuu swore. He didn't see any other way.

He made bandages from the rags he was wearing and wrapped them as tightly around Rei as he could. They soaked through with blood immediately, but he figured it was better than nothing. In a better world, Ryuu would have been able to throw her over his shoulder, but if he did that his shoulder would be right in her wound. He would have to carry her in his arms. She was light, but it was a long way to the top of the hill.

Ryuu grimaced as he picked her up. His ankle flared up, and he almost stumbled and dropped her. His vision went fuzzy for a moment before it returned to normal. Ryuu found the energy that surrounded him and fell into it once again, feeling the strength return to his exhausted muscles. He started walking, one step at a time, each one a grueling test of his will and focus.

Ryuu didn't dare release the energy, drop out of the state he was in. He was sure that if he did he would have nothing left. All that mattered was getting Rei help. His mind flashed back to Takako, dying right in front of him. He didn't want to live through that again. He wasn't sure that he could.

Even bringing in all the energy he could, every movement he made was torture. He could feel the cut on his back widen under the pressure it was experiencing. He worried his ankle would break. More than anything, he wanted a dayblade to be somewhere in Akira's camp, even though he knew it was impossible. The blades needed to come back, all of them, to the Three Kingdoms.

Ryuu was halfway back up the hill when his focus abandoned him and he collapsed. He tried to move, but wasn't even able to move his own body. He lay there, face in the dirt, trying to summon up the strength to keep moving.

Then he sensed them, Akira's soldiers, moving down towards them. Ryuu looked up and moved his hand to wave, but then his world went black.

When he came to, he was lying on his stomach while a medic stitched his back together. Ryuu swore loudly, startling the doctor. He heard Akira's distinctive chuckle.

"They thought you'd sleep for days. Apparently not so much."

Ryuu managed to form words. Everything in his body seemed sluggish to him. "What happened?"

"When you left, I had men follow you to the perimeter of the camp and watch your battle. As you can imagine, the outcome was of no little importance to me. They saw you defeat Renzo, although they admit they couldn't actually see much of the battle in the dark. When you started carrying Rei back to our camp, they came back to report. I sent men to retrieve you. I apologize. If my men had some more initiative, they would have prevented your climb back up the hill."

Ryuu nodded, the small motion causing pain to blaze throughout his body. "Thank you."

"It's the least I can do. I figured Renzo would be coming for me if you failed, so I'm grateful you succeeded."

Ryuu could feel the darkness pressing in on him. Akira dismissed the medic, finished with his work, and knelt down next to Ryuu.

"I've been talking with my generals, Ryuu. We're going to surrender when the sun rises. I hate it more than anything, but you are right. Thank you."

"You're welcome."

Then the blackness claimed Ryuu before he could even ask what had happened to Rei.

CHAPTER 32

Akira stood in the early morning sun and looked at the two nightblades recovering in their tent. Ryuu would live and heal. He was cut, and his cuts were deep, but there wasn't anything fatal. It was Rei he worried about. Her arm hung limp, and the healers had told him they weren't sure it would ever be functional again. He wondered how she would feel about it. She had been so happy, so positive about everything. But if she lost her movement, her ability with the sword, what was left for her?

Akira hated seeing the two of them in this condition. He had become fond of them, fond of their strength. Akira had known how strong Orochi was, and Ryuu had killed him. Renzo, whoever he had been, must have been incredibly strong to do this to both of them.

Looking in on the nightblades gave Akira the strength he needed. He hadn't slept at all the night before, and this morning the battle lines were being drawn up. Akira had spoken with his generals. They knew what was coming.

It was the damn Azarians. Akira had cursed and raged when he had gotten the news, but no amount of anger changed the facts he faced. He had never imagined so many Azarians. Never imagined they would be backed up with hunters. Not even Moriko had made it out alive, and Akira was sure she'd been strong.

He wanted to give the order to charge. He wanted to make the soldiers of the Western Kingdom pay in blood for every step they'd taken on his land. But he wouldn't do it. His men thirsted for the blood of the invaders, but they wouldn't taste it today. Not with the danger they would be facing. Today he would surrender his kingdom to Tanak. It was the hardest decision he'd ever made.

Akira left the tent and found his honor guard. He mounted his horse and looked with pride upon all the men who had assembled to fight and die for him.

They raised a white flag as a banner and Akira rode down the hillside. They rode to the center of the field and waited for Tanak to come. In time he did, bearing his own white flag of truce. Akira motioned to his honor guard to stay in place while he rode to Tanak. Tanak did the same, and the two of them met in open field, alone. Akira thought, just for a moment, he would cut Tanak down where he stood, but the moment passed. No good would come of it.

"Good morning, Akira." Tanak dropped the honorific.

"Good morning, Lord Tanak." Akira swallowed his pride, as much as it pained him to do so.

"It's a lovely morning for battle, isn't it?"

Akira shook his head. "No. No morning should be ruined by the sound of the battle calls." He paused. "I've received a message that concerns us." He handed Tanak the same report he'd received from the Three Sisters. Tanak read it quickly and threw it to the ground.

"Please, do you think to get me to turn back now, just because you show me a letter?"

"No. I would like you to turn around so I can send my men down to the pass to protect it."

"It will never happen, Akira."

"Damn it, Tanak! If we fight here today, no matter who wins, our armies will be broken. We don't have the strength to stand against a force this size."

Tanak looked Akira right in the eye. "My men will meet yours in battle, and after you are gone, we'll go down and protect all Three Kingdoms. We can stand before them without a problem."

Akira couldn't believe what he was hearing. Surely Tanak wasn't so delusional as to believe what he was saying?

"You won't turn back?"

Tanak shook his head.

"Then I need to negotiate my terms of surrender."

The grin on Tanak's face made Akira want to draw his blade again, but he resisted. "What are your terms?"

"With the threat from the Azarians, I ask that my men are allowed to disband and go home, keeping their weapons. None of my men are to be tried for any crime, and they will be allowed to keep their organization. If you need them, they will come to your call to protect the land. Also, grant me the title of your second-in-command, so that my men will accept this peace."

"So you can stab me in my sleep and take the throne that way?"

Akira glared at Tanak. "You know I wouldn't stoop to such tactics."

Tanak thought about the terms for a moment. "That is true. If nothing else, you are honest. There is one thing more I require."

"What is it?"

"The head of the nightblade in your camp."

Akira spun around, making sure no one was close enough to overhear. But they were alone on the battlefield, their honor guards dozens of paces away. "Come again?"

Tanak spat. "Don't play games with me, Akira. I know you have a nightblade with you. Renzo told me before he went to assassinate you. I'm assuming Renzo fell to him, given that you're here in front of me. I want his head. Renzo deserves it."

"And how do you expect me to kill a nightblade?"

"That's your problem. I'll agree to your terms, but you must bring me his head."

Akira debated for a moment. "I will try to kill him myself. That way, even if I fail, your price will be paid."

Tanak smiled. "That's good enough for me. I agree to your terms."

Akira cursed to himself and rode away. Now he had to tell his men why he had surrendered his kingdom before they'd even fought.

CHAPTER 33

After over two moons in the Azarian prairie, the fort at the southern tip of the Three Sisters seemed like a gift from the fates. Moriko hadn't been sure she'd ever see it again. She was flooded with relief. It wasn't home, but it was good enough.

Even at first glance, Moriko could tell Toro hadn't wasted his summer. There was an extra wall built around the fort, and the existing walls had been built higher than they had been when she had left. As she approached she could see the soldiers at work, drilling and building. She kicked the horse. She wanted to be inside the walls.

Moriko was greeted at the wall like she was a hero of the people. She gazed from face to face. She saw fear and hope in the eyes of the soldiers. A summer without battle had taken their toll. Moriko was brought to Toro right away. She started with the most important news. The hunters were real, they were in charge of the tribes, and they were coming. Moriko estimated they had a half-moon at the most to prepare. Toro's face paled when she spoke of the capabilities of the hunters. His scouts had spotted the Azarians, but the hunters were news to him.

She had to give Toro credit. He set aside all his disbelief and listened to what she was saying. They spoke through the afternoon and into the evening. But before the moon broke the horizon, he held up his hand to stop her.

"This is much to take in. I will start to make preparations as I see fit, but we can continue this tomorrow. It's obvious that you are exhausted."

Moriko graciously accepted his hospitality, falling asleep in the offered tent instantly and sleeping better than she had in ages. Her time in Azaria had taught her not to take safety for granted. When she woke, she was brought to Toro, and he began a careful questioning, bringing out details Moriko hadn't even realized were important. She realized she had learned much more than she thought she had, just by living with the Azarians.

Throughout their interview, Moriko knew the camp was more alive than it had been in some time. Toro had taken her story to heart, and defenses were being prepared. Walls were reinforced. Blades and arrows were sharpened and honed, all on her word. The First was preparing for war. They were interrupted regularly by dispatches that Toro answered quickly. Moriko was in awe. She could destroy him in single combat, but this man was a leader, preparing his army for a battle Moriko thought was hopeless. She couldn't take his place, no matter how strong she was.

They talked through the night, reaching the point of Moriko's story when she met Nameless for the first time. The moon was high in the sky when Moriko finally left the general's tent. She breathed in the night, feeling it filling her with strength. She hadn't been sure she would survive, but here she was, stronger than ever.

Moriko slept soundly that night as well, rejoining Toro for another day of interviews. They went almost through the entire day, ending just before the sun set. When they were done, Toro dismissed her quickly, needing to get back to the work of commanding his army. Moriko knew that somehow her story was changing how he was managing his defenses.

In the privacy of her tent, Moriko watched the moon come up over the horizon. She had returned a different person than when she had left. More different than she had expected. She thought about Ryuu and about the world they were caught in. She thought about what was next.

War was coming to the Three Kingdoms. Not the petty civil war that was currently tearing the land apart, but a war that would destroy the very identity of the Three Kingdoms. There was a part of her that admired the brutal traditions of the Azarians, but she recognized it was because of her own strength. She was accepted among them. But they would bring destruction upon the kingdoms, not because they were power hungry or because they sought to cause destruction. They would destroy because they were weeding out the weak. They would consider it a favor. If they would barely lift a finger to save their own kind, how much less would they do to save the lives of the average citizen of the Three Kingdoms?

Moriko saw all this. It wasn't a vision, from her perspective, it was simple inevitability. There wasn't any force in the Three Kingdoms prepared to face what was coming their way. The problem was, Moriko didn't care. She could hear Ryuu's voice in her head, telling her they had to protect the weak, but Moriko didn't agree. She had spent her life confined within the monastery walls. After Ryuu had rescued her and reached a truce with Akira, they'd had freedom for a time. The reason Moriko had gone south was to regain that freedom, but with the Azarians coming north, there wouldn't be any safety in the Three Kingdoms. They would be hunted until Nameless was sure they were dead. The Three Kingdoms wouldn't be home, not for long. If she elected to serve Akira, or any Lord, she would be bound by chains as confining as the monastery walls she'd grown up in.

She was saddened, but she also knew she was right. She wouldn't be able to go back to Akira and wait for Ryuu. If she did, fate would embrace her again, and she'd be brought into the battle. It was time for her to leave the Three Kingdoms.

That evening Moriko sat down to write a letter to Ryuu. She told him that she was heading back to their hut and would wait there until spring. She figured it was the longest she could stay before the Azarian invasion made it too dangerous to travel. Every word was slow to come, but she persevered. He had to know, had to understand why she was making this decision. She explained why she wouldn't serve any of the Lords, and she asked Ryuu to join her. He had until spring. She sealed the letter and took it to Toro. It was addressed to Ryuu, in care of Lord Akira. It would reach him.

Toro begged her to stay. He wanted her strength, but it wasn't his to command. She almost found it amusing that when in danger, he wanted a nightblade at his side, where a few moons ago he would have been just as happy to kill her. Danger made for strange partners.

Toro offered her a horse, but she refused. They would need every horse for their defense, and Moriko felt like a long walk would do her good. Toro wrote her passes to get her past any checkpoints. Moriko left the fort the next day, heading north. She took one last glance at Azaria. She wouldn't, couldn't forget her time there, but she was glad it was behind her.

Moriko turned and started walking home, the home she would soon be leaving forever.

CHAPTER 34

Akira stood on the ridge, Ryuu standing well back in the crowd. Moving was hard, but this he had to see. Ryuu had to admit, Akira was a true Lord. He had turned a surrender into a victory among the men. Celebrations had broken out yesterday, and today he assembled them for a speech. Ultimately, the men were overjoyed today wasn't their day to die. Akira had never seemed more the leader. It seemed that by losing his power, he had found his center. He had come to the pinnacle after walking through the assembled troops, bowing and congratulating them.

The sun was beginning to set, and the sun illuminated Akira as he spoke. Ryuu imagined Akira's armor could be seen all the way down the hills to Tanak's armies, breaking camp below. Despite the crushing hits the Southern Kingdom had taken this cycle, the men still looked up to him. Ryuu was impressed.

Akira spoke softly, but his voice was penetrating and carried well in the crisp autumn air.

"Men of the Southern Kingdom."

Akira paused for effect, looking out over all the men assembled. He looked like a proud parent as he looked on his men. Ryuu knew it wasn't an act he put on. He was genuinely proud of his men.

"We have reached a truce with the Western Kingdom. The treaty is not yet official, but the basics are already settled. The Western Kingdom and the Southern Kingdom will become one Kingdom, one people once again."

There was an excited murmur that ran through the crowd, one barely silenced by Akira's call. He waited for the excitement to die down.

"Each of us, every single man here, has dreamed we might see the day where the glory of the one Kingdom may be restored. Gentlemen, I believe that day will soon be upon us."

He paused again and his face turned from one of pride to one of sorrow.

"But, while I celebrate this merging of our kingdoms, our fight is far from over, for news of an even greater threat has reached my ears. An invasion from the Three Sisters is imminent. I have heard word of it from General Toro directly. All of Azaria is coming to the entryway of our kingdom, and they bring with them a type of warrior we call hunters, warriors who have skills similar to our nightblades of old."

The former Lord of the Southern Kingdom looked over his men. "I know that many here consider the nightblades to be nothing more than a myth. We have trained to hunt them, but all of us hold that speck of doubt, that doubt that we have created a phantom that doesn't really exist. We doubt their skills can truly be all the legends speak of."

"I stand before you today to tell you that nightblades do exist, as do the Azarian hunters, and they are more dangerous than any of us can imagine. I fear for our kingdom, so newly unified."

There was one last pause.

"This war is over. You may all go back to your homes and set your affairs in order. Help with the harvest and save all the food you can. Prepare for war, for I fear you will be called back before the winter is over. And this time we don't fight among ourselves. We fight instead for our very survival, because the Azarians want our land, and they don't need us to be on it when they arrive."

"My men, my friends, I wish you all the blessings of a bountiful harvest, but the Great Cycle continues to turn, and we must go to war again soon. Don't let the rust get to your swords."

There was a low murmur running throughout the crowd. Akira bowed deeply to his men, kneeling and putting his face to the ground, and Ryuu was sure the gesture moved many to tears. These men would die for him. Of that Ryuu had little doubt. Ryuu was certain they would have their chance soon enough.

Akira came to Ryuu that night as he sat by Rei's side. Ryuu wished he had the power of the dayblades, the power to heal her arm and her body. He wanted to take her back to the island so she could rest and heal. But he couldn't move her until she was stronger.

Akira bent over Rei and brushed the hair out of her face. Ryuu had never known Akira as anything other than a Lord. Seeing him as a lover was disconcerting. Akira turned to Ryuu. "This came for you today."

Ryuu snatched the letter out of Akira's outstretched hand. He recognized Moriko's handwriting at once. He read through the letter and then read it again, not believing what he was reading. She had survived! And she was leaving.

He knelt to the ground as the information sank in. She was planning on leaving the Three Kingdoms, their home, for good. It felt like a betrayal to him, like she was turning her back on everything they had built together. He had sensed, from a distance, that she had become different, but he had never imagined she would reject their lives like this. He saw her invitation to come with her, but Ryuu wasn't sure he could. The Three Kingdoms were his home. They were her home.

Something broke in Ryuu then. He couldn't take the loss of Moriko. She grounded him, held him together. She understood him in a way no one else could. First Takako, now Moriko. Great, heaving sobs wracked his body, but his eyes were dry. No tears would come. He wanted to dig a hole and hide from the world forever.

"I'm sorry, Ryuu."

Ryuu turned to the sound of a sword being drawn. Ryuu expected his sense to warn him of an attack, but it was gone. He suddenly realized he couldn't sense anything at all. He turned to see Akira assume a fighting stance and move to cut him.

Ryuu dove out of the way, feeling his back open up again as he rolled on it. He cursed loudly as he came to his feet.

"What are you doing?"

Akira stepped and cut again, and Ryuu stepped out of the way. He couldn't sense Akira's attacks, but he had still trained in swordsmanship every day of his life since he was five. Even without the sense, he was a strong fighter, but he couldn't figure out why Akira was attacking him.

"This was the final condition of the treaty. That I bring Tanak the head of the nightblade who killed Renzo." Akira thrust wildly, and Ryuu saw the desperation in his eyes.

He saw something else too, something he'd been too distracted to notice earlier. Akira's eyes were red, his body broken. Something clicked in Ryuu's mind and he knew Akira had given up hope.

Ryuu drew his blade and deflected a cut. Akira slashed again, not caring how slow or how obvious his attacks were. Ryuu stepped inside his guard and hit him with the side of his blade, knocking Akira backwards. He came back to his feet, a wild grin on his face, and Ryuu saw Akira had lost everything that mattered to him.

Akira charged, sword raised high above him. Ryuu stepped in and sliced, causing a sliver of scarlet to open up from his shoulder to his stomach. Ryuu cut twice more, each cut a perfect strike. He finished with a kick to Akira's chest, knocking him backwards.

Akira started to get up, but Ryuu brought the tip of his sword to Akira's neck. "No."

Akira looked like he was about to move, but Ryuu pushed the tip closer, drawing blood. He worried Akira would try to impale himself if he got the chance. "I know what you're trying to do, but I won't kill you. You haven't failed, and your people need you. They'll need you more than ever in the next few moons."

Akira broke down, his manic state gone. The tears fell, mingling with his blood on the ground. "End it, please."

Ryuu shook his head, snapped the blood off his blade, and sheathed it. He looked around the tent, focusing on Rei. "What about her?"

"He doesn't know about her."

"Good. When she comes to, tell her I said thank you." He turned to leave.

"Ryuu, wait."

Ryuu turned at the door.

"Where will you go? What if I need you?"

"I don't know, Akira. I'll become an outlaw to save your treaty. Hunt me if you must. I'm not sure where I'll go. I'm not sure there's any place left for me. But you can't give up. Don't ever give up."

Without another word, Ryuu left the tent. He still couldn't use his sense, and the fear in his gut was that somehow he had lost it for good. He walked into the night, hunted by the Azarians and the soldiers of the Three Kingdoms.

Before you go, I just wanted to take a moment to say thank you for reading. If you liked the story, please take a moment to go over to Amazon and review this book. Small independent authors like me rely on reviews to help spread the word about our work.

Finally, if you're interested in being among the first to know about upcoming releases, get behind-the-scenes glimpses of the company in action, and get FREE STUFF, please head on over to my website: www.waterstonemedia.net. You can sign up for my newsletter and catch up on all the latest news.

With Gratitude,

Ryan